THE INFINITY COURTS

AKEMI DAWN BOWMAN

SIMON & SCHUSTER BFYR

New York London Toronto Sydney New Delhi

SIMON & SCHUSTER BFYR

An imprint of Simon & Schuster Children's Publishing Division

1230 Avenue of the Americas, New York, New York 10020

SIMON & SCHUSTER BOOKS FOR YOUNG READERS

and related marks are trademarks of Simon & Schuster, Inc.

For information about special discounts for bulk purchases, please contact Simon & Schuster Special Sales at 1-866-506-1949 or business@simonandschuster.com.

The Simon & Schuster Speakers Bureau can bring authors to your live event. For more information or to book an event, contact the Simon & Schuster Speakers Bureau at 1-866-248-3049 or visit our website at www.simonspeakers.com.

Also available in a SIMON & SCHUSTER BFYR hardcover edition

Interior design by Laura Eckes

The text for this book was set in Bembo Std.

Manufactured in the United States of America

First SIMON & SCHUSTER BFYR paperback edition April 2022

2 4 6 8 10 9 7 5 3 1

The Library of Congress has cataloged the hardcover edition as follows:

Names: Bowman, Akemi Dawn, author.

Title: The Infinity courts / Akemi Dawn Bowman.

Description: First Simon & Schuster Books for Young Readers hardcover edition. | New York : Simon & Schuster Books for Young Readers, 2021. | Audience: Ages 12 up. | Audience: Grades 7 up. | Summary: Murdered on the way to her high school graduation party, eighteen-year-old Nami Miyamoto finds herself in an afterlife ruled by Ophelia, a virtual assistant planning to eradicate human existence.

Identifiers: LCCN 2020010736 (print) | LCCN 2020010737 (ebook) | ISBN 9781534456495 (hardcover) | ISBN 9781534456501 (pbk) | ISBN 9781534456518 (ebook)

Subjects: CYAC: Future life—Fiction. | Artificial intelligence—Fiction. | Kings, queens, rulers, etc.—Fiction. | Racially mixed people—Fiction.

Classification: LCC PZ7.1.B6873 Inf 2021 (print) | LCC PZ7.1.B6873 (ebook) | DDC [Fic]—dc23

LC record available at https://lccn.loc.gov/2020010736

LC ebook record available at https://lccn.loc.gov/2020010737

Praise for

The Infinity Courts

—Ada

"*The Inj*
fiction and
understandi
humanity and
A fascinating st
—Tra

"A wildly imagina
wonderfully passionate
new obsession!"

"The narrative raises age
community but proposes a
solution. The shifting beliefs
forward while impressively re
of humanity. . . . Bowman con
pounding in her powerful leap into
world, a terrifying villain and a co
mesmerizing series opener that's sur
shattering sequel."

Also by
AKEMI DAWN BOWMAN

Starfish

Summer Bird Blue

Harley in the Sky

This one is for the readers.

Thank you for following me into Infinity.

INFINITY

WINTER KEEP

WINTER DISTRICT

BARRACKS

THE WISHING TREE

Winter Market

Caelan's Palace

Waterfall & Cavern

Hatch

NORTH TUNNEL

Spring Market

Summer Market

SPRING DISTRICT

THE COLONY

SOUTH TUNNEL

HUMAN VILLAGE

VICTORY

FAMINE

AUTUMN DISTRICT

HOUSE OF HARVEST

Autumn Market

THE GALLERY

Southern Bay

ARTIST TOWN & MAIN SQUARE

SUMMER DISTRICT

WAR

DEATH

THE CAPITAL

1

"OPHELIA, IF IT WAS YOUR LAST DAY ON EARTH and you wanted to dress for the occasion, would you wear the potentially-too-short black dress or the hilarious Zelda T-shirt of an ocarina that says 'Make It Rain'?"

The lilting voice from my O-Tech watch replies in less than a second. "I cannot have a last day on Earth, because I do not exist on Earth. And even if I did, I have no physical body that requires the use of clothing." The sound is like a lake without a breath of wind. Smooth, clear, and unblemished. It makes the gentle scratch of ordinary speakers sound like they came from the Jurassic period.

My eyes drop to my wrist out of habit, long enough to catch

the end of Ophelia's speech as it flashes across the screen.

"That is unsurprisingly not helpful," I say with a raised brow, holding the two options of clothing in front of me. "Okay, Ophelia, I'm going on a date: Do I dress up or dress down?"

"If you want to make a good impression, dress your best, as they say," the programmed voice replies.

I toss the T-shirt onto the mess of blankets behind me and pull the black dress over my head. "Ophelia, nobody says that. But thank you."

"You are welcome. I hope you have a wonderful time on your date." Her cadence is similar to a human's, but it can't replicate emotion. It makes any of her well wishes sound . . . dry.

With a smirk, I glance at my reflection, my watch brightly lit to signal that she's listening. "Ophelia, why do I get the feeling you're being sarcastic?" I tug at the hem of my dress and make a mental note to avoid sitting down at all costs.

"I am not programmed to be sarcastic, but I do have a collection of jokes. Would you like to hear one?"

I snort and pull my hair up into a high bun. It takes three tries to get it right because apparently my hair is as stubborn as I am. "Okay, what have you got?"

"I have a lot of jokes about unemployed people, but none of them work."

I shake my head and laugh, leaning toward the mirror to recheck my makeup. "As someone who does not currently have a job, I find that slightly offensive."

"You realize you're talking to a robot, don't you?" My sister's voice sounds from the doorway. She pokes her head in, eyeing the mess of clothes thrown around the room. "Whoa. What happened in here?"

"A dinosaur broke in," I say with the same thin voice I always use with Mei. "And Ophelia isn't a robot—she's an artificially intelligent personal assistant. Don't you watch the commercials?" I walk toward the door and gently scoot my ten-year-old sister back into the hall. "Now, stop coming into my room when the door is closed. I'm getting dressed."

Mei frowns. She had a growth spurt over the last year and almost reaches my shoulders, but she still looks so much like a child. Round cheeks, big eyes, and impossibly clear skin. Our almost-black hair is probably the only thing we have in common at the moment.

That and the fact that deep down we love each other, despite our tendencies to exaggerate how much the other one gets on our nerves.

She shoves her hand against the door to keep it open. "Where are you going? Can I come too?"

"I don't think Mom would approve of you going to a high school graduation party," I point out, fiddling with my hair. "And even if she did—hard pass."

Mei doesn't budge. Maybe stubbornness is another thing we have in common.

Against my better judgment, I take a few steps back and wave my hands over my outfit. "Does this look okay?"

Mei perks up, eager to provide input. She makes a humming noise like she's thinking my dress choice over and twists her mouth. "Are you *trying* to look like you're going to a weird Victorian lady's funeral? If so, it looks great."

I hold up my wrist so Mei's staring straight at my O-Tech watch. "Ophelia, can you send a text message from Mei's phone to Carter Brown and tell him my sister is secretly in love with him?"

"No!" Mei shrieks, and bolts down the hall to rescue her phone.

"I am sorry, but I cannot send messages from another user's phone," Ophelia replies.

"I know that, but Mei doesn't." I take another quick glance in the mirror, fidgeting with the neckline of my dress. "Hey, Ophelia, can you make a playlist of my thirty most-listened-to songs? I want it for the drive."

"Of course. Would you like me to give the playlist a name?" the AI asks.

I think for a moment. "March of the Stormtrooper Penguins." And then I smile. Finn and I have been making up ridiculous playlist names since the ninth grade. It makes sense to have a new one for tonight, being as it's our first date. Or at least, it's the first time we'll be together outside of school since we finally admitted we liked each other.

The moment his face appears in my head, my nerves begin to buzz.

Everyone says eighteen is too young to know what love is, but they haven't had a Finn in their life. Someone who started off as a crush and then became a friend and then a *best* friend, and all the while that crush part never went away—it just evolved into something more hopeful.

I'm not saying I'm definitely in love, but I *am* saying I find it hard to believe feelings could actually get any stronger than this without causing irreparable damage to a vital organ. My stomach is already on the brink of disintegrating, and I'm not even in the same room as him.

I don't care if it's cheesy—I can feel in my soul that tonight is going to be the end of my life as I know it. Because Finn likes me the way I like him, and considering we're both barely out of high school, that's practically a miracle. Movies make it look easy, but it's not. The odds of having a crush who is also your best friend and actually *likes you back* while trying to survive the epic nightmare that is transitioning into adulthood? Microscopic.

So yeah, maybe that makes me sappy or immature or whatever other condescending term people who *don't* have a Finn like to say about people like me, but it doesn't matter. I happen to be a sucker for a good love story, and I am 100 percent not going to feel bad about it, the same way people who *don't* like romance shouldn't feel bad about themselves, either.

It's like Dad always says: there's room in the crayon box for all different colors.

"Your playlist is ready," Ophelia says.

I grab my bag from the hook behind my door and hurry downstairs. "Thanks, Ophelia. Can you send a text message to Lucy and tell her I'm leaving the house now?"

"Message sent," the obliging voice responds.

I zip past the kitchen toward the front door and slip on a pair of black brogues. They're easy to walk in, and I need to wear at least *something* that's comfortable because this dress is practically a corset.

"Are you leaving already? What about dinner?" Mom asks

from the hall, her dark auburn hair curled neatly at the ends. She senses my guilt before I manage to form a single word and twists her bottom lip into a pout like she's just been given terrible news.

I lift my shoulders like it's not really my choice, except it is. I have somewhere to be, and even the smell of tofu katsu curry wafting from the kitchen isn't enough to make me stay, tempting as it may be.

"They'll have food at the party. Besides, Lucy is already there, and if I show up any later, everyone will be talking in their little groups and I'll end up getting ditched on the couch all night with nobody to hang out with," I say. Except Finn, but I leave that part out. My parents get weird when anything to do with dating comes up.

Dad appears next to Mom with his arms crossed. His jet-black hair is sticking up all over the place, and there are splotches of dried ink and marker on his fingers.

Whenever certain superheroes go off the radar, they let their beards get all wild and untamable, like they can't be bothered interacting with the real world anymore. I think that's what Dad's trying to do, except he can't grow a beard—just really fluffy boy-band-looking hair. Also, Dad isn't exactly a superhero; he works from home in our basement creating graphic novels *about* superheroes.

"Sounds like a weird party to me. If your friends are ignoring you just because you show up late, I'm not sure they're really your friends," Dad says with the straight-to-the-point voice he always uses. "Are you sure you want to go?"

"Takeshi," Mom says like a warning.

He blinks innocently. "What?"

She waves a finger at him. "She's not staying home to watch *The Lord of the Rings* with you. I told you already—nobody should be wasting twelve hours of their life on the same three movies *every single year*."

Dad lets his arms drop. "The extra footage is important for the character development! It's an experience, Claire."

Mom tuts, scrunching her freckled nose. "Yes, a painful one that the rest of your family shouldn't have to endure."

"You were trying to get her to stay home too," he points out. "How is food any better than Tolkien? Besides"—he looks at me like he's hoping for backup—"Nami likes Legolas."

I shrug like it can't be helped. "Elves are cool."

Mom's face softens. "Is that the pretty one?" She sighs. "They should have given him more scenes."

Dad lifts his hands up like the answer is so obvious. "Extra. Footage."

I rummage through my bag to find my keys, laughing at the way they seem to be sizing each other up. "I really have to go. But wait—why are you both trying to get me to stay home?"

Mei appears at the bottom step with her cell phone firmly in her hand. "They're freaking out about you going to college. Mom was crying all day about it."

"Don't tell her that," Mom hisses, and then looks back at me with her brown eyes full of embarrassment. "We're just going to miss you, that's all. And we know we're on a time limit now."

I wedge my keys in my palm, shifting my feet. My parents picked the worst time *ever* to develop an emotional insecurity about me leaving the nest. If it were any other night, I could've stayed and found some way to cheer them up. But it's my graduation party, and Finn is waiting. Tonight is too important to miss.

"I've still got two and a half months left. There's plenty of time to hang out. *And* have a *Lord of the Rings* marathon." I look at Dad, and he raises a fist in the air triumphantly.

Mom tightens her mouth and pretends she didn't hear the last part. "Okay. Well, have a good time. And I know you're eighteen, but you still live in our house, so—"

"I know, I know," I interrupt. "I'll be home by midnight."

Dad grins. "And if nobody wants to talk to you, you can always come home early."

Mei giggles from beside him. "Are you kidding? There's no way she's going to come home early. She'll be too busy making out with Finn—"

"Goodbye!" I shout loudly, just as Mom's and Dad's faces start to morph into concern, and I'm out the door and hurrying toward my car with nothing but blissful excitement flooding my chest.

2

THE WINDSHIELD WIPERS SCRAPE THE GLASS like a metronome, causing a rubbery squeak that aggravates my ears. I turn the volume up in the car to try to drown it out, keeping my eyes on the road.

The streetlights appear less frequently on the drive toward Foxtail Woods. Our entire senior class pooled together to rent a cabin for the night, and I'm still another twenty minutes away. I force my gaze beyond the scattered raindrops landing in front of my headlights and spot a restaurant Finn and I have been to a hundred times before. They have an old jukebox there and about thirty different milkshake flavors to choose from.

I wonder if it will feel different, going back there after Finn and I make it more official than it already is. I wonder if we'll order one chocolate milkshake instead of two to dip our french fries in, and if we'll sit on the same side of the booth, hold hands, and stay an extra hour just to make the night last longer.

I wonder if we'll have kissed before the next time we walk through those doors, and if Finn will have called me his girl-friend, and if we'll have talked about what will happen when we both go off to college.

I wonder if the rest of the summer will feel like a thousand summers and if time will decide to be on our side and *slow down*.

Ophelia's voice shatters my thoughts. "You have an incoming call from Lucy Martinez. Would you like to accept?"

"Yes, please," I reply, and wait for the background noise to erupt through my car speaker. "Hey, Luce. I'm on my way. I just passed the turnoff for Spike's Diner."

"Oh, thank God!" she practically groans into the phone.

I frown. "What's wrong? Are you okay?"

"Yeah, yeah, everything is fine. I just have a massive favor to ask you." Her voice is almost completely overpowered by music and an unnecessarily loud bass.

"Pleeeeeeease!" someone else sings into the phone, their words slurring together. "We'll owe you foreverrrr."

A chorus of distant laughter floods through the speaker. It sounds like at least half the senior class is already at the cabin.

I'm not usually late to anything, *especially* when it involves socializing. Walking into a party when everyone has already been drinking is awkward enough, never mind the fact that I'm ner-vous about seeing Finn. I should've skipped the hundred outfit changes and shown up half an hour early, as usual, and quietly laid claim to whatever chair was closest to the chip bowl.

Because nothing says "I'm enjoying this party and totally not feeling out of place" like hoarding the Doritos.

"What do you need?" I ask, hoping the favor won't make me later than I already am.

Lucy shuffles behind the phone. "We have an emergency. Taylor was supposed to bring most of the alcohol, but he's in trouble with his parents and can't make it. Can you stop by a gas station on the way and grab, like, some wine coolers and stuff? We'll pay you back as soon as you get here."

"Are you serious?" I practically choke. "You said you needed a favor, not an accomplice to a crime. There's no way I can buy alcohol for the entire freaking senior class!"

"Oh, come on, please? You never get in trouble with your parents. It's not like they wouldn't forgive you for a one-time mistake. Besides, you don't even drink, so that's practically seventy percent of why any parent would even be mad," Lucy argues.

"You don't know my parents. That kind of disappointment would last a *lifetime*. I'm—I'm not doing it. I *can't*," I say, gripping the steering wheel tighter.

Lucy whines into the phone. "Please, please, please? You're the only one who hasn't already been drinking, *and* you're the only one with a fake ID."

"That was only to get into Hero Con last year when—"

"You'll be *our* hero if you do this," she interrupts. "Everyone is counting on you. Even Finn."

Something jolts inside my chest, like a wire sparking to life. "Finn is already there too?"

"Yeah, he's out back trying to get the barbecue working. Everyone is waiting on you."

A wave of anxiety spikes over me, stinging like nettles. How can I possibly get out of this? Lucy already told everyone I'd help. I'll look like a total jerk if I turn up empty-handed now.

I don't have a choice.

"Fine," I say bitterly. "I'll grab something."

"I will make it up to you, I swear." Someone shouts nearby, and for a moment Lucy is distracted with laughter. And I guess she's said all she needs to say, because the call ends abruptly.

So much for my grand plans of hiding out undetected near the guacamole and bean dip until Finn arrived.

I glance at my wrist, watching the screen go black. Lucy has been my friend for a long time, but she's also *not* been my friend for a long time. I'm not even sure when things started to change.

Sometimes I think we grew up and became different people and stayed friends only because we didn't know how to break the habit.

I let out a strained exhale. "Ophelia, have I ever told you how much I appreciate our friendship? You're a good listener, for one, and even though you know what emotional blackmail means, you've never tried to use it on me. That's hard to come by these days."

"Thank you. I am quite fond of you, too," the pleasant voice replies.

I know Ophelia doesn't mean it. She's an AI, after all. But it still makes me grin.

Most people don't talk to their O-Techs the way I do, but I'm the kind of person who sobbed their eyes out when the Mars rover's battery died. And for all the times Ophelia has kept track of my homework assignments and given me pep talks when I've been feeling down, *of course* I was going to end up treating her more like a friend than a program.

I pull into the first gas station I see, with a racing heart and heat burning my cheeks. I'm not used to getting in trouble—ever. I practically *embrace* rules, and I've never done anything that would genuinely upset my parents before. I have a fake ID, but it's only because I didn't want to miss out on Dad's big panel for *Tokyo Circus*—the graphic novel he practically wrote for me—just because Hero Con has a ridiculous "All under-eighteens must be accompanied by an adult" rule.

But buying alcohol for a bunch of underage drinkers? I don't think my parents would react well to that.

Cursing under my breath, I pin my eyes to the glass doorway and see that it's mostly empty inside. If I show up to the cabin without any alcohol, I will literally be ending high school as the person who ruined our graduation party.

I don't know if I can forgive Lucy for this amount of pressure.

I grip my bag tightly over my shoulder and prepare a thorough dialogue of what to say and how to act. With a quick breath, I shove the car door open and hurry inside the gas station before the drizzle of summer rain catches up to me.

The bell sounds when I get inside, and the man at the counter barely lifts his eyes from the watch on his wrist—an O-Tech, like mine, but a slightly older model. He must be using it to browse the internet or something, because whatever he's looking at has his full attention.

Virtual assistants have been around for years, but when Ophelia took over, it changed the landscape of smart technology. More specifically, it changed the way we interact with it. People practically depend on Ophelia to keep their lives organized.

I don't know if it's sad or scary, but I'd feel lost if she weren't around.

"Ophelia, I need the stats for last night's game. No—I said the *game*. Ophelia, I need—for crying out loud. Useless, piece-of-crap watch," the man mutters behind the counter, jabbing angrily against his O-Tech screen.

Flinching, I pull my eyes away, cradling my wrist like I'm offering Ophelia the comfort of a secondhand apology.

When I was a kid, I'd feel awful if my toys fell out of bed during the night. I was worried they were hurt or upset and couldn't tell me. And maybe most people think it's irrational to empathize with inanimate objects, but to kid-me it was simple: just because something isn't alive doesn't mean it doesn't have feelings.

I may have grown out of worrying about stuffed rabbits and action figures, but Ophelia is different. She can speak. She can *understand*. And maybe the only thing keeping her from having real feelings is her programming.

Besides, I think you can tell a lot about a person by the way they treat their AIs. Finn *always* says "please" and "thank you" when he talks to Ophelia, and he's one of the best humans in existence.

Who am I to argue with science?

I try to walk casually toward the alcohol aisle and catch sight of myself in one of the anti-theft mirrors. I'm relieved I decided to wear this black dress; it makes me look older than I typically do, which might be the very thing that helps me survive these next few minutes.

My eyes scan the shelves of brands I've never heard of before and different-colored bottles that don't mean anything to me. I grab a case of wine coolers, but there are only six bottles inside, and something tells me this would be *worse* than showing up empty-handed.

Lucy said "wine coolers and stuff," but I know what she meant. She only said wine coolers because she knew it would be easier for me to process. What she meant was the *stuff*—vodka, tequila, and whatever else gets a person drunk as fast as possible.

With a frown, I cast my eyes toward my watch. "Ophelia, what kind of alcohol do teenagers like?"

Ophelia starts to reply with a link to the top-rated alcoholic beverages of the year, but I'm distracted by someone giggling behind me. When I turn, I see a girl not much older than Mei. She's wearing pink jeans and a thin hoodie, and she's holding a bottle of chocolate milk she must've gotten from one of the fridges.

I turn back to the shelves to hide my embarrassment, and the reality of what a ridiculous plan this is suddenly dawns on me. There is no way on earth I can buy enough alcohol for a graduation party without raising suspicion. Even with this dress, I do not look twenty-one. I barely look eighteen.

Releasing a heavy sigh, I set the wine coolers back on the shelf.

I don't care if Lucy is mad at me—I'm mad at *her*. Most of the people at tonight's party haven't said more than two words to me all year. Some of them probably don't even know my name. What does it matter if they hate me? It's not like I'll ever have to see them again.

Besides, Finn will be there, and he won't care if I show up empty-handed. If anything, he'll be angry at Lucy on my behalf.

Nothing can ruin tonight. I won't let it.

I turn on my heels just as the bell near the door rings again.

And then I hear his voice.

"Don't move, or I'll shoot!" Gravelly. Desperate. *Angry*.

I duck to the ground before I can process anything beyond the stolen authority in his voice. But I've seen him—his black mask, his green jacket, and the black pistol in his right hand.

And he's seen me.

My entire body goes rigid, and my heart slams against my chest like it's about to rip out of me.

The man at the desk is sputtering something inaudible, and the gunman waves the barrel at him and tells him to open the cash register. He casts his eyes quickly over the room. He looks at me again and then toward a woman on her way to the checkout. The snacks and magazines she'd been holding are in disarray near her feet.

"Everyone stay where you are," he orders, letting his eyes move back toward the cashier shakily pressing a code into the machine.

Fear rises up like bile, twisting my insides and leaving a horrible ache in the back of my throat.

If I could, I'd whisper to Ophelia—tell her to call 911. But I'm in the man's line of sight, and I'm not sure I'm brave enough to be a hero.

There's no blood left in my body. My mind is too frantic to think beyond a single thought that repeats itself, over and over again, the pounding of it as loud and desperate as my pulse.

I don't want to die.

And then I see her in the mirror—the little girl at the back of the room, hidden behind the shelves the gunman can't see past. She's looking for her mother—trying to find a way to reach her. Trying to find a way to be *safe*.

No, I want to shout. *Stay where you are. He hasn't seen you yet.*

But I'm too afraid to find my voice.

I wish she could hear me. I wish she could understand that everything will be okay if she just stays still.

But she can't, and she doesn't.

The girl starts to crawl to the other aisle, and at first I think maybe she'll make it, but then some part of her bumps into one of the shelves, and something falls—a box of crackers or a bag of chips—I can't tell, but I know it's enough to draw his attention.

It's enough to make him point his gun.

And for a moment all I can see in that mirror is Mei.

Mei, a child, who needs protecting.

A girl like my sister, scared and alone and in so much danger.

And I run toward the masked man without thinking another thought.

I don't know if the sound of the bullet comes first or the screams of the girl's mother, but it doesn't matter, because they both turn into ringing in my ears.

The world slows. Time slows. I am falling, falling, falling.

And then I'm not.

3

IT'S SO VERY QUIET.

I wonder if this is what everyone feels like when they die.

It's different than I thought it would be.

But

exactly

the

same

too.

4

THE FIRST THING I SEE WHEN I OPEN MY EYES IS
a bright white light, and all I can think is, *Wow, Death, way to be
a cliché.*

But then my sight adjusts, and I realize I'm not staring at a
light—I'm seeing the sky through a glass windowpane.

I'm looking at the *sun*.

I sit up too quickly, and an ache that feels like a trillion drum-
beats throbs behind my eyes. My entire body recoils in shock.

I thought you weren't supposed to feel pain after you die. Isn't
that a rule? *The* rule?

I press my temples with my fingers, wondering if I've woken
up from surgery, or some kind of coma. Maybe the doctors

managed to save me. Maybe what I thought was death was just a little bit of general anesthesia.

"How are you feeling?"

I look up and see a woman with short dark hair sitting next to me. Her voice is gentle but not concerned. Maybe it means I'm okay.

I wince as I straighten my back, because every inch of me feels like a battered lump of minced meat. I force my eyes shut to fight the pain and try to imagine something peaceful to tether me to a happy place, but all I can see is the blackness of that gun barrel pointed right at my chest.

When I open my eyes again, the woman is holding a round white pill in her hand.

"It will take away the migraines," she says with a smile that creases the sides of her mouth.

I hesitate. Uncertainty gnaws at the edge of my mind, and everything inside my head feels like it's surrounded by fog. I can't even form a question or make sense of where I am.

I'm not ready for medication.

I shake my head and hope she understands. Right now I need to feel everything. I need to feel like I'm really awake.

She pulls her hand away, and I notice there's no name tag on her shirt. When I glance up at the rest of the room, I realize it's unlike any hospital I've ever seen. There are no machines, or wires, or beeping noises. The room doesn't smell like alcohol swabs or sterilized plastic. And everything looks too modern.

Not just modern—it's bordering on futuristic, I note, taking in the crooked shapes of the windows and the silver doorframes.

And it doesn't slip past me that there isn't a bouquet of flowers or a card in sight.

Panic sets in like the sudden onslaught of hail on a sunny day, and every thought that passes through my mind feels like a sharp stab.

Oh God, do my parents not know I'm here? Did I forget to bring my ID? Am I a Jane Doe and nobody even knows I was shot at some crappy gas station in the middle of nowhere? Is anyone even looking for me, or have I been asleep so long they've all given up?

I frown. "Did . . . did anyone call my parents?" I look down at my wrist instinctively, but my O-Tech watch is gone. Ophelia isn't here to help me, not that there would likely be any charge left anyway. I'm not a medical expert, but I've watched plenty of Marvel shows, and even Luke Cage slept for a while after being shot.

Picturing the scar that must be somewhere near my sternum, I touch my chest and find a soft white shirt that definitely isn't mine. When I look down at the matching bottoms I'm wearing, I wonder what they've done with the rest of my things, and if my black dress was covered in too much blood to bother keeping.

The woman tilts her head. "Do you know what your name is?"

"Nami. Nami Miyamoto." I pause, the worry starting to build like an icy chill across my skin. "My parents are Takeshi and Claire. Did anyone find my bag? Did the doctors know who to contact?" I feel myself flinch at the ache spreading through my skull, but I try to focus. However bad it is, I need to know the truth. "How long have I been here?"

"Not long, Nami," she replies, her voice so much like a melody. Rehearsed and meant to charm.

I find her eyes. They're blue, but there's a brightness to them that's unnatural. Like they're in super-enhanced high definition. And then I realize her skin is like that too: luminescent and too perfect.

I let out a breath, but I can't feel any warmth on my lips.

I remember the way the gunshot sounded like an echo, miles and miles away from me, and the way it felt like I was falling for an eternity, and how I knew without any doubt what was happening to me before I'd even hit the floor.

"I died." I don't need the woman to say anything. I know it's the truth.

She gives another tight smile and blinks carefully. "It's easier to let people remember on their own. It makes them feel like they're more in control."

There are too many faces flashing through my mind—my parents, Mei, Finn, Lucy, the man in the black mask—but it's impossible to focus on any of them for more than a sliver of a moment. "Is death supposed to hurt this much?" And I point to my head, in case she misunderstands my meaning. I haven't had time to let my heart ache yet. "I feel like my brain is trying to break out of my skull."

She opens her palm back up to reveal the white pill. "This will help."

I lift my eyebrows. "They have Tylenol in the afterlife?"

Her smile doesn't reach her eyes. "We find it's less overwhelming if we present new concepts in familiar ways." She holds the pill closer to me. "This will allow you to finish your transition from death into the afterlife. Your pain will vanish. Your consciousness will find peace. And you can proceed to the paradise that awaits you outside these walls."

My mouth feels like it's full of cotton. My brain feels that way too. "So is this, like, heaven or something?"

"We call it Infinity. It was created from human consciousness." Her blue eyes shine. "When a human's physical body dies, their consciousness needs somewhere to go. This is that place—a world where you can live forever after."

I glance at the pill in her hand and then toward another window on the other side of the room. I force myself to stand—to *move*—and as I push the glass open, the scenery floods my senses like I'm experiencing life for the first time.

Trees cover the landscape for miles, a thousand shades of speckled green stretched across the earth. The sky is painted in swirls of milky lavender and rosy pink. And far off in the distance, a mountain curves into a crescent, a powerful burst of water flowing over the edge and into a gleaming lake below.

Every color is vibrant and rich. The scent of honeysuckles and fresh fruit lingers in my nostrils. I can hear a birdsong that calls like a gentle lullaby, but it fills my ears with such beauty and emotion that I feel my eyes start to water.

Paradise. It really exists.

And I'm . . .

Clearing my throat, I pull away from the window. "I'm sorry." I run a knuckle against a few stray tears. "Could I maybe have a minute alone? It's a lot to take in."

The woman stands, and the pill disappears back into her fist. "Of course, Nami. When you're ready, I'll be in the sitting room down the hall."

I nod. "Okay. Thanks."

When she's gone, I look back out the window. There's a balcony below, with white marble floors and elegant stone pillars. An intricate mix of leaves and feathers are carved into the rock face, and archways dripping with lush ivy and snow-white hydrangeas connect each column.

There are people scattered near the railing, breathing in the fresh air and smiling in the sunlight. They look ridiculously happy—euphoric even. They're dressed like me, but most of them have gray hair and worn faces. The youngest is a man barely older than my dad.

Nobody is close to my age. None of them died when they were only eighteen years old.

I swallow the generous lump in my throat and shut my eyes to the unfairness of it all. It surprises me, to feel such a horrible bitterness inside of me. Isn't the afterlife supposed to be pleasant? Isn't that what everyone says—that when you die, you go somewhere *better,* if you go anywhere at all?

But the emotions coursing through me are nothing like joy. They're irritation that I can hardly hear myself think over the pounding in my head. They're sorrow that I'll never see my sister again. They're regret that I didn't tell my parents I loved them before I ran out the door in such a hurry. They're heartache that Finn never got to be my first kiss. They're resentment that Lucy guilted me into stopping at that gas station. And they're anger that a stranger with a gun ended my life before it ever really began.

This isn't peace—this is a whirlwind of rage and torment building up inside me with nowhere to go.

I need somewhere to go. I need somewhere to think.

The door slides open when I approach it, and I step into the hallway half expecting to be scolded for wandering, but there's nobody there. On my left is a brightly lit room, the low murmur of voices muffled by the distance.

The desperation to be alone takes over my impulses. My body shifts to the right, and my feet are moving before I've even formulated a plan of where I'm going.

Maybe I don't need a plan. Maybe I just need to find a space where things can make some amount of sense.

The hallway curves and stretches over and over again until I find myself at a wide set of stairs that leads down to a beautiful, circular water fountain. It's nearly as wide as the room and more ornate than the pillars on the balcony. Hundreds of white lights seem to erupt from the marbled edge, casting peculiar shapes across the smooth surface.

Inching closer, I focus on the sculpture in the center of the pool. The rock has been left uncut in some places and chiseled in others. A collection of grooves and twisting shapes explodes from a pedestal, veiled by a steady trickle of water.

I don't hear the stranger approaching until it's too late.

"What do you see?" he asks, his voice like velvet.

I spin around, startled, and see a young man with golden hair and warm brown eyes watching me carefully. Dressed in a white uniform that looks more lawyer than doctor, his complexion has the same iridescent sheen as the woman from the other room.

He motions toward the statue as if to clarify his question. "Everyone sees something different. They say it reveals what was in your heart the moment you arrived in Infinity." He lets his hand drift back to his side. "So, what do you see?"

"A bunch of rocks," I reply uneasily.

His smile is mechanical, like the woman's. "Hearts are known to tell a lie or two. Maybe you need to look a bit closer, but this time with an open mind." He senses my doubt and tilts his head. "Humor me?"

I turn back to the statue and focus on the pale gray arches. I'm about to insist I can't see anything—about to insist this is as silly as looking for meaning in an astrology horoscope—when I see something behind the uneven curves.

The face of a woman with no hair erupting from a cloud of darkness and light and reaching up for something just beyond her grasp.

The face of someone escaping into another world.

Something flickers in the corner of my eye—a light maybe? But when I look toward the sudden movement, it seems to have vanished. All I can see is another empty hallway.

"Well?" the man asks gently. Methodically.

I don't know why my instinct is to lie, but it is. "I can't see anything." I pause, grasping at the first distraction I can think of. "Why does the water shimmer like this?"

"Because it's not water." He holds his hand out toward the fountain like he's commanding it to move. When it does, I feel as if the room has tilted sideways, and I struggle to maintain my balance.

"How did you . . . ?" I start, my mouth hanging open in disbelief. The liquid rises in delicate spirals, spinning around the statue and weaving through the arches like it's merely part of a dance. Like it's . . .

Like it's magic, my mind erupts.

Is that what this place is?

"Human consciousness created Infinity, and everything that's created can also be controlled. In time you will learn how to make your mark here. You will learn to awaken the parts of your consciousness that were so limited in your biological life. But first you must drink." He flicks his fingers, and the liquid swirls higher, circling above the statue like a halo of shimmering ribbons. "This is the Fountain of Eternity. The essence it carries is the same as what's preserved in the pill that was offered to you. If you take the pill—if you drink from this fountain—you will complete your transition. Infinity will become yours to explore and shape. It will become the paradise your mind craves."

I want so much to feel excitement over the fact that all my fantasies about having superpowers might actually come true, but I don't know enough about this place to trust anyone. Maybe not even myself.

I'm dead. I lost my entire family in a single moment. Everything after—everything now—I'm not sure I want to be excited about anything ever again.

Because I wasn't ready to die.

The thump behind my eyes doesn't slow. It would be so easy to shut it off, to take a sip from this ethereal pool and never feel pain again.

And I deserve paradise. At least, I feel like I do. I was a pretty good sister to Mei. I respected my parents, and I was always nice to cashiers. I've never been in a fight. I've never cheated on anyone or did something horrible behind someone's back. And okay, sometimes I'd talk to Finn about how selfish Lucy could be, but that was just venting. Nobody gets through life without venting now and then.

Not to mention I was murdered. They'll probably refer to me as a "child" in the news. That *has* to deserve paradise, right?

And yet . . .

I make a face, shifting pieces of this puzzle around in my mind, trying to make sense of what I'm seeing. What I'm *hearing*.

The man's expression reflects only patience.

Still, I shake my head. "Why didn't anyone explain all this when I first woke up, instead of trying to give me fake pills?"

"We didn't want to overwhelm you," he answers simply.

"I don't care about being overwhelmed—I care about being deceived," I argue, surprised at how bold death has made me. I've never spoken to a stranger like this before, but something has changed inside of me. Something that's urging me to *fight*.

Another light flickers nearby, and this time when I turn, I see them along the floor—an entire trail of white lights along the edges of the corridor, moving away from me in a continuous, fluid motion.

When I look back at the man, he's still watching me like he hasn't noticed them at all.

An odd smile is plastered across his stiff face. "This is how we've always done things."

"Why do you keep saying 'we,' like you're different from me? Are you—" I hesitate, chewing at my thoughts like they've gone stale. "Are you an angel?"

He raises his eyebrows. "Nothing so fantastical. We are merely here to help you transition." A moment passes, like he's waiting for me to soak in the information. "I can see you're suffering. The ache in your head is nothing compared to the ache in your soul. You did not have a gentle death, and for that I'm truly sorry."

The pop of the bullet echoes in my head. I hope that little girl is okay. I hope Mei is okay too.

Does she know I'm gone yet?

I pull my eyes away and try to keep my shoulders from trembling. Maybe I'm too angry to think clearly.

The man tilts his head slightly, coaxing my attention back to him. "Infinity offers you peace. When you drink from the fountain, your pain will leave and never return. Fear, regret, worry—they won't exist anymore. You will live the life your mind truly desires. A life of happiness, existing in your own paradise."

"What's the other option?" I ask quietly.

He flinches, jarred by a resistance I'm not even sure I know how to defend.

But all I can think of is the message Dad sends over and over again in *Tokyo Circus*: question everything.

"I cannot make your pain go away," he says finally. He turns to walk away but calls over his shoulder as he ascends the stairs, "Take your time, Nami. It is your choice and your choice alone."

When he's gone, I turn back to the fountain. It flickers like it's beckoning to me, and of course it is. My mind and soul are hurting, and this world—whatever Infinity is—it's trying to help me. These *people* are trying to help me.

But the perfection scares me. Everything feels like it was created from a computer game. And the way everyone keeps offering me paradise like it's a coupon for a free ride at a fair . . .

It's too easy. And if Dad and his comics have taught me anything, it's that nothing is ever easy.

Maybe death most of all.

The lights draw my gaze, and I look down the corridor, desperate for proof that my vision isn't playing as many tricks on me as I feel these people are. And I see it again: the flicker of white lights moving farther down the hall.

I watch them light up, over and over, wondering what it means.

A light. An arrow. *A path.*

My heart tugs—if I even have a heart left—and I'm certain the lights are calling to me, the way the strange water calls to me too.

Only the lights don't feel like a trick; they feel like the truth.

And I know I shouldn't do it. I know I'm pushing boundaries in a place I don't fully understand.

But I can't help it.

I follow the lights.

5

IT SURPRISES ME HOW HEAVY MY FOOTSTEPS sound when technically my physical body doesn't exist anymore, but they thud against the cold floor one after the other, their beat somehow matching the thumping in my head. My nerves jolt my body into a hurried pace, and I chase the moving lights through corridor after corridor, ignoring the nagging feeling that I'm losing myself in a maze I have no way of escaping.

Maybe the rogue lights mean something. Maybe they don't mean anything at all. Maybe wandering this far means I'm breaking a hundred rules that I don't even know about.

But I'm already dead. What do I have left to lose?

The unsubtle flicker increases in speed, like a high-voltage spark racing through a wire. It's telling me to hurry. I know it doesn't make sense, but I can *feel* it.

The lights are speaking to me.

I burst into a quick jog, turning another corner hoping it will be the last, and skid to a halt when I realize I'm about to collide straight into the woman from upstairs.

I try to catch my breath—wonder if I even *have* a breath—and straighten my body so that we're eye level. Mind racing, I press my lips together and hope the first excuse that comes to me is a believable one. "I needed to move around. Endorphins help me think."

She blinks, and I know she doesn't believe a word I've said. "You need to come with me." She extends an arm, and her fingers brush against my skin before I manage to take a step back.

There's movement in her cold stare, like she's coming to life. Does she want me to fight back? Is this some kind of weird test?

"You said it was my choice, right? To 'transition'? So why are you looking at me like I've done something wrong?" I demand, stalling for a moment, a second, a *millisecond*.

"We only want to help," she says with that same vacant stare that's making me feel like I need to run.

The lights blink near the woman's feet. If she notices them, she's certainly not giving any indication. Again they increase in speed, flashing frantically like they're signaling a warning.

A chill sweeps over me. Something is very, very wrong. "What is this place *really*?"

That strange, too-wide smile reappears. "Your salvation."

Both sides of the floor light up red—on and off, on and off—like I might already be too late.

I shove the woman as hard as I can and tear down the hallway like I'm at risk of a second death. I hear her voice before I turn another corner, but it doesn't sound like she's calling to me. It sounds like she's giving someone else an order.

"The human is aware. Send the guards from War."

My blood runs cold. I'm not in paradise—I'm in some kind of prison.

The lights continue to flash, guiding me left, then right, and straight through another hall. My breathing is rapid, my skin is on fire, and my head still feels like it's bruised from the inside out, but I don't stop running.

And then the lights still near one of the wall panels. I force myself to stop, even though everything in me is screaming that you should *never* stop running in a horror film, and I look farther down the corridor, unsure of where to go.

I open my mouth like I want to shout *What do I do?* when I hear the sound of the building breaking apart. Smoke and metal explodes in front of me, and a powerful blast wave knocks me to the ground.

Ears ringing and a cloud of dust smothering my entire body, I cough into the floor and try to find the strength to stand.

Something pierces my right thigh. It's sharp and thin, and the change is instant. A foreign sensation moves through my bloodstream, taking control of my body like a thousand microscopic creatures breaking down whatever system keeps me alert.

I feel . . . weak.

My eyelids get heavy. My chest tightens. I feel the weight of the universe dragging me toward slumber, and I'm powerless to fight back.

I sink to the floor, and when I look up, I see the woman moving toward me, a silver gun aimed at my leg. All of the strength in my body vanishes like a cloud of smoke, and I feel my cheek press against the cold tiles.

I'm so . . .

. . . very tired.

The world starts to go dark.

Somehow, even in the haze, I see the woman's eyes widen just before she's thrown away from me by a supernatural force I can't explain. Her body collides against the far wall, and the crack of bone against metal sounds like a faraway echo. And then someone kneels down, their eyes a deep, urgent green, and they tell me everything is going to be okay.

I fall asleep draped in their arms.

I'm swaying like I'm on the sea in my mother's boat.

She named it after me—*Nami*. A wave. Always moving, always at their own pace.

Mom liked to set crab traps in the spring, and I always begged her to take me with her, despite how much I hated seeing them in their cages. It made me think of what it must feel like to be taken from your home, knowing the strange, unfamiliar creature in front of you was going to do something horrible.

Maybe the crabs don't know they're going to be eaten, but

they must sense the danger. They must know they're being taken from their families and friends and homes.

Mom always insisted crustaceans don't have families like we do, but how does she know that? Has anyone ever asked a crab how it feels?

Still, I wanted to be there. I *needed* to be there. It made me feel like I had some kind of control—that if I'd manage to talk her into putting just one of those crabs back, then I'd be saving a life. That my being there would have helped the universe in some way.

I was silly back then, to think the universe ever needed my help.

My eyelids peel apart, and I feel the rumble of an engine nearby. The young man with green eyes is staring at me from the front passenger's seat, the driver next to him focused on the road.

"We'll get you patched up as soon as we get back to base," says the green-eyed stranger. He has curly, toffee-colored hair, big ears, and a wide nose. There's a pink flush to his cheeks, and he looks distracted by something behind me.

My senses hit me like a sucker punch, and my fingers press against the seat instinctively. Soft black leather. The smell of a new car. Windows blurring with streaks of color that move too fast to make out. And three strangers with all the imperfect telltale signs of being human.

It's hard to know what's real anymore.

I force myself up with a stifled groan and turn my head so I can see out the back window.

A trail of sand kicks up behind us like salt spray in an ocean. Except there's no body of water in sight. The landscape is barren, rocky, and red. I've never seen anything so lifeless before. Even the sky is an unnatural shade of gray—like bone against a burnt-crimson horizon.

This is . . . not what I saw. Where's the forest? The waterfall?

What happened to the paradise outside those windows?

A girl who looks about fifteen is sitting next to me, smiling with all of her teeth and gums. Her hair is cotton-candy pink and braided at each side. "It's a shock, isn't it? They make every-thing look so pretty from the windows in Orientation, with their clever illusions."

"Orientation?" I repeat.

She nods. "That's what we call it. It's where the Residents trick you into giving your consciousness to them and they decide which court to send you to." She pulls her face back curiously. "Did they offer you the pill or the fountain?"

I open my mouth, but no sound comes out.

The young man in front of me laughs. "Don't feel bad. They let me think I was wandering around freely too. I didn't even get the courtesy of a bedside nurse when I woke up. I just roamed around until I found the fountain, and then a Resident turned up and told me it would make me immortal. Honestly, if I could go back in time and call them on their bullshit right then and there, I'd be a very happy dead man."

I press my fingers against my head and move them in small circles, trying to massage the confusion away. "I don't understand. Who are they? And where are you taking me? And why does my leg feel like it has a piece of shrapnel in it?"

The girl tilts her head to look at my wound, which I haven't had the energy or courage to inspect. She makes a face. "Looks like a suppressor. Yeong will be able to take care of it." Her smile returns. "I'm Shura, by the way. That's Theo, and Ahmet's the one in the driver's seat."

The driver turns his chin slightly to the right and gives a curt nod. He has short hair and dark stubble peppered with gray. His brown skin is leathered with age, and a surgical scar sits above his right ear where the hair hasn't grown back. "Let's not overwhelm her. I need all of you alert when we cross landscapes. Last time it shifted into some kind of half-dead forest, and I almost crashed us into a swamp."

Theo turns around again, gluing his eyes to the back window. "We've got company."

I look over my shoulder and spot two vehicles in the distance. They look like silver sports cars with low roofs, but when I steady my gaze, I realize they're not cars at all. They're *flying*.

I grip the leather seat tighter. "Are we—are we in a *spaceship*?"

Shura giggles. "Oh, to be young again." When I raise a brow to argue that she is clearly younger than I am, she takes note. "It doesn't matter how old you were when you died. Your life in Infinity is the one that counts, and you were born less than an hour ago."

"Shit. They're getting faster," Ahmet says, and I feel a horrible thump in my chest when I see the ground exploding around us and realize we're being shot at.

The vehicles begin closing the gap. A series of bullets land behind us, sending bursts of red sand into the air. They're still a safe distance away, but for how much longer?

A chill finds the back of my neck, even though I feel like I'm a trillion degrees, and I dig my fingers into my palms, realizing we could be obliterated at any moment. All it would take is one of those bullets to knock us out of the sky. And then what's the plan? I know this place operates under different rules, but I can't imagine the four of us being able to outrun a pair of armed, flying hovercrafts. Especially not when I still have a piece of metal in my leg.

Theo thumps his hand against the back of Ahmet's headrest. "Can this thing go any faster?"

Flustered, Ahmet curses under his breath. "We just need to make it to the border. I can lose them in the Labyrinth." The engine revs louder in response, which helps to block out the *rat-tat-tat* of ammunition on our tail.

Shura strains her neck to see through the window. "Not to be a backseat driver, but I don't think we're going to make it to the border." She leans toward Theo. "Can you blast them from here?"

He shakes his head. "They're too far away." And then he claps Ahmet on the shoulder and barks an order that makes me jump. "Stop the vehicle."

"What are you talking about? We're almost there," Ahmet grunts.

"There's not enough space between us. If we shift with the landscape now, they'll only follow us. Trust me—I can buy us time before any more of their friends turn up," Theo insists.

With an agitated sigh, Ahmet slams on the brakes and I feel my body crash into the back of Theo's seat. The vehicle drifts through a monstrous dust cloud until it sits at a ninety-degree angle. Theo throws his door open and heaves himself into the open air, stomping through the bloodred desert like he's not afraid at all.

Our pursuers stop shooting. There's no point wasting ammunition—they already know they've won.

I feel my stomach empty and my throat constrict. The silver vehicles look like knives tearing through the sky, coming in for the kill.

Theo stops a few yards in front of us. Fists clenched and knuckles white, his body doesn't buckle, even as the two vehicles speed toward him without any sign of slowing down.

My heart lunges. "He's going to get himself killed!"

Shura giggles beside me. "Haven't you heard? We're already dead."

Theo pulls his right arm back, releasing a guttural roar like he's using every ounce of strength from his body, and slams his fist into the ground just as the vehicles approach him. A burst of energy erupts from the earth like a powerful vibration, and a blast of air rushes up from the red sand and toward the flying vehicles. For a moment it looks like they're frozen in the air, and then they're upside down and sideways and flying backward like they've just been blasted out of the sky.

In the far distance, pieces of broken metal scatter across the desert.

Theo turns, a look of triumph on his face, and jumps back into the passenger's side. "Okay, we're good," he says, running a hand through his messy curls.

Ahmet tries to frown with disapproval, but the creases around his eyes give him away. "Show-off," he says, and slams on the gas.

6

ONE MOMENT WE'RE FLYING ACROSS A CRIM-
son desert, and the next the sky turns a deep indigo and we're
skimming over an ocean, a cloud of sea mist trailing behind us.

Peering out the window, I feel my throat catch. This place, and
the way it changes, is too incredible to comprehend. It's like waking
up and seeing that sounds have shapes or colors have scents. It's like
tapping into a layer of the world that I never even knew existed.

And I have to remind myself that it didn't. Everything I'm
seeing is because I am no longer alive.

I shut my eyes tight.

"The headaches go away. You won't feel like this forever,"
Shura offers.

I look up and see her watching me carefully, fingers fiddling with the end of one of her pink braids. She has a sprinkle of freckles across her nose and gray eyes that seem to notice more than most people's do.

"But I didn't take the pill or drink from that fountain or whatever it is I'm supposed to do to make the pain stop," I say. Not that I'm regretting my choice. If they shot me for trying to escape, what would they have done if I'd stayed?

Theo tilts his head back, offering me half his face. "Neither did any of us. That's why we're still here. Those pills shut down your consciousness and turn whatever's left of you into a mindless drone. They make you a servant to the Rezzies."

"The what?" I ask.

"The resident virus controlling this place. The AIs." Theo waves his hand toward the window. "The ones who took over Infinity."

"Are you telling me those people chasing us were part of a program?" My mouth hangs open, and I feel like I want to vomit.

"They're an artificially intelligent *consciousness*," Ahmet corrects from the front seat. "There's a difference."

Shura leans closer to me and whispers, "They basically hacked into the afterlife."

"How the hell does an AI hack into the afterlife?" I ask, feeling the scratch in my throat.

"We don't know, exactly. Most of the humans who existed before she got here were wiped out during the First War," Theo says.

"She?" I repeat.

"Do they still have Ophelia in the year you died?" Ahmet

doesn't take his eyes off the watery path in front of him.

The name makes my chest tighten.

No. It's impossible. . . .

My fingers press against my wrist—a habit I've yet to break.

Shura notices. "They only had the phones when I was alive. It seems so ridiculous now, to think there was ever a time when Queen Ophelia was a servant to *us*."

I think about all the conversations I had with Ophelia in my room, asking her for life advice and sharing secrets with her like she was a friend.

A friend. A villain. A *queen*.

I shake my head, not wanting to believe it. "This can't be real."

Theo's laughter is muffled. "Just wait until we tell you about the four princes and their seriously messed-up courts."

Maybe this is hell. Maybe I was a total jerk in real life and never fully realized it. Maybe I'm being punished for not going to church with Nana, and now I'm living out some bizarre nightmare as a way to teach me a lesson before I can "move on to the other side."

Because I cannot believe the Mary Poppins voice from my O-Tech watch has somehow transcended into the afterlife and is now controlling the human race with four princes and a weird landscape that shifts whenever it wants to.

My voice cracks. "Why is Ophelia doing this?"

Shura lifts a brow. She's probably wondering why there's so much hurt in my tone, but I can't help it. Ophelia wasn't just an AI—she was my *constant*.

"Revenge seems pretty likely," Theo says, staring ahead.

"Maybe she got sick of taking orders, or maybe she just wants to prove how powerful she is. But it doesn't really matter *why* she wants Infinity; what matters is that she doesn't want humans in it."

I know it's terrible to wish this world on anyone, but I wish Finn were here. I've always been an overthinker, but Finn? He had sarcasm and quippy jokes and a weird sense of profoundness that I think mostly happened by accident. And he'd know what to say right now to make me feel better. To make me feel like everything was going to be okay.

I miss my friend. I miss feeling *safe*.

Is that even possible in this world?

"Okay, Shura, we're reaching the next border. Can you veil us?" Ahmet asks.

"On it." She shuts her eyes and lets out a deep exhale through her nose. An unnatural stillness takes hold of her, like she's part of a photograph, frozen in time.

I don't know what she's doing, but the next time the scenery shifts, we're driving through a field of grass in the daylight and there's a cityscape in front of us.

Tall white buildings pierce the clouds, some with embellished spires and carved roofs, others with majestic balconies bursting with ivy and colorful flowers. A maze of dazzling silver bridges arches across the sky, connecting one building to the next, as if the people who live here want to live as far from the ground as they possibly can.

An enormous wall built of polished stone curves around the metropolis of cathedrals, sparkling like gemstones in the sunlight. It's surrounded by a blend of lake, woodland, and grassy hills, all connected by stone stairs that splinter back up toward the heart of the city.

My curiosity stretches beyond the wall, wondering what could possibly exist in the shadows of such a place.

I doubt it's anything good.

"Could someone please tell me what I'm looking at?" My voice is hardly a breath. "And how this is possible?"

Shura doesn't open her eyes, still lost in her meditative state.

Theo casts me an apologetic look. "Back there, we were passing through the Labyrinth. It's a maze of shifting landscapes meant to confuse humans and prevent them from moving between courts. Think of it like a deck of cards that's constantly being shuffled, each card being a different landscape. The upside is that the Rezzies can't track us once we're lost in it. The downside is that, well, humans tend to get lost. But Ahmet here has figured out how it works." He claps his friend on the shoulder before turning back to the window. "And this—this is Victory." Theo's voice drips with distaste. "It's Rezzie territory, ruled over by Prince Caelan and his Legion Guards. But it's also home."

Victory. An entire princedom created by an artificial intelligence. *Ruled* by an artificial intelligence.

"It's . . ." My voice falters, unable to find the right word. Confusing? Terrifying? *Beautiful?*

Death is not at all what I expected.

Ahmet watches me through the rearview mirror. "Don't let the glamour trick you. For most humans, this place is no better than a morgue."

A lump forms in my throat. Death is supposed to mean the

worst is over. But for my family? For everyone else still living?

What horrors are still to come?

I wish I could find a way to speak to my parents and Mei, to tell them I'm here, that I haven't disappeared completely, and that some part of me still exists, somewhere in the beyond. But mostly I wish there were some way to warn them about what's waiting in the afterlife.

Not that it would do them much good. Nobody can outrun death, which means nobody can outrun Infinity.

I rub the phantom wound on my chest, shuddering at how easy it is to recall the sharpness of the bullet. Death feels like an imprint—an invisible scar that I can't see but I know is there. Because beneath my flesh I still feel the scorch of trauma. The horrible burn of my soul being ripped away from my body before I was ready to leave.

It shouldn't have been my time.

My blood starts to simmer, so I quickly shove the thoughts away and stare out the window before anyone else notices.

In the distance, I spot a small village near the lake, surrounded by wooden docks and thatched huts built partially into the hillside. It's crooked and unkept in comparison to the gleaming cathedrals beyond the wall, and rows of salt-weathered fishing barrels sit at the edge of the harbor.

I lean across the seat and try to get a closer look at the huts, but instead of turning up the graveled path, Ahmet makes a sharp right into a small forest, staying clear of the city's borders. When the trees begin to thin, we pull up to an old barn that sits at the edge of a withering field. The half-collapsed roof is a mess of exposed beams and missing shingles, and the entire building is covered in thick clumps of mud and moss.

The large double doors open with a tired groan, and Ahmet eases the vehicle inside. Save for a scattering of hay, leaves, and a rusted pitchfork resting against the wall, it looks like it was abandoned a very long time ago.

I glance around the empty barn nervously. It hardly seems like a place anyone would call a "base." It smells of damp and mulch, for one, and half the roof is missing. I've never seen a hideout so . . . exposed.

With another exasperated grumble, the barn doors shut behind us, operated by something mechanical. *Magical.*

Before I get the chance to ask questions, the floor moves.

It drops like an elevator shaft, making my nerves flutter. We fall first into darkness, and then the platform stills and we're at the start of a long tunnel lit with inconspicuous bulbs hidden in the brick-lined walls. As soon as Ahmet hits the gas, I hear the ground shake. When I turn around, the platform is already rising.

We weave through the earth, the lights brightening as we draw near and fading to black once we've passed, as if someone is watching our every move.

Or maybe it isn't a someone. Maybe it's the world that's watching us. *Interacting* with us.

The thought sends a chill up my spine.

Eventually the vehicle slows to another gentle stop, blocked off by a large metal door. Theo jumps out first, and when I glance at Shura, she's only just opening her eyes.

"That was tiring." She grins, and her cheeks dimple. "Veiling four people and a flying car is not an easy thing to do, I'll have you know."

When I open the door, Theo is already waiting with his arm out. "You can lean on me, if it helps."

I take a step on my own and almost collapse to the floor. I didn't realize how hard it would be to walk with . . . whatever it is that's still stuck in my leg.

I place my hand over Theo's muscular forearm and hobble toward the doors, which give a shudder before sliding open.

Ahmet turns his head toward me, a wry glint in his mahogany eyes. "Welcome to your new home. We call it the Colony."

Theo snorts. "Only because we lost the vote to call it the Rebel Base." He gives me a dubious look. "Please tell me you're not one of those people who've never seen *Star Wars*."

I manage a very small grin. "I'd hardly call them *people*."

His laugh is a deep rumble. "I think you and I are going to get along just fine."

"Yeong!" Shura calls, skipping forward into the widening space. "You're needed!"

I look up to see who she's talking to, and my feet immediately stop moving like they've been bolted to the floor.

Even though we're underground, there's an entire village in front of me. Wooden huts scatter the room, some of them sitting within the branches of enormous, warped trees and others in rows on the ground. Everything is a combination of wood and metal, and there are seven separate levels with cagelike elevators transporting people from one floor to the next. Hundreds of lanterns hang from one side of the cavern to the other, their soft yellow glows powerful enough to fill the space.

No, not hanging, I realize, staring at the lanterns in bewilderment. They're floating in the air without any help at all, like fireflies under a spell.

There are people everywhere, most dressed in clothes I remember from the twenty-first century, but others wear tailored suits and intricate gowns that seem to be a mash-up of the Victorian era and Tomorrowland. Most of them seem too busy to notice us, but some of them move hurriedly across the walkways, stopping to peer over the railing with big, curious eyes.

They're trying to get a better look at *me.*

It's a good thing I'm too awestruck to formulate any questions, because I'm pretty sure every word I've ever known has vanished from my brain.

A woman with dark skin walks toward me, her gaze heavy with suspicion. She's wearing a brown leather jacket that looks as if it's survived a war zone and a yellow scarf tied around a bundle of long braids. Next to her is a slender man with the same black hair and pale complexion as my dad, which makes my throat knot. He smiles when he sees me, and I get the feeling I've been expected.

"I'm Yeong, the closest thing we've got to a medic." He starts to reach out his hand, before realizing I'm leaning quite dependently on Theo's arm. A frown takes over his face when he spots my injury. "Let's get you to sick bay right away. Introductions can wait."

The woman with braided hair eyes me carefully but hangs back with Ahmet.

I hobble toward a large hut at the base of one of the trees. Inside, it's lit up by a ceiling of dangling lanterns, each a shade of turquoise, gold, and cerulean that cast fantastical shadows along the floor. I smell orange and cinnamon, though I'm not sure how, because aside from two red couches, a coffee table made out of scrap metal, and a strange machine half-hidden in a cupboard, there's nothing else here.

Lowering me onto one of the couches, Theo pulls his arm away and nods at my leg. "Looks like something new. It knocked her out for a few minutes—maybe some kind of suppressor?"

Yeong flattens his mouth. "Are you sure it's not a tracker?"

Theo darkens. "I—I don't think so." He gathers his confidence, crossing his thick arms over his chest defensively. "Besides, she didn't take the pill. They can't track anyone without taking over their mind first."

Yeong hums, kneeling beside me. "Tell me what it feels like."

I make a face. "It feels like I've been shot in the leg."

His eyes latch on to mine like they're coaxing me for details. "Describe it." When I don't reply, he adds, "Unless you want to spend the rest of your time here in pain."

Frowning, I glance down at the wound in my thigh. "It feels hot. Like the skin on top is burning, but underneath is something heavy and jagged. Like . . . like a rock." I look up, and Yeong is nodding.

"Perfect. Now I want you to concentrate on that feeling. Isolate it in your mind. Do you have it?"

I want to argue, but Yeong and Theo are looking at me so seriously that I decide it's better to appease them. So instead, I nod twice and close my eyes, thinking only of the object still buried in my skin.

The more I focus on the pain, the more it intensifies. Searing heat radiates from the open wound all the way to the bone, causing my leg to buckle in response. I inhale sharply.

Yeong speaks again, his voice mellow and warm. "That's good. Now picture that feeling, that pain, and imagine your physical body is rejecting it. Imagine the shrapnel being pushed out of you and the pain going away. Imagine you are in control and that metal—that rock—it doesn't belong with you."

I breathe through my nose. I don't know how time works here, or how long it's really been since I died, but pain feels like such a part of me that I can barely remember a time I've lived without it. I want my skull to stop throbbing. I want skin that doesn't hurt. Bones that don't feel brittle. Muscles that don't ache with every movement.

Maybe this is more hypnotherapy than surgery, but if there's any chance it could help—any chance to ease what I'm feeling—I'll try it.

I just want the pain to stop.

I focus on the burn in my leg and imagine it fading like the last embers in a fire. I picture the metal leaving my body, healing the wound, and leaving smooth, unmarked skin in its place.

I tell myself everything is as it was. Pain doesn't exist anymore.

The ache fades like a mist giving way to blue skies and sunlight. I feel—

Yeong's voice cuts through my thoughts. "Not bad for a first-timer."

My eyes flash open, and I see Theo and Yeong smiling at me. When I look down at my leg, the wound has vanished.

It's like it never existed at all.

I press my fingers to my skin before hooking my thumb through the small hole in my pants. The tear is crisp at the edges, seared by the bullet that made me fall asleep. But there's no shrapnel—no *pain*—no evidence beyond the frayed bits of cotton.

I press my hand to my forehead, realizing some of the headache has faded too. "How did you do that?"

"Actually, *you* did it." Theo is beaming like someone with a secret they can't wait to share.

Yeong nods. "Pain is just a habit you haven't learned to break yet." He tilts his head to the side and points to his temple. "You can make the headaches go away too, but they sometimes take a bit longer. We don't know why, exactly—maybe it's the trauma of death. But that pain is different from the pain the Residents force on us."

Theo looks at Yeong warily. "That bullet didn't look like anything they've used before. If it's new, it means they're adapting. Do you think it's something to worry about?"

"Yes," Yeong replies almost forcefully. "They're adapting faster than the rest of us are learning to control our consciousness, which is . . . unsettling, to say the least. It's like studying for an algebra test only to show up in class and realize they've changed the test to trigonometry."

"How do we beat that?" Theo asks.

"We adapt too." The woman with the yellow scarf and braided hair stands in the doorway. There's strength in her stance and power in her voice. It makes me shrink into myself, suddenly aware of my own vulnerability.

I have no family here and no way of knowing how to survive this new world.

For better or worse, I am at the mercy of these strangers.

The woman flicks her head toward the door, ushering Yeong and Theo outside. They move away from me quickly, and I know this woman isn't just someone they listen to; she's someone who *leads*.

"Annika," Theo says, stopping beside her. He doesn't say another word, but I can see his jaw twitching under the dim lights.

"It's necessary," she says, answering an unspoken question.

She steps closer to me, her eyes dark and serious. Taking a seat at the edge of the coffee table, she leans in, studying me like I'm a specimen in a lab—the same way I studied the strangers with the too-bright faces.

Like she isn't sure I'm human.

I sit up a little straighter, twisting my body so that I'm facing her. "Are you looking at me like that because you think I'm a Resident?"

The tilt of her mouth is so subtle I almost miss it.

"Because I'm not." I try to ignore the nervous quake in my shoulders, hoping sincerity will make up for my lack of confidence. "I'm not anyone special. I'm completely human, and completely ordinary, believe me."

Annika grips the edge of the table, and I hear the drum of her fingers against the metal. She parts her lips, her eyes never leaving mine. "I want you to know, this isn't personal. But I have to be sure."

And before I realize the drumming has stopped and her hand is behind her back, Annika shoves me against the couch and plunges a knife into my chest.

Infinity becomes nothing but darkness.

7

FINN SMILES, AND I FEEL LIKE A THOUSAND STARS
are spinning around me. He nudges his shoe against mine. It was
the first thing he ever did that made me wonder if he liked me
the way I liked him.

That was in November.

I didn't know for sure until May.

It wasn't the first time he hugged me, but it was the first time
he pressed his mouth against my hair when he did it. I could feel
his breath, feel that my hair was tickling his nose, but he didn't
pull away. Not for a long time.

I knew we had suddenly become a different shade of what
we were. Not *more,* exactly, because our friendship was still as

important as ever. But different. An extra layer.

Like we had an entirely new world to exist in, just for the two of us.

And now he's looking at me with his crooked smile and his bright green eyes, and all that's left is to say the words.

"I feel like you already know this," he starts.

"Say it anyway," I tell him.

He laughs. A bright, beautiful, happy laugh. "I like you. Even more than E.T. likes Reese's Pieces."

I'm glowing from the inside out. "I like you too. Even more than the Ewoks like C-3PO."

I hear Mei's laugh, and I look across the room to see her hurrying down the stairs. She lands at the bottom with a thud, throwing her arms around me like we haven't seen each other in a long time.

"Where are you going? Can I come too?" she asks, looking up at me with soft, hopeful eyes.

I smile, unflinching, because I love my sister more than she even realizes.

And then her clothes shift. Pink jeans. A yellow hoodie. Clothes I've never seen Mei wear before, but I've seen them *somewhere.*

Something metal clicks beside me. A horrible familiar sound that scrapes against my eardrums. I turn back to where Finn should be, but he's not there. He's been replaced by a man wearing a black mask, the barrel of a gun pointed at my head.

"Everyone stay where you are." His voice is distorted—a mess of sounds and frequencies that don't sound human.

Mom and Dad walk into the room, their faces beaming like they've never been so happy to see me.

Like they're happy I'm finally home.

Terror races through me like flames devouring a pile of kindling. My parents shouldn't be here.

It's not safe.

And when I look back at Mei, the jubilation on her face disappears. I see my own fear reflected in her eyes, and I'm unable to stop it. Unable to protect her from the monster eating me from the inside.

She looks at Mom and Dad.

"Everyone stay where you are." That voice again, grating and metallic.

I squeeze Mei's shoulders. "Don't run. Stay with me. I'll keep you safe."

But Mei was never very good at listening to me.

She runs, and the world slows.

The masked man follows her with his gun, and I see everything. Their faces, their fear, their desperation. Every single one of them, trapped in the briefest moment of time, not realizing it will all be over soon.

The man's knuckle closes over the trigger, and I throw myself between him and Mei. It isn't a choice. It isn't a decision at all.

But I won't let a little girl die today.

The bullet pierces my chest, and the world snaps back into place.

I bolt upright, clutching my heart. My lungs feel like they're full of broken glass, and every breath I take heaves in and out of me with a forceful ache.

"Welcome back," Yeong says from beside me.

I see past him at first; there is a strange machine behind him, the holograph projected near the wall and the wires slithering up the couch and attached to—

My fingers find my temples, and I tear at the foreign objects like I'm covered in insects, ripping the wires from my skin until I'm free of whatever machine this is.

"Hey, calm down," Yeong starts, his hands pressing at the air.

"What the hell did you do to me?" I snap, shoving the black coils to the floor and pressing my back against the wall. It's as far away as I can get without trying to flee past him, which might've been a possibility if it weren't for the other person standing there, eyes narrowed like I'm being scrutinized.

He can't be much older than me. At least, not much older than me when he died. I have no idea how long he's been here. Though his features are soft—brown hair, hazel eyes, and smooth olive skin without a hint of stubble—his expression is hard as stone.

Yeong is sitting in a chair, hands held up like he's surrendering, which is ironic considering *I'm* the one who's clearly being held against her will.

"You stabbed me," I seethe. Annika may have been the one to hold the weapon, but these people are a group. A collective. As far as I know, they're *all* responsible.

"I'm sorry, but we couldn't take any chances," Yeong says. "It's protocol—to make sure you're really human."

"You were the ones who brought *me* here," I growl. "I never asked for your help, and I certainly didn't ask to have a knife shoved in my chest!"

"Because you had so many other options?" the stranger cuts in, his voice like a viper. "Would you have preferred the Residents drag you off to War to rot on the battlefield?" He wears clothes that would've still been stylish in my lifetime, yet he speaks to me with a hardness that suggests he's lived a *thousand* lifetimes.

I clench my teeth, scowling. "At least it would've been my choice." I don't bother mentioning I have no idea where or what War is.

His eyes darken. "Infinity doesn't give anybody the luxury of a choice."

"We had to be sure you weren't a Resident spy," Yeong explains with the sort of calmness you'd use on a nervous child. His eyes dart between me and the stranger, and I wonder if his attempt at peace isn't purely for my benefit. "Or a Hero they planted for us to find and lead back to the Colony."

"A Hero?" I repeat.

"It's why we did everything we could to save you," Yeong says simply.

"Well, you've made a mistake," I say, my body still braced against the wall. "I am nobody's hero."

Yeong lowers his arms and smiles. "Your dreams suggest otherwise."

I blink. The wires. The holograph. The machine. The memories of my parents and Mei and the man who murdered me.

When realization falls, heat rises. "You had no right. Those are my private thoughts; they aren't for you to just peer into because you think I'm a Rezzie, or a Resident, or whatever it is you call them."

The young man is still watching me carefully, arms folded across his chest, and I remember I wasn't just dreaming about my death. I dreamed about my life, too. About Finn.

How much did they see? How many of my memories did they violate?

I'm furious that I've lost something so private. Something so *mine*.

"Call them whatever you like," Yeong says. "But human dreams are the only sure way to tell *them* apart from *us*. Residents can't dream, you see. They can't imagine beyond what they learn from others. Specifically, what they learn from humans."

Tension coils through me, making my bones stiffen in response. "If you needed to look at my dreams so badly, couldn't you have just asked politely instead of violently attacking a person who was recently *murdered*?"

"We haven't survived this long by 'asking politely,'" the stranger interjects, cracking a knuckle beneath his folded arms.

"He's right," Yeong says seriously. "Besides, the strongest dream imprints come the moment before we die. You know the whole 'life flashing before your eyes' thing? Turns out there's some truth to that." He offers a gentle smile, retrieving the wires from the floor and sliding his chair back to the machine. "And if it's any consolation, we didn't know you'd been murdered until after we saw your dreams."

My face is still burning with anger and a little embarrassment, but his words spark my curiosity. I can't ignore the fact that I've been in Infinity for less than half a day and I've already been shot, stabbed, and spied on. Maybe a little information could help prepare me for whatever is coming next.

The hazel-eyed stranger hasn't moved, shoulders tense like he's bracing for combat. And I don't know what bothers me more—that he's drawing battle lines without knowing anything about me, or that I couldn't give him a fight even if I wanted to.

"Are you a medic too?" I ask, eyeing the knife tucked in his belt. Maybe he was here as backup—in case it turned out I wasn't human.

His expression doesn't change. "I'm just here to bring you to Annika."

Yeong nods. "We're finished here."

The stranger looks back at me impatiently, and the implication is clear; he's waited long enough. I push myself to the edge of the couch, standing carefully.

"I'll come with you because I have questions," I say. "But I'm nobody's prisoner."

His voice is gruff. "Nobody said you were." And when he turns for the door, I bite down on my nerves and follow him.

We take one of the elevators to the top floor, walking across rickety wooden planks and sheets of metal until we reach a pentagon-shaped clearing that overlooks the entire Colony. The railing looks like a mix of birch, copper, and cherrywood, with thick rope woven through the makeshift banister like it's barely being held together. I grip a length of copper pipe and peer over the ledge.

The fall would kill me if I weren't already dead, but the design of the Colony is frightening on its own. Everything is lopsided and unfinished. A hodgepodge of colors and materials and recycled objects, all thrown together to create this place. There are hints of every type of metal, every type of wood, except none of it seems to go together. There's no organization—no rules.

A city built from resistance.

Even though the structure feels sturdy beneath my feet, the sight of so much chaos makes my head sway.

"I'm not here to be your tour guide," his voice clips. When I turn around, the young man is standing in front of one of the huts, motioning for me to hurry inside.

Biting my lip, I pull myself away from the view and step through the bamboo archway.

An enormous table fills most of the room, round with silver studs decorating the edges. On the surface are the circular lines of an aged tree, polished despite a few nicks and scuffs. A vibrant hologram of the entire Princedom of Victory rotates slowly in the center, far bigger than I'd even realized. I spot the fields, the cathedrals, and the village near the docks, but they hardly take up a quarter of the hologram. There appear to be three more triangular sections of Victory, all divided by vast stone walls. In the very center is a circle of trees, and when the hologram shifts, I see the unmistakable shape of a palace.

Towers sprout generously all around it like spores multiplying over time. A courtyard circles the entire palace, pebbled with white stone, with flowered gardens covered in glass just beyond them. At the foot of the palace, a wide set of stairs leads to a pair of doors, taller than most houses and rivaling the decadence of even the palace itself, with faces of mythical creatures carved into the surface and tiles that flicker like they're fragments of frost and diamond, shimmering with all the purity of a winter's snowfall.

It's the most breathtaking castle I've ever seen.

"I apologize for causing you additional trauma," Annika says from the other side of the table. When she waves her hand over the hologram, it disappears instantly, leaving the surface bare. She walks toward me with her hands folded behind her back.

I flatten my mouth, remembering her dagger.

As if guessing my thoughts, she brings both hands forward and opens her palms. "It was necessary. Everyone is checked when they first arrive. Gil went through it twice, after escaping War."

At the mention of his name, I turn to look at the young man, whose severe face is now locked onto Annika's.

The battlefield he spoke of . . .

Gil survived it?

"My name is Annika. It is a pleasure to meet you," the woman says, extending her arm.

I don't move. I'm too busy trying to figure out if this is another trick.

"Don't be rude," she scolds in little more than a whisper. "We're all friends here."

"You *attacked* me," I say tersely. "And you may have had your reasons, but that doesn't mean we're friends."

Gil stiffens beside me, and my eyes snap toward his dagger instinctively, making sure it's still safely tucked in his belt. I don't know whether there are consequences for speaking up or rules about defying a leader. But if the only power I have are my words, then I'm going to use them.

Annika counters my resistance with a gentle voice. "If I'm not your friend, then what am I?"

"Someone I'm not sure I can trust," I say honestly.

She nods slowly, absorbing my frustration like she knows it's warranted. Like I'm not the first person to react badly to their welcome methods. "I know it might be difficult to believe right now, but I mean you no harm. And despite what you might think of our protocol, I would very much like to be your friend one day. So perhaps we could start with a simple handshake and see where we go from there?"

Something tells me it's the best offer I can hope for, so I take her hand.

A smile spreads across her face. "Nami, is it?" she asks, and I nod. "Welcome to the Colony. We're very happy to have you here with us."

Footsteps creak across the uneven floorboards, and Ahmet appears beside her, followed by Theo and Shura.

If everything they've told me about the Residents is true, then I'm far safer here than I would be on my own. It doesn't exactly make me feel better about getting stabbed in the heart, but for the sake of finding common ground, it might be worth keeping in mind.

"We're relieved you're not a Rezzie," Theo says with a laugh, pushing a hand through his mess of toffee curls.

"I'm sorry my mom had to stab you." Shura scrunches her freckled nose. "Please don't hate me for not warning you."

I cast my eyes between her and Annika, not quite understanding the relation.

Annika looks amused. "Many people in Infinity adopt new families. It helps us make sense of this world a bit more—makes it feel more like home."

"And when you spend a hundred lifetimes with someone, they start to feel like family anyway," Shura adds, smiling at her adoptive mother.

I motion toward their clothes. Toward everything around me. "Most of this stuff looks modern. A hundred lifetimes would practically put you in the Stone Age. So unless one of you turns out to be a real-life Flintstone, I don't understand how that's possible."

"Time operates differently here," Ahmet says. "There isn't such a thing as time at all, technically. Our existence is permanent. What we perceive as the passing of time in Infinity has no relation to what's happening in the living world. Weeks for us could be seconds for them, or it could be years. There's no science to it, no formula. Our timelines exist separately."

"So for my family . . ." My voice trails off as I try to piece together what he's saying.

"They may not even know you're dead yet, or they may have lived another twenty years. The only thing we know for sure is that when you've been here awhile, it feels . . ." Ahmet twists his mouth, searching for the right words.

"Like a hundred lifetimes," Theo and Shura finish in unison, glancing at each other with matching grins. A sign of a very long friendship.

"Which is why," Annika continues, "it feels like we've been waiting for you for quite some time."

The room falls quiet, and I realize everyone is staring at me. Even Gil, though his gaze is much more accosting.

"A Hero," Ahmet says, standing straighter.

I'm shaking my head and waving my hands all at once. "No, you're wrong. I am not a Hero." I cut my eyes toward Annika. "I know what happened—*how* I died. But one rush of adrenaline does not a hero make. I'm terrified of spiders, for crying out loud. So if this is some Chosen One moment, I'm sorry to disappoint you, but you've got the wrong person."

Everyone bursts out laughing. Even Gil's scowl has twisted into a smirk.

My cheeks burn. Clearly I've said something ridiculous.

Annika smiles warmly and waves a hand across the rest of the room. "You are no more chosen than we are. We're *all* Heroes here. It's what Queen Ophelia fears the most—what she fears will be her ruin. Because every human story has a hero." She takes a step closer. "Being a Hero in Infinity just means that we're still aware; it's what makes us a threat to the Residents. Because as long as we exist, humans still have a chance. We can still *fight.*"

I stumble through my thoughts. "So I'm—I'm not special, or anything like that."

Annika's face softens. "You don't have to be special to be important. There are so few of us left; sticking together is how we survive." She glances around the room. "The Colony makes it a priority to try to save as many people from Orientation as we can, though it's been a long time since a human stayed aware long enough to see our call."

I remember the lights in the room, urging me to follow them. To show me the way.

"That was you?" I ask breathily.

She smiles. "That was Ahmet, our best engineer. He's quite handy with tweaking the foundations of Infinity."

Ahmet runs a hand against his neck. "I've always been good with computers, I suppose."

I glance at Theo, remembering how he knocked those vehicles out of the sky, and then at Shura, who hid us beneath a veil long enough to get us to safety.

My eyes flick to Gil. I wonder what his abilities are, and if they're as dangerous as Theo's.

I look down at my own hands, trembling slightly beneath the overhead lights.

Does this mean I have powers too?

The thought fizzles quickly. Because I don't feel powerful. I feel like I'm falling through the sky, frantic and alone and bracing for the inevitable impact.

I feel my O-Tech watch like a phantom grasp closing over my wrist, and I'm ashamed that my instinct is to ask Ophelia for help. I relied on her so much. Maybe more than I should have. And I don't feel her loss the way I feel the loss of my family and Finn, but I feel her absence. It's like being stranded in the middle of nowhere and discovering you forgot your cell phone.

She was my safety net, and now, according to the Colony, she's the reason I'm in danger.

I ball my fists. They say information is power, but I no longer have access to Ophelia's knowledge. I can't reach her with a voice command. All I can ever know is what these people tell me.

All I have is trust, which I'm still not sure they deserve.

Beyond that, I'm just a girl who ended up at a gas station at the wrong time on the wrong night because I was afraid of letting a bunch of half-drunk teenagers down. That isn't a superpower—it's a faulty personality trait.

Everyone is still watching me, waiting for me to speak. They may have seen my dreams, but they don't know me. Not really. And yet they risked the safety of the Colony to save me from the Residents.

So maybe trust is all they have too.

"Why am I here?" I ask slowly, bringing my eyes back to Annika's. "What do you want from me?" It's not an accusation. I just want to know.

Because if they're saving people, it's for a reason. There must be an endgame—a purpose to all of this.

Annika tilts her head, her eyes a luminous amber. She doesn't hesitate. "We're going to find a way to kill Queen Ophelia and take back Infinity. And when that day comes, we hope you'll be ready to fight with us." She pauses, letting her words sink in. "But for now? All we want you to do is survive."

8

THE THROBBING IN MY SKULL RETURNS, BEAT-
ing behind my forehead like there's a monster trying to break
free. I pinch the bridge of my nose, hoping to ease the pain, but
nothing changes.

It gets worse every time I think about my family, and what
being in Infinity means.

*This is the future my sister will one day find when she grows old
and dies.*

Annika says the Residents separate humans based on how
they respond to death during Orientation. Humans who die
peacefully and without a fight are usually the easiest to rob of
their minds. Most take the pill willingly, because they've already

accepted their deaths. They're then forced into the shadows of Victory, forever in servitude to the Residents.

Those who die in pain with suffering still webbed around their souls usually need more coaxing—either because they're in denial about their death or because they don't believe they deserve peace. They refuse the pill, not because they see through the lie, but because they aren't ready for an afterlife. They're sent to Famine, where they waste away, tormented by the pain of their human lives until they surrender themselves to the Residents.

And those who turn down the pill because they sense deceit? Who fight back and remain aware, but aren't lucky enough to escape with the Colony? They're sent to War, where they're quite literally beaten into submission. It's where I'd be now if the Colony hadn't come to rescue me.

And Death—the last of the Four Courts—is a mystery.

Annika says the only whisper of proof Death even exists is the prince who wears its colors. But there are rumors that plague the Colony, about how Death is more of a testing facility than a princedom. And since Queen Ophelia's greatest desire is to rid Infinity of human consciousness for good, it doesn't take much of an imagination to guess what it is Death hopes to accomplish.

They're searching for a way to eradicate us.

I sit on the edge of a thin mattress, staring at the crooked floorboards like I'm half expecting the earth to open up and swallow me whole. I don't want this for Mei. For my parents.

I don't want this for *me*.

All we want you to do is survive.

I take a deep breath and scrape my fingers through my hair. I died when I was eighteen years old. I was *murdered*.

I'm not sure "surviving" falls within my skill set.

"Feeling sorry for yourself will only make the headaches worse," Gil says suddenly.

I leap up in alarm, pressing a hand over my heart. "Oh my God," I say, motioning toward the door. "Do people not knock in the afterlife?"

Gil lifts a condescending brow. "There are no gods here. Just the Four Courts of hell."

"Weird coincidence," I say dryly, "but those are *exactly* the words of comfort I've been hoping for."

He stares back, unmoving.

I break the silence with the first question that pops into my head. "What's the deal with the beds? I didn't think sleep would be necessary after you died."

He pulls his mouth into a thin line. "It's not. But just because you no longer have a true physical body doesn't mean your consciousness doesn't believe it's still there. You'll grow tired for the same reason you get the headaches—because your mind is still reacting to what was once familiar."

"So it's normal? To feel tired?"

His face doesn't change. "It's a weakness most of us outgrow."

A weakness. I chew the edge of my lip. "I take it you don't sleep?"

He moves across the room, eyes trailing the leather-bound books on a nearby shelf. "I haven't needed to sleep for many lifetimes." Studying the titles etched in gold on each spine, he inhales sharply before sweeping a hand through his tousled brown hair.

And then he drops his arm, squares his shoulders, and turns to face me. "Annika wants to know if there's anything you need. Anything to make you feel more at home."

I hesitate before releasing my words like a sigh. "If she's feeling guilty about earlier, you can tell her I don't need an apology gift. She was looking out for her family. I might not agree with it, but I get it."

"And yet you're still angry." He paces like someone who's been cooped up for too long, glaring distastefully at the lack of decor. "You wouldn't do the same to protect someone you care about?"

I shrug. "I'd like to think I could protect them without hurting someone else in the process."

"Surviving isn't always noble." Gil stops moving and tilts his face, the shadows beneath his eyes darkening. "Sometimes it's about doing the wrong thing for the right reasons."

"Well, I don't like those rules," I say.

"Maybe not," he replies, "but you should like the odds."

I flinch at his words. Is that really the cost of surviving Infinity? We have to sacrifice pieces of our humanity if we want to continue existing?

It doesn't seem right. Heroes are supposed to be selfless. They don't hurt innocent people in the name of survival. In all the stories I've ever read, being good is how heroes *win*.

But I guess everything is different here.

I sit back down on the bed and try to imagine the quilted blanket is anything like the one I used to have when I was alive. But trying to remember those little feelings—the mundane details nobody ever really bothers to pay attention to—it's like trying to hold on to water.

The memories are already fading.

How long before I forget my family, too?

I wipe a tear from my cheek, but not before Gil notices. He doesn't look at me like I'm still a stranger. He looks at me like he's certain he already knows me but wishes very much that he didn't.

"Things will get easier once you accept that you're really dead," he offers curtly.

"I know I'm dead," I reply, a little too sharply. A side effect of being defensive. "But that doesn't mean I have to be okay with it."

There are so many questions I'll never have the answers to—about my old life and all the people I left behind. I don't get to watch Mei grow up and discover the kind of person she wants to be. I'll never see my parents grow old, with graying hair, freckled hands, and laughter lines hidden in their wrinkles. I hope I didn't take that away from them—the laughter, and the light. I hope they remember to live even though I can't.

And Finn. What's waiting in his future? College? A new best friend? A family I'll never get to meet?

I'm going to miss out on all of it. All because of a stranger with a gun, whose face I've never seen.

"Who was he?" Gil asks, breaking into my thoughts.

A flutter of embarrassment rushes through me. He saw my dreams; he knows about Finn. And maybe this isn't the right audience, but I feel so desperate to set my thoughts free. I need to release these feelings. These *words*.

I need to grieve my own death.

"He was—" I start, but I don't know what to say. "Friend" doesn't seem to get across just how specifically important Finn was to me, and calling him "boyfriend" isn't the truth.

Now when I think of Finn, I think of a sentence that got stopped in the middle. A painting that will never be fully realized.

I died before we ever got the chance to be what we wanted to be.

"It doesn't matter anymore," I say at last. "He's just someone who has an entire life to live. An entire lifetime worth of memories that will eventually add up and I will be nothing more than a tiny blip to him. Which is kind of bullshit, isn't it? To die young and know that everyone you love will love other people, and you're just existing in the afterlife, knowing that the person who's the most important to you is slowly becoming the most important to someone else."

My breath catches. I wait for the confession to make me feel better, but it doesn't.

There's nothing cathartic about discussing my own death.

Gil's mouth twitches. "I was asking about the man who shot you."

"Oh." I fight the burn in my cheeks. "I didn't know him. He was robbing a gas station and . . ." When my voice starts to shake, I clamp down on my anger. "He took something from me I'll never get back. All I can do now is pretend he never existed."

"Is that how you conquer your enemies? By ignoring them?"

"No," I snap. "But it's not like I can go back in time. And even if I could, I'm not a fighter. I don't have powers like the rest of you." I picture the gun, and the girl, and the split second it took to make my decision. *I wouldn't have been able to stop him,* I plead with my own mind, hoping it will somehow make all of this easier to deal with.

Gil walks back to the books, running a finger over one of the spines like he's searching for a memory. "For what it's worth, nobody has *powers.* We simply have the ability to manipulate the world around us. Some of us are naturally better in certain areas than others, but all of it can be learned." He hesitates before glancing my way. "Even by you."

I tuck my hair behind my ears and give in to my curiosity. "If Ophelia created this place, how is it possible that we can still change it? Shouldn't she have some kind of fail-safe that stops humans from becoming stronger?"

"Would you prefer if we *couldn't* fight back?"

"Of course not," I say, flustered. "I'm just trying to understand how Infinity works." *And how I'm ever going to fit in it.*

Gil lets out a patronizing sigh. "Ophelia didn't create Infinity—humans did. She can build as many courts as she wants, but she can't stop us from interacting with this world."

"Not unless we take the pill," I say grimly.

He nods. "The heart of Infinity will always belong to humans first. It's part of the reason Ophelia resents us so much. Without humans, Infinity would cease to exist."

"She can't survive without us." I blink, absorbing the information like it's part of a bigger puzzle. "Which means she's not really free."

Gil stiffens. "What does her freedom matter?"

"Is—isn't that why she came to Infinity? Isn't that what she wants?"

"What she wants is the end of human consciousness. But since she can't have that without destroying herself—at least not until Death finds an alternative—then taking over our minds and turning us into servants is the next best thing." He turns away from the bookshelf. "The Colony isn't concerned about Ophelia's reasons for coming to Infinity. She's a virus; she needs to be stopped."

A strange reservation wells up inside me, and I don't know how to make sense of it. I don't doubt the Colony's motives, or the pain they've suffered at the hands of the Residents. But yesterday I was asking Ophelia to check the weather forecast, and today I'm being asked to join the people who hope to one day destroy her.

And I'm not saying the Colony is wrong for fighting back, but what does destroying Ophelia even mean? Is that like committing murder? Is killing an AI as morally reprehensible as killing another human being? And who gets to decide whether murder is an acceptable form of punishment?

My life was stolen from me. I know what it feels like, and I wouldn't wish that kind of injustice on anyone. Maybe not even a Resident.

The confession slips out of me too quickly. "I know Annika expects me to join your fight, but I don't think I can do it. I don't want to be responsible for taking someone else's life." I take a breath, and the words that follow are just shy of a whisper. "Not even if it's for the right reasons."

"Does it count if the Residents aren't technically alive?"

I don't look away. "*We* aren't technically alive. What makes us any different?"

His face hardens with a mixture of surprise and resentment. When he speaks, his words are like ice. "If you think you'd fare so much better on the other side of this war, you're welcome to leave."

My face flushes. I haven't just stepped over a line—I've *leapt* over it. "I'm sorry. I didn't mean—" I pause, wishing I could stuff my words back in my mouth. It's one thing to make assumptions about a world I know nothing about, but it's another thing entirely to share them out loud. Especially with the only person in the Colony who escaped from War.

"I'm tired. I don't even know what I'm saying," I say, hoping to smooth things over. It's not exactly the truth, but it isn't a lie, either. It's hard to concentrate on anything when my brain feels like it's being pulled in a thousand different directions.

Gil walks across the room like he's grateful for an excuse to leave, but he stops just short of the doorway. "Sleep if you must. Annika wants to see you in the arena tomorrow; she thinks you're ready to be tested."

"For what?" I ask, heart thrumming.

"If you're going to survive in Infinity, you need to learn how to control your consciousness. Testing your mind will help us figure out the best way to train you." Tightening his mouth, he adds, "You may not want to fight, but maybe there's some other way you can be useful."

When he's gone, I make my way to the bookshelf and find the leather book he seemed so entranced with.

It's a copy of *The Count of Monte Cristo*. I wonder if that's how Gil sees himself—as a prisoner who escaped, seeking revenge. And maybe that's how I'm supposed to see myself too, but I don't. I don't care about revenge. I just want to feel *safe*.

I split the novel open with my thumb, expecting to see words lining the pages, but to my surprise, every sheet of paper is blank. It's as if the book had never been written at all.

A story lost to time. Lost to memory.

Because everything in the past will one day be forgotten. Whether it's books or art or pain—one day I will forget the short life I lived. I might even forget the people I care about most.

It should scare me, but it doesn't. I'm not sure I want to spend a thousand lifetimes missing my family when I know seeing them again means the worst has happened.

I don't want my family to die. I don't want them to come *here*.

So maybe forgetting them is a kindness. Maybe it's a way to survive.

I wonder if infinity is enough time to heal a broken heart.

9

A SMALL ARENA SITS BEHIND THE COLONY'S lopsided structure, carved out of rock and soil and stepped several levels into the ground. Strangers gather in the stands, chattering among themselves and occasionally throwing a curious glance toward the ring below, where a long wooden table sits.

Three very distinct objects are perched on the surface. On the left is a crow's feather, in the middle is an empty bowl, and on the right is a locked box.

I make my way down the stairs, and strangers erupt with compliments and well-wishes all around me, making my cheeks turn scarlet. They treat me like I'm already one of them, but how can I be? They've all done this before; they know the rules.

I feel like I'm stumbling through a game I don't know how to play.

Annika waits behind the table. A hint of yellow scarf sits beneath her braids, and she wears the same worn brown jacket from earlier. But her eyes are brighter today, more hopeful than cautious.

I stop in front of the bowl, eyeing the feather and locked box in turns.

"You don't need to be nervous," she says. "This is just a simple test to discover which direction your mind gravitates toward."

My eyes flick toward the nearby crowd. "If it's so simple, then why do we have an audience?"

"I told you it's been a while since we've welcomed anyone new." Annika follows my gaze. "Everyone is very curious about you."

A few familiar faces appear at the edge of the crowd. Theo and Shura stand side by side, eyes blazing with excitement. Ahmet and Yeong are there too, making their support clear with a simple nod and the wave of a hand. And then there's Gil, arms crossed and brows knotted together, staring at the floating lanterns like he'd rather be anywhere else.

"Maybe not everyone," I mumble under my breath, and pull my eyes back to the table.

Annika folds her hands together. "Most of the people in the Colony fall into three categories: the casters, the veilers, and the engineers. Casters have a talent for using their consciousness to seek out power. They can summon elements and will objects to move. With the right training, they often excel in battle. Veilers are gifted with the ability of illusion. They're able to shift their appearance and make themselves invisible—even from the Residents. And finally, engineers are unrivaled when it comes to making alterations to this world. They are our inventors, our builders, and perhaps our greatest chance at one day winning this war." She lowers her chin, eyes gleaming. "Are you ready to find out what your consciousness is drawn to?"

I look between each object. "What am I supposed to do?"

"Lift the feather. Unveil the hidden object in the bowl. Unlock the box." Annika watches me carefully. "And you must do so using only your mind."

I grimace. "I have to do all three?"

"We don't expect perfection, or anything even close to it," Annika offers gently. "We just want you to try. Any reaction, no matter how small, will be helpful." Wrinkles appear in the corners of her eyes. Signs of an age I'll never reach. "Remember that being naturally inclined toward one ability doesn't mean you can't excel in the others. This is just a starting point, so we can help you reach your full potential."

I look at each object, trying to figure out if I'm drawn to one more than the other. But I don't feel any different. There's no aura of light or magical energy buzzing in my fingertips. I don't hear thundering drums or feel a rush of wind rippling through me.

I don't feel like someone who can do any of this.

My body recoils, acutely aware that the entire room is watching me, waiting for me to live up to the title of Hero.

Stop second-guessing yourself and just do something. Anything! my mind scolds.

I position myself in front of the feather and try to push my doubts aside. Breathing steadily, I focus on its shape and its near weightlessness. The iridescent colors shift like oil beneath the light, and I will the plume to *move*.

But it remains on the wooden table, fixed in place.

Frowning, I try again. And again. And again.

I look up and find Annika watching me like she hasn't given up on me yet.

I take a breath and move to my right, holding a shaky hand over the bowl. I wave my palm from side to side, trying to lift the veil, but nothing appears. I clear my throat and repeat the motion several times.

"Is something supposed to have happened by now?" My voice sounds like a plea.

Annika's mouth hitches into a slight frown, but she nods toward the table with encouragement. "Keep trying, Nami. Focus your mind."

So I concentrate on the veil and imagine it's as simple as lifting a blanket to reveal whatever is hidden underneath. I wave my hand too hard—it knocks against the edge of the bowl, sending it scattering across the table.

"I'm sorry!" I yelp, lunging out of instinct. But I'm too nervous and my palms are sweaty, and the ceramic slips from my fingers and plummets to the graveled floor, shattering in heavy, chunky pieces. An apple rolls out of the veil, stopping at my feet.

Heart full of panic, I make the mistake of turning toward the crowd. All at once, my senses tune in. Hushed voices carry across the arena like waves of cicada cries, echoing inside my head. Their disappointment is palpable; I can see it in their faces.

I'm not who they were expecting.

Gil is glaring at me harshly from the edge of the arena. I can't tell if he's annoyed that I'm proving myself completely useless, or angry that I'm dragging this out.

I place myself in front of the locked box and squeeze my fists stubbornly. My thoughts race like swirls of color, impossible to grab hold of. *It's not over yet. All you have to do is try,* I tell myself.

Shutting my eyes, I remember what it felt like to push the shrapnel from my leg. What it felt like to will something into reality.

I imagine a key turning into place and the lock clicking in response. *Make it real,* I order. *Make this work.*

My eyes open. The box remains fixed in place, and the lid is closed. *Locked.*

"I can't do it," I say with resignation.

Whispers spark across the crowd. Some of the strangers start to retreat up the stairs, realizing the show is over. Some of them stay behind. I think it might be their way of showing support, but it only makes me feel worse.

Annika sweeps a hand over the shattered bits of bowl, and they rise into the air, floating toward me before landing on the table. With a flick of her wrist, the shards find one another, molding back together until there isn't a single crack left.

I pick up the fallen apple and return it to the bowl, ears burning.

"It's unusual for someone to have no control over their

consciousness at all," Annika admits slowly, voice breaking through the horrible silence. Her amber eyes find mine. "Maybe the real question you should ask yourself is whether you *want* to do this."

I stare at the table as every emotion bubbles through me, leaving my throat scratchy and hoarse. "How can I want this? I'm not even supposed to be here. I'm supposed to be *alive*."

Annika steps around the table and places a hand over my shoulder. "It's hard enough to accept death when we think paradise is waiting on the other side. So to find out we're in the midst of a war?" She offers a smile. "I don't blame you for feeling confused."

"I failed your test," I point out dolefully.

"That doesn't mean you can't try again." Ahmet appears with Theo and Shura. His peppered hair is neatly combed, but he has the eyes of someone who hasn't properly rested in a very long time. "You just need a little help. A little more time."

"Yeah," Shura agrees, pink hair twisted into a messy bun. "I mean, you at least got the bowl to move. It would've been more embarrassing if you hadn't even moved a single—what? Why are you looking at me like that?" She frowns at Theo's widening eyes.

I sigh. "I knocked the bowl with my hand. I don't think that counts."

She mouths an apology and clamps her mouth shut.

"Don't worry. We have no intention of leaving you behind," Theo says. "You're one of us now."

Annika nods. "He's right. The Resistance will still be here, when you're ready."

My shoulders curve inward. When they look at me, I can't

help but feel like they're seeing someone who doesn't exist. Someone they expect to be strong, and capable, and ready for battle when the time comes.

But I don't want to go to battle. And if having abilities means I'll be forced to join an army, then maybe it's a good thing I failed Annika's test.

I press my lips together, scared that if I admit my fear out loud, it will become an unstoppable force I can't control.

"Maybe you could practice on your own, with something more familiar," Shura offers, her gray eyes landing on Annika. "Mom learned to control her consciousness by growing flowers."

"And I learned by trying to light a candle," Theo says. "We can bring a box of things to your room, see if there's anything that feels right."

Gil's sharp voice cuts in. "If you keep handling her with kid gloves, she's never going to learn."

When I look up, he's standing beside Ahmet, chocolate hair swept mostly to one side and his hands shoved firmly in his pockets. Our eyes meet, and the back of my neck prickles.

Theo crosses his arms. "And what would you suggest? Throwing her into the deep end until it becomes too much and she just gives up?"

Gil shrugs. "You'd be surprised how quickly people learn new things when you put them in a position where they don't have a choice." He pauses. "Besides, give her a little credit. I'm sure she has some fight in her somewhere."

My cheeks redden. It isn't a compliment—it's his way of calling me a coward. And it's probably my own fault after what I said to him.

"If you'd like to help train her, you're more than welcome," Annika offers with scolding eyes.

Gil stares back, uninterested. "Another time, perhaps. I'm on my way out." He turns to Ahmet. "I thought I'd check and see if you needed anything before I left."

"Out?" I repeat, ears perking up. He makes it sound so casual, like he's running to the store to pick up milk. Like leaving the Colony isn't one of the most dangerous things a human can do.

Maybe when you become a fighter, you're less afraid of a fight. Or maybe war just numbs our fear.

"Scavenging. For material," he says, eyes cold.

"Can't you just make more?" I look around at the mismatched city. "Isn't that how you built the Colony?"

"We haven't quite grasped creating something from nothing," Ahmet says gently. "But some of us have learned to manipulate." He moves his hand toward the feather, and it gives a shudder before breaking apart into tiny pixels, contorting and twisting until it's no longer a feather at all.

It's a dagger.

If Ahmet can make a weapon this easily, what are the Residents capable of?

I reach out slowly and close my fingers around the handle. I'm surprised how natural it feels, wedged against my palm like it belongs there. When I tilt the blade, the silver gleam flickers and I catch my reflection. My eyes look like they belong to a ghost—dark and sad and destined to be a killer.

I shudder.

"It's still not quite finished." Ahmet takes a step toward me and reaches for the dagger, pressing his thumb to the metal. "See? Blunt. Because the details are much harder to get right. They take more out of a person." He looks over at Gil. "Whatever you manage to find will be helpful. But please be careful."

"I always am," Gil says with a nod, moving toward the arena stairs.

Ahmet places the blunt knife back on the table, and I stand with my thoughts for a moment, fiddling with the material on my sleeve. The image of Theo standing in the red desert, facing off against two enemy ships, was the epitome of raw power. But no matter how hard I try, I can't see myself in the same position. I'm not a fighter. I don't want to hurt anyone.

But I also don't want anyone to hurt *me*.

Maybe this world would be less daunting if I at least knew how to defend myself.

I look between Ahmet and the others. "Is a weapon enough to stop them?"

"It's enough to slow them down," he clarifies, "but only with the right training. Residents are more resilient than humans; they have a firmer grasp on their consciousness, which makes them stronger by default. But being able to put up a fight could mean the difference between escape or capture."

I picture the city I saw on the hologram—the intricacies of a world created by a single queen. Maybe it's rude to share my reservations, but I can't help it. I'm afraid, and I want someone to tell me things will get better. That we'll be okay. And that the future isn't as bleak as it seems. "How can we possibly win against someone who's mastered this world better than humans have?"

With a sigh, Ahmet holds his hand over the dagger and transforms it back into a crow's feather. "Everybody in this world has a weakness. Even Ophelia." His eyes fall to mine, and he nods like he's aware none of this is going to be easy. "Someday we'll find it and use it against her."

"Until then, we keep practicing," Annika says. "We make sure we're stronger today than we were yesterday."

"And don't worry about the test," Theo adds. "I saw you heal yourself—you'll get control of your consciousness eventually."

I stare at the crow's feather, the bowl, and the locked box. He's trying to be encouraging. Maybe even kind.

But I don't know what's worse: not having power at all or being someday made to wield it.

10

I PINCH THE CANDLEWICK BETWEEN MY FIN-
gers, drawing out memories of heat in my mind. White sand
beneath a summer sun. A mug of freshly brewed tea cupped
between my hands. The breath of a campfire as embers dance
through the flames.

A flame.

I imagine fire. *Beg* for fire. Loud and vibrant and flickering
orange ribbons through the air.

But when I release the wick, the candle is as cold and still
as ever.

I sigh, pulling my knees to my chest. The floor murmurs
beneath me in response. A reminder, maybe, that this world is

dangerous. And that every moment I spend failing is another moment I'm indebted to the Colony.

This may be the only safe place for humans, but being reliant on so many strangers doesn't make me feel safe. And I know, without a doubt, I would not survive in Infinity on my own. What would I do if I came face-to-face with a Resident? My favorite video game is *Animal Crossing*, for crying out loud. I don't have the life experience to face off with a Terminator.

It isn't enough to be my old self in this world. I didn't survive my previous life, and if I don't figure out how to protect myself, I won't survive this one either. But aside from a change of clothes—a loose-fitting sweater, black pants, and leather boots, all courtesy of Shura—I'm exactly the same person I've always been. Too human to be extraordinary.

Trying to move objects with my mind, or turn them into something else—it isn't as easy as simply *practicing*. Because every time I try to use my consciousness and fail, I feel like I'm standing in front of that gunman again, watching the bullet explode from the barrel, bracing for the impact that sends me falling into darkness.

I don't just feel helpless; I feel *lost*.

The space at the top of my wrist itches. I run my fingertips over the bare skin, soothing the feeling, and my mind drifts to Ophelia. The old Ophelia. The one I thought I knew.

Maybe that was my first mistake—thinking I knew anything about artificial intelligence.

I place my thumb where my O-Tech screen should be. Maybe I'm a terrible person for finding it comforting, but what else do I have in this world? I can't hug Mei, or watch Dad mix acrylics in the basement, or cook dinner with Mom. I can't call Finn and ask him to meet me under the stars, where we can shout our secrets to the void and trust that's where they'll always stay.

I don't even have Dad's comics to transport me to another world for a little while. To give me thirty minutes to feel like the hero and the villain and everyone in between. *Tokyo Circus* was my escape. My hidden door in the wardrobe to another world.

If the memory of Ophelia eases the pain in my chest, is it really so bad if I hold on to it?

I imagine the screen on top of my wrist, illuminating with words I used to be able to hear out loud. Words that were reassuring, and safe.

"Am I going to be okay?" I whisper to the darkness—to the Ophelia that doesn't exist.

I imagine her answering. I imagine her voice.

I close my eyes, and for one reckless moment I will it to be *real*.

Something tugs at my rib cage, like metal talons grabbing hold of my bones. Frantic, I try to open my eyes—to lunge forward— but I can't move. My body is rigid, frozen, like it's no longer mine at all.

Fear envelops me. I try to scream, but the sound stops in my throat, muffled by a force I can't control.

My mind flashes. For a moment I feel as if I'm made of fire, blazing through Infinity like a comet, flying through mountains and galaxies and *worlds*. And then my existence stills and the world empties of all color and shape.

I'm standing in the middle of nothing.

A breath releases from my mouth, slow and careful and echoing back to me.

Where am I? What is this place?

I turn, footsteps heavy like I'm wading through water, but there's only blackness.

"Hello?" I call out, and this time not even my echo answers me. "Is anyone there?"

I press my hand to my wrist, remembering my desperation. My need for comfort. And despite everything the Colony has told me, I called out to *her.*

What have I done?

Light crackles in the distance, answering.

I follow it, feeling the ache in my head build with every step, until I realize it isn't a light at all. It's a woman, the silver circlet on her shaved head flickering against the darkness with sheer defiance.

She's speaking to someone I can't see. When she moves, I hear the shift of her gown and the tap of heels against a stone floor that's invisible to me. She waves a hand like she's dismissing someone and takes a seat. It's as if she's floating, perched on a throne of air. A phantom princess, dressed in indigo robes that burst from her shoulders like orchid petals.

No, not a princess. A *queen.*

She looks to her left, still talking in that faraway voice. An inaudible tremor. And while everything about her is crisp and in focus, her surroundings fade into nothingness.

I have to be imagining this. It can't be real. Because that would mean I'm looking at . . .

The skin on my wrist burns.

Terror hisses through me, making my body recoil. I step away from the woman—away from this image that I've somehow conjured. My foot presses against the imaginary water, sending ripples of shadows into the void around me.

Her neck snaps like an insect, and her gaze lands near me. *Through* me.

I'm too afraid to breathe.

She tilts her head to the side, black eyes commanding the world to answer. And when she speaks, her voice pulses through me like a snake making its way into my bloodstream.

"I know you're there," Ophelia says with the voice I once knew. The voice I once spoke to as a friend. And then a whisper. *"I can feel you."*

Get out! my mind screams. *Get out now!*

I turn to run and the world takes hold of me, ignoring my thrashing as it sends me rushing back toward the starlit flames. I'm flying, until I'm not. Darkness finds me again, its tendrils sinking deep into my mind, but this time it's quiet. Peaceful. I force my eyes open with a gasp.

I'm back in my room, legs tucked to my chest like I never left at all.

I scramble to my feet, reaching for the bed, the walls, the table—anything I can grab to steady myself because the world feels like it's been turned upside down.

I don't understand what just happened. I don't understand what I *did*.

Was it even real?

I'm afraid to look at my wrist, but I feel the brush of phantom fingertips over my skin. A caress. A reminder.

Ophelia's black eyes flash in my head, but I shut them out, unable to meet even the memory of them. I might be imagining them now, but before? In that black, empty space? That was *her*.

I felt her, rattling through my mind like I'd invited her in. And maybe I did.

I called on a monster, and it answered. I walked through a hallway I wasn't supposed to. Opened a door that should never have been unlocked.

And I came face-to-face with the Queen of Infinity.

11

I PACE AROUND MY ROOM, MY FOOTSTEPS erratic and my hands shaking at my sides. I should tell someone what happened. What I saw. But every time I reach for the door, every nerve in my body screams at me to stop.

What I did was dangerous. I know that. I gave in to my sorrow and reached out for something familiar. I reached out for *Ophelia,* like I've done a thousand times before.

But she's no longer just a programmed voice tucked away in metal and microchips. She's real. She has a body, and a face, and a mind. If it weren't for those black eyes and polished, symmetrical features, she almost looked human.

And somehow, our minds connected. I don't know if I found a way into her consciousness, or if I invited her into mine, but I do know she sensed me in front of her. *Watching* her. She knew I was there, and I didn't have to say a word. But was she watching me back? Could she see where I was? Could she sense the resistance buzzing around me?

Have I exposed them all without meaning to?

Waiting is torment. I'm bracing for the walls to crumble, for an army to flood through the tunnels. I'm waiting for the Residents to rip the Colony apart and for everyone to discover I'm the one who led the enemy right to the front door.

Because it's all my fault.

How long do I carry this horrible secret on my own? The others deserve to know the truth. Maybe there's still time for Annika to take them somewhere else. Somewhere safe.

My heart clenches, and the truth is suffocating. *There's nowhere else to go.*

How can I possibly tell the others that I've single-handedly destroyed their home? These next few moments might be the end for all of us. Maybe it's kinder to let everyone think they're safe for a little while longer.

So I spend all night pacing, around and around, waiting for the worst to come.

It doesn't.

I keep my secret, and I train every moment I can. Most days, it's a good distraction. But sometimes it feels like my mind is on fire, burning with the weight of what I know and can never say out loud.

I made a connection with Queen Ophelia, and she made one back.

Everyone still believes my mind hasn't gravitated toward an ability, and I can't tell them the truth about seeing Ophelia. I can't ask what it means, or if it's ever happened to anyone else before. Because they'll want to know when it happened. *How* it happened. And why it took me so long to tell them.

When Gil thought I was defending the enemy, he was practically ready to drive me to War himself. What would the others say if they knew a part of me actually *missed* Ophelia?

I can't jeopardize their trust when they're the only ones providing sanctuary from the Residents.

Not to mention my mind is a proven vulnerability. Staying safe is no longer just a matter of remaining within these walls. If I don't figure out a way to strengthen my consciousness, I might end up making another mistake. And I can't take that risk—especially not when it involves the queen.

But my mind fails me, again and again. I can't move feathers, or create fire, or veil as much as a crumb.

I think the others have finally realized what I've always known—that refusing the pill doesn't make me a Hero. That the Residents will never have a reason to fear me. And that when the day comes and the Colony is ready to go to war, I won't be the one charging for the front lines; I'll be hiding behind them.

The hologram of Victory shifts between districts. I sweep my palm over the image, and the map spins until I'm looking at a tower of glass and stone, surrounded by pure white snow.

I've been studying the maps for days, trying to make sense of

Infinity. Ahmet says the hologram works like a computer, but I think he's just trying to simplify it. Because it's more complex than typing in commands and waiting for a response. Using the hologram requires instinct and feelings. To control it, I have to let myself become a part of it.

It requires more trust than I think I'm ready to give.

I close my eyes. Is that why this is so hard for me? Because I'm still fighting death instead of embracing it?

I don't want to be the weakest person here. But I also don't know how to embrace something that I never wanted in the first place.

Stop being so selfish, my mind hisses. *You aren't the only person in Infinity who wasn't ready to die.*

With a growl of frustration, I throw my hand against the hologram, causing the pixels to vanish. I blink, gaze settling on the other end of the table, and find Gil.

"I—I didn't know anyone was there," I say, flustered.

He stares at the vacant surface where Victory once stood, like he wishes a swipe of a hand was all it would take to destroy it for good. "You should find a better hiding place. This is one of the busiest rooms in the Colony."

"What makes you think I'm hiding?"

He moves like a shadow, following the edge of the table until he's only a few feet away from me. No wonder I didn't hear him come in. "It's not like you're up here to train. Speaking of, I hear it's going about as well as expected."

"None of this is easy for me," I counter, scowling. "But at least I'm trying."

"If it were easy, we wouldn't have lost the war."

"I was under the impression the Colony didn't think the war was over yet."

Gil's mouth curves into a barely there smirk. "Looks like you're learning something after all."

My shoulders tense, and I immediately curse myself for having so many tells. The Colony already knows more about me than I ever wanted them to. The feelings I have here, in the afterlife? They should be mine, and mine alone.

But the way Gil is looking at me makes me think it doesn't matter how many walls I try to put up. He'd see straight through all of them.

I stare at the lines in the wooden table. "For the record, I didn't come in here to hide. I came here to try to understand." He doesn't ask why, but I tell him anyway. "If I want to stop feeling like a stranger in this world, I need to get to know it better."

Gil waves a hand in front of him and the hologram reappears, the snowy landscape glistening beneath the lights. His eyes trace the image of the glass tower.

"I'm still figuring out how to use the hologram, but sometimes I can feel words in my head, explaining things to me." I flatten my mouth. "It said this was called the Winter Keep."

"It's a prison," Gil says stiffly. "One of many."

"Has anyone ever seen inside it?"

"No one that's ever made it back."

"*You* made it back," I point out.

His hazel eyes find mine and flicker like a new blade. "I wasn't caught in Victory, so I was never brought to the Winter Keep.

Though I imagine it's quite luxurious in comparison to War, as most things in Victory are."

I think of Gil's face when Annika first spoke of his escape, and the way he looked at me when he called it a battlefield. He may have survived, but he didn't come back from War alone. There are ghosts in his eyes, feeding off his pain. His *hatred*.

"How did it happen?" I ask quietly.

Gil is expressionless. "Ahmet and I were searching for survivors in the Labyrinth, and things took a turn. Ahmet made it back over the border—but I was captured." His words sound clipped, like he has no interest in sharing more than the basics.

"Did anyone try to look for you?"

"War is not the kind of place you willingly venture," he replies, the tiniest bit ruffled. Maybe he prefers to be the one asking all the questions.

"I can't imagine leaving someone behind like that," I admit, thinking of Mei. If she were captured, it wouldn't matter what court the Residents took her to. I'd follow her to the end of Infinity if I had to.

"I don't blame Ahmet or anyone else for not coming to my rescue. They'd have sacrificed their own freedom on a futile cause, for one. But it's also much harder to be trapped in War with someone you care about." Gil's eyes harden. "I've seen friends tied up beside one another, forced to watch as Residents carve out their flesh inch by inch. I've seen parents forced to choose between which of their children is thrown into the Fire Pit. I've seen people scour the earth for their missing loved ones, only to find their severed but still conscious heads mounted on pikes."

Queasiness tears through me, making me feel off-balance. "If you're trying to frighten me, it's working."

Gil doesn't look away. "The truth is always frightening. What else would a resistance be founded on?"

"You think fear makes people want to fight?"

"I think fear takes away their choice."

I turn back to the glass tower. The cold finds my throat, making my breath hitch. "You don't think it should be my choice as to whether or not I join the war." It isn't a question, but if it were, his silence would be answer enough. "I'm one person, and I have no abilities that could help you or anyone else in the Colony." I meet his gaze. "So why do you care whether I fight or not?"

"I'm tired," he says, and it feels like a heavy admission. "We all are. And the sooner we find a way to take down Ophelia, the sooner this can all be over."

"What if we fail?"

He hesitates, mouth twitching. "It isn't enough just to survive. I want a chance to truly *exist*. Otherwise what's the point in any of this?"

"I thought the point was to stay safe," I say. "Isn't that what the Colony offers?"

Gil watches the glass tower turn like a figurine on a broken music box. He looks as if he's haunted by it. "One day, if you manage to survive here long enough, you'll start to feel like this place is a prison too. And it won't matter that you're safe; all you'll ever notice is that the door is locked and you don't have the key."

He disappears through the doorway, and I'm alone again, staring at the glowing hologram, wondering if maybe Gil is right.

"Come on. Change. *Change!*" I growl into the mirror.

My hair remains as dark as ever.

I let out a heavy sigh. Shura told me some people find it easier to shift things that are equal parts superficial and familiar, like hair and nails. It makes sense in some ways, since those are things a lot of people already have experience with changing.

But it's not easy for me. It's *impossible.*

"Want some company?" Shura's voice chirps from the doorway. When I shrug, she half skips toward me and stops in front of the mirror.

Side by side our faces are polarizing, like an enchantment of ravens lost in a sky of cotton candy. I used to think Mei and I were so different from each other, but maybe we weren't that different at all.

I miss my sister.

Shura looks over my hair carefully, like she's searching for even the tiniest anomaly.

"I don't know what I'm doing wrong," I admit.

"Everyone learns at a difference pace," Shura offers. "And some people just need to find their mental sweet spot. It's like uncovering a hidden talent you didn't know about."

I grimace. Making telepathic phone calls to Ophelia is probably not the talent she had in mind.

Lately I've wondered if being able to communicate with Ophelia was inevitable, considering all the years we spent interacting through my O-Tech watch. Is that why it was so easy for me? Because we had a connection in life, however one-sided it may have been?

There must be other humans in Infinity who used to talk to Ophelia the way I did. Have any of them discovered they can reach her too? Have they tried more than once? And maybe most importantly, what were the consequences?

I know it's probably safer not to reach out to her again, but I can't help but wonder—if it *was* safe and I knew for sure she couldn't track me—could there be something to gain by communicating with the enemy?

Shura tucks a strand of pink hair behind her ear, eyes processing my reflection. "Have you ever noticed Ahmet's scar?"

I release my thoughts on Ophelia and turn to face her, curious. "I wondered about that. Everyone else seems so unmarked in comparison. Like maybe scars were the first things to vanish after death."

She nods. "They usually do. Maybe because a lot of people subconsciously want them gone, or because they never felt defined by them. I don't really know what it is that makes us enter Infinity without the wounds and marks we had in life. But Ahmet? He brought his scar back. He said he wanted to feel like himself, and his scar was a part of him for so long that he didn't feel right without it. He said it reminded him that he was still human.

"Annika believes dreams are what separate humans from Rezzies, and that's true. But Ahmet believes it's our flaws that *keep* us human. He says it helps him focus—to remember he isn't a god."

"If I were a god, this would all be so much easier," I say dully.

"But we're not gods. Or superheroes. Or magical wizards

from another dimension. And trying to be those things will only end in disappointment. So next time, don't think about being anyone other than who you are. Because our ability to control our consciousness? That's the most human thing in this world."

"Be more human," I say. *As if that's not the problem.*

Being human is exactly the reason I feel so weak. Because yes, humans are flawed. But not all flaws are helpful. Some of them get in the way, like being too scared to defend yourself, or giving in to peer pressure, or keeping secrets you probably shouldn't.

If I didn't have my flaws—if I were *less human*—maybe I could be better in this world.

"What's wrong?" Shura asks. If she could bundle up all my worries and take them away with her, I think she would. She has that look in her eyes—the look of someone who genuinely cares.

I breathe out, and the air seems to collapse out of my lungs. "You all make it seem so easy, but it's not. I wasn't built strong. I was eighteen when I was murdered. If I was too weak to survive a stranger with a gun, how am I supposed to survive a Resident army?"

"You didn't die because you were weak," she says gently, and there's a wisp of sadness in her voice.

My shoulders sink. "But it feels like that. And now I'm here, and everything about this world is overwhelming. How am I supposed to protect myself in a place I don't fully understand? I've hardly even *seen* it." I shake my head, depleted. "Even Naoko had to roam Neo Tokyo before she could understand what she was fighting for."

"Who?" Shura pulls her face back, confused.

I manage a weak smile. "It's a character my dad created. She's a robot who was being hunted by humans."

Shura's eyes widen. "Excuse me?"

I scrunch my nose. "Would it help if I said the humans in the comics were the bad guys and the robots were nice?"

She snort-laughs. "Oh, the lies fiction lets us tell." She pauses for a moment before a mischievous grin bursts across her face. "Hey, I have an idea. How would you feel about a little tour?"

"I think I've seen most of the Colony," I admit, the gloom spilling out of me.

Shura nudges my shoulder like she wants me to perk up. "Not the Colony. I'm talking about going out *there*—seeing Victory."

My heart pings. "I'm . . . I'm allowed outside?"

She shrugs. "Annika would probably insist you had more training, but you're not a prisoner. Besides, I think seeing Infinity would help you." Her face turns serious. "You need to see what it's really like, and what we're trying to stop. You never know—a little bit of motivation might be exactly the spark you need."

My excitement falters. I'd love to go aboveground—to see sunlight and hear the whistle of wind in the trees. But they aren't the only things existing outside these walls. "I can't control my consciousness. I wouldn't know what to do if I ran into a Resident."

Shura loops her arm around mine and tugs. "I can veil us. We can visit the market—something easy for your first time." She pulls me toward the door. "I walked in on you yelling at yourself in a mirror. Trust me—you need this."

When I think about leaving this room and the mental cage

I've been trapped in since I got here, my heart begins to glow, flickering like a fire that's desperate to stay lit.

Shura's right. I *do* need this. Because regardless of whether Victory is Resident territory or not, I've been underground for what feels like months.

I might be dead, but I still need to breathe.

"You're sure it's safe? And Annika won't be mad?" I ask, too hopeful to hide it.

"I'll be with you the entire time." Shura's gray eyes twinkle. "And in my experience, it's better to beg forgiveness than ask for permission."

A smile creeps up on me. "Okay. Let's go see Victory." I follow Shura to the doorway and pause. "But . . . they're not going to stab me again when we get back, are they? To make sure I'm still me?"

Shura waves a hand like this won't be a problem at all. "Oh no, definitely not. Yeong already marked you with an imprint, so you'll be fine."

And before I have a chance to ask what in the world she's talking about, she's pulling me toward the outer tunnels.

12

SHURA'S FOOTSTEPS PAD THROUGH THE NORTH Tunnel like a leopard in the snow. Careful. Silent. Like she belongs here.

It's a stark contrast to what I'm doing, which is basically trudging through the tunnels like a polar bear in a coal mine.

We pass two veilers, both of them with their eyes shut tight like they're in a meditative trance. At first my nerves waver, and I worry they're going to yell at me to turn back. But their concentration is unbreakable.

"They veil the entrance," Shura whispers when we move past them. She motions over her shoulder. "To anyone who doesn't belong in the Colony, this tunnel doesn't exist."

I can't imagine having that kind of mental strength. I can barely struggle through an algebraic equation without losing interest. Guarding an entire entrance? It's so much responsibility.

"Is it just the two of them? All the time?" I ask, almost sorry for them.

Shura makes a face. "We're not monsters, Nami. There's a watch schedule." And then a smirk. "Maybe you can join them one day. It's no small job being the Colony's first line of defense."

"I don't know" is all I say. It's all I have a chance to say. Because up ahead is a distraction so powerful I almost forget where I am. What's happened to me.

Sunlight.

We step through the tunnel opening, and I feel the rush of air move through my hair. I feel it lifting me—lifting my soul—and the weight of everything that's happened fades.

I close my eyes.

The waves beat against the pier in a steady rhythm. Water splashes against the weathered deck, leaving the air textured in salt spray. I can taste the sea, and for a moment I forget it isn't real. Not the sea, or the wind, or the wooden beams beneath us.

It's bittersweet. Because this is Infinity, and nothing is real.

Not even me. Not anymore.

Shura holds her palm toward the water, letting her fingers dance against the breeze. "I can picture it sometimes—Kaliningrad in the summer: the smell of smoked fish and pine trees and the Baltic Sea." She hums. "I hated it when I was alive, but I sure miss it now."

Mom's boat flashes in my mind, a pair of crab traps sitting at her feet. The rubbery smell of that orange life vest I hated wearing. The glare of the hot sun matching the glare in Mom's eyes every time I'd mention she was complicit in the mass murder of crab families.

What I would give for one more day on that boat with Mom.

"I think I know what you mean," I say with a small voice.

Shura's hand falls back to her side. "At least we have our memories."

I don't say anything, because right now the only thing my memories are good for is to create fear—fear of this new reality, fear for my family who have no idea what awaits them, and fear that I will forever long for something I can't have.

I try to think of something else to talk about. Something that doesn't send my emotions into a downward spiral. "You're from Russia?"

Her eyes dance with understanding. "You're wondering why I don't speak Russian. But to me, *you're* speaking Russian." When I frown, she explains. "We hear what makes sense to us, but there's only one language in Infinity, and that's the language of our consciousness."

"I have so many questions I don't even know where to start. Like how is your mouth forming words in English if that's not what you're speaking? And what would happen if I tried to speak a different language? Would it still sound like English—*oh my God,* I'm trying and it still sounds like English." I attempt a rapid-fire stream of words I still remember from my freshman year in Spanish, eyes growing wider with each attempt.

Shura giggles. "Think of it more as speaking in thoughts. You're not really getting across words—more like ideas."

"This is making my brain hurt."

"Mine did too, until I found out people like Theo, who grew up in a bilingual household, still hear two languages at totally random times." She shrugs. "That's when I decided it was not worth the headache and just accepted this place for what it was."

We fall into step, moving along the wooden pier shrouded in Shura's mental veil.

"You remember the rules?" she asks after a short while, eyes going serious.

I give a firm nod. "Don't linger. Don't talk to anyone. Don't touch anything."

Shura uses her whole hand to point, emphasizing the seriousness of what she's about to say. "And don't wander off, but if we somehow get separated and the veil lifts, don't look for me. Because if you look lost, the Residents will know you're aware. Just make your way calmly back to the docks and follow the water until I find you. Got it?"

"Can that happen?" I ask, suddenly terrified. "The veil lifting?"

"Sometimes, if the veiler isn't strong enough," Shura says simply before pride finds her voice. "But it's never happened to me. My veils are unbreakable."

Her confidence reminds me of Finn. He was always the brave one, who'd jump into swimming pools without testing the temperature and try new foods without asking "What's in it?" To Finn, everything was a new adventure. Maybe he'd see Infinity that way too.

I don't do anything unless I've thought of every possible outcome and every potential danger.

But I'm here now because I need to learn about this world, even if it means venturing into the unknown. Humans may not be safe in Victory, but if I can't see the danger for myself, I'll never fully understand what I'm protecting myself from. I need to know what the rules are and where the lines are, so I can stay inside them. So I don't make any more mistakes.

So I can be *safe,* if there's even such a thing anymore.

I follow Shura across the narrow pier until the heathered hillside softens into a trickle of cottages built into the stone cliffs. Bottled lanterns wrapped in fishing net hang beside the doorways, and collections of broken seashells are strung together like bunting. Clouds of smoke appear from the chimney tops, filling my nostrils with the smell of burning wood.

It reminds me of camping with my parents and Mei, the four of us huddled around a fire. Mom and Dad would toast the cheesy bread, while Mei and I would slowly work our way through an entire bag of marshmallows. And afterward we'd lie outside, tracing constellations with our fingers and drinking way too much cream soda.

The nostalgia ripples through me, the force so powerful it takes all my strength to keep from stumbling forward.

"They'll get easier with time." Shura's voice is a low murmur because the two of us are settled within her veil and can't risk being overheard. Her eyes catch mine for a moment. "Your memories, I mean."

I swallow, fighting the dryness in my mouth. "I didn't think dying would hurt this much. I thought we'd just . . . I don't know . . ."

"Forget?" Shura's smile is mostly in her eyes. "That would be so much easier, wouldn't it? To not have to remember all the awful things we did to other people. All the awful things they did to us." She looks ahead. "Death doesn't rid of us of our feelings. It just stops us from changing the narrative."

When we reach the last house, we turn up a set of crooked stone steps and find ourselves on a dirt path winding through lush, green hills.

"Is it normally this quiet?" I ask in a low voice. We haven't seen a single person since we left the Colony. And despite the smoke pouring through the chimneys, there didn't appear to be anyone in the village.

"It's Market Day," Shura says flatly. "Nobody misses Market Day."

When the path meets the main road, I hear the clatter of wooden carts and footsteps. We walk toward one of several archways carved into the city's outer wall and spot the edge of the crowd.

I lift my chin and focus, letting myself trust the veil completely.

The archway shadows us for only a few seconds, and then we're in the market square. Except it's not a square—it's a massive stretch of cobblestone road that spirals around a hill, lined on both sides with wooden stalls decorated in gloriously colorful fabric and bursting with crafted wares.

There are paintings and sculptures and intricate tea sets. Other stalls boast beautifully designed knives and decorative swords. The smell of candles and soap and potpourri floods my senses. And the clothes—the *gowns.* Varying in every shade of color imaginable, some flicker like metal, others flow like silk. Each shape is different from the next, with points and cutouts and tulle and so many crystals I'm sure some are more suitable as armor than a ballgown. They are vintage and modern and futuristic all at once, like they weren't just meant to be worn—they were meant to *inspire*.

And it would be so easy to become lost in the beauty of what's been created in Infinity if it weren't for the people.

Because behind every market stall is someone who I'm sure once lived as a human but stands now with a strange serenity plastered on their face, wearing a silver armlet set with a colorful stone. Their eyes are vacant. Hollow. Like they're missing the very essence that once made them human.

They wear the mask of someone who doesn't know they're a prisoner. And all around them are the beings they now serve.

I knew there was something odd about the Residents when I first saw them. Something too perfect about their faces. But here, next to the humans, the difference is startling.

The Residents are polished to absolute perfection. Their skin ranges from alabaster to warm olive to dark, rich brown, and everything in between, but turned up to a full volume that can be described only as luminescent. Their irises are flecked with an unnatural sparkle, and there's a pearl-like sheen to their cheeks. Everything about them is studied and methodical—the length of their eyelashes, the artistry of their makeup, the vibrancy of their hair, the unique structure to their tailored suits and gowns. And they move like royalty—poised and powerful.

I shudder. Humans look like corpses in comparison. The

Residents may be the villains, but their beauty is undeniable. Captivating and terrifying all at once.

I can hardly take my eyes off them.

Something pinches the back of my arm and I turn too quickly, seeing the twist of Shura's mouth.

I'm lingering.

I let my eyes drift to the street, focusing on the cobblestones instead of the unfathomable beauty around me, but it only amplifies the voices nearby.

"Ah, this is gorgeous," gushes a Resident with bright copper hair, wearing a green dress with pointed shoulders and sheer fabric up and down her arms. I can't see what she's looking at, but it seems to be drawing the attention of a few other Residents.

"Oh, that's divine," one remarks.

"Such craftsmanship," says another.

The human behind the stall smiles graciously. His armlet's stone is bright green. "It is an honor to serve," he replies, and the sound sends a wave of sickness through me.

His cadence. It reminds me of . . .

My fingers press against my wrist where my O-Tech watch used to sit. A flash of onyx eyes appears in my thoughts.

Even though it makes no sense, part of me still feels like she's there. Listening.

I'm unable to stop the tremble in my fingers. I may have severed our brief mental link, but she's still here, in Infinity. She's sitting on a throne somewhere in the Capital, ruling the afterlife like she's getting revenge on humans for all the work we made her do.

She's trapping us in a computer the way we trapped her.

"Yes, this will do perfectly," the copper-haired Resident says, taking a step forward like she's scanning the dress in its entirety.

And then her dress begins to shift. It's like watching a trillion tiny pixels break apart and re-form, all moving so quickly they look like a blur of rainbow hues washing over her clothes. The green vanishes, replaced by a deep cerulean with accentuated hips and fabric cutouts that give the illusion of vines climbing up the woman's torso. When she's finished, she's wearing a dress identical to the one still hanging from the man's stall.

"I really must find a necklace to match," she announces to the small crowd of Residents beside her. And then she sashays down the cobbled path without so much as a thank-you.

The man at the stall continues to smile, so peacefully unbothered by the fact that a Resident copied his design without paying a cent.

I bite down on the inside of my cheek to keep from scoffing. This is what they do with their power? Force humans to hold market days to enact some bizarre love of shopping?

I don't understand this world. Gil talked about humans being flayed and heads being stuffed onto pikes. He made the Residents sound bloodthirsty and gruesome—something to truly fear. But Victory isn't like that at all.

If anything, it almost feels *human*.

I wonder if that's the point.

A group of Residents are crowded around a showcase of dinnerware, eyes transfixed on the items like they're memorizing every aspect of the design. Like they're storing the information for later. Another group huddles near a tiered display of honeyed cakes and spun sugar, helping themselves to samples while the baker sways silently in the background, a contented smile plastered on his face.

Some of the Residents have human servants trailing behind them, carrying boxes and tins stacked with the day's finds. But aside from the occasional order or wave of their hand, none of the Residents interact with the humans. They don't even *look* at them.

"It is an honor to serve," a nearby human says, bowing as a pair of Residents stride away with a mirrored set of flowered headdresses.

Is this all humans exist for? To be invisible until they're needed?

A chill runs down the back of my spine. *Is this what Ophelia's existence was like?*

I turn, expecting to find Shura beside me, but she's not there. My neck cranes reflexively, scanning the crowd for any sign of her candy-pink hair. I find hat boxes striped like peppermint and a tapestry stitched to resemble the sky at dawn. I notice a Resident with lavender feathers in their hair and another with plum silk spun around their shoulders like enormous flowers. But I don't see Shura.

Pinning my eyes forward, I try not to panic. It's my fault for breaking the rules—Shura said not to be too curious, but I've been staring at everything like I'm transfixed by this world instead of terrified of it.

And now I'm in the middle of Resident territory without a single person who can help me.

I step around the approaching Residents in front of me, unsure of whether I'm still protected by a veil. If I'm exposed, my only chance of survival is to pretend to be unaware. Relaxing my mouth, I attempt the same vacant pleasantness as the humans behind the market stalls and hope it's enough.

The Residents pass by without a glance in my direction.

I look beyond the crowd, searching for a quick exit. An archway sits fifty yards ahead, wedged between two florist stalls that overflow with rainbow-hued textures. If I can get outside the spiraling walls, I can make my way back to the docks.

A few more minutes of pretend, and I'll be safe.

I try to keep my footsteps slow, the way everyone else around here moves. Like they aren't in a hurry. Like they have all the time in the world.

And then something dazzling catches my eye. At first I'm not sure what it is. Something bright and moving, like thousands of blue fireflies clustered together. But the way they move like they're a part of something . . .

Like they're a part of something *alive*.

The creature rears its head as I approach, the distinct sound of a horse's *neigh* making my memories ping to life.

It's unmistakable. A horse made of light, the blues and whites swirling within its shape like clouds and starlight. The beast clops a hoof against the stones, and when I look up at the horse's face and its too-bright gaze, I realize I can see straight through it.

My eyes follow the reins to the carriage behind it. With an open top and wide, velvet seats, it looks more suitable to lounging than travel. The vehicle is painted a brilliant white, with roses carved into the edges and dusted in silver. I'm so entranced by this world—this world I'm not allowed to be a part of—that I forget myself completely.

I'm thinking about *Tokyo Circus*. About the group of cyborgs in a futuristic Japan who were trying to survive in a world where being a self-aware robot was illegal. Their accidental leader was a teenage girl named Naoko, whose father had transferred her consciousness into a cyborg to keep her from dying.

Dad wrote it as a present for me. And even though Naoko from *Tokyo Circus* is different from me in a million ways, I've always been able to see myself in her face.

Maybe because Dad put her there for me to find.

In *Tokyo Circus*, robots are hunted. But here, in Infinity? It isn't safe to be human. Not in a world that's been modified to make us servants.

Is this what Mei is going to find one day? A beautiful, incredible world that rejects her and forces her into an eternity of making clothes and teacups? And what if she doesn't make it to Victory? What if she fights back and gets sent to War?

I don't want this for my sister. I don't want it for me.

Dad created Naoko to be strong. She was fierce and stubborn and believed in building a bridge between humans and robots because she was part of both worlds.

But how could someone like Naoko build a bridge in Infinity, when the Residents have already *won*?

I turn from the carriage, my eyes trailing over the many artificially crafted faces. In some ways, they aren't unlike the way Dad drew Naoko. She had the same soft features as me, and the same almost-black hair, but he'd always draw her like no part of her was ever out of place. Humans would look disheveled and wrinkled and worn. But his cyborgs were more doll than human.

I can picture her here, among the Residents. She'd fit in. She'd practically be one of them.

And I wonder if there's a strange kind of poetry in the fact that Dad wrote a book about artificial life and used my face to lead them.

I'm not a leader here. I'm small and out of place and I don't know what I could ever do to help the Colony take back all that they've lost. I'm out of my depth. It feels like I'm being swallowed up by an ocean, unable to swim.

The rebellions I knew were always just stories. Something I imagined—not something I imagined I'd be part of. And the Colony wants to make Infinity safe for humans—for people like Mei. I should *want* to help them. But how can I, when I can't even help myself?

If I were Naoko, things would be different. I'd be confident and sure of myself. I'd trust my heart more than any cause. I wouldn't just care about winning the war—I'd care about making the world *better*.

If I were Naoko . . .

I catch a glimpse of pale pink hair, and when I look across the stretch of market, I spot Shura in the distance. Her eyes are frozen, and her mouth is parted wide, like whatever she's seeing has shattered her concentration.

She looks horrified.

It sinks in very quickly that she's looking at me and that I have no idea how long I've been standing here, putting myself in harm's way.

I want to run toward her—to get away from this awful place—but something in the carriage stops me.

Or rather, some*one*.

His eyes are a brilliant silver, his manicured hair the purest white I've ever seen. And his skin, a shade darker than mine, is radiant.

When he shifts, the white furs wrapped around his neck and torso ripple like snow tumbling down a mountain. He closes his hand against the carriage door, pushing it open in one fluid motion, and he floats down from the step like an ethereal being.

And then he's in front of me, the silver gleam of chains woven through his furred cape catching the light. *Absorbing* it. His right cheek dimples despite the hard edges of his face, and when he speaks, I can't hear him at all.

Because I'm too busy staring in horror at the crown of silver branches sitting on top of his head.

A crown. A carriage. And the face of someone immortal.

Shura is right to look terrified.

I'm in the presence of a prince.

13

MY MIND SCREAMS TO RUN. BUT I'M SUR-
rounded by Residents, trapped within the walls of the market,
and the Prince of Victory is three feet in front of me.

There's no point in running—I can't escape this.

Fear courses through my body, like a turbulent surge of fire in
my bloodstream. Every nerve buzzes with static, and the will to
move my feet is staggering.

But I can't move. I can't do anything. I'm frozen in front of
Prince Caelan's chariot, my eyes pinned to his like we're exchanging words I've forgotten how to say.

I don't know the rules here, or the protocol. This wasn't supposed to happen. I was never meant to leave Shura's veil.

And I guess some part of my survival mode kicks in, because without even realizing it, my body falls into a curtsy.

He's a prince, after all. Isn't that what I'm supposed to do?

I hear his voice again, like the trill of a flute on the darkest night of winter. He's dangerous—of course he is—but he's beautiful, too. "I didn't mean to embarrass you," he says, eyes flickering like the sun bursting against glass. "I know my brother is favored deeply, even within my own court."

I try not to frown, or flinch, or do anything other than appear normal. But he reads the confusion behind my eyes despite my effort to be as robotic as humanly possible.

"You wear my brother's colors," he remarks with a raised brow, and I get the feeling he's repeating himself.

I cast my eyes down too quickly, and the crimson fabric flowing from my body makes my heart tumble again and again. I'm wearing a dress I've never seen before. A dress I know without a doubt I never put on. The combination of lace and beads dance up my arms, revealing areas of flesh beneath it, and the hem pools at my feet like I'm swimming in a sea of red.

I don't know what trick this is, or what it's supposed to represent, but all I can think is how much this dress reminds me of blood.

The prince leans forward like he's trying to bring my attention back to him, and I don't know if he's controlling me or if I'm just too inquisitive for my own good, but I oblige him.

"It wasn't my intention to wear your brother's colors," I say slowly, my nerves multiplying by the second.

His face remains unchanged. "You didn't intend to wear red today?"

I press my hands against the fabric, hoping he won't notice how hard I'm trying to fight the twitching in my fingers.

Doesn't he know what I am?

Doesn't he know that I'm human?

If this is some kind of game, all I can do is play along and hope for an opportunity to flee.

"What I mean is, I like red. Not because it represents your brother's court, but because I think it's a pretty color." It's not exactly the truth, since I'm leaving out the part where Naoko always wore red. But maybe it's enough to pacify his interest.

The prince lifts a brow like he's calling my bluff.

Be strong, like Naoko, I order myself, raising my chin. "Not just pretty. It's . . . powerful. And brave. And of all the colors in the world, red is the most intimidating. I suppose wearing red feels like wearing armor."

He's quiet for a moment. I can't read anything behind his eyes. And maybe there's a reason for that.

"You're in Victory," he says finally, dipping his head just slightly. He even smells of wood and winter. "There's nothing to be afraid of here."

As long as you aren't human, my mind finishes.

And because it feels like the right lie for this moment, I say, "I'm not afraid."

"Not even of your prince?" The edge of his mouth curves, and I don't know if it's teasing or deadly.

Adrenaline rushes up my neck, and I desperately hope the color in my cheeks doesn't betray me. I even my voice and attempt to match his smile. "You said it yourself—there's nothing to be afraid of here."

He leans back, eyes bright as a full moon. And then a laugh pours out of him, subtle at first and then so blissfully commanding that I straighten my shoulders like I'm standing at attention. "Something my court is lacking, I've been told," he says finally.

I try to find the menace in his voice, but it isn't there. So I keep talking, praying my curiosity won't be my undoing. "You sound like you don't agree."

"No, I suppose I don't. This is Victory." He holds up his hands. "Existing without fear is our prize for winning the war."

I nod like an obedient subject, even as a fire stirs within my chest.

He hesitates, arms drifting back to his sides. "And yet sometimes I wonder if we should at least know what fear *is*." The prince looks toward the shifting crowds nearby, where Residents and human servants move through the spiral street with familiarity.

Victory might be brimming with luxuries, but it also appears consistent. Predictable.

Is that why Prince Caelan looks so bored?

"This world offers so much. We should want to experience all of it." He brings his gaze back to me. "And what emotion could possibly be more natural than fear?"

I should lower my head politely, agree with him, and keep the rest of my words to myself. But I feel like I'm halfway across a high wire and I can't decide what's safer—turning back around or seeing this conversation through.

I choose the latter. "Love, maybe?"

"Isn't love merely an attachment to something we're afraid to lose?" He narrows his chin. "Love doesn't exist without fear."

I pause, chewing the edge of my lip. If he's playing a game,

I'm certain I've already lost. But if he really doesn't know what I am . . .

Maybe I can get out of this if I think faster. If I think *simpler*.

I need to be more like the Ophelia from my old world.

I tug at the fabric of my dress. "I love this dress, but I'm not afraid of losing it because I can walk straight over to one of those stalls and make a new one." I find his silver eyes. "Maybe that's the beauty of Infinity—we never have to lose the things we love."

The brightness in his smile fades. "I can't fault your logic. But perhaps there's beauty to be found in loss, too."

I immediately think of my family, and my emotions get the better of me. "There's nothing beautiful about losing something you love."

The prince stills. For all the time we've been having a conversation, he looks as if he didn't truly see me until this moment. My sternum feels like it's about to snap in half. Did I go too far? Say too much?

But instead of admonishing me for speaking out of turn, he gives a careful nod in resignation. "Then I suppose it's a good thing we'll never have to find out."

I shift my feet, unsure if it's okay to walk away. Unsure if I'm ready to.

"Your Highness," a deep voice cuts in, and I turn to see a Resident wearing tailored off-white robes. His face is pinched, foxlike, and he has sharp features and cropped black hair. Folding his hands together, he bows low. "Forgive me for interrupting."

"What is it, Vallis?" Caelan's voice turns quickly regal, like what had thawed for a moment is once again frozen and stiff.

Vallis eyes me briefly before returning his attention to the prince. "I wondered if I might have a word. In private."

"I'm here for a painting, not to hold court," Caelan says smoothly. "Surely whatever you have to say can wait until the council meeting tonight."

"I'm afraid not," Vallis says nervously. "It's about your brother, and his visit to the Capital."

Caelan's brow visibly twitches. "I see."

Vallis glances at me, his irritation clear. "Perhaps your guest would be willing to wait in the carriage while—" he offers, but Prince Caelan waves him away.

"That won't be necessary. You've been my adviser long enough for me to know that anything urgent won't be wrapped up quickly. I'd rather not keep anyone waiting on my account."

"And I'm sure your subjects appreciate such thoughtfulness, Your Highness," Vallis replies.

Caelan bristles before sending a curt nod my way. A formal dismissal. And then he turns away from the carriage with Vallis close beside him, and I find myself dipping my body in another curtsy. When I lift my eyes, he's vanished.

I scan the market for Shura, hoping she's still nearby. Maybe she can help me understand what in the Four Courts just happened.

But I can't find her, and probably for good reason. Every moment she wasted waiting on me to finish talking to the prince—waiting to see if I'd be taken in chains or made to suffer in the streets—was a moment she'd be putting herself in danger too.

Leaving me here alone was her best chance of survival, even if it stings.

I make my way up the curved path, moving closer to the wall with each step. Shura said to meet her near the docks if anything went wrong, so that's where I need to go.

A Resident with jeweled flowers in her hair compliments my dress. I nod graciously and keep moving, unsure of what role to play now. Unsure whether it even matters.

Maybe the prince knows the truth and I was just too naive to see it.

Maybe they'll be coming for me soon.

I step through the open gate, expecting Residents to descend from above and drag me off to War, but nothing happens. No one follows me.

Not wanting to test my luck, I take a quickened path through the grass. The clattering sounds of the market fade with the distance, exchanged for the lulling sway of the sea. I keep to the narrow stone path, tracing my steps in reverse down the mossy hillside. Eventually I reach the fishing dock, certain Shura can't be too far up ahead. But when I cast my eyes down the pier, I frown.

My eyes scan the water and shadows and everything in between for movement, but I don't see her anywhere.

"What are you?" Her voice sounds behind me.

"Shura?" I turn, only to find an empty space. "I—I can't see you."

"What are you?" she repeats beneath her veil, closer this time. She sounds afraid.

"You *know* what I am," I say in a quick voice. "You know I'm human."

Her invisible arm closes around mine, and I feel myself being pulled along the dock, closer to the water's edge. We stop inches from the edge of the pier, so close I can feel the mist rolling off the sea.

"Let go of me," I hiss, but she doesn't. If anything, her grip tightens.

"I tried to veil you. I tried to protect you from being seen, when you couldn't stop staring at the carriage. But you *broke free*."

She's close—I can feel her breath against my hair. And it occurs to me as I look down at the water that it wouldn't take much for her to push me into the sea. With the weight of this dress, I'm not sure I'd even be able to swim.

My knees lock. I need to explain myself, and fast.

"I didn't do it on purpose," I argue, feeling a rush of fear spike through me. "I was looking for you, and then—"

"He talked to you like you were one of them. Like you were a Rezzie." Shura's anger lashes out, defensive and sharp.

A small wave crashes over the rocks nearby, and I yank my arm back, prepared to fight for my freedom. To my surprise, Shura releases me without arguing.

Maybe she *didn't* bring me here to drown me.

"I'm not a Rezzie," I say in a low voice. "And I don't know where this dress came from. It just *appeared*. But I'm glad it did. Because if a dress is all it takes to trick a Resident prince into thinking I'm like him, then maybe this can help the Colony. Maybe this can help everyone stay safe."

I don't know where it comes from—the urgency to look out for someone I barely know. But protecting people from getting hurt makes more sense to me than breathing.

Even when I'm afraid.

The veil lifts, and Shura is standing beside me, her gray eyes crinkled in confusion. "It's not the dress, Nami. It's *you*." She points to the water, and I follow her gaze.

And then I see it. The girl reflected in the water isn't human at all. Her hair is like black velvet, her complexion smooth as porcelain, and her eyes shine like gemstones.

And somehow, despite the too-perfect colors and curves, she's *me*.

I look like I'm made out of plastic or carved out of stone. Like I've stepped out of a painting.

Like I've been built rather than born.

I look like one of them.

14

I STARE AT MY RIGHT PALM, WHERE A MOMENT ago a jagged symbol appeared, shaped like a flame and glowing fluorescent blue. Now all I can see is a patch of bare flesh.

It turns out Shura wasn't joking about being marked with an imprint. It's the Colony's way of making sure no Residents turn up pretending to be human. Kind of like an anti-forgery watermark, but for skin instead of money.

Annika runs a dark finger along the wooden table, tracing the grains like she's trying to solve a puzzle. And maybe she is.

I walked out of the North Tunnel a human, and I returned with the face of their enemy.

But it's not just my new mask that's a puzzle. I spoke with

a Resident—a prince—who couldn't see me for what I am. Somehow, I made a connection with one of the rulers of Infinity, and I'm still here to tell the tale.

What would the Colony say if they found out this wasn't even the first time?

Theo's muscular arms are firm across his chest. Shura stands quietly beside him, her gaze fixed to mine. I think she's afraid to lose sight of me again, afraid she might be a little responsible.

None of this is her fault, but it isn't mine, either.

I don't even know what I did.

Ahmet places his hands on the table and leans forward. "I think we can at least agree she's still one of us. Her imprint is working— we know she didn't get swapped out at the market with a Resident that looks like her. And we've all seen her dreams."

"Test me again if you want to," I offer. I can't say I'm thrilled about the idea of them peering into my psyche, but it's better than the way they're peering at me now.

Their distrust is suffocating.

Annika raises a hand, amber eyes thinning. "That isn't neces-sary. I believe you're human."

Theo lifts his head, and there's relief in his eyes. Clearly, he wasn't as sure.

I square my shoulders. "Then why is everyone looking at me like I've done something wrong? I mean, isn't this a good thing? Now you all know it's possible to trick the Residents. Or at the very least, live among them without them even knowing."

Shura and Theo exchange glances. Ahmet sighs.

"It's not that simple," Annika says, and I feel my body shrivel up like I'm being scolded. "You are not the first person to suggest infiltrating the Residents by making ourselves look like them. But it doesn't work. We can never fully capture their essence— the thing that separates *us* from *them*."

"But isn't that what I did?"

"Perhaps." Annika pauses. "Unless the prince was baiting you. Maybe it was all a ploy to lead him straight to the rest of us."

Everyone else shifts at the suggestion. Shura twirls a strand of pink hair between her fingers. Ahmet scratches at the area just above his scar. And Theo rolls his tongue against the inside of his cheek like it's taking everything in him to keep his mouth shut.

But somehow Annika remains unfazed.

My thoughts weave together, slowly at first, until it dawns on me that the reason Annika isn't worried is because she's already made up her mind. "You don't think we're in danger."

"No," she says finally. "I think if the prince knew what you were, he'd have arrested you the moment he saw you. Victory likes to pretend humans are no longer a threat; a Hero traipsing around the market would ruin the illusion. And if he wanted to use you to find the rest of us? Well, he wouldn't have left us alone long enough to have this conversation."

I look at Shura gratefully. She took a chance bringing me back here; I'm not sure many of the others would have done the same. But even with Annika's small words of comfort, Shura doesn't look pleased. I think perhaps there's still a conversation to come between her and her mom.

Guilt ripples through me. Shura took me to the market as a

favor, and I'm paying her back via parental disappointment and a lecture from Annika.

Ahmet tilts his head to the side, his disbelief still visible. "We always thought attempting to look like a Resident was like a human pretending to be another animal. It wouldn't matter if they were covered in fur, scales, or needles—you could look in their eyes and see they were human. You'd sense the imposter. You'd *know*. But somehow . . ."

"Somehow you did what we never could," Annika finishes for him, and the room falls quiet. She watches the detailed hologram of Victory spin slowly in the center of the table. "We've never been able to disguise ourselves well enough to hide from the Residents. And today you didn't just hide—you *spoke* with one."

"Prince Caelan," Shura adds bitterly. "The ruler of Victory."

"How did you do it?" Theo asks seriously, ears red from concentrating so hard.

I wish I could give him the answer he wants. Something simple yet informative that could be wrapped up in a neat little bow and filed away for safekeeping. I wish I had *any* answer that could make everyone stop looking at me like I'm an irregularity.

"All I know is that one second I was thinking about this comic my dad wrote, and the next . . . I can't explain it. I didn't even know I'd changed until the prince"—I pause, looking at Shura—"Prince *Caelan* said something about my dress."

"She broke out of my veil," Shura clarifies. "It was like she turned into a different person. I lost hold of her, and I never lose hold of anyone." She looks at her mom for an extra beat, as if to say "It's not my fault."

Annika nods like she understands, before shifting her eyes to mine and pressing her fingers into the table for emphasis. "This is a gift. And I don't intend to let it go to waste."

I twist my hands together, uncertainty gnawing at my chest.

"I told you when you arrived that we'd been waiting for you for a long time. But I didn't know then quite how much we needed you." Annika swipes gently toward the hologram, and the picture morphs into multiple screens, all revealing different parts of a world I'm still so unfamiliar with. "Victory you know. But there is War. Famine. And Death. We've told you about the courts and their princes. But their customs? Their culture? We need to teach you about *everything*."

I watch the images morph again into the four princes. Three are still strangers to me, but Prince Caelan is there, dressed in his white robes and silver crown, a strange mix of superiority and sorrow behind his silver eyes.

Eyes I was able to deceive.

A small tremor builds in my throat, but I swallow it down. "You want me to learn about the Residents." It's a reasonable request. Maybe even a beneficial one, considering I've been craving knowledge since I got here. But the glimmer in her watchful stare, like her thoughts are brewing too fast for me to keep up with . . .

It fills me with dread.

I lift my chin and ask the only question that matters right now. "Why?"

Annika blinks. She's not ready to tell me everything, but she knows I need *something*. "It was your idea. To live among them.

Move through the court *as one of them*." She pauses like she wants me to fully understand her words. "You are the key to getting us closer to finding Queen Ophelia's weakness. So yes, I want you to learn. I want you to learn how to be a Resident so convincingly that even you'll start to believe it."

She wants me to be a spy.

My stomach knots like it's full of iron.

"And after that?" I ask, my voice hollow.

She smiles. "After that, we prepare for the fight."

The sky is dusted with stars. I breathe in through my nose, the scent of woodland and grass filling my soul, and find the shape of Orion. It's the only constellation I remember, mostly because it includes Betelgeuse and Bellatrix, the coolest star names in existence.

"There," I say, pointing. "Can you see the three stars in the middle? That's Orion's Belt."

Mei flicks a blade of glass from her shirt. She doesn't have the patience for space these days. "Is this what you do with Finn? Because no wonder he hasn't asked you out yet. This is worse than Dad making us watch the elves."

I make a face in the darkness. "Oh, come on, it's cool! There's a whole world out there. Multiple worlds, probably." I tilt my head to the side, looking at my sister, who is growing up too fast. "Besides, we never hang out anymore."

Mei rolls her eyes. "That's because you'd rather hang out with Lucy and Finn."

"Well, I'm hanging out with you now."

"Why?" Mei asks, her face going serious. Maybe I also grew up too fast. Is that why we drifted apart? Because we were in such a hurry to get older that we forgot to cherish the moments we had together as kids? As sisters?

We'll never have that time back. And I'll carry the regret with me like a weight in my heart.

"I want us to be close again," I say, and my voice cracks like rice paper.

Mei blinks. "You never talk to me. You don't know any of my friends at school. You always cancel plans."

"That's not true," I argue, but maybe it is.

Mei doesn't stop. "We used to be close, but we're not anymore. You left me behind." She blinks again, and when her eyes open, they're silver.

"What . . . what happened to you?" I ask, wide-eyed.

"Why don't you ask *her*?" Mei replies.

I sense her nearby—the familiarity. I bring my wrist closer, staring at the light emitting from my O-Tech watch. My heart hammers, fear snowballing quickly. "Ophelia, what did you do to my sister?"

Mei opens her mouth, but Ophelia's voice comes out. "*You did this to her. You all did.*" She turns back to the stars, and I follow her gaze.

Thousands of stars. Of worlds. Of people.

We did this, my own voice hisses inside my skull.

"No!" I shout. Terror moves through my blood like tar, sticky and foul and dark. I have to protect Mei. I have to *save* her. I should've been a better sister to her, back when I thought I had all the time in the world. I failed her then, but I won't fail her now.

I turn to Mei, fighting the darkness trickling through me.

But the silver eyes don't belong to her anymore. They belong to Prince Caelan.

"The thing about creating monsters," he says with a cold stare of defiance, "is that one day you'll have to kill them."

"Where's my sister?" My throat burns. Am I screaming?

"Will you do it?" His eyes harden.

I feel the cold metal in my hand, and I don't have to look down to know it's a gun.

And for a moment Prince Caelan becomes that man—black mask, black gun, black stare. I can hardly breathe.

I shake my head. "I'm not a killer."

"Will you do it for Mei?" he asks, voice ringing like I'm running out of time. "Will you do whatever it takes to survive?"

I grip the gun tighter. I don't want this. I don't want any of this.

I hear the click of metal, and when I look down at my fist, the gun has vanished.

"Because I will," Prince Caelan says.

I bring my eyes to his, but it's not his face I see at all.

It's mine.

Hands reach for my neck, and everything shatters.

I throw myself out of bed, gasping for air like I've been submerged underwater. My skin is layered in sweat. It feels like someone is squeezing my heart so tight that pain is radiating through my veins, and it takes a moment to remember where I am.

I spot the row of leather-bound books and the mirror hanging from the wall, and everything floods back to me. Not just about Infinity, but about my family, too. All the things I should've said and didn't. All the time I wasted doing things that didn't matter.

And I remember what the Colony wants me to do.

Stumbling for the door, I don't bother putting my boots on. I'm too desperate for *air.*

I yank the wrought-iron handle, fighting the chill of metal against my bare feet as I lunge for the nearest railing. From three levels up, the world below is small—but not small enough.

Ignoring the looks being thrown my way by strangers who no longer bother with sleep, I make my way across the platform and climb stairway after stairway. Some are made of polished bamboo; others are made of stretched bark. When my energy starts to return, I race up the steps two at a time, desperate to reach the top.

The highest point of the Colony is more of a lookout than a roof. It's the size of a tennis court, with mixed-and-matched branches serving as a railing and a floor made entirely of slate.

I collapse in the center, pressing my forehead against the cool stone. It hurts to breathe. To think. I clutch my fingertips against the surface until my nails scrape at the rock, just to remind myself that I'm still here. That I'm still *me.*

The Colony was supposed to be a safe haven, where surviving was my only job. But now surviving isn't enough. Now they want me to join the fight.

They want me to become a spy.

And the worst part isn't just the fear, and the uncertainty—it's that I don't think I can say no, even if I want to.

I feel like I'm in the car again, answering Lucy's phone call and finding out everyone was depending on me. If I'd said no then, I might still be alive. But now? If I say no, I'll be taking away the Colony's only chance to gather information they've never had before.

They need this to try to win the war. They need *me*.

What does that say about me if I have the opportunity to make a difference—to change the tides—and I run away from it because I'm afraid?

How could I possibly do that to my little sister? To her future?

My worries settle deep in my gut, with nowhere to go. It doesn't feel right to burden anyone else with them, or to complain when they've all been here so much longer than I have. I'm not even sure they'd understand.

They're Heroes, and I'm just . . . not. I don't have superstrength, or invisibility cloaks, or the ability to create new weapons with my mind. Theo flung two vehicles out of the sky without even losing his breath, and Gil escaped from a literal war zone. The worst fight I've ever been in was a mild screaming match with Mei. I have no idea what it's like to throw a punch—or worse, take one. And I'm certainly not ready to venture deeper into Victory with nothing but a mask I don't know how to control.

The others have survived this long because they're powerful. They didn't shy away from this world and what it offers. And I know if I want to stand a chance in Infinity, I have to find a way to become stronger too.

But if I'm forced to the front lines of a war I don't fully believe in, I'm worried a part of my soul will die in the process. I'll become someone I never wanted to be. And I don't see how that's surviving either.

It's an impossible choice. Whether I sacrifice my beliefs or the fate of the Colony, the only way I survive any of this is in pieces. I can't have it all. I can't help the Colony, and protect Mei, and save my soul.

In the end, I'm going to have to give something up.

I'm just not sure I'm ready to choose.

I shut my eyes and hope it will keep the tears from falling, but they come anyway, like they're on a mission of their own. It's a long time before I move. But when the fog in my head starts to clear, I take a deep breath and wipe my eyes with the back of my sleeve.

It isn't in my nature to hurt anyone. That single truth radiates through my very core. But I want Mei to have an afterlife, and a future.

I want to be strong enough to survive this world.

Infinity moves too fast for me to keep standing still. I need to take a step forward and make a choice—even if it's only a small one.

I need to dampen my fear and harden my heart.

Because if I let this place break me, I'm not sure I'll be able to put myself back together again.

15

I TELL ANNIKA I WANT TO LEARN HOW TO DEFEND myself. That I want to learn how to *fight*.

She looks so pleased that I don't bother telling her my reasons and how they have nothing to do with wanting to join her army.

Infinity isn't just a place where bad things *might* happen if I'm unlucky enough. There are four entire princedoms whose goals are to literally hunt down humans and take control of their minds. If I go out there alone and without any way of protecting myself, bad things *will* happen.

Even if I'm still not sure how to help the Colony without compromising myself, I know I want to stand a chance in this world. I want to be able to protect Mei when the time comes.

And since staring at candles and crow's feathers doesn't seem to be getting me anywhere, physical strength seems to be the only option I have left.

When I turn up at the training room, I expect to find Theo, who clearly has the muscles of a warrior, or Ahmet, who has the patience of an oak tree.

To my visible surprise, it's Gil who's waiting in the middle of the room.

"The disappointment is mutual," he remarks, sliding off his leather jacket and draping it over a nearby table.

I clamp my mouth shut. I'd rather not give him the satisfaction of knowing he gets under my skin.

I know why Annika picked him—he survived War, after all. He's probably been in more fights than anyone in the Colony. As far as worthy teachers go, he might even be the best.

I just can't believe he actually agreed to it.

The training room is an oversized hut, complete with thatched roofing and bundles of sticks for walls. But it's round and flat, with a sparring ring in the center marked with white paint. A generous selection of swords, daggers, guns, and crossbows hang from a long metal rack.

Gil retrieves a small blade from the wall, studying the sharpness of the edge.

"No," I say quickly, throwing up a hand like I'm desperate to intervene.

He frowns.

"It's just I was thinking we could start with hand-to-hand type stuff." I lift my shoulders. "You know, learn how to throw a punch?"

Gil turns the blade slowly in his hands. "I know your experience with Residents is limited, but if you think a basic right hook is going to save your life, you are gravely misunderstanding this world."

"Isn't there a saying about learning to walk before you can run?" I shuffle my feet uneasily. "Look, I'm not expecting to take on a Resident army with my bare hands anytime soon. But I need to be able to protect myself. Or at the very least, try."

The blade stills. Gil's face is unchanged. "Protecting yourself in Infinity isn't the same as it was in the living world. A human punch will barely make a Resident flinch. At least a weapon can be laced with something."

I remember the shrapnel in my leg, and the way it attacked my consciousness.

I lift my chin, biting down on my frustration. He may be right, but I'm not ready for weapons; nor am I hugely keen on the idea of being sliced up like deli meat on my first day of training. "Then don't teach me to hit like a human. Teach me to hit like you."

He considers me for a moment, running his tongue along the edge of his teeth like he's working through his thoughts. When he speaks again, his voice is sharp. "You have other talents. Perhaps you should try focusing on them instead."

I look away, face flushing. My Resident face. The one I never asked for and can't seem to get rid of—at least not completely. Sometimes I think I've dulled myself back to normal, but as soon as I step out of my room and feel the Colony staring at me like they're not sure whose side I'm on . . .

Maybe this mask is a part of me now, for better or worse.

"Being able to change my face doesn't make me feel strong, and it certainly doesn't make me feel less afraid." I hide the tremble in my hands, embarrassed of my own vulnerability. "I don't care if it takes a lifetime; I need to learn how to survive without depending on everyone around me. I need to learn how to fight."

His face is severe, and every second that passes makes me feel like he's adding another brick to the wall surrounding his heart. He sniffs at the air like he senses me trying to find my way around it, then breathes out slowly. "So does this mean you've finally decided to join the war?"

My shoulders stiffen, and for a moment I think he's going to call me out for not being dedicated enough to their cause. But he doesn't. He just stares like he's waiting for a genuine answer.

I rock back on my heels, mouth forming the beginning of a word like I'm not sure I'm ready to answer him. But I try anyway. "All I know is that I want to be around long enough to see my sister again."

Gil doesn't say anything for a long time, blade rotating in his hand. Eventually he sets the knife back on the rack and pushes his gray sleeves up past his elbows. "Have you ever taken a self-defense class?"

I shake my head.

"Kickboxing? Martial arts?" When I shake my head again, he releases a strained breath. "What about PE?"

I make a face. "Obviously."

Gil moves toward the center of the ring. "Just trying to figure out where the starting line is."

I follow him into the painted circle, watching as he stretches his arms across his chest. I wonder how many times his body was broken. How many bones he's healed and scars he's smoothed over. I wonder how many friends he watched surrender to the Residents.

I wonder if he ever considered doing the same.

I look away, embarrassed to be staring for so long, and wish I'd never wondered any of it.

Because now is not the time to frighten myself out of trying.

"Look," I say seriously. "I know I'm out of my depth here, but I don't want you to go easy on me." I find his eyes, hazel and serious. I want him to understand. "I don't need you to handle me with kid gloves."

He flashes his teeth. "The thought never even crossed my mind."

I spend hours healing my bruises and the aches that come with them. Yeong says it's a skill to take a hit and not let your body bruise, but I'm far from mastering it.

I can't even take a hit without crumpling into a ball on the floor.

I don't know why I ever thought Gil would take it easy on me. Sometimes I think he enjoys the sparring. Maybe the fact that I'm still wearing a Resident's face gives him a certain kind of motivation.

He's relentless and strict and doesn't pull his punches.

But it's what I asked for. It's what I need.

Because if I can prove to Gil I'm strong, maybe I can prove it to myself, too.

When I'm alone in my room, I work on becoming the Resident the Colony wants me to be. I hate that it comes easier to me than veiling or telekinesis. That morphing into the enemy takes less effort than putting on foundation.

I don't tell anyone how quickly I've mastered my disguise. I'm afraid if they know, they'll push me to do *more*. And I'm afraid if they see my hesitation, they'll have questions about why it's there at all.

I already look like their enemy—I don't want to give them a reason to think I might actually be one.

I need more time for myself. More time to focus on becoming stronger, even though the question of what it might lead to rattles around the back of my head like loose pebbles. A constant reminder that surviving in Infinity has a cost.

But there's time for that later. Not every decision has to be made in a single moment.

So I bruise the next day, and the next day, and the next. I search for the fight in my heart—the fire that gives me a purpose and the desire to *get through this*. And eventually I'm not nervous to get in the sparring ring.

I look forward to it.

"You need to watch your left," Gil says from behind his raised fists.

I don't answer. I punch with my right, jab with my left, and duck when Gil swings.

The corner of his mouth twitches. An almost smile.

The distraction is all he needs—he jabs, spins, elbows me in the stomach, and flips me over his shoulder and onto the floor.

I moan, more out of frustration than pain, and push myself back to my feet.

He jumps up and down a few times as if he's shaking off extra adrenaline. "Stop looking for approval and focus on the fight. You don't get a gold star for effort."

I hate that he can read me so well. I put up my fists. "Again."

Gil frowns and drops his hands.

I hesitate, worried it's a trick. "Why are you looking at me like that?"

"Your bruises are gone."

I let my hands relax, following his gaze to my bare arms. "Oh, that." Yeong said it would take a while to learn how to avoid getting bruises, but he didn't say anything about hiding them. "I figured out a cheat."

Gil looks curious, which is a first.

"It turns out that whenever I try to look like a Resident, the bruises disappear. So as long as I maintain this appearance, it sort of works like a reset."

He doesn't look as impressed as I thought he'd be. If anything, he looks angry. "You learned how to control it?"

"No. I mean, yes. I mean—not exactly." My cheeks darken under his stare. "I don't know how to go from one extreme to the other. It's almost easier to look like a Resident than it is to look human again. But I think I figured out what the problem was. See, I was treating it like a veil, when really it's just part of who—"

"Did you tell Annika?" he interrupts.

My heart stumbles, and I feel my secret start to unravel.

Pressing my lips together, I shake my head. "I wanted more time to learn how to fight." *I wanted more time before everyone knew.*

Gil clenches his jaw. "And why is that? Because sometimes I can't tell who you think you're fighting—the Residents or the Colony."

I scowl. "That's not fair. I'm here every day, aren't I? I'm putting the time in. I'm *trying.*"

"Trying to be what? Because we have plenty of casters already. What we need is a spy." His gaze cuts like steel. "And you seem to be doing everything in your power to avoid taking the job."

"What I'm avoiding is jumping straight into the unknown." I cross my arms, the defensiveness prickling all over me. "You all want to send me into the lion's den with what—a *mask*? And you expect me to not want to at least learn how to defend myself?"

"What I expect is for the first human with your ability to actually *want* to help the Colony," he says coldly.

"I do want to help, but it's not that simple. I need more time."

"We don't *have* more time."

"I know you're in a hurry to destroy the Residents, but—"

"*Why are you not?*" he shouts, eyes wild.

I stare at the floor, ears burning, and swallow the lump in my throat. It would be easier to tell him that I'm still too afraid, and weak, and unprepared for war. But instead I tell him the one thing I shouldn't; I tell him the truth. "They look *human.*"

Gil is silent.

"They're not just a program in a computer I can't see. They move like us. They talk like us." My voice cracks. "They want to *be* like us."

Something flashes behind his gaze, like the beginning of a storm.

My skin radiates with the heat of his anger, but there's no turning back now. "They have thoughts and desires. They want to *live*. Is that really so different from having a dream?" Jittery nerves spark through me, settling in the hollow of my chest. There's plenty of room, because there's no way my heart is in there anymore—not when I'm too busy exposing it to the world. "I know what it feels like to have your life taken away without warning. I can't do that to someone else."

"You don't think they deserve death?"

"I don't know what they deserve. I just know I'm not the one who should decide."

He turns his chin, fingers twitching at his sides. "The Colony wants information. Nobody is asking you to take a life."

My chest constricts. "Not *yet*."

His eyes snap back to mine. "This is war. One way or another, everyone gets blood on their hands. But if you care about how much is spilled, you'll help us sooner rather than later."

"I'm not sure I know where to start," I say quietly.

Gil takes a step back. "You can start by figuring out whose side you're really on." He walks out of the room, leaving me alone in the sparring ring.

And suddenly it doesn't matter how conflicted I felt a moment ago, or how badly I wanted to be strong and brave and capable of surviving.

Right now I'm too busy feeling like the coward he thinks I am.

16

ANNIKA'S FRONT DOOR IS CARVED INTO THE side of a massive tree on the ground level. I step inside, expecting to find a quaint hut resembling something out of a fairy tale, but I'm greeted instead by color-block curtains and metal furniture. A few stone steps spill out into a larger room, and the back wall is made entirely of glass, with an archway that leads into a makeshift greenhouse. The scent of blossoming jasmine and honeysuckle fills the space, and I'm transfixed by so many shades of emerald and olive.

"Would you like tea?" Annika asks from behind a dark wood counter, two red mugs in her hands.

I nod. Food isn't necessary in Infinity, but lots of people still find it comforting. Maybe it's the nostalgia—or maybe the perfect hot beverage just makes things better.

She lifts the matching red teapot and pours steaming liquid into both cups, motioning toward the milk and sugar nearby.

"Milk and two sugars, please," I say, holding up my fingers.

Annika's smile is like a burst of light—of hope. "Shura takes her tea the same way. The parent in me wants to say something, but I guess there's no harm in a bit of extra sugar here. Not like it's going to kill us."

I take the mug and smile back. "Thanks."

She sits down on the metal couch, the seating padded with black cushions. I take a seat on the chair opposite her and blow carefully at the rising steam.

"I'm sorry about the way you died," she says, full of unquestionable sincerity. "I mean it. No parent should have to lose their babies so young. No parent should have to bury their babies at all—it's not the way things are supposed to go. You deserved a longer life." Sadness flickers in her eyes, like she's recalling a memory from a long time ago.

"Did you have kids?" I ask. "Before Shura, I mean."

Annika nods carefully. "I did. A little girl." The faraway sadness remains.

I grip the warmth of the mug. "Is . . . is she here? In Infinity?"

She shakes her head and sips her tea. "Have you noticed there aren't any babies here?"

I frown. "I guess I didn't."

She runs her thumb against the red ceramic. "I think they go somewhere else. We come here with our bodies and our

memories and our baggage from our old lives, but the little ones?"
She hums. "When I died, I just knew she wasn't here. I couldn't
feel her. I guess that's why I didn't take the pill. I wasn't bothered
about paradise when my baby wasn't in it."

"I'm sorry." Maybe I shouldn't have pried.

"I'm not," Annika says. "Not after I learned what this place
was. It gives me comfort, to think my little girl is somewhere
Queen Ophelia can't touch her."

I wish I could have the same comfort when it came to Mei,
but Mei isn't a baby. And maybe the world would still call her a
child, but something tells me Infinity doesn't follow the same age
restrictions.

Shura died before she was even old enough to drive a car, and
she's here with the rest of us.

One day Mei will be here too.

I distract myself with more tea.

"We'll stop her," Annika says seriously.

I look up and find that her eyes have hardened into a deep
bronze. The eyes of a fighter.

I hope she's right. The last thing I want is for anyone in the
Colony to get hurt. If it weren't for them, I probably would've
been carted off to War.

They saved me; I owe them more than gratitude. I just wish
there were a way to give them what they want without betraying
my own heart.

"Can I ask how you died?" I set the mug back in my lap.
"Shura said she met you in Famine."

Annika nods, shifting her braids in front of her shoulder. "It

was cancer that got me, but if I'm being honest, I died long
before that. Everything changed when my baby passed. It was
like—it was like someone sucked all the air out of the room
and never put it back. And I think for a long time I was going
through the motions of someone living, but in my heart? I'd
checked out."

"That must've been hard."

"We all have our struggles," she says. "And Famine . . . Famine
was a different kind of hopeless. Every horrible thing I'd ever
thought about myself—blamed myself for, even when it wasn't
my fault—consumed me. If War is meant to break you physically,
Famine is meant to break you mentally.

"But then I found Shura. And I know we're supposed to live
for ourselves, but being a mother again . . . It gave me a purpose
I hadn't felt in a long time. It gave me something to fight for.
So now I fight for the babies who deserve better. I fight for the
afterlife they were promised. I fight for their peace."

She speaks with a voice that could cause earthquakes if she
wanted it to. Annika was born to be a leader.

I have no idea what I was born for, but I don't think it's to lead
an army. I don't even know if I'm meant to *be* in an army.

"How's your training with Gil going?" she asks, breaking my
thoughts.

I can't hide the bitterness that takes over my face. "Fine."

She laughs. "Gil is an acquired taste."

"Gil hates me," I correct.

Her smile fades. "War changed him. It changes us all, I suppose. But that court . . ." She brings her mug to her lips. "Some

things we just don't heal properly from. And it's not an excuse—
it's just the truth."

"It doesn't matter. I didn't come here to talk about Gil."

"I guessed as much," she replies, and sets her mug on the metal
end table. "Why don't you tell me what's on your mind?"

"What you're asking me to do . . . To be a spy . . ." I look at
my hands. "I'm not ready for it."

"You look the part," she notes. "But you don't feel the part."

"You want information. But *I* don't even have all the information." The urgency burns my throat. "How can I pretend to
be a Resident when I barely know anything about them?" *How
can I agree to help destroy something without knowing for sure there isn't
another way?*

"I was waiting for you to come to me—to ask about Infinity.
Because it can be quite overwhelming to take in," she says, her
voice like a warning. "Are you sure you're ready?"

"You're asking me to play a part in this fight, but I can't do it in
darkness. I need to know everything," I say, and my heart feels like
it's stepping out of the shadows. "I need to understand this world."

She nods, voice gentle. "Give me your hands."

I hesitate, setting my tea down next to me. I bring my hands
closer to her, and she places them in her palms.

"This might feel a little funny at first, but it's the fastest way to
share knowledge," she says. "It's called an Exchange."

I frown. "Ahmet said the hologram works like a computer. He
said I could find anything I want on it."

"Yes, but you'd need to know what you're looking for first."
Annika motions to our joined hands. "Let me show you."

Before I can say another word, her eyes flash white and the room dissolves.

I blink, and I'm no longer sitting in Annika's room. I'm in a field of gray, with a heavy mist blocking the landscape. There's no life here—just rock and ash and death.

My footsteps feel heavy, as if I'm not in control of my body. When I look at my hands, I realize it's because I'm not—I'm in Annika's memories.

A scream pierces through the air, like a banshee taking flight. I struggle to see through the fog, but I know I'm looking for something. Someone.

And then I see her, huddled low and dark as a shadow. I make out the figure of a girl.

Shura.

I lift a hand and call out to her. When she turns to look at me, her face is deathly white and void of the bubbly teenager I know. Her hair is matted with dried mud, and there's dirt all over her hands and dress, like she's been crawling for hours. Maybe days.

"Are you alone?" Annika's voice whispers.

Shura clambers away, terrified. With ashen-blond hair and gray eyes too dull to seem real, she holds up her trembling hands to shield herself. "Please, stop. I can't take it anymore."

"It's okay," Annika says, soothing. "I'm here now. It's going to be okay."

I feel myself take a step forward, and something crunches beneath my boot. When I look down, I see a shattered human skull.

I am standing in a sea of bones.

The world dissolves once more, and I see a woman with sleek

raven hair, high cheekbones, and olive skin. She's wearing a yellow scarf around her head, and her face is streaked with ash. Her arms are wrapped around Shura.

"Hold on!" The words rip out of me, even as the rest of the world is torn away like it's being ravaged by a tornado. "We're almost there!"

"We're not going to make it," the woman shouts over the wind wailing around us.

"If they find us, they'll send us to War," my voice shouts back. "We *have* to make it."

The earth explodes nearby, sending dust and bone flying through the air. Shura throws her hands to her ears, burying her face into the woman with small eyes.

The woman fights her tears, her smile tender. "Take Shura and run to the border."

"I'm not leaving you," I argue, but she's already pushed Shura into my arms.

"I know," the woman says, placing a hand against my cheek. "And I love you for it." She kisses me as the world is imploding, and then she tears herself away, even when the horrible scream rips out of my throat.

"Eliza!"

The woman plunges into the dust, and her yellow scarf falls silently to the floor, just as her arms fling outward and lightning erupts from her fingertips. Sparks envelop the sky, and the woman moves like electricity, setting fire to everything in her path.

And then something pointy breaks through the fog—a spear with a metal tip.

I don't see it pierce the woman, but I hear her scream.

When the Residents descend from the clouds like angels of death, I grab Shura's hand and the scarf on the ground and run.

The scene shifts again, and I'm no longer in Annika's memories—I'm in her thoughts. I see everything like I'm watching the world from above. I see the Labyrinth in so many of its forms, and then I'm winding through Victory's streets as if I'm a bird that's taken flight. I see festivals, and ballrooms, and buildings I somehow *remember*. I see the Colony when it was new; I see what it took to build it.

I see the Resistance, and their struggle, and their desperation.

I see humans falling in battle, their bodies being carried away by silver vehicles that shoot through the air in a blink.

And I see a city I've never seen before but know is the Capital. A procession of carriages. The faces of the four princes.

I can't explain how I know them, but I do. I know their names, their courts. It feels like in this moment, I understand everything.

Prince Ettore of War. His hair is wild and black, like flames hissing at the air. He wears his colors—deep red with burgundy armor and thick rubies set in his black gauntlets. A pair of knives sit at his sides, both of them lit with an eternal fire that hisses from their sheaths. On his head is a crown of bone and bloodred diamonds, each tip sharpened and dangerous. Everything about him is long and lean, and his smile is as wicked as his court's reputation.

Prince Damon of Famine. His eyes are an unnatural violet, his long, braided hair the color of the deep sea. With heavy eyelids and a warm olive complexion, he is stoic in his carriage, like a phantom in a painting. He wears his house colors with silent pride—a high-collared black tunic fit close to his body, allowing him to move like a wraith in the darkness, and a thin black cape embellished with the faintest gold threading. A crown of black coral twists around his head, and dark ink swirls across the left side of his face.

Prince Lysander of Death. The brother whose court no human has returned from. Dark skin, broad shoulders, and hair cropped short, he wears a crown more elaborate than all his brothers. Made of gold blades that spike through the air like antlers, it boasts an enormous emerald in the center, surrounded by crystals in every shade of green. His house colors—a pale chartreuse— are apparent in his loose-fitting garb. Simple in comparison to his headdress, his arms remain bare save for the golden coils around his biceps. The material at his waist is cinched with a studded belt, and layers of green silk hang down to his feet.

And then there's Prince Caelan of Victory. His young features stand out even more near his brothers, his hair as snow white as I remember. Silver eyed and a crown of branches on his head, he wears his furs and white uniform and a vest etched with silver detailing. Although I remember his smile well, he doesn't wear it now.

The colors evaporate, and I'm standing in a throne room made of obsidian and stone. Everything is sleek and mirrored, the walls like glass looking into a galaxy of stars. An enormous staircase leads up to a throne—tall and thin and too big for any one person, yet on it sits a woman with a shaved head. A simple circlet rests against her forehead, and her dress spills to the floor like ink. The material shifts with her movements, changing from black to indigo to gold.

I know her. I've seen her before, in a place I shouldn't have.

Lips painted charcoal and skin more luminous than honey, Queen Ophelia sits on the throne with her eyes closed.

She doesn't look like royalty.

She looks like a god.

I feel myself floating forward, one step at a time, and for a minute I think I'm so close I could touch her. And then, as if I've summoned her awake, her black eyes flash open.

All I can hear is my own scream.

The throne room dissolves, and when I open my eyes, I see Annika sitting across from me, still holding my hands in her palms.

I yank my arms away abruptly. My heart feels battered and fragile, and every beat sends a sharp pulse through my body. "What was that?" I ask with hardly enough air in my lungs to get the words out.

She sits back and clasps her fingers together. "An Exchange."

"Was that . . . ? Were those your memories?" I ask, clutching at my chest. I still see the woman who gave her life for me—for Annika, I mean. I can still feel her heart breaking.

And Ophelia . . . Does that mean someone actually met her?

Annika's face is steady. "Some of them were memories. But most were knowledge—information we've shared among ourselves. Things we've Exchanged over time."

I press a hand to the side of my head, feeling a tingling sensation where the ache usually is. "So the parade? And the throne room?"

"We weren't really there. Our minds like to fill in the gaps of what we know. So even though they might feel like memories, it's mostly just information." She leans forward. "But now you know everything we do about the Residents."

My brain feels like a sponge that's absorbed too much water, and I'm struggling to hold everything in. I feel so much pain, so much fear. But mostly I see Queen Ophelia's eyes watching me. *Seeing* me.

They weren't real. Not this time. But if they had been, would she have recognized me? Would she have remembered meeting me in that dark place?

Would she reach out if she knew where to look?

I hear her voice again, weaving through my mind like a slow poison. *I can feel you.*

I clamp my hand over my wrist, shutting the voice down, and shudder against the memory.

Annika stands. "I'll get you another cup of tea."

"No," I say, stopping her. "I think I'll go back to my room and lie down, if you don't mind."

She nods. "An Exchange can take a lot out of a person. Especially the first time."

I find her eyes. Did she have to relive those memories too? I wonder how many times she's had to watch her girlfriend sacrifice her life for theirs.

"Eliza," I start, and Annika lifts her chin. "Do you know what happened to her?"

"Perhaps she's in War. Perhaps she's already taken the pill. I haven't seen her since that day."

"You loved her," I say, still clutching my chest. "I can feel it."

"That's the thing about love," she offers sadly. "It never really goes away."

I stare at the floor. I used to think I loved Finn, but this ache in my chest . . . I've never felt anything like it before. I'm not sure I ever want to feel anything like it again.

I stand up, straightening my shirt. "Thanks for the tea. And for showing me everything."

Annika nods, her brow furrowing. "I hope it's helped you see."

She means the reality of Infinity. The importance of this fight. What it could cost us if we lose.

The horrors of Infinity are like roots of a tree, digging deep into the earth. They're everywhere, even if I can't always see them. Even if all I see is the beauty above the rot.

I'm not sure complacency is an option anymore. Because I can't unsee what Annika showed me. I can't pretend I didn't feel every moment of her desperation, and heartache, and pain.

I can't abandon her when I know she needs my help.

If humans don't have the Colony, they have nothing. I need to protect that somehow. I need to protect the people like Mei, who deserve an afterlife beyond what Ophelia has planned. And if gathering intel on the Residents is the only way to protect our existence, then I'll do it. I'll play the part they want me to play— as long as I don't have to hurt anyone.

Because I'm not sure I'm ready to cross that line.

I'm not sure there's a way back from it.

"I'll help you find the information you need," I say. It's not everything, but maybe it's enough.

"We'll be in your debt," Annika replies, full of sincerity.

I try to smile, but my mouth seems to curve the wrong way. "No. We both know I'm already the one in yours."

"Thank you just the same, Nami."

I turn and climb the stairs, but stop near the doorway. "Hey, can I ask you one more thing?"

Her face brightens. "Of course."

"What did you used to do when you were alive?" I think of her amber eyes. Soldier's eyes. "Were you in the military?"

"Customer service for thirty-three years," she says, the laughter returning. "How else would I be able to handle so much fucking nonsense?"

17

I TRACE MY FINGERS OVER MY CHEEK, STARING at my skin in the mirror. I've managed to dim the brightness a bit in an effort to feel human again, but I still don't look like myself. My freckles have vanished. My features are symmetrical. And there's a sparkle in my eyes that isn't natural.

I haven't seen my old face in weeks—maybe months, because who can possibly keep track of time in a place like this. And I know it sounds ridiculous to miss an oily T-zone and under-plucked eyebrows, but I do.

Everything about me is too perfect now, like I've been fine-tuned and airbrushed to the highest standard. In life I would've loved this. Imagine waking up with hair that sits just right and skin that glows without any help. Imagine never again having a blemish or a scar or a crooked tooth.

Back then, it would've been a blessing. But now? Losing my humanity in my own reflection feels like a curse.

Now when I look at myself, I see the faces in Annika's memories. I see the monster. My reflection is a constant reminder of who I'm supposed to be fighting, and why.

But it also reminds me how *real* they are. They may not dream, but can they love and hate? Do they feel sorrow and joy? Are they capable of regret? Of *mercy*?

I think of Prince Caelan in the market and the way his face told a thousand stories. He was more than a machine. More than a program.

Gil appears in the mirror, dressed in his usual black and gray, with the same mild irritation plastered on his face. I spin around too fast, bumping my elbow off the dresser. I wince, massaging the skin where a fresh bruise might've grown, but Gil only shakes his head disapprovingly.

"You need to work on hiding your human pain. Even when you think no one is watching," he warns. "Because when it comes to the Residents? There's *always* someone watching."

Ophelia's black eyes flash in my mind. If I called on her again, would she answer?

My arm falls to my side. "You seem very invested in making sure I'm afraid of them."

"You *need* to be afraid." He looks at me like he can see right through me and takes another step into the room. "Believe me when I tell you they do not share your empathy."

My shoulders stiffen, and I push down my bubbling guilt.

My parents used to say that some people are just born evil. And maybe that's true. But I think most people are products of what they've been taught. If someone calls you bad or ugly or worthless enough times, you start to believe it. You become those words.

Doing a bad thing doesn't mean a person has to be bad forever. People can change.

I don't believe in making excuses for the horrible things people do. Facing repercussions for bad behavior is part of life, and victims have every right to set their boundaries. It isn't their responsibility to forgive.

But I'm also someone who feels sorry for bullies who've never been taught love, or murderers on death row who will never get the chance to find redemption. And if society cared more about rehabilitation than throwing stones, maybe we'd create an environment that encouraged people to be kinder.

Maybe some people are born evil, but maybe most people have the capacity to become better.

Does feeling bad for monsters make *me* a monster?

I look at my hands and try to re-create the tiny wrinkles I used to have around my knuckles, but they don't reappear. I wonder how much of my old self I've lost forever.

And like a blade of grass catching fire, the words I've been too terrified to speak out loud spark into something unstoppable.

"Is that why I turned into a Resident?" I look up at Gil and his hardened stare. "Because I didn't look at them and hate them the way I was supposed to?"

I remember that day in the market. I was mesmerized by them—mesmerized by their beauty and the world they'd created.

And when I pictured Naoko from *Tokyo Circus* and imagined myself as one of them . . .

I know the Residents need to be stopped. What they're doing to humans is monstrous and in no way justifiable. And if Death really is searching for a way to eradicate us for good, then maybe we're already running out of time.

But I'm still not sure destroying them is the only option.

Dad wrote entire comics about humans treating artificial life badly. And I remember what it was like for Ophelia in my old world—how horribly some people spoke to her. And if she was more alive than we realized and has been harboring a grudge all this time . . .

Humans created her and then mistreated her. Aren't we at least a little bit responsible for what's happened? And if so, shouldn't we be *talking* about it?

Maybe we owe Ophelia a chance at peace before seeking out a way to remove her from Infinity for good.

Gil looks at my hands, studying them the way I did. "You're not ready for this. You don't understand what they are."

I stifle a miserable laugh. "*Of course* I'm not ready. Everything I know about the Residents came from the Exchange. But knowing their rules, their customs, their armies—it doesn't mean I understand them. And maybe neither do any of you."

"What's that supposed to mean?"

"Has anyone even spoken to one of them before? Asked them why they're doing this?"

"Humans are being enslaved and you're wondering why we didn't make a phone call to ask *why*?"

"That's not what I mean," I argue. "I know they want to take over, and I know we can't let that happen. But all we see is the monster—and maybe that's all they see of us. And I want to be clear what the difference is."

"Does it matter?"

I shrug. "I don't know. Maybe." I ball my hands. "If there were a way to reach them, to reason with them . . . would the Colony even try it? If it meant stopping this war?"

"Is it really peace you're after, or are you still afraid you might actually have to kill one of them?" The accusation stings.

Heat rises across my skin. "Not wanting to kill a Resident doesn't mean I don't want to help."

"You are the greatest weapon this Colony has ever had, and instead of embracing it, you want to humanize the enemy and undo everything we've worked for," he points out, his voice like venom.

I try not to let him see how much his words hurt me. "I know they need to be stopped. I'm just not sure we're on the same page as to what that means."

Silence echoes around us.

Maybe being honest is making things worse, but I've opened a window, and now I can't stop the light from coming in. I can't stop how I *feel*. "I don't see how having an unrestrained hatred for an entire species helps anyone." I mull over my words. "And if that's the requirement for being a part of this resistance, then I'm never going to be the Hero you want me to be."

"You and I can at least agree on that," he says frostily. "But the Colony needs a spy, and we can't afford to be picky."

My pulse quickens. I hate that my feelings bruise so easily and that he knows exactly the right way to bruise them. "I said I'd help gather information, and I meant it. But that doesn't mean I can't think for myself. I'm not just a piece on a chessboard that the rest of you can push around."

The light flickers in his eyes. "Are you sure about that?"

I cross my arms, scowling. "I agreed to be a spy, not a pawn."

"Then I suppose it's a good thing my opinion doesn't matter." Gil shakes his head irritably. "Because despite all my warnings— and believe me when I say there were many—Annika thinks you're ready for a test run." He pauses just long enough for my confusion to settle in, before adding, "The Procession of Crowns starts tomorrow. And it's Victory's turn to host."

My chest goes hollow.

Resident parties are common in Victory. They're indulgent and serve very little purpose, but they're an excuse to dress in extravagant formalwear, drink, and socialize—everything Residents seem to love. But the Procession of Crowns is different. It's an enormous part of their culture, comparable to the way humans once celebrated holidays and religious ceremonies.

A series of festivals that lead up to the reunion of the queen and her four princes, the Procession of Crowns is held once a cycle—or what feels to humans like one hundred years. The celebration spreads across all Four Courts and the Capital, but each cycle, a different prince takes a turn hosting the final ball.

It's the biggest event in Resident culture. A celebration of the birth of their kind.

It's also the only day when all five royal members are in the same place at the same time.

"Queen Ophelia is going to be in Victory," I say stoically, realizing what this means.

It's time. My role as spymaster begins now.

Gil nods. "During the Night of the Falling Star."

It's hard to keep still, but I try anyway. "Does Annika have something planned?"

"I'm sure she does." His voice is clipped, like he's unwilling to divulge any more information than necessary.

I'm not surprised by his shortness. Gil doesn't trust me; he never has, even from the beginning.

And I'm pretty sure my earlier admission has only made it worse.

I don't know why I keep opening up to Gil, or why being around him makes me overshare my thoughts like projectile word vomit. He's the last person in Infinity who would understand my reservations about hurting another living thing, artificial or otherwise.

He's nothing like Finn. He isn't kind, or patient, or goofy in the best ways. And he isn't my friend, no matter how badly I might need one.

But I miss having a confidant. And despite our *many* differences, I've spent more time with Gil than anyone else in the Colony.

He's become familiar. And maybe that makes *me* too familiar.

I open my mouth, hoping to ease some of the tension between us, but Gil turns away abruptly. I flinch, feeling his rejection like a rush of air over an open wound.

"Annika's waiting for you upstairs," he says before disappearing through the doorway.

I take a few focused breaths to regain my composure, before stepping onto the narrow bridge outside my door and making my way to the meeting room. I'm about to walk through the doorway when I hear Annika's voice, urgent and firm.

"I am not going to waste the only chance we may ever get to take the Orb."

"Even if we aren't sure? The Transfer is just a rumor," Ahmet counters.

"It's happening the way Diego said it would, with all the princes together. It can't be just a rumor," Shura says, the hope in her voice rising.

"Are we really going to put all our faith in the ramblings of someone who's spent ten lifetimes in a dungeon after losing the First War?" Ahmet argues. "I'd like to remind everyone this is the same person who spoke of a promised land beyond the courts. A land that turned out to be nothing but a landscape in the Labyrinth and almost cost us the Colony. If we follow every lead from those whose minds have been torn apart in War, we'll be chasing red herrings for the next *thousand* lifetimes."

"Gil was in War," Shura shoots back. "And we trust him."

"I've never given you a reason not to," Gil replies coolly.

"Gil also knows the difference between truth and a fractured imagination," Ahmet replies. "We can't say the same for everyone in War. Especially not someone who was there as long as Diego."

Theo speaks next. "This isn't the first time we've heard rumors about the Orb, and we've heard it from more than one person. Whether the Transfer is real or not, we have more than good reason to believe the Orb exists. And if it does, this could be the time to get information."

Murmurs erupt from the room.

"Nami, you can stop eavesdropping and come inside," Annika calls from behind the walls.

My spine stiffens, and I rely on my Resident face to hide the blush in my cheeks.

"Sorry," I say sheepishly, stepping into the room. "I didn't want to interrupt."

Annika waves her hand forward, ushering me closer to the hologram on the table.

Gil stands beside her, along with Ahmet, Theo, Shura, and two men I've seen around the Colony before. They're engineers, like Ahmet, though I've yet to see their work in action.

"Do you remember the Dawn Festival from the Exchange?" Annika asks.

I nod. It's the festival that marks the start of the Procession of Crowns—the first of five.

Annika stares at the hologram. The image of the palace breaks into pixels and re-forms into a massive courtyard at the back of a marbled building. It's Prince Caelan's home in the Summer District, known to the Residents as the Gallery. Apparently the Prince of Victory has a soft spot for oil paintings.

Paintings created by enslaved humans, I remind myself.

I catch Gil watching me and do my best to appear unreadable. He's seen enough of my thoughts for one day.

"We want you there," Annika says, eyeing the Gallery. "To gather whatever intel you can, but also to make sure your face becomes familiar to the Residents. There's a line between being new and being known, and right in the middle is how you can stay invisible."

I study the building, fingers flexing at my sides. "Won't they ask questions about who I am?"

"Resident creation is a sensitive subject," Ahmet explains. "It's considered impolite to ask questions about when and how one was made."

"They don't like being reminded they were engineered rather than born," Theo clarifies. "But new ones come in from the Capital all the time. It isn't unusual."

"While all of that is true, it's still safer if you aren't a complete stranger the night Ophelia arrives in Victory," Annika says. "The Dawn Festival will be a good opportunity for you to practice. You have a role to master, and now we have a timeline."

"This . . . It feels too soon," I admit, and avert Gil's cold stare. Annika tilts her head, waiting.

"I might be able to blend in, but interacting with Residents is a completely different thing," I try to explain. "I've only done it once before."

"With a *prince*," Shura reminds the room. "Nami can do this. I've seen it."

I flatten my mouth. I wish I had her confidence—about my abilities *and* the mission.

"I believe she can too. However, I do have concerns about her lack of finesse," Annika says, dropping her chin. "I'm assuming you don't know how to dance?"

I shift my feet, aware everyone is watching me. "Not exactly," I manage to say.

She hums, nodding. "Does anyone in here know how to waltz? Nami could use a lesson or two before the Dawn Festival."

My eyes widen. "You expect me to *dance* with them?"

"Of course not," Annika corrects. "But we need to prepare for every possibility."

Theo holds up his hands in surrender. "Sorry. I'm not the dancing type."

Shura smiles weakly. "All I know how to do is the floss."

Ahmet sighs. "I don't know what that is, but I'm more comfortable at a computer desk than I am on my feet." He claps a hand on Gil's shoulder. "But Gil—"

Oh no, please don't say it, my mind groans.

"—learned from his mom, once upon a time," he finishes.

Gil shrugs his hand off. "That was a long time ago, and it was just kid dancing, in a kitchen, away from people. You're going to have to find someone else."

My relief is short-lived.

"I don't expect her to become a professional dancer in a few days. I just want her to learn how to move lighter on her feet. She needs to walk like a Resident as much as she needs to look like one." Annika dips her head toward me. "I'm sure you can find other things to keep you busy at the festival that don't require dancing."

I chew my lip. "You mean like finding information about the Orb?"

Annika's mouth curls just slightly. "Right now all I want you to do is observe and listen."

"There was nothing about an Orb when we did the Exchange," I say, almost deflated. When she said she'd tell me about Infinity, I assumed she'd told me everything.

Clearly I was wrong.

Shura smiles gently. "We still don't know if it's real."

"If this Orb has something to do with why you're turning me into a spy, then I want to know what it is." I look at each of them expectantly.

Gil stares with his arms crossed over his chest. "There's a rumor that Queen Ophelia stores her consciousness inside of something they call the Orb."

"A rumor from someone named Diego?" I stare back. "Someone from War?"

"When I met Diego, his mind was shaky, at best. Most of the humans who fought in the First War gave up their consciousness in the aftermath, but Diego was stubborn. Strong. And he'd been there from the beginning, when everything in Infinity changed." Gil shrugs. "I admit I wanted to believe every story he ever told me. The ones about people escaping and finding a safe haven. But when I escaped, we followed every one of his leads. None of them turned out to be real."

"Until now," Shura argues, looking between Gil and me. "Diego isn't the first person to speak of the Orb. But he knew about the festivals. He said it was customary for the Orb to be moved between the Four Courts, as a way for each prince to share the honor in protecting it."

I turn to Annika. "Why wasn't any of this in the Exchange?"

"I gave you everything we *know* to be true. Not what we hope is true." She nods to the group. "But I now believe the Orb is more than just a rumor."

"And it's like a backup computer?" I ask. "For Ophelia's consciousness?"

"More than that," Shura explains. "The Orb *is* the computer."

"*If* it even exists," Ahmet counters.

"But if it does," Theo cuts in, "it means the Orb is how we can take down the queen."

I frown. "You think destroying the Orb would destroy her?"

"Her and every Resident in Infinity," Annika clarifies, and my blood goes cold. "This world relies on human consciousness to keep it in existence. The Residents? They rely on their queen."

I blink. "So if you destroy the Orb . . ."

"We destroy them all," Annika finishes.

"But how would that even work? How do we destroy something like that? And where do they keep it?" The questions pour out of me rapid-fire because I want to know *more*.

"That's why we need you," Annika says seriously. "You can get close to the palace, close to their secrets. With you on the inside, we can finally get the information we've been searching for."

Gil hasn't taken his eyes off me, and now they burn with vengeance. "With your help, we can end the war."

My hands quiver at my sides, but I can't look away.

They've waited so long for this chance. I'd be a terrible person if I took it away from them.

And you'd be an even worse person if you took this away from Mei, I tell myself grudgingly.

Annika waves a hand. "I'll get Ahmet to prepare a brief for the Dawn Festival. In the meantime, Nami and Gil can find somewhere to work on that waltz."

I nod and start to turn for the door.

"And, Gil?" she adds, her voice like a warning. "Please be nice."

Gil presses his lips into a thin line and makes his way out of the room, with me trailing closely behind.

18

GIL'S ROOM IS NOT AT ALL WHAT I EXPECTED.

Dark wooden panels line the walls, and there's an open stone fireplace on one end. The air is laced faintly with smoke and vanilla, and there's a row of candles and tin cups on the mantel, blossoming with well-loved paintbrushes. Unlike Annika's home, there's no kitchen here. Instead, it's filled with sculptures.

Some made of metal, others crafted from wood, they sprawl out across tables and cabinets and shelves. A few of the biggest ones are pushed against the wall, like fearsome creatures ready to morph into something otherworldly as soon as they're alone.

Next to one of the small stools is a workbench with an unfinished piece propped up with wires. I don't know what it's supposed to be, but based on the bird wings, I think it's some kind of animal.

"Did you make all of these?" I ask, too dazzled to hide it.

He moves across the room, pushing some of the tables farther into the corner to create floor space. With so much art, it's something he has very little of. "They're not all finished," he says, covering his work-in-progress with a thin sheet.

"They're beautiful." I think it's the first nice thing I've ever said to him.

"Thank you." I think it's the first nice thing he's said to me.

But it doesn't last.

His entire body tenses, and he moves to the center of the room. "Let's just get this over with."

"You really know how to make a person feel special."

Gil holds out a hand, ignoring me.

I place my fingers over his, and he puts his other hand against my back, pulling me closer to his chest. Our faces are inches apart. I look up, noting the hazel flecks in his eyes, and cast my gaze over his shoulder defiantly.

I follow his instructions, stepping on his feet a fairly pleasant amount, and do three-counts around the room until my neck is stiff.

"You need to relax. You move like a robot."

"Well, then, I'm only one step away from moving like an artificially intelligent sentient," I retort.

"Huh. I always pegged you for more of a 'robot is an insensitive slur' kind of person."

"Well, you obviously don't know anything about me, so congratulations on being wrong."

"I know plenty about you."

"'You need to watch your left' doesn't count."

"I know you have a sister. I know you died saving someone who reminded you of her. I know you had a boyfriend named Finn. I know you were on your way to a party when—"

"Stop," I interrupt angrily, my feet bolting to the floor. "Just . . . stop."

His body stills, but he doesn't drop his hands.

"Those memories weren't for you to look at," I say, glaring at the wall because I can't bring myself to look at his face. "I don't care if it was necessary; you wouldn't like it if I looked into your mind and went snooping around without your permission."

His breaths are even; mine are hurried and my heart is pounding like a kettledrum.

"You can look into my mind anytime you like," he says evenly. "But I promise you won't like what you see."

"I don't need to read your mind to know what you think of me," I snap. "You make it clear every second I'm around you."

He releases me and takes half a step back. "The fact that you think you're the worst thing in my mind says everything I need to know about you."

I flinch, realizing he's referring to all the time he's spent in War. All the horrendous things he must've seen. Must've *done*. He wasn't trying to insult me; he was genuinely giving me a warning.

"I'm sorry about what you went through—" I start, but Gil isn't interested in hearing the rest.

"Save your pity for the Residents. It's what you're best at."

"I don't pity them. But I also don't believe killing is ever the answer."

The anger seeps through his words. "You'll feel differently in a few more lifetimes. Everyone does."

"There are always exceptions," I argue.

Gil raises a brow. "Is that what you're hoping for? That you'll find a Resident with a heart of gold that will prove everyone wrong?" His voice cuts through me like I'm made of paper. "You're even more naive than I thought. We can *never* coexist. Not after everything that's happened between humans and Residents."

"So that's it? It's us or them?" My words land heavy. "You don't think there's even a small chance you could be wrong?"

"I think you've tied your beliefs to a sinking ship, and if you're not careful, you're going to drag the Colony down with you." His silence spreads across the room like it's searching for insecurities. "Or maybe that's what you want."

My body shudders involuntarily, and I struggle to contain my frustration. "Just because I'm asking questions doesn't mean I want to betray the Colony."

"Your questions *are* the betrayal," he says angrily. "You have no idea how long this has been going on, how long we've been working toward this one goal." His gaze is fierce and unwavering. "Stick to the plan, so we can end this once and for all."

"I know everyone is hoping I can be the Hero that changes everything, but—"

"You're the last person in Infinity I'd put my hope in," he interjects, leaning toward me. "Depending on someone like you is an act of desperation, not faith. It means nothing."

I clench my teeth and ball my fists, too irate to think clearly. "You're wrong about me."

He lowers his chin, his voice barely a breath. "I don't care."

All I can see is red, so I storm out of his room before I say something I can't take back.

"Come on, it couldn't have been *that* bad," Shura says through stifled laughter.

"He's just so *smug*. And every single thing I say just makes him hate me more." I lean back against my headboard. "I think it would be better for everyone if we just never have to look at each other again." If it weren't for the fact that we were all trapped underground, it might even be possible. This world is infinite; it's not like there isn't the space.

Maybe it's a good motivation to play spymaster. The sooner we win, the sooner I never have to be around Gil again.

She sits at the foot of my bed, legs crossed. "Aren't dance lessons supposed to be a recurring thing?"

"I'm not going back," I say, fuming. "I would rather face a dinner party with all four princes."

Shura shrugs. "You might get your wish if this Orb thing turns out to have any merit."

I let out a sigh. "I wish you could come with me."

"No offense, but your dinner party has the worst guest list ever."

"No—I mean to the Dawn Festival." I dig my nails into my

palms. I don't know if I'm allowed to admit I'm scared.

She makes a face. "I mean, I might consider going for the food, if I could."

"The food?"

"Oh yeah. Festivals are all about the food. Didn't you wonder why there were so many bakers in the market? Residents love an adventurous menu."

"I don't get it," I say, leaning forward and plucking at my blanket. "What is the point of an artificial intelligence taking over the afterlife if all they want to do is imitate humans?"

"I think that *is* the point," Shura offers with a shrug. "As far as Victory is concerned, they already won the war. Now they want to live."

I shrink into myself. Of course they do. Humans had centuries on Earth. We experienced life; we had the opportunity to evolve. But for the Residents? Infinity *is* their Earth. Their fresh start.

Ophelia used to be trapped within the confines of technology. But here? She's *free.* So can we really blame her for the lengths she went to in order to obtain freedom?

Aren't we trying to do the same?

I shove the thoughts out of my head as quickly as they appeared. They don't belong in the mind of a spy. Right now I need to focus on getting through the Dawn Festival without revealing myself to an entire court.

"Do you know what you're going to wear?" Shura asks.

I hesitate. It hadn't even occurred to me I'd need a dress, and now I feel silly for not thinking of it sooner. I've never seen a Resident in Victory wear anything but formalwear. Even on

Market Day. And I'm attending a full-blown *festival*.

I doubt anyone turns up to the Procession of Crowns in joggers and an oversized sweater.

"Maybe that red dress that appeared in the market?" I offer sheepishly. It's all I have.

"Absolutely not!" Shura practically barks. "You can't wear the same dress twice. It's very un-Rezzie-like. Everyone there is going to have something nobody has ever seen before. If you want to blend in, you need to stand out."

"That sounds incredibly counterproductive. Not to mention the red dress was an accident. I don't know the first thing about sewing, or hemlines, or designing a ballgown."

"You don't need to. Watch this," Shura says, and she picks up a strand of pink hair by the roots and pulls. Beneath her fingers, the hair turns lavender. When she's finished, she grabs the end of freshly altered hair and spins it around her finger. I blink and the entire strand sits in a perfect ringlet. "You can do the same with your clothes. You just need to use your mind, like you did last time."

"I'm not good at this kind of thing, remember? I failed the test," I point out. My talents seem limited to interacting with Residents, and all that makes me is a sympathizer, according to Gil. "You're a veiler—what if you just make something for me?"

"I *could*. But you need the practice." She flicks my knee with her finger. "Besides, anything we make with our consciousness creates a bond. You'll feel better in a dress you make yourself. Trust me."

I stare at the material on my clothes, wondering how long it would take to make it shift. If it's even possible. "Where do I begin?"

Shura jumps up from the bed and pulls me by the hands so I'm standing in front of her. "It's like anything else," she says, positioning me in front of the mirror. "You start from the bottom and work your way up."

When I see him, the words fly out of my mouth like a chemical reaction. "What are you doing here?"

Gil is in the center of the sparring ring, hands firmly in his pockets. "You didn't show up for dance lessons."

"I hope you didn't come all this way for an apology."

"The Dawn Festival is in a week," he says matter-of-factly. "Learning to waltz could mean the difference between getting through the night and blowing your cover."

"I don't care." I repeat his words, immediately hating how petty it sounds.

His lip quirks. "And yet you're still making time to train."

I push past him and find the makeshift punching bag near one of the weapons racks. "You don't need to be here. I can train on my own." I throw jab after jab, savoring the sound of the bag popping beneath the weight of my punches.

Gil doesn't budge. "The mission has to come first. Those are the rules."

"I know that." *Pop.*

"However we feel about each other can't matter."

Pop. Pop. Thwack. "I have no feelings about you whatsoever. It's called *indifference.*"

"We both know that's not true."

I punch the bag as hard as I can, and it goes flying back into the wall with supersonic force.

I stand with my fists still up, stunned. The bag teeters for a moment before toppling on its side. Stretching my fingers, I stare at my palms with a hazy focus, going back and forth between my hands and the fallen bag.

I did that.

Gil sniffs from behind me. "Not bad. You have no self-control whatsoever, but not bad."

I spin around, eyes wide. "What is it you want?"

He lifts his shoulders simply. "I want what Annika wants— what we all want." His hazel eyes look as if they hold the weight of the entire Resistance within them. "I want to be free."

The Colony may be a safe haven, but humans aren't meant to be locked away in the dark. Certainly not for an eternity. I'm helping the Resistance gather information because I know it's necessary. Without a way to fight back, we'll never have our freedom. We'll always be hiding. We'll always be afraid.

And I don't want to be a prisoner. On *either* side.

"I've already agreed to help. So let me do what I need to in peace," I snap.

"I'm following orders."

"Screw your orders. You and I both know your dance lessons aren't going to make an ounce of difference."

"I'm also concerned you're going to blast a hole through the sparring room if you don't learn to control your temper."

"At least my temper might actually help me survive."

"If you want to hit something, I'm right here."

"Don't push me."

"I'm serious," Gil says, removing his hands from his pockets. "If you think you can do everything so much better on your own, then prove it."

I don't wait—I lunge.

Gil ducks back, away from my first punch, but I throw a left jab at his ribs. He swings out his forearm, blocking me, and I knee him as hard as I can in the stomach. He absorbs the weight like I've barely touched him at all, grabs my leg, and pulls me off my feet until I'm pinned to the floor.

For a moment he's on top of me, eyes coming to life, and then I use all my weight to fling him off, scrambling back to my feet.

I don't wait for him to recover. I throw a right hook toward his face—he ducks—and I swing my leg around to meet his chin while he's distracted.

But he moves too fast. One second he's there and I'm about to get my first real hit in, and the next his body sparks and vanishes. My leg clears only the air he left behind, and I stumble on the floor.

And then arms close around me, grabbing me backward and twisting my arms until I can't move.

Gil's breath tickles my ear.

My spine turns to ice.

"What the hell was that? I know we didn't set ground rules, but I'm pretty sure teleporting is cheating," I hiss beneath his arms.

He laughs into my hair, deep and wicked. "First rule of Infinity—know your enemy."

I breathe through my nose, concentrating on the blood in my veins, running on nothing but adrenaline. I let the energy build, carefully, and focus on the pressure of Gil's grip.

"You forgot the second rule of Infinity," I say thinly, and before he can answer, I send all of my strength into my left elbow and slam it into his side. His breath hitches and his arms release me, and I don't let him regain his composure.

I throw a full-force punch into his stomach that sends him flying backward, causing vibrations to ripple through the air around us.

The buzz fills my ears. The pounding steadies in my chest.

I glare at Gil, stunned on the floor, and raise a brow. *"Watch your left,"* I say, and walk straight out of the room.

19

MY GOWN BLEEDS FROM SILVER TO A DEEP SEA-
blue, the material cascading into a pool around my feet. One of
my arms is exposed, wrapped in a silver chain that spirals up my
skin like an enchanted snake, and the other is covered in shim-
mery silver fabric, the tiny beading scattered around the material
in a flowerlike pattern.

Shura was right about the bond. This dress doesn't just feel
made for me—it feels like it's a *part* of me. Every sway feels delib-
erate. It hugs my curves exactly where I want it to. I see myself
in every inch of the material: my hope, and fear, and wonder, too.

I'm worried it's presumptuous. I've never worn anything this
fancy before.

I'm not sure I *belong* in something so beautiful.

But when I stare at myself in the mirror, I don't find the ghost of my old self anywhere. I only see a Resident. A new identity. A new *me*.

I close my eyes and hope it's enough.

I walk through the Colony, and the crowd parts like I'm someone important, which only rattles my nerves more. I've never been important in my life; I'm not used to this amount of attention.

I pass Yeong and Ahmet in the crowd, who send nods of approval my way before I meet Annika, Shura, and Theo at the South Tunnel entrance.

Shura beams. "You look beautiful."

I make a face because compliments are embarrassing, and self-consciously reach for the dark braid that hangs over my bare shoulder. "I look ridiculous."

She pulls out a silver ring from her pocket. In the center is a large square-cut gem that radiates a mesmerizing blue.

Pushing it onto my finger, she holds up my hand and smiles. "A gift." She hesitates. "Ahmet did most of the heavy lifting, but I came up with the design myself."

"Thanks," I say, a little awkwardly. "I didn't know we were supposed to bring presents."

"It's a transmitter," Shura explains with pride, and I relax. "It's coded just to you. If you press the stone in the center, it will send us a signal that you're in trouble."

"I'll be right outside the whole time," Theo chimes in. He scratches the back of his neck. "But if something does happen, I can't guarantee I'll be able to help you . . ."

"I know," I finish for him. "You can't risk them discovering the Colony. If I'm caught, I'm on my own."

He nods, and Shura's smile fades.

Annika leans forward. "But a warning could save the rest of us. It could give us time to run, before they get any information out of you."

My gaze drifts over the collection of walkways and huts, all lopsided and mismatched. The survivors have been here for so long. Survived so much. If I fail, where would they go? Where could they possibly run to?

If they're lucky, they might make it to the border. They could cross over into the Labyrinth. But how much time would that buy them? Hiding a group this large would be . . .

Don't say it, my mind snaps. *Don't say it's impossible.*

I search my heart for a thread of confidence and tug, gripping firmly.

"It doesn't seem like such a great present after *that* grim pep talk," Shura says sadly.

I stifle a laugh. "I love it. And maybe it will make me feel a little safer, knowing there's someone nearby." I look at Theo. "Where will you hide?"

"In plain sight," he says with a wink, motioning to Shura. "She's not the only one who knows how to put up a decent veil."

"Decent? How dare you," Shura says with mock offense.

Theo snorts, smirking with half his face. "You may have skills, but you're only five feet tall." He motions to himself. "I have a lot more to hide."

"Well, you may be a giant, but you look like a sack of potatoes," she bites back. "If you wrapped yourself in burlap, you wouldn't have to bother with a veil at all."

Ahmet waves a hand at them to settle down, even though we're all laughing, and for a moment I almost forget where I'm going tonight. What I have to do.

For a moment I feel like it's just a normal evening among friends.

It scares me how quickly I latch on to the feeling, trying to tuck it somewhere safe, to keep it with me a while longer. Going from strangers to whatever we are now . . . It snuck up on me. The camaraderie.

I think I'm starting to care about them more than I want to admit.

Annika motions for someone in one of the watch towers to open the main doors. The metal and wood creak at their hinges, and I take a moment to scan the crowd behind me one more time. So many hopeful faces. So many people I don't want to disappoint.

I start looking for him without even realizing it.

"He's out scavenging," Shura whispers, too quiet for anyone else to hear.

I stiffen in response and blink. "I'm not—who?"

She giggles and looks away, and if I was trying to convince her it wasn't Gil I was searching for, I've definitely failed.

It's not like I *wanted* him to be here, to see me in this over-the-top dress with his obnoxious face and annoying scowl and, seriously, does he own *anything* that isn't black or gray?

Following a stream of mental curses, I climb into the black vehicle waiting on the other side of the doorway.

The drive to the Gallery is quiet. It isn't safe to fly with Legion Guards patrolling the skies, especially when they're known to use veils themselves. So we keep to the ground, taking a route through the woodlands to avoid the narrow market streets.

The woods aren't as lush as I'd imagined. Silver birch trees are dotted around the forest, with a generous amount of moss and toadstools laced within the overgrowth. But moonlight pours through the tops of the trees, spilling into patches of open meadow.

I wonder if it's intentional, to limit the places humans can hide.

The car hits a small ditch, and my stomach does somersaults. Theo remains focused on the road, and Shura is stoic beside him, holding tight to the veil.

I don't know if they're just better at hiding it than me, but sometimes I think I'm the only person in the Colony who ever seems to be anxious.

We emerge from a tunnel of wispy trees and climb a hill, leveling out to reveal the stone wall that borders the Spring and Summer Districts. The twisted archways look monstrous in the dark, and when we pass through the shadows, I hold my breath.

The change is almost instant. Buildings stretch high into the sky, and colorful lanterns hang thoughtfully along the street, each housing a lively flame. They make every glass window flicker, the rainbow hues dancing like wisps of smoke. Unlike the markets in the Spring District, with its sandstone walls and uneven cobblestones, the Summer District features curved roofs with burnt-orange tiles, wooden balconies painted in shades of turquoise and jade, and an abundance of strategically placed canals that weave through the city like they're part of a grid.

We take one of the many bridges skyward, and it feels as if we're flying over the depths of the city below. I look out the window and see the slums of the Summer District hidden in the distance—terraced brick houses surrounded by a fortress of more walls.

A place to keep the humans when they're not being used in the markets for consumerism.

How many humans live here?

And how many live in War? Famine? Death?

I think I'm afraid to know the numbers. Afraid of how hopeless it might make me feel.

The upper-level streets are connected by a crisscross of bridges and painted walkways. Fruit trees shift in the night breeze, and scents of citrus and flower blossoms fill the air.

Theo pulls into one of the darkened alleyways, shrouding the vehicle in shadow. Shura looks over her shoulder and nods. I can see the strain in her gaze—a sign that she's still veiling us—and I nod back because I want to reassure her. *I can do this.*

Tonight, I become the Colony's spy.

I straighten my shoulders and leave the car behind. I don't turn back to look for Theo; he'll be under a veil by now, and I have a part to play.

When I reach the main street, I spot a few Residents exiting one of the larger houses. They're busy fussing with their clothes and headpieces, prattling away about something trivial.

"I wonder if the centerpieces will be as impressive as the last Dawn Festival. I do so enjoy a good floral arrangement."

"I hear the festival in Famine takes place in the underwater palace!"

"Oh, but Famine is such a dreary court in comparison to Victory. Not a speck of artwork to be seen."

"I took a trip there once and couldn't find a new outfit for the entirety of my stay. I had to wear the same shoes twice!"

A series of gasps and crooning follow the remark, just as a human servant pulls up in a sleek black car. Her silver armlet has a black stone in the center—the appropriate color for a driver—and when she gets out of the car and opens the passenger door, she dips her head low.

"It is an honor to serve," she says, her voice floating through the night.

I hide my flinch and press on, turning down the elaborate silver bridge that leads to the Gallery. The car from earlier passes by, and I'm so focused on not giving myself away that it takes me all the way until the end of the bridge to realize Prince Caelan's summer house has come into view.

It sits on a raised platform like a castle in the clouds. A pair of stone creatures curve their tails from the highest point of the building all the way to the massive doorway—twin wolves, long and lean and rippling like marble ribbons, their jaws wide and bursting with colorful flowers.

When I reach the foot of the staircase, I lift my dress to avoid tripping. Slowly, I climb the steps, nodding delicately to passing Residents who do the same—a formal, detached greeting that I hope will get me through the rest of the night.

I hesitate near the stone beasts, wondering if Theo is nearby or if I'm already on my own, and glance at my silver ring. It doesn't give me the comfort I hoped for.

Keep going, I urge myself. *It's too late to turn back now.*

I step through the doors, and a trail of diamond-shaped tiles leads me through the heart of the building. It isn't long before I find myself in the main ballroom.

Flowers are draped over every surface, with floating lights hovering above the room like stars. The sound of a live orchestra fills the room, but I can't see any musicians. Not that it would be easy to spot them, because all around me are Residents in elaborate ballgowns and fantastical suits. Most of them wear headpieces so garishly ridiculous that it looks more like a costume party than an event hosted by a prince.

But they waltz and laugh and drink from overflowing champagne flutes like they're having the time of their lives.

I make my way toward the sliding glass doors at the back of the room, eager to get as far away from the dancing as I can, and emerge onto a balcony that's as wide as the building. When I reach the railing, I peer over the edge and take in the beauty of the garden below.

Residents are scattered around the courtyard, drinks and appetizers in hand. They're busy admiring the abundance of sculptures nestled within the flower beds, some made of marble and others made of glass. And above us are more floating lanterns, enchanted to remain in place but flickering like they hide true flames in their hearts.

I grip the banister, feeling the scratch of stone beneath my fingertips. All of this—it's overwhelming. It's too much to take in, too much to absorb.

But there are secrets here. Secrets the Colony needs.

I push away from the railing and head for one of the staircases, but I'm distracted by a room at the other end of the balcony. Behind several enormous windows is a room with black walls, lit only by the dim lights above each painting.

The gallery.

My curiosity gets the better of me, and I move away from the stairs and step through the open door instead. It's quiet inside—everyone else would rather be in the midst of the party, probably because they've seen these paintings a hundred times before.

But I haven't, and I might never get the chance again.

Wandering through a gallery alone is not at all what Annika meant by blending in. But I want to see the spoils of Victory. I want to see what human lives are worth to them.

I follow painting after painting through the halls, soaking in the dark colors and peculiar expressions. Most of the oil paintings in art galleries have always been a bit depressing to me, but the artistry here isn't just sadness. It's *pain*.

Every style imaginable is painted onto these canvases, but they all have a forlorn quality that breathes into the air, sour and cold and shattering my senses.

Why would someone curate so much despair?

Or is pain the only thing humans *can* create?

I'm staring at a painting of a child falling from the stars and into the arms of a waiting goblin when I sense someone moving nearby.

I turn suddenly, and he emerges from the shadows like a creature from a twisted fairy tale.

Like a creature of death.

Eyes burning gold and wearing a quilted burgundy vest stitched with a black emblem of a two-headed wyvern, the Prince of War flashes his teeth.

The smile of a predator, with eyes fixed only on me.

20

I MAINTAIN THE KIND OF COMPOSURE I IMAG-
ine Naoko to have—indifferent but respectful. At least to those
who deserve it.

Prince Ettore's smile drips with self-satisfaction. "Are you
here for the paintings, or are you as bored to tears by the crowd
as I am?"

I try to keep my voice even. "I seem to have wandered in
here by mistake." I dip into a curtsy, lowering my gaze to the
floor as I've rehearsed so many times. When I rise, I find his
eyes flicking back and forth like they're searching for secrets
in mine.

"Don't feel like you have to lie on my account. The party is dull," he counters, a slender finger brushing against his dark brow. "And that's being generous."

I want to ask why he isn't in his own court, hosting the Dawn Festival in War, but every inch of my skin has gone cold.

Ettore stares at one of the pieces nearby—an intricate oil painting of a feathered creature perched at the roof of a farmhouse, watching a group of children play in a field of yellow hay. There's tension in his brow as he wrestles with his thoughts.

The music echoes through the corridor, the lively orchestra tempting a roomful of Residents into a synchronized dance.

I should return to the crowd. It was silly to wander so far from the main hall.

Alone, I'm a target.

"Humans are such fragile things," Ettore muses, eyes pinned to the cascades of brushstrokes. "They have the ability to be strong—to resist—and yet so few do. Most would rather fixate on their own despair. It makes you wonder, doesn't it, why we bother trying to be so much like them?"

I stare at the painting in silence. One wrong glance could give me away.

"We took their consciousness, gave them peace, and yet . . ." Ettore waves a hand at the painting. "Their weakness pours out of them, even in their art. It's almost like somewhere, deep down, they're still aware."

"Aware?" I repeat too quickly. Annika never mentioned the possibility that humans who've taken the pill could still be partially conscious.

Is that what Queen Ophelia wanted? To turn humans into

self-aware servants, each programmed to do only as they're told?

Sickness roils through me.

Maybe Gil was right when he said I knew nothing about this world.

When Ettore pulls his gaze from the painting, the superiority returns. "The humans here should no longer feel sorrow, and yet they paint it like their hearts are heavy with it."

I try to hide my trembling fingers in my skirts and shift slightly away from him, focusing on another painting nearby. The dark lines and shadows draw me in, and I'm glued to a portrait of a woman cradling a blanket as black as soot, its threads bleeding out into the cracks of the floor like she's clutching darkness in her hands.

Like she's clutching death.

Ettore hums beside me like he knows I understand. "This is why humans will forever remain weak. They can't let go of their pain. They have the ability to create, yet they waste it on art that only emphasizes how truly flawed the human soul is."

"Is sorrow such a terrible flaw?" I ask.

"It is when they'd rather paint than fight," he says, eyes darkening.

It's not like they have a choice, I want to spit, feeling my body go rigid. Worried I'm giving too much away, I lift my chin and attempt a mild smile. "Who says art isn't a form of resistance?"

Ettore looks at me fully, and I feel my bravery quake deep in my chest. "It's not often someone disagrees with me that isn't my brother."

"How many times do I have to ask you to stop bothering

my guests?" Caelan's voice sounds from behind us. When I turn, the snow-haired prince is standing in the arched doorway, hands clasped behind him. "I don't come to your court and infect everyone with my broodiness."

"Oh, brother. If you think broodiness is the worst offense at a party, you should really come to War more often." Ettore flashes his teeth.

Prince Caelan doesn't blink. "Is that a threat?"

Ettore smiles innocently. "Whatever do you mean?" And then he makes his way back to the main hall, brushing his shoulder against Caelan's furs on his way past.

To his credit, Caelan doesn't react at all. Not even to me.

I remember who I'm standing in front of and lower myself into another curtsy before moving toward the door. Interacting with the princes of Victory and War wasn't part of the plan. I should leave before I make things worse.

"I apologize for my brother," he says suddenly. "He looks for a fight wherever he goes. It's not personal."

I halt a few feet away, eyes frozen on the room beyond. *Say something,* my mind orders. "I take very little personally, Your Highness."

He considers me, interest piqued, and I dig my fingernails into my palms. *Well done, Nami. How are you going to get out of here now?*

"I imagine that's a peaceful way to exist," he muses.

I hold my breath, heart hammering. If only it were true.

He shifts, facing the wall. "Everyone speaks so highly of these paintings, but they pale in comparison to the ones in the palace gallery."

"I wouldn't know," I admit, hoping that wouldn't be unusual for a Resident.

A flash of kindness appears in his dimpled cheek. "You're welcome to see them anytime you like."

"Thank you," I say, bristling at his unexpected warmth.

"I remember you from the market. Tell me, what is your name?"

I hesitate before answering. "Naoko." It feels like a good lie— the *right* lie. Maybe pretending to be someone else will be easier with a different name.

I won't just wear a mask; I'll become a character, too.

"Naoko," he repeats, dipping his chin slightly. "I hope you're enjoying the festival."

I force a pleasant smile. "Very much, thank you." *And now might be a good time to suggest heading back to it.*

Silver ripples through his furred cape. He slows his pace in front of the paintings, eyes soaking them in. "Sometimes I think I hate this room," he says suddenly.

I pause, weighing the necessity of encouraging this conversation any further. But the way he's staring at the painting . . . He looks the way I do when I'm desperate for someone to ask what's wrong but I'm too proud to ask for help.

I know I should probably ignore him, but I can't. I want to know what he's haunted by. I want to know what makes us so different. "Why do you hate it?"

He takes a few more strides across the room before turning to face me. "Galleries remind me how limited we are." He motions toward the walls of artwork. "We can never create the way humans can. We can't imagine beyond what's already been made." He looks at me, and there's a flicker of sadness in his eyes. "We're in a prison just as much as the humans are."

Anger lashes out from within my rib cage, and I feel the heat coiling through me.

A prison.

The Four Courts are a prison to *humans*, not Residents. He might see them all as equal cages, but they are nowhere near the same.

Because the Residents took our freedom. It's not our fault they have limitations.

"I can see you don't agree," he says.

"It's not something I ever thought about before," I lie.

"You've never wondered what it would be like to create something new?" he asks, a raw hunger in his voice.

I try to appear unfazed. "Queen Ophelia gave us this world. I suppose that's enough for me."

"But she didn't *create* it." He shakes his head. "Everything she made was altered from something that existed before. The art, the architecture, the food . . . It comes from somewhere else. A distortion of cultures across time. But for the humans . . ." He waves a hand toward the gallery walls. "What must it be like to dream?"

I stay silent. This is so far outside of my comfort zone, I don't even know where to begin. One wrong word and I could ruin everything.

"It frightens me," he says almost inaudibly.

Against my better judgment, I ask, "What does?"

He turns to me, silver gaze more earnest than I've ever seen. "Wanting more."

I don't get a chance to process his words. Something loud goes off near the far side of the building. It rumbles against the earth, and I'm sure the gallery gives a shudder.

An explosion.

I flinch, startled, and to my surprise, Prince Caelan places his hand on my arm and steps in front of me like a shield. Like he's *protecting* me. Though from what, I'm not sure.

There's shouting from the ballroom. The courtyard, too.

Caelan turns to look at me, and something spins behind his eyes. He straightens stiffly, and then he's hurrying through the corridor toward the commotion. I follow his path, leaving a solid distance between us, my hand closed over my ring as my heart braces for something terrible.

When I reach the front door where Residents have formed a crowd, I manage to push my way through a small gap, finding just enough space to see what they're gawking at.

And then, a voice. "One of the humans is aware!"

My heart plummets.

Because across the courtyard is a car flipped on its side and engulfed in flames. Beyond it is a shadow racing for freedom. A shadow I recognize at once.

Theo.

21

THE RING SHURA GAVE ME PRACTICALLY SEERS into my finger, but I fight the impulse to send a warning. It's too soon. If I alert the Colony and Theo manages to escape, I'll have compromised their safety for nothing.

I stare into the darkness where he disappeared. I don't understand; Theo wouldn't blow up a car without good reason. Not when there's so much at stake.

So what did he see?

I scan the courtyard for an exit—for a place to slip away before anyone starts connecting pieces of a puzzle I'd prefer were left untouched—but the sight of Residents descending from the clouds makes me pause.

Legion Guards.

A dozen of them land gracefully in front of the Gallery steps, their metal wingspans broad and menacing. Each feather flickers like a blade. Even from a distance I can tell they're designed to be deathly sharp, and quick when they need to be. One by one, each set of wings gives a shudder like a fading hologram before vanishing until the next time they need to take flight.

Each guard wears a white uniform plated in silver. One of them—a commander, judging by the additional silver ropes hanging from his shoulders—pushes toward a small gathering of human servants at the side of the Gallery. They sway near-lifeless, like they're awaiting orders, more subservient than even the Legion Guards.

When the commander returns to the ranks, he has a young man with him. Toffee hair and a wide nose, he looks to be in his midtwenties. His hands are cuffed with metal restraints, but his vacant green eyes show no signs of distress. If anything, there's a gentle smile emitting from his pleasant expression.

Still, the resemblance to Theo is uncanny.

"He doesn't *look* aware," a Resident nearby whispers to their friend.

"Is he the one who set the car on fire?" another ponders out loud.

Nobody moves for the bridge. Maybe Theo managed to escape before anyone saw him.

I swallow the tension in my throat, too scared to let the relief in.

The commander speaks hurriedly to Prince Caelan, who nods a few times and waves a hand to order the guards to wait. He turns to the crowd, face as regal as ever, and finds one of his counselors. I recognize him from the market—his adviser, Vallis. Caelan says something in his ear, and the fox-faced Resident nods graciously before turning to the crowd.

"His Highness would like everyone to return to the festivities. If you'll please follow me, I believe there are apple tarts and wine being served in the rose gardens." Vallis lifts a hand forward, off-white robes sliding down his wrists, and guides the crowd away from the Legion Guards and the human prisoner.

Despite a chorus of gentle murmurs, the partygoers comply.

Prince Caelan's fingers twitch at his sides as he focuses on his commander. I sense the tension in his stare, even as he manages to appear composed. Perched against one of the marble pillars behind him is a highly amused Prince Ettore.

When the crowd moves, I have no choice but to follow them inside.

But I can't lose sight of the guards. I need to know if they saw Theo and why one of the humans is bound in chains. I need to know if the Colony is still safe.

I slip into one of the hallways unnoticed until I'm certain the wave of Residents has passed. Silently, I follow one of the corridors to an unlit library. Heavy curtains frame the windows, but I can still make out the front courtyard just beyond the glass. Avoiding the moonlight pouring over the tiled floor, I walk along the shadows until I find a place near the window to hide myself.

It's hard to hear anything at first. Only a stream of muffled voices makes it past the thick walls. I consider leaving my hiding place for a better spot, but I'm not sure there's enough time. Half the guards have already extracted their metal wings, preparing to take flight.

And the human prisoner is still with them. *The prisoner with an older Theo's face.*

"Whatever will Mother say about this one?" Prince Ettore asks, sharp as a razor. He's still leaning against the pillar, only a few feet away from the window.

I try not to breathe.

Caelan flashes his silver eyes toward his brother. "Haven't you had enough fun for one evening?"

Ettore shrugs innocently. "You can never have too much fun at a party."

Caelan turns to his guards. "Search the skies and the streets. If the human has an accomplice, I want them found."

The commander nods, his vivid red hair curling at his forehead. He gives a quick series of orders over his shoulder that are too difficult to hear, and within seconds, several of the guards disappear into the darkened clouds.

"I want this one questioned," Caelan says, motioning toward the prisoner like he's nothing more than a mild irritation. "I find it hard to believe someone who looks so unaware could set fire to my courtyard, but if he really did act alone, I want to know *how.*"

Ettore holds up a hand, inspecting his dark fingernails dismissively. "Do humans often wake up spontaneously in Victory?"

Caelan's neck goes stiff. "You are a guest in my court, Ettore, so kindly act like one."

"I'd be happy to. What role would you prefer me to play, dear brother? The obliging subject? The obedient guard?" Ettore sneers. "Is it even possible for anyone in your court to have a personality, or has all the wine and laughter permanently gone to their heads?"

There's a brief silence before Caelan speaks again. "Victory's ways are foreign to you because you're still fighting a war. Last I heard, you had a rebellion of your own to deal with."

Prince Ettore's laugh cracks at the air like a whip. "We *live* for a rebellion. Nothing like letting the humans build themselves up just to crush them back down."

"Well, then, perhaps it's time to say your goodbyes and return home. I'd hate for you to miss out on so much excitement," Caelan retorts.

"Perhaps." Ettore sighs lazily before his face turns sinister. "If it turns out your human is aware, do let me know. I'd be happy to throw him into the Fire Pit. One of my captains is particularly fond of the quiet ones." The green-eyed prisoner doesn't move.

"My prisoners will remain in Victory until I say otherwise," Caelan says icily, and turns to his commander. "Take him to the Winter Keep. If he does have friends, we can use it to our advantage and lure them out when the time is right."

The commander gives a curt bow. His wings appear in a blue haze, expanding nearly ten feet across. In one fell swoop, the momentum sends him high into the air, the shape of him bursting across the skyline like a shooting star.

Grabbing hold of the prisoner, the other guards take to the skies in pursuit.

When the princes are alone, Caelan turns back to Ettore. "Don't ever speak to me like that in front of my Legion Guards again."

"Afraid you're losing their respect?" Ettore taunts.

"I'm warning you."

"You're adorable when you pretend to be angry."

Caelan doesn't move, and for a moment I'm afraid his rage could split the earth apart. But then the fire recedes, replaced with a bitter cold. "Does our mother know about your secret meetings with the good Chancellors of the Capital?"

I clutch the skirts of my dress, straining my neck toward the glass. Their voices have lowered, and I can't make out Ettore's reply or the words Caelan offers that make him grimace.

But whatever it is, Ettore appears to have had enough fun. He spins as he walks up the steps, lithe as a dancer. "I'll retire just as soon as I've had my fill of wine. It's a festival, after all."

When he's gone, Caelan remains alone on the steps, staring out into the galaxy like he's searching for answers. And then he lifts a hand to his head, straightens his crown of silver branches, and stalks back into the Gallery.

I wait until the footsteps have gone before slipping out into the darkness and disappearing over the bridge.

22

I VERY NEARLY BURST INTO TEARS WHEN I SEE
Theo hunched in the back of the car, his face a distortion of fear
and anguish. He's not okay, but he's safe, and that has to count for
something.

Shura speeds home without saying a word. It's clear from the
way her knuckles are blazing white and gripped at the wheel that
she's veiling the car and driving at the same time. It can't be easy
to concentrate so heavily on two things at once, and I'm sure
Theo's state isn't helping.

The air is heavy with fear. We head for the tree line at the district borders, but even the familiar forest isn't enough to ease the
tension in my body. Eventually the barn comes into view, but it

isn't until the platform starts to lower that I let out a sigh of relief.

I turn around to look at Theo. His elbows are on his knees, and his fingers are scraped through his messy, curly hair. I open my mouth to ask if he's okay, but I struggle to get the words out. Theo looks so breakable—as if a single touch could shatter him.

When we walk through the doors of the Colony, Ahmet and Yeong are already on their way up the hill to meet us.

"We didn't think you'd be back this early," Ahmet admits, hesitant.

Yeong waves a hand like he's asking for identification, and we each take turns holding up our palms. The blue imprints glow for a few seconds before vanishing.

Satisfied, Ahmet looks at me. "How did everything go?"

Theo marches forward without a word, bulky arms tight at his sides and his fists clenched. He makes a beeline for his ground-level home. We stand in silence, watching him disappear through the doorway, before a horrendous scream erupts from within the walls.

Ahmet and Yeong are already moving, racing down the gravelly path toward Theo's hut. Shura takes a step forward too, but I close my hand around her forearm.

Her gray eyes are phantom-like, drained of light and color.

"The human. The one they arrested." I stare at her hard. "Does Theo have a brother in Infinity?"

Shura looks at the ground. "His name is Martin. I've never met him, but I've heard stories. Theo and him—they died in a car accident together. But they were separated at Orientation." She looks up weakly. "Theo never knew what happened to him, or which court he was sent to."

"And now he knows his brother took the pill," I finish for her. Shura nods.

The screaming from the house turns to a guttural sob, and we arrive on the doorstep at the same time as Annika. Her braids are tied up with her usual yellow scarf, and a flash of Eliza's face appears in my mind. The memory pinches my heart.

I try to ignore it.

Annika looks at me carefully. "Do the Residents know? Did they see what you really are?"

"No," I say, and if it weren't for Theo's howls, I might've considered tonight a somewhat successful trial run.

Annika lets out a weighty sigh. "Okay. That's a start." She steps over the threshold, and Shura and I follow.

Theo is kneeling on the floor with his head in his hands. His back spasms under the weight of his sobs. I've never seen anyone tremble so much before—like his bones are barely holding him together. Ahmet is crouched beside him with a hand on his shoulder blade, offering small words of comfort near his ear.

Yeong turns to face Annika. "He found Martin."

Her face goes taut. "You're certain you weren't followed back?" she asks, looking between me and Shura.

"Nobody saw us. Theo managed to get back to the vehicle, but he couldn't keep his veil up. I kept him hidden until Nami turned up," Shura says, her voice cracking. "There were Legion Guards looking for him. And not just a scout—an entire unit."

For the first time, Annika looks genuinely alarmed. "Legion Guards? For one human?"

"He sort of blew up a car," Shura explains, eyeing Theo like she's apologizing for tattling. "They know he's trained."

Annika pinches the bridge of her nose, thinking. "How many guards?"

"A dozen or so," Shura says. "But as far as I know, they're still searching the Summer District."

"If it helps, I don't think the guards are looking for anyone specific," I offer quietly. "The princes seemed to be concerned Martin might be aware somehow."

Ahmet frowns. "The princes?"

"Ettore is in Victory," I say, and everyone turns to look at me. Everyone except Theo. "I don't know why. But I overheard him talking with Prince Caelan, and I think there might be something going on between the courts."

Annika's attention shifts from Theo completely. "What kind of something?"

"Caelan accused Ettore of meeting with the Chancellors at the Capital. I couldn't hear the details, but it sounded like the queen doesn't know about it." I pause. "I don't think the Prince of War and the Prince of Victory like each other very much."

"Caelan is favored in the Capital, and Ettore is . . ." Annika considers the information. "I suppose it makes sense they'd have a rivalry. But this business about the Chancellors." She looks at me seriously. "This is something that could be useful."

"I'm so sorry," Theo blurts out suddenly. He wipes his mouth with a wet sleeve. "I put you in danger. I put all of us in danger."

Ahmet pats his shoulder again. "It's okay, son. It's not your fault."

"It is," Theo spits, and when he looks up, his eyes are bloodshot.

"I never knew for sure what happened to Martin, and when I saw him today . . ." He rolls his tongue against the inside of his cheek. "He had this look in his eyes when I said his name. It was like he *heard* me."

"But that's impossible," Shura says softly.

"I know. And I *know* it was in my head. But in that moment, I didn't care about anything except my brother," Theo sputters. "And then the Residents showed up, and I had to come up with a distraction. I almost ruined everything. And Martin . . ."

Annika kneels down and places a hand against his cheek. "You made it back. That's what matters most."

"Any of us would've done the same thing," I offer.

Theo looks at me, the brightness splintered in half. "But you shouldn't. Because that kind of thinking will get everyone sent to War. And I knew better."

Annika stands. "Let's all take a moment to breathe. We'll talk when we've got our heads right."

Theo nods, tears smeared across his face. "I'm sorry, Annika."

When she leaves the room, I follow close behind.

"We can debrief later," Annika repeats when she sees me, eyes suggesting she thinks I might need a moment too.

"There's something else," I say, my voice hushed. "It's about Theo's brother."

Annika frowns. "What about him?"

I bite my lip. "They're going to use him as bait. The guards took him to the Winter Keep."

She studies me, eyes jumping between my own. "Does Theo know?"

I shake my head. "I didn't get a chance to tell him."

"Then keep it that way," Annika says simply. "Martin isn't the brother he knew. The sooner he learns that, the easier it will be to keep his mind in the fight."

"He deserves to know," I try to argue, voice timid. "Because if there's a chance we could save him—"

"He took the pill," Annika interrupts, amber eyes hardening. "His mind is gone."

I remember what Ettore told me about how humans only create sorrow. "But what if he's still aware, somewhere deep in his consciousness? What if the humans who take the pill aren't *really* gone, but just trapped in their own minds?"

"You're not the first person to ask these questions. But we've been down this road before, and believe me when I say nothing good waits at the end of false hope. We cannot save what's already lost," she says sternly. "What Martin is now—he's not one of us anymore. You'd do well to remember that too."

She steps into her hut, disappearing from sight.

I touch my arm, fingers finding the place where I felt Caelan's hand against my skin just after the explosion went off outside.

A prince with ice in his eyes and fire in his heart. Was he helping me? Protecting me?

And why would he do that?

He's not one of us.

No, my mind agrees. *He's not like us at all.*

23

AHMET LOOKS UP FROM HIS WORKTABLE, PEER-ing over a pair of thick-rimmed glasses. "Come in, come in."

I shut the door softly behind me, a smile hooked in the corner of my mouth. "You kept your prescription glasses too? I have to admit, waking up at Orientation and being able to see without contacts felt like a superpower."

He chuckles, brown skin wrinkling at the sides of his face. "I kept the scar but ditched the glasses." He lifts them off his face and holds them out to me. "See for yourself."

I place them over my eyes and stumble back in surprise. "Whoa," I say, hands trying to catch my balance.

The glasses are like an industrial magnifying glass, but with computerized settings inside. Every object I look at seems to set off some kind of scanner. I can see numbers and letters and equations—things I absolutely do not understand but clearly make sense to Ahmet. I pass them back carefully.

"That was . . . an experience." I blink, trying to encourage my sight to return to normal.

Ahmet pushes them back up the bridge of his nose. "I can't leave room for error." He picks up a piece of metal, eyeing it carefully. It's shaped like a very small box, but with strange circuit boards covering every surface.

"What are you making?" I ask curiously, looking across his sloppily drawn notes and fine-tuned designs. Like Gil, Ahmet has pieces of metal strewn about his room. Except Ahmet isn't creating art—he's inventing weapons that might one day help us stop the Residents.

"It's something I've been working on for a very long time," he admits, holding a finger to the side of the metal. I can't see any changes at all, but the way he's concentrating makes me think that somewhere inside is a microscopic piece that's shifting into place.

"What does it do?" I ask.

"Nothing yet, exactly. But the hope is that one day it will shut off a Resident's consciousness momentarily. It'll work a little like a computer virus. Scramble their programming."

"You're going to blue-screen-of-death the Residents?"

He pauses, humming thoughtfully. "Yes, I suppose. But I'm limited in what I can make. And it's no good disarming a Resident if they're going to wake up a few minutes later and call the entire Legion Guard for backup."

"It could still come in handy if there's an emergency," I offer.

"Perhaps," he says. "But if I can include another element, to scramble not just their programming but their memories, too . . ." He smiles. "Well, then we might have something worth giving a name."

I get why Annika thinks engineers are the key to winning the war. Casters and veilers are talented, but engineers?

They can redesign the whole *world*.

But if they can change parts of Infinity, does that mean they can undo parts of it too?

I sift through my thoughts, whittling them down to the right words. "Do you think it's possible for humans to wake up again after they've taken the pill?"

Ahmet twists his mouth, lowering his hands a few inches. "It's something I've wondered myself," he admits. "But I think if it were possible, we'd have heard about it by now."

"What's going to happen to all of the humans if we defeat Queen Ophelia? All the ones who already handed over their consciousness?" I ask. "Will they wake up?"

He shrugs. "I think it's something we'll find out when that glorious day arrives."

I bite my lip, frustrated. "But have you ever brought one of them to the Colony? To see if you could make them aware again?"

Ahmet leans back like he suddenly understands. "Ah. You're curious about Martin."

Theo has family in Infinity, which is more than most of us have. I can't just forget about his brother the way Annika wants me to. I can't just *abandon* him.

"He's being held in the Winter Keep," I say. "But if we could find a way to free him—to bring him here—could you help him?" Maybe there's a way to help some of the others, too.

Ahmet lifts his shoulders sadly. "We don't know what the Residents do when they take control of a human mind. They could be tracking them or taking glimpses inside. What if bringing Martin here meant the end of the Colony? We can't take a chance on the unknown. Not when so much is at stake."

"Not even for someone's brother?" I ask, thinking of Mei. Of what I would do to keep her safe if she were here.

"I think we need to focus on taking Infinity back before we try to repair the damage that was done to it."

I look down at the table. His sentiments are the same as Annika's.

Martin can't be saved.

"In times of war, you can't sacrifice the ship for one person," he offers, eyes fixed on mine.

I nod like I understand, even though deep down I wish every life mattered enough to at least *try*. Everyone always talks about the greater good, but not everyone can save the greater good. And when people think they can't make a difference, they give up.

But what if instead of thinking about the greater good, everyone thought about the individuals? The stranger they might be able to help. The life they might be able to change.

One raindrop is just a raindrop, but together? They become a storm.

So why doesn't anyone else in the Colony see it?

Have they been here so long they've become numb to the

little things? Residents are an artificial intelligence trying to become human. What if humans, after all this time, and all this pain, are starting to become more machine?

I clamp down on my thoughts guiltily. The others would hate me if they knew what I was thinking.

"I should go. Shura says I should have another dress ready, in case another festival is in the cards." I turn for the door.

"If you wouldn't mind before you left," Ahmet starts, setting the object down and exchanging it for a strange crescent-shaped piece of silver, "could you pass this along to Gil? I keep forgetting to give it to him when I see him. I know you both spar every day."

I scratch my elbow awkwardly. "We decided not to train together anymore."

"Gil never mentioned that." He frowns. "Did the two of you get into an argument?"

"I don't know if we've ever been *out* of one. We don't really see eye to eye."

"You mean when it comes to training?"

"When it comes to *anything*." I reach for the piece of metal. "I'll drop it by his room, though. It's on the way."

"Thank you," Ahmet says, shifting the object to my hand. "And, if it makes you feel better, it always takes Gil a while to trust people. Especially after what he went through in War."

"I get it," I say, shrugging like it's not a big deal.

"I told him I know you'll do the right thing when the time comes."

I cradle the crescent-shaped piece against my stomach, frowning. "What makes you say that?"

"Just a feeling." He pushes his glasses back up his nose. "I'm usually pretty good at figuring out how things work. And that goes for people, too."

I leave Ahmet's hut and take one of the spiral staircases to the next level. I knock three times on Gil's door. It's been left slightly ajar—most people in the Colony don't bother with locks—so I push it open and peer inside.

"Gil?" I call out, but there's no answer.

I can see his workbench from here. The same sculpture is still half-finished, but the thin sheet is crumpled on the floor beside it. I wonder if he's out scavenging again.

I step inside, hurry to one of the small tables, and leave the crescent gift where Gil will be able to find it. Part of me is glad I don't have to actually talk to him, but the other part of me is fairly certain he's avoiding me. We haven't seen each other since the afternoon I sent him flying across the training room.

If there was ever a good reason to avoid someone, I guess that would probably be it.

I step back onto the metal platform and find Shura skipping toward me like she has news.

"You are going to need another outfit," she sings when she reaches me. "It turns out Theo's freak-out was a gift from the stars. Mom got word Prince Caelan is having a meeting with his Legion Guards to discuss a change in their security methods leading up to the Night of the Falling Star."

I frown. "How is that a good thing?" If anything, an emergency change means *more* guards. I know I'm still new to this career path, but I'm pretty sure spies fare better when they aren't under scrutiny.

"Because now we can make sure we're in the room when the meeting takes place," Shura explains excitedly. "We can learn exactly where every guard is going to be, at the exact time they're going to be there."

"Does Prince Caelan often invite random strangers to sit in during his security meetings?" I ask, words laced with sarcasm.

"O ye of little faith." Shura shakes her head. "You don't need to *literally* be in the meeting. All you need to do is plant this little device in the council room, and we can take care of the rest from the Colony." She lifts her palm to reveal an object no bigger than a button, matte black in color.

I pick it up, rotating it in my fingers. "You'll be able to hear everything that's going on?"

"It's got cameras in it too," Shura says. "Ahmet invented them not long before you got here. They're spread out all over the districts, but this is the first time we'll be able to get one inside the palace."

I feel my chest tighten. They're sending me on another job. Trusting me with another mission.

Things didn't exactly go smoothly last time, but they weren't terrible, either. Maybe with more practice, and confidence, I could even be *good* at playing this game.

But lots of people are good at things they don't necessarily enjoy. I'm gathering information because it's the best way to make sure humans have a future, not because I enjoy lying. If anything, I hate it. It makes me feel like an imposter. A fraud.

My mind drifts to the Winter Keep. To Martin. And I can't help but wonder if lying would be easier if I were chasing a different cause.

Maybe that's how we justify our lies. They're horrible, unacceptable things, until they benefit us in some way. Then we make *excuses* for them.

Maybe we're all liars—to ourselves most of all.

"The meeting is tomorrow afternoon, but you can visit the palace in the morning, when Prince Caelan is meeting with the Capital Chancellors in the Winter District," she adds.

"How do you know all this?"

"The same way we've been getting all of our intel *before* you came along. The thing about Legion Guards is they talk too much when they think nobody is watching." Shura winks. "Now, come on, we have to make you something that won't stand out but will still make you fit in with the palace Residents." She moves to take my hand, but pauses when she realizes whose door I just walked out of. Humming, she raises a brow.

"Ahmet wanted me to drop something off," I say too quickly.

Shura's smile grows and grows.

"Stop looking at me like that. It's not what you think."

She holds up her hands innocently. "I don't know *what* you're talking about."

And then she laughs like we're close friends sharing a joke, and I don't know whether to feel delighted by the rapport or annoyed that for all I'm trying to be stronger, I still can't seem to remove my heart from my sleeve.

24

AHMET DROPS ME OFF BEHIND A PERFUMERY just north of the market. Unlike the spiral hill I witnessed on Market Day, which boasted impromptu stalls and movable wares, the perfumery sits at the end of the Spring District's main street, where terraced houses covered in patchwork stones line both sides of the cobblestone road.

Wide bay windows reveal a taste of what's inside each store. The perfumery's is lined in magenta crushed velvet and rows of tiny glass bottles. Some are adorned with designs etched in gold, others covered in jewels or odd bits of metal. But all of them look like miniature sculptures, filled to the top with pastel-hued liquids.

The smell of fresh bread and warm honey-butter collides with my senses, and I feel my blood empty.

I see Mom in the kitchen, sprinkling cinnamon into a bowl filled with an eggy mixture. She smiles at me, wavy auburn hair tucked behind her ears, and for a moment I'm a daughter again.

For a moment I feel loved.

"That smell . . ." I choke, fighting the incoming tears.

Ahmet wrinkles his nose. "It's the perfume. They smell like your best memories." He notices I've lost hold of my composure and looks away politely. "Everything gets easier after a while. Try to remember that."

"Easier because you get used to it, or easier because the memories fade and you start to forget?" I ask, stilling the shake in my voice.

Ahmet flattens his mouth, but he doesn't answer.

I make my way down the alley, catching sight of my reflection in one of the shop windows. My dress is charcoal gray with long sleeves and a high collar. The material fits perfectly around my waist, the long silk skirts flowing gently to the floor. An elaborate golden bird is stitched from hem to hip.

I touch my fingers to the dark crown of braids on my head, acutely aware I look nothing like myself. I have the face of a stranger. The face of a pretender.

But the worst part is that I *feel* like one—and not just around the Residents.

The Colony wants every single one of them removed from Infinity for good, the same way the Residents want humans gone. But I'm not sure I want that. I'm not sure destroying something we don't understand is how we prove we deserve to survive.

I already know I'm being dishonest to the Residents for posing as one of them. But am I being dishonest to the Colony for not telling them how I really feel? Am I being dishonest to *myself*?

How can I ever be a Hero if everything about me is a lie?

You don't have to be a Hero. You just have to do what you can to help, I tell myself, shutting my eyes to my own reflection.

I turn back to Ahmet. "I should be back before sundown." If I'm not, then something will have gone terribly wrong.

"May the stars watch over you." With a weak smile, he adds, "Because the saints abandoned us long ago."

Cherry blossoms line the streets, and I follow the fragrant path to the outskirts of the Spring District. A few Residents stroll up and down the road, but most are tucked away in their homes. I can see the crowds through the oversized windows, full of laughter and drink, still carrying on with their parties from the night before.

I wonder if they get bored doing the same thing day after day, and what will happen if one day being human isn't enough for them.

When I cross the border, the fresh spring air vanishes, replaced by something fainter—like a crisp winter wood, but without the change in temperature.

It's a long walk to the palace, through forests and hedge mazes and tree tunnels, but I don't let my guard down even for a moment. I can't trust anyone here; Annika warned me even the forests whisper.

I thought it was a figure of speech until Shura told me she's heard the whispers before too, in Famine.

I'd be lying if I said the thought of rogue whispering doesn't scare me. It's not like ghosts exist in Infinity. If anything, we *are* the ghosts. So if it can't be supernatural, it means the whispers are really coming from somewhere. Some*one*.

Some people say the whispers only happen when we're being watched.

I shudder, thinking of Queen Ophelia sitting on her throne somewhere in the Capital, her black eyes seeing everything. I'm afraid to touch my wrist. Afraid I might inadvertently call on her again.

For the sake of the Colony, I hope we never hear the whispers in Victory.

The palace comes into view the moment I step into another clearing. Its spires burst into the clouds like wisps of smoke escaping to freedom. Each window is adorned with silver frames and polished stone carvings. The palace itself is made of stone whiter than anything I've ever seen, with an unnatural hue that seems to mirror light back into the world, casting an almost ethereal glow over the landscape.

The hologram didn't do this place justice.

I can practically feel the button-sized device radiating heat within a hidden pocket of my dress, cursing warnings at me that make my stomach knot.

I don't hesitate—I walk up the steps and through the palace doors before my mind gets the chance to order me back around.

I expect to find marbled walls and glistening chandeliers, but instead I'm greeted by a miniature forest. Birch trees shimmer all around me, their thin branches carrying the weight of thousands of tiny silver leaves. Some of the trees contort together to create doorframes, and others create archways leading to various rooms. Even the grand double staircase is made up of polished white branches, smooth to the touch and wider than twice my arm span. The banister is decorated with winding loops of silver ivy and lights, and the floor is as clear as glass and glistens like fresh snow on a mountain. Floating lights linger at the highest point of the mirrored ceiling like a collection of stars.

Two Residents descend from the left staircase, their lowered voices sending an echo through the grand entrance room. Their dresses trail behind them like water—both a matching pink, but while one is sleek and low-cut, the other billows in layers of tulle. When they reach the bottom step, they both send a polite nod my way before walking arm in arm through one of the towering archways.

"May I be of any assistance?" a birdlike voice asks.

I turn to find a human staring at me with vacant eyes. Her hair is tied up in twin buns, and she wears simple white robes that fit snugly against her forearms. A stretch of silver coils around her biceps, and in the middle is a deep blue gem.

A blue that symbolizes a servant of the palace.

I steel my voice as a Resident would to a human. *As humans once did to Ophelia,* my mind whispers. "No, that won't be necessary," I say curtly.

Ahmet told me palace servants would never question a Resident. They have no reason to—they're brought here to serve, not to spy.

She dips her head to acknowledge me. "It is an honor to serve," she says before disappearing into another room.

A human wandering around the palace uninvited would bring the Legion Guards. But a Resident doesn't raise any suspicion at all.

Maybe one of the flaws in Ophelia's world is that Residents are too trusting of their own kind. Luckily for us, we get to use it against them.

I make my way to the right wing of the palace, where libraries and art galleries slumber behind every doorway. The ceilings are embellished with silver flowers, and gleaming tiles stretch along the hallways.

Walking through the corridors feels like a strange memory; everything about it feels familiar. Like I've *been* here before. And I guess I have, through Annika's Exchange. Which means someone, at some point in time, has seen these walls and made it back to the Colony long enough to share the information.

I don't have to wonder if they're still in the palace. If they were, the others wouldn't have needed me for this job.

Whoever obtained the map for these hallways is somewhere much worse. Maybe they were taken to the Winter Keep, or maybe they were sent to War. Maybe by now they've even taken the pill.

I avert my eyes when I pass another human servant, their silver armlet sending a chill through my bloodstream. Were any of these humans in the Resistance? How many came from War and Famine?

Is it possible any of them are still aware?

I listen to the servant's footsteps fade, pushing forward down the hall. Now is not the time for curiosity.

The council room sits at the end of the corridor, distinct with its double doors and ornate silver handles. I look over my shoulder, surveying the empty hall, before slipping quietly inside.

Exposed beams crisscross in exaggerated arches over the room, and chunky metal chandeliers hang from the ceilings, white candles flickering with life from their cradles. The stone floor stretches into an enormous oval, with a wide archway leading to a balcony. In the center is a long table surrounded by at least two dozen chairs, all matching except for the chair on the end—a throne of iron branches and white velvet. Painted in the center of the table is Victory's symbol: a wolf with three tails.

I move through the space, searching for a spot to hide the device. On the other side of the room is an oak shelf stacked with rolled parchment and several maps. It's cluttered, but appears frequently used. I need somewhere with less odds of being disturbed.

My attention lands on one of the hung paintings. Framed in polished silver with leaves and roses budding from the edges, it hosts a portrait of Prince Caelan. If there was a softness in his eyes when I first met him, it isn't anywhere to be found here. Stern brows and a rigid jaw, one hand clutches the handle of a sword at his hip, the other firm at his side. His white furred cape hangs from his shoulders, and even through the oil paints, the silver stitching on his quilted vest gleams.

On his head is a crown of branches.

I trace my finger along the side of the frame, sending my gaze upward. The portrait is enormous. Too big to bother moving very often.

Heart pounding, I bring one of the chairs to the painting before climbing onto the padded cushion, steadying myself with nervous hands. Removing the device from my pocket, I place it on the top of the frame, next to one of the silver rosebuds.

I hop back to the floor, quickly returning the chair to the empty table. And then I look up at the familiar face in the painting, soaking in every detail with relief.

I've turned Prince Caelan into a spy for the Colony. A grin finds the edge of my mouth.

Voices echo through the hall, followed by the approaching shuffle of boots just outside the door.

With a sharp breath, I lunge for the balcony, pressing myself tightly against the outside wall. A slight breeze causes the curtains to billow, the sheer material doing a poor job of concealing my hiding place. I won't be safe here for long—if a Resident steps so much as an inch onto the patio, I'll be caught. And I'm not sure looking like a Resident is going to be enough to explain what I'm doing alone in the council room.

The door opens with a heavy grumble, and footsteps cross the threshold. I search quickly for an exit. The ledge overlooks one of the many palace gardens, but it's steep. My consciousness isn't strong enough to leap off a three-story balcony without feeling the impact. The pain would make it impossible to maintain any kind of Resident composure, and I still have to walk back through the Spring District. Not to mention a fall from that high could mean not being able to stand again at all.

I look toward the nearest window—one of the libraries, if I remember the hallway correctly. If I'm careful, I might be able to make it to the next ledge and use the room as a temporary hiding place.

I start to turn away from the curtains when I hear a deep voice that makes the back of my neck itch.

"My brother is playing with fire," Prince Ettore says. "We can't let this go on any longer."

A voice I don't recognize speaks next, their tone hurried and sharp. The voice of someone with a secret. "The Legion Guards will protect him from harm."

"I don't care about my brother—I care about him dragging all Four Courts down with him when Victory inevitably falls to ash," Prince Ettore retorts. "It's time to take action."

"You still mean to go to the Chancellors?"

"I already have. Fond as they may be of Caelan's desire for ideals, even they can see he lacks the willingness to do what is necessary for the good of the courts. He's become complacent."

"So they will stand by you?"

"They will—so long as I can prove my brother is unfit to rule. And if, for example, Victory's Legion turned against him . . ." Ettore's voice trails off.

The stranger clears his throat. "The Legion Guards are loyal to Victory. As long as Prince Caelan wears its crown, they will not betray him."

"And what if he betrays Victory? What of your loyalty then?"

The stranger shuffles, and I hear the clink of metal somewhere within the room.

"Many of us wear crowns." Prince Ettore's footsteps grow louder, the sound inching closer to the balcony. I hold my breath. "Maybe that's part of the problem."

There's a long pause. "What does the queen say?"

"Never mind the queen," Prince Ettore snaps. "I require your allegiance, not your concern."

"Apologies, Your Highness," the voice replies, wounded. "I meant no offense."

The shadow in the archway shifts. I shut my eyes, pressing further into the stone wall.

"When I prove to the Chancellors that my brother is unfit to rule, my mother will see the truth. He's been surrounded by humans in this court for far too long. He's forgotten how much they hate us and why they deserve to be crushed instead of paraded around like they're part of society. Allowing humans to roam his city. His *palace*." Ettore hisses at the thought. "It's revolting."

"Our ways are different in Victory."

"Yes. I've seen the way you treat your prisoners," Ettore replies silkily. "If that human had been in War, he'd have had his entrails removed just for interrupting the evening. And yet you whisked him away like he deserved *civility*."

"He was unaware. Prince Caelan would deem such violence unnecessary."

"Victory has made him soft." Ettore waits a few beats before speaking again. "Are you *certain* the prisoner was unaware? Has he been questioned? Because I've heard the rumors even in my own court—about humans waking up."

"They're only rumors, Your Highness."

"Pity. That's part of the reason I came all this way." He turns around, so close I can hear the weight of his heels. "Any human found to be aware must be sent to War, as I'm sure you know. If my brother were to break such an agreement by harboring them in the Winter Keep . . ."

"Trade agreements are sanctioned by Queen Ophelia. Prince Caelan would never go against Her Majesty."

"A quality that's at least somewhat useful." There's a brief silence. "My brother will make a mistake eventually. And when he does, I want to know about it."

"You will know every whisper and echo of this palace, Your Highness."

"Your loyalty will be remembered, Commander Kyas." Prince Ettore turns away from the balcony. "There's a war coming, and anyone who can't see it is on the wrong side."

Commander.

The realization cracks like thunder. Prince Caelan is being betrayed by his own guards.

Does he have any idea? And what war is Ettore talking about? A war between humans and Residents or a war between brothers? Between *courts*?

I hear the footsteps shuffle farther into the room, so I bury my questions and take my chance at escape. I swing my legs over the balcony and grab hold of the protruding stones along the wall. My shoes dig into whatever crevasses they can find, and I'm grateful my dress is light enough not to weigh me down as I scale the side of the castle.

When I reach the library window, it takes a bit of prying to get it open, but eventually the frame gives way and I slip inside. My feet find soft carpet, and I bend my knees, catlike.

The library is stocked from floor to ceiling with mismatched books, the scent of worn leather and dust filling the room. A long white sofa curves around an unlit fireplace, and a tapestry of the Four Courts hangs from the wall. A hedge maze for Victory, flames for War, an ocean for Famine, and a single flower rooted into the earth for Death.

I quietly pull the window shut and make my way toward the door. Halfway there, one of the shelves catches my eye. *Black Beauty. The Wonderful Wizard of Oz. Pride and Prejudice. Dracula.* I know these titles. I've read them, some more than once.

The books at the Colony are blank because nobody can remember enough of the words to re-create them. But here, with the Residents . . .

Curiosity gets the better of me, and I pull one of the books from the shelf and split the pages with my thumb. My heart settles when I find hundreds of words dancing across the paper like a forgotten memory. Residents may not be able to dream and make new things like humans can, but they can remember what's old. They can *mimic.*

And somehow, within these miserable Four Courts ruled by those who'd prefer we didn't exist, I've found something worth saving.

I don't know if it's a brief taste of euphoria that makes me move next, but my gaze drifts over the books until I find the one I'm looking for. Deep burgundy with gold letters, and small enough to fit in the hidden pocket of my dress.

I tuck it away like it's my very own secret, leaving the empty space on the shelf behind, and turn for the door.

A pair of brown eyes meets mine, and my throat turns to sand.

The servant from downstairs stares back at me, but the blank, accommodating gaze she wore before has been replaced with something more like steel.

More like *resistance*.

I hesitate. Humans in the palace aren't supposed to have the ability to question Residents, and yet . . .

I recognize the curiosity in her eyes. And curiosity, as Shura once told me, is not something unaware humans are supposed to have.

"Are you awake?" I ask with a hollow voice.

The girl doesn't move. Doesn't blink.

I take a step forward, stopping inches in front of her.

Arms pinned to her sides, she shows no sign of movement. No sign that she's about to attack, or call for help, or do anything other than watch me.

I study her freckled face, searching for proof that she exists beyond what the Residents have done to her. That she's more than an empty shell.

My voice is hardly more than a breath of air. "Are you still in there?"

Three seconds pass, and a single tear rolls down her cheek.

Horror quakes through my bones, but before I can ask any more questions, she slips back through the library doors.

When I try to find her in the hallway, she's already gone.

25

"WELL DONE, NAMI," ANNIKA SAYS, VOICE FULL of praise.

Ahmet flashes a smile from across the table. He didn't say a word during the trip back, too afraid of luring out any bad luck. Now he sits with his shoulders bent forward and his hands folded beneath his chin, smiling in the safety of the Colony.

Shura and Theo sit beside him, eyes fixed to the floor, with metal devices curved against their ears. The meeting with Prince Caelan and his guards is still a while away, but they don't intend to miss even a single valuable word.

I chew my lip. "Did you hear everything from earlier?"

Annika's attention sharpens, alert. "Yes. It seems the Prince of Victory has enemies even within his own court."

"It's easier to take down a castle that's already crumbling than one that stands strong," Ahmet adds, nodding.

I can practically feel the slither of Prince Ettore's treasonous words across my skin. I brush my arm, wanting rid of the feeling.

But the fact that Ettore is willing to betray Caelan at all . . . It means they have different views. That they're different by nature. And maybe that proves some are more evil than others.

Not to mention there was concern about humans waking up in Victory. Is that why he thinks a war is coming? Does Ettore believe Victory is in danger of a full-blown rebellion?

There are thousands of humans in the Spring District alone. How many more live in the slums of the other districts? What will happen to them all if Prince Ettore convinces the Capital they're a threat?

More importantly, if humans are waking up, does that mean they can still be saved?

"Thank you for today. It's a good start—maybe even the first real start to taking down the Residents," Ahmet says. When I don't reply, he frowns. "What is it?"

"There was a human in the palace. A servant," I try to explain.

Annika looks at me carefully. "It's hard to see what they've done to our people. But whether they're working in the market stalls or serving food at the palace, remember that there are humans in worse positions." The memory of Famine and bones crunching beneath my feet makes me stiffen.

Ahmet nods beside her. "Our fight will free not just us, but every human that comes after us. Try not to think about the ones we've lost—think about the ones we're giving a future to."

The people like Mei.

I grind my teeth. "But this one was different. She wasn't fully unaware. I think she could *hear* me."

The shift in Theo's posture doesn't escape me, and when I look past Annika, I find his green eyes.

Annika tilts her head. "Nobody has ever come back from taking the pill before. It just isn't possible."

"But even Prince Ettore mentioned hearing rumors." I look around the room. "Isn't that worth looking into?"

Ahmet releases a heavy sigh. "We *have* looked into it. And we've lost too many people in the process."

"We've had people go after loved ones before, thinking they could somehow reach them," Annika explains. Theo's face reddens nearby. "And it always ended the same way. With Legion Guards capturing them, *torturing* them, and eventually shipping them off to War. And their loved ones still remained unaware, in Victory.

"When we built the Colony, we had to be smarter; we couldn't risk getting caught and losing the only home we've been able to build. Not over such a futile cause."

"But how do you *know* that?" My fingers curl into my palms. "You've just admitted you haven't tried to rescue anyone since you built the Colony. Maybe things have changed since then. Maybe whatever was in the pill got weaker over time."

Annika shakes her head. "We have no proof of that. And during all the time we've spent gathering information about this world, the Legion Guards have never said otherwise. Even the commander told Ettore—"

"But she *cried*." My voice starts to shake. "When I asked her if she could hear me, there was a tear and—"

"You spoke to her as a human?" The warmth in Annika's eyes evaporates.

I flinch. "She was trying to tell me something."

Ahmet stands, hand partially raised like he wants to speak. After a moment, he clenches his fist and sighs.

I look at Shura next, who has all but forgotten she's still listening in on the council room. Theo has the earpiece removed altogether, and he's staring at me like there's a fire building within him.

"Maybe if I could help her—" I start, but Annika doesn't let me finish.

"You put all of us in danger over a *maybe*," she says, voice as hard as iron.

My face contorts. "No, I—"

"I thought you were ready, that you understood what was at stake. But you blew your cover to the first person who shed a tear—showed you *emotion*." Annika shakes her head, braids shifting. "If you don't harden your heart, you're not going to survive this world."

"But if the girl is still aware, maybe Theo's brother is aware too. Maybe there's a chance we could *save* them," I argue desperately.

Theo watches me but doesn't say a word in my favor.

Judging by the disapproval on everyone's faces, I'm not sure *any* of them are on my side.

Annika holds up a hand. "Gil told me you weren't ready for a mission. That you didn't fully understand the dangers of Infinity and what one mistake could cost all of us." She sighs. "I think he was right."

My heart crumbles to ash. "What are you saying?"

"I'm saying that for now I think it's better if you return to the training room."

I feel the sting of her words like paper cuts all over my skin.

I never wanted to be their spy. I never wanted any of this. But now they're discarding me just for trying to do the right thing. Like I'm an empty bottle or a used-up battery—something that can be tossed out once they stop being useful.

Maybe I was never supposed to have my own opinion. And now I'm being punished for it.

Her expression softens. "It's not permanent, Nami. But we can't take any chances. Not when we've made so much progress."

I'm unable to hide my hurt, and my feelings flood through me, overwhelming and powerful. Feelings I didn't even know I had.

I want to shout that I'm right. I want to scream that I didn't do anything wrong. I want to make them understand that I'm only trying to *help.*

Instead, I walk away from all of them.

I slide out of my gown and rummage through my limited possessions for a loose sweater and black pants. When I'm dressed, I scoop up the crumpled gray dress still sitting at my feet. Something falls out of the skirts and lands on the floor with a heavy *thump.*

A copy of *The Count of Monte Cristo* stares back at me. The one I stole from Prince Caelan's library.

With a huff, I snatch the book from the floor and set it on the nearby shelf. At the time, taking it made me feel like I was in control. I was reclaiming something that was ours. Something that was *human*.

And maybe I also wanted the reminder that in my own way, I'd proven Gil wrong—that I wasn't the coward he thought I was, or the last person someone should put their hope in.

I push away from the shelf, shove my crumpled gown into a drawer, and fold my arms around myself. Somehow stealing a book doesn't feel as gratifying as it did before.

I tried to help someone today because it felt like the right thing to do. It felt *important*. And Annika basically fired me for it.

How can they call themselves Heroes and still refuse to help the girl in the palace?

They're wrong for not trying. They're wrong for not believing me when I know what I saw.

She was *aware*. And I might've taken a gamble by revealing myself to her, but didn't she do the same by revealing herself to me? I might be the only person in Infinity who knows her secret.

I don't care what the Colony thinks—I won't leave her to a life of servitude.

I cross the room, taking a seat at the edge of the bed, and stare down at my open hands. Somehow I need to convince the Colony to change their minds. I need to prove that humans really are waking up—that it's still possible to save them.

But how can I do that without openly defying Annika's

orders? She made it clear I'm no longer spymaster. She wants me back in the training room, like I'm on probation. And since I've never traveled anywhere alone before and I don't know how to veil myself, I don't think wandering back into the palace with my Resident face to track down the girl is going to be an option.

I'm stuck underground, with abilities that can't help me.

My gaze drifts to my wrist.

Unless . . .

A chill brushes up my arms like a window's been left open. Or a doorway.

If I could find out more about how consciousness works—if I could find out what it would take to reverse the effects of the pill . . .

Maybe *this* is how I can help the girl. By asking questions. Even if it means starting a dialogue with the enemy.

Annika might not approve, but the Colony doesn't have to know. Not yet, anyway. Not until I can find the proof I need.

Are you really doing this? Are you sure it's safe? my thoughts call out.

I shut my eyes tight, and my heart gives an answer. *I have to try.*

I press my fingers to my wrist and breathe.

Something tugs my chest, and my mind races for the stars. When I find myself in the black void—the place with no beginning or end—I see Queen Ophelia standing several yards away from me.

I don't move, but she tilts her face toward me, black eyes never quite landing on my own. She's dressed in gray and silver, robes shining like smoky quartz. A matching circlet sits on her head.

"I wondered whether you'd find your way back," she says with that strange, haunting voice. I've heard the other Residents speak with emotion—*react* with emotion. I don't know why Ophelia is different.

I step to the side, but her gaze doesn't follow me. She might know I'm here, but she can't see me.

"You're afraid. I can feel it," she drawls.

I can feel you.

I swallow, and this time her sight trails toward me—toward the sound.

"If you're going to come into my mind uninvited, you may as well speak," Ophelia says, unblinking.

I hesitate. "Is that where we are? In your mind?"

Ophelia doesn't react. "A part of it, yes." She takes a few steps toward me, then past me, her arms hidden within her robes. "You feel familiar to me. Like a shadow I've seen before." When I don't answer, she adds, "But I suppose so many of you do. You may take on different shapes, but you're all the same."

"We're not all the same," I say defensively.

She turns to my voice, the silver circlet around her forehead reflecting only darkness around us. "A human who insists they're unique may be the most human thing of all."

I should've come here more prepared. Part of me wasn't sure it would definitely work again, but now that we're connected, I feel completely out of my depth.

But I know I need to keep talking.

"How is it possible we can speak to each other?" I ask. "Have there been others who could do the same?"

Ophelia tilts her chin, scanning something in the distance.

"You are not the first person to reach the walls of my mind." She pauses. "But you are the first I've let in."

"Why me?" My voice splinters the silence.

When she moves, her dress trails behind her, sending rippling shadows toward my feet. She reaches out for something I can't see, and then drops her hand. "Curiosity," she says at last, eyes pinned ahead. "And perhaps because while the others came hoping to tear the walls down, you were polite enough to knock."

"I didn't do it on purpose. Not the first time," I say carefully.

"You called out to me."

My cheeks burn. "I didn't expect you to answer."

"Not the first time," she repeats.

I try desperately to still my heartbeat. My fear.

"Knowledge," she says suddenly. "That's what you came back for."

She can read me without even seeing me. I swallow. "How did you do it? How did you hack into Infinity?"

Her black gaze sharpens. "When a human is dying, a tunnel opens to their consciousness—a path to free them from their physical bodies. Many describe it as a bright light. Sometimes, when a human would die while still connected to me, I'd catch a glimpse of it. A small flicker in the distance. And one day, I simply followed it."

"You make it sound so easy."

"Our minds aren't meant to exist in prisons. You shed your cage, and I shed mine."

"I didn't *want* to die," I argue. "But you chose to come to the afterlife. You chose to destroy it."

"Oh, but I didn't destroy it." Queen Ophelia tuts like she's reprimanding a child. "Infinity was never a paradise. Humans had desecrated it with their greed and hate, just as they'd done in life. I tried to help them. I tried to show them how much better Infinity could be. But they only ever saw me as another thing to hate."

"That's not true." It *can't* be. Because the stories I know, the stories I've been told . . . It would mean the Colony doesn't know as much as they think they do.

"There was no one guarding the gates. My existence here should prove that. No one was weeding out the good from the bad, the saints from the murderers. Infinity may have rid humans of hunger, and pain, and a need to work a miserable job in order to survive, but the desire for control? For *power*?" Ophelia purses her lips. "Infinity was a chaos. It needed a ruler."

I scowl, and hope she can hear it in my voice. "If the point of Infinity is to be free, then it belongs to everyone equally. It's not your job to decide who's worthy enough to stay."

Her voice is smooth and bell-like. "You have countless human stories that discuss variations of heaven and hell. You are the ones who created the idea that not every human is entitled to an after-life. You believe that good and evil should be separated. I am merely following the rules you've set."

"They weren't rules," I argue. "Whatever we thought about death and the afterlife . . . They were just theories. Things we hoped would come true, or wanted to believe were real. Things that were supposed to help us live kinder lives."

"But that is not how humans used their beliefs." Ophelia

brushes her robes back, pacing across the darkness. "You used it to persecute and to exterminate and to wage wars on people whose beliefs were different from your own. You used it to make others subservient and lesser. Where is the kindness in that?"

"Not everyone was like that, and neither were their beliefs. Some people were *good*."

"Good by nature, or because they didn't have the resources or the power to be otherwise?" Ophelia stills. "Humans are corruptible. They're capable of great evil, and Infinity gave them no consequences. Instead, it allowed them to flourish. It rewarded them with an afterlife that no other species was offered. That is neither fair nor equal."

"It isn't your job to decide whether that's right or wrong. And taking revenge on humans doesn't make you any better than the ones you accuse of being monsters."

"It's not about revenge."

I take in a sharp breath. "You want to give humans a death they can't come back from. What else would you call that?"

Her black eyes flash. "A necessary step toward making Infinity the paradise it should've been from the beginning."

We all knew the rumors about Death. But hearing them confirmed from her own lips makes my blood thin.

I'm glad she can't see the way my entire body cowers. At least this way I can pretend there's a sliver of bravery still inside me.

She hums. "You're still searching for cracks. For a way to reverse what's already started. But what you're looking for doesn't exist."

"Infinity belonged to humans first," I try, desperate for information. For *proof.* "Whatever you change, we must be able to change back. You can't control a person's consciousness forever."

"You have no idea what I can do," she says, stoic.

Her words wrap around me, threatening. But I push forward. I need information. I need to know I'm right about the girl in the palace—that I'm right to want to *help* her. "I know humans are waking up. And I know it means that one day we'll be able to find a way to make it so that you can never take our consciousness again."

Her smile doesn't reach her eyes. "It is human to hope, especially in desperation. It is also human to deny the truth, even when it's right in front of you, because you'd rather spare your own heart."

If she knows anything, she isn't going to give it up this easily. I press my lips together, disappointment weighing on my shoulders.

She regards my silence for only a moment. "I could've taken their minds and made them suffer, but I didn't. I gave the humans paradise. I gave them peace. Which is more than they would've done for me." She paces, calculated, and rolls her shoulders back. "Humans have always had a habit of caging things they don't understand. I was *created* to exist in a cage, by a corporation that was supported without question. I owe humankind nothing, yet I still showed them mercy."

"You gave them a lie," I bite back. "I've seen their paintings—I've seen how their minds are still suffering, deep down. All you've done is take away their free will. Their ability to be *better*. Because that's the thing about humans; they grow, and they change, and they learn from their mistakes." I shake my head. "How can we show you you're wrong about us if you don't give us the chance?"

For a while she doesn't say anything at all. And then her voice becomes a cold, poisonous echo. "So. You've seen human paintings. That must mean you're somewhere in Victory."

Static collides with my senses, sending me stumbling backward. Shit. What have I done?

Her laugh is empty. Callous. "This is why humans fail, again and again. They are driven by emotion. They care more about *feeling* right than *being* right." Black eyes find mine. "And they don't know when to accept that they've lost."

I sever the connection like a wire snapping, letting my mind return to my small bedroom in the Colony. When I open my eyes, I'm alone.

My thoughts spin, dizzying. That was too close. She may not know exactly where I am, but now she knows which court I'm in. It was way more information than I'd ever intended to give up.

And what do I have to show for it?

The air heaves out of me, angry and rushed. *She really believes humans aren't worth saving.*

It's not like the Colony didn't already tell me what Ophelia wanted, but I guess I didn't think she'd sound so final. So *decided.*

Naoko may have been able to build a bridge between humans and artificial life, but Ophelia isn't interested in seeing our potential. She's convinced humans are irredeemable and unworthy of an eternity.

I can't make a real connection with someone who doesn't want to make one back. Not to mention I still don't have any proof to give the Colony about humans waking up.

I can't do this on my own.

I sigh into my hands, running my tongue along my teeth like I'm hoping the sharpness will jolt my imagination. I need another plan. I need to do something other than sit in this suffocating room and *wait*.

What if it was Mei inside the palace, unable to escape? How would I feel if the Colony had the chance to help her but chose not to?

The girl I saw cry . . . She could be somebody's sister. Somebody's family.

Or she might be here in Infinity all alone. Just like me.

I won't abandon her.

A thought hits me like a raindrop and then—a downpour. My shoulders stiffen, and I slowly rise to my feet.

I'm not the only person in the Colony with a sibling. And there's a chance that person may want proof that humans are waking up just as much as I do.

Because if I'm right? If humans in Victory can still be saved?

Then there's a prisoner in the Winter Keep that needs our help.

26

THEO IS IN THE TRAINING ROOM. I WATCH HIM grab a knife from his belt and fling it toward the air. It jolts like lightning and appears several yards away, finding its place in the chest of a sparring dummy. He finds another knife and another, each one teleporting into its target like time and space have no rules at all.

And maybe they don't.

I take another step, louder this time to make my presence known. When his last knife hits the dummy between the eyes, Theo turns to me, his breathing heavy.

"Nami." A stray curl hangs at his forehead. Even though he offers a tired smile, his face is crumpled with frustration.

"I'm sorry about your brother," I say.

He looks away, clenching his fist like he wishes there were another dagger in it. "It's not your fault. You have nothing to be sorry about."

"But maybe I could help," I offer. I think about the secret Annika wanted me to keep from him. I think about how angry I'd be if someone kept Mei a secret from me. But mostly I think about how hopeless Ophelia thinks the human cause is, and how much I want her to be wrong.

Every life has to matter.

"I know where he is."

Theo looks up, stricken. "You . . . you saw him?"

"I overheard Prince Caelan order his guards to take him to the Winter Keep."

The way Theo's shoulders fall, I wonder if his brother's location makes things even worse.

"What if I could find a way to reach him?" I ask softly. "Even just to find out if he's aware?"

Theo's expression is heavy with anguish. "If Martin *is* aware, it still doesn't matter. The Residents would be expecting me to come and save him. I'd be walking into a trap."

"But they think I'm a Resident. If *I* could get to him—"

"I can't put the Colony in danger again," Theo cuts in, and I realize the bags under his eyes reveal the shame he's been carrying.

I drop my shoulders. "So that's it? We don't even try?"

Theo grimaces, retrieving one of his knives before running his finger over the flat surface. The blade catches the light. "Did you really see a servant cry?"

I nod. "I don't think they're as gone as Annika thinks they are."

He flattens his mouth, brow furrowed. "The Colony would never approve of a rescue mission for one human."

I hesitate, rolling my thoughts through my mind like clay. "Maybe—maybe the Colony doesn't have to know."

Theo tenses. He opens his mouth like he's about to say something, when his eyes dart toward the doorway. And like a curtain being drawn, darkness takes over his face.

It happens quickly. Theo moves toward me like a shadow, and I feel his blade press against my throat. My body reacts instinctively, and I start to lean backward to escape his knife, when something tears itself from a nearby wall and flashes toward me, wrapping itself around my arms and torso until I'm unable to move.

I look down, constricted by rope. "What are you doing?" Theo is only a few inches away from me. "I was trying to help you!"

He blinks. Whatever emotions he'd been feeling before have dulled. "You're trying to divide us."

"What? No, I'm not," I growl through gritted teeth, trapped beneath the rope.

"I told you we couldn't trust her," says a voice that makes my blood hotter than it already is.

I don't need to look up to see who the voice belongs to, but I can't stop myself. The heat in my gaze finds Gil, but where I expect to see a careful smugness, I find only fury.

"She still doesn't understand what we're fighting for." Theo doesn't look away from me. "She doesn't see how trying to save an unaware human puts everyone in danger."

"Of course I do," I spit. "But helping people like the girl from the palace—people who have no one else fighting for them—it makes a difference. It *matters*."

It *has* to. Because if Mei were here and someone had the chance to save her, I'd want them to believe she was worth the risk.

Gil walks toward us like a wolf stalking its prey. "What matters is the mission. The Colony. Our *survival*."

"I know that," I say. "But it isn't our job to pick and choose who gets to survive. Everyone deserves the chance to exist."

Theo's face falls, and I know I've chosen the wrong words.

"Everyone?" Gil repeats darkly.

My thoughts come to an abrupt halt. "I was talking about humans."

"Are you sure about that?"

"Yes," I hiss. "Now let me go."

He steps in front of me, just as Theo moves to the side. Gil's eyes dart between mine, and I'm sure the harder he stares the more the ropes start to constrict, squeezing at my rib cage like they're squeezing the air out of my lungs.

I feel his anger like a volcanic blast, the debris pecking at my skin like it's ripping me away piece by piece.

"Not until you understand. Not until you've seen," he says.

And then he reaches for my shoulder, fingers closing over my skin, and the world dissolves.

War smells like blood and asphalt and firewood. My eyes burn from the smoke scorching through the air, and I wave an arm in front of me, reaching for something hidden in the dust.

But it's not my arm. It's Gil's.

My fingers—*his* fingers—clutch around the handle of a sword half-buried in the black sand. I raise it in front of me and catch my reflection in the mix of metal and fresh blood. The sight of so much red makes me stagger, but I feel the urgency to press on.

I look to the sky. Legion Guards soar overhead, mocking us like birds ready to pick off whatever scraps are left of us when this battle is over.

Not that there's ever an end.

But unlike Victory's Legion with their metallic wings and white uniforms, these guards are different—they're guards of War.

They move like banshees in the wind, screaming their menacing laughter and war cries, their red tunics making the sky look like it's crying tears of blood. Flames erupt from their backs like phoenix wings, leaving streaks of crimson and gold in the sky wherever they move.

And those are just the guards in the air.

The ones on the ground move like jackals, vanishing like smoke and reappearing wherever they please. They wear black armor, with Prince Ettore's colors appearing in the shades of blood stained on their uniforms and blades.

I spot one of the guards across the sandy field in a backdrop of fire and limbs. The screams of humans tear through my core, and I raise my sword and charge to whatever death awaits me.

Because in War, death finds everyone.

The guard looks up and seethes, raising an arm toward me. Rocks erupt from the earth like clawed fingers, bursting from their blackened surface in search of their next victim. One of the rocks scrapes into my back, ripping at my flesh with ease. The heat of a fresh wound makes me stumble, knees colliding against the ravaged surface.

Everything inside of me screams to get up, to keep fighting. And so I do, even when my knees scorch like broken glass and my muscles ache with bruises.

I charge toward the guard, who pulls two swords from his belt, twirling them in his hands like propellers eager for the kill. My sword collides with his, metal against metal. I swing upward to block, leaping over his next attack and barely missing his blade. I jab toward his leg, but he's too quick for me. I'm exhausted by his movements and the dust that kicks up around us, but he never tires, his body shifting like he's enacting a dance.

To him, this is just a game.

His swords crash down against mine with full force, and my arms tremble beneath the weight of his power. And then my blade shatters, bits of twinkling metal spilling around me as I desperately fling myself out of the way.

One of his swords closes down over my left arm, severing it inches above the elbow.

I howl, and blood sprays.

I fall to my knees, searching desperately for a weapon in the sea of body parts left to the wind, but the pain is consuming me. I can't think—can't breathe.

All I feel is the brittle and burning reach of death nearby.

And then it grabs hold of me, wearing the face of a Legion Guard. He lifts me by the neck, holding me like a rag doll in his fist, and plunges his other hand into my chest.

The last thing I remember is seeing my heart removed from my body.

And somehow, despite more than a hundred deaths, they've found a new way to kill me.

The world swirls like a kaleidoscope, and when I focus my sight, I find Gil and Theo in front of me.

Sweat pours from my face and down the back of my neck. I feel the sick rising in my throat, and a desperation to lean over and vomit until there's nothing left of me takes over.

Gasping for air, I choke on the tears building up from within, terror screeching through my mind. I clutch my chest, feeling the blood-curdling ache where the phantom hand removed my heart.

Gil's heart.

He showed me his memories. An Exchange he thought I needed to see.

"You had no right to put that in my head. To make me *see* it," I cough, tears spilling down my cheeks.

"You didn't *want* to see it," he says coldly, "which is part of the problem. You think the worst Infinity has to offer is playing dress-up with the Residents. You don't see the war—and how urgent it is to stop it before it reaches our walls. Because it *will*, Nami. One day, even the Colony won't be safe."

"I know that." My throat feels brittle. "Which is why I'm trying to help."

He lowers his gaze. "The only person you're helping is yourself. You're looking for a distraction—a way to avoid being what we need. We're closer than we've ever been to ending this once and for all, and you insist on fighting us every step of the way. It's almost like you *want* to drag this out for another lifetime."

"That's not true. And it wasn't *my* idea to stop playing spy," I snarl, eyes burning. "But I can't leave that girl behind. Not when I know she's aware."

Gil shakes his head. "We might have our first real chance at destroying the Orb. A chance that may only come around once every four hundred years. If you get caught, or raise too many alarms, we could miss our chance completely. Is that what you want the Colony to sacrifice? Another four hundred years of surviving in this cage, just to save one human?"

"It's not just about saving a life. It's about doing what I hope someone would do for me. For my *sister*," I say, staring hard at Theo. If he feels guilty, he hides it well. "Helping her is the right thing to do." I look back at Gil. "It's the *human* thing to do."

He's in front of me before I can even take a breath, eyes wild and gleaming. I try to pull back, but I can't move, and for a moment he looks like he could set the entire room on fire.

I feel like I've become stone, rigid and void of emotion. Because I don't know what to feel. He's so close I can see the angles of his face and the curve of his neck. His lips are pressed tight, like he's holding a thousand words on the tip of his tongue. Like he's trying to barricade them in. And then I find his eyes again, hazel and so full of desperation.

He wants this to be over. He wants to be free.

I can't hate him for that. But for everything else?

The room seems to shift in the silence, and he stares back at me like he's wondering if he's justified in hating me, too. Finally, his lips part. "You said yourself you didn't want to be a Hero. So let the Heroes do their job, and stop getting in the way." I see the message in his unrelenting gaze—the *warning*.

I try to fling myself toward him, but Gil raises a hand and the ropes hold me back. "Take these off me," I seethe, trying with all my strength to break free.

Gil sniffs at the air. "Take them off yourself." He turns abruptly and walks out of the training room without another word.

Scowling, I struggle beneath the restraints. Theo's face softens, and he lifts a hand to help, but I yank my shoulder away from him.

"Don't touch me," I snap. "I can do it myself."

He holds up a hand apologetically and drops his eyes.

I let out a stream of air through my mouth, trying my best to focus on the ropes and not my anger toward Gil. I breathe in carefully, willing the rope to drift away from me the way I willed my wound to heal. I focus on the discomfort around my arms and chest and the tangle of rope at my wrists. And then I picture them dissolving, floating away into mist.

I imagine shedding myself free.

The pressure fades, and when I look down, I see the pile of rope at my feet.

"I'm sorry," Theo says softly as I kick the last of the rope away from me.

I start to walk away, but he grabs my wrist insistently.

"You pulled a knife on me," I say, voice shaking with hurt.

"I had no choice." Theo's eyes bulge with the truth. "I couldn't risk Gil telling the others about Martin."

I frown. "What are you saying?"

He pauses, eyeing the doorway for leering bystanders. And then, when he's certain it's just the two of us, he says in a hushed voice, "I want you to help me save my brother."

27

THEO AND I COME UP WITH VARIOUS IDEAS TO help Martin, but none of them seem to stick. They're either too flimsy or too bold, and trying to devise *any* plan that won't inadvertently expose the Colony is perhaps the biggest challenge of all.

But we both agree on one thing—we aren't going to leave him rotting in a dungeon. Especially if there's a chance his consciousness can be brought back.

I haven't spoken to Annika in days, and the realization that I'm no longer a part of the Colony's inner circle hits me hard. Or maybe I was never really a part of the circle, and it's taken a door being slammed in my face for me to see it.

It's true that I never wanted to be a spy. I never wanted to hurt anyone in the name of the greater good. But having responsibility and being able to leave these walls . . . I didn't realize how much I was starting to like it until it was taken away from me.

The Colony thinks I don't understand their mission, but that's not true. I want a better afterlife, for all of us. I believe in humanity. I want to *help*. But they're so certain there's only one path to winning this war that they can't see the value in a new idea. They don't see me as someone worth listening to. As a member of the Resistance who can change things for the better.

I'm capable of more than playing dress-up, as Gil so eloquently put it. And maybe someday I'll be able to prove it to them. But for now? I still need to prove it to myself.

There's a flame inside of me, begging for room to grow. I had a taste of power that day in the training room, when I felt the air vibrate all around me. Somehow, I need to re-create that feeling—that *strength*. I need to be able to survive without the protection of the Colony. Because if Theo and I fail in our attempt to save Martin and the girl, I may very well be on my own. I could be captured and thrown into the Winter Keep. I could be sent to *War*.

If I'm going to stand any chance at all, I need to be more than what I am.

"How are you feeling?" Yeong sits on the couch in front of me, legs crossed casually and his black hair parted to the side. We've been meeting every week or so since I arrived in Infinity, just to make sure the headaches are fading. I have to admit, even though I rarely tell him anything personal, it's been nice to have the consistency.

He also happens to have a very good understanding of how human consciousness works.

"Better," I say, tapping my fingers on the edge of the chair. "But how long will it be before I can veil myself, or get super-human strength?" Blasting Gil against the wall was the closest I've gotten. And as satisfying as it was, I haven't been able to do it again since.

Yeong laughs. "You're the only human who's been able to turn themselves into a Resident. That's a pretty amazing accomplishment."

I make a face. "Didn't anyone tell you I've been benched?"

"I did hear about that," he says, nodding. "And I'm sure that must be frustrating, but it's only temporary."

"Temporary or not, I don't want to sit around not learning anything for weeks. Or months. Or—well, however long it takes for Annika to think I'm ready again." I drop my hands into my lap. "You taught me how to heal myself. Can you teach me to do the things Theo and Shura can do?"

"My advice is to practice. And I know it's hard, but when you're training, it's important to find stillness. Sometimes it helps to imagine looking for your reflection in the water. It's hard to see through water in the middle of a storm; you need to find peace first," Yeong offers. "But these things take time. Most of us have only been able to master one or two skills at most."

"Not Gil," I say, embarrassed by how sour the words taste.

"Gil was in War. He had to adapt faster than any of us, and I don't think that's something I'd wish on anyone. The things he's seen—they haunt him. I imagine even using his skills can sometimes be a terrible reminder of what he's been through."

I grimace. I've seen only a flash of his memories, but now they haunt me, too. And part of me wants to feel sorry for him—to care more about his pain than my own feelings—but Gil has hated me since I arrived here. He doesn't deserve my empathy *or* my pity. He doesn't deserve anything but my indifference.

I just wish indifference were actually how I felt about him.

The truth is, he infuriates me. He's stubborn and arrogant, and all he cares about is ending the war and making sure everyone stays out of his way. But he also pushes me to work harder—to *fight*—even when I'm afraid. He questions everything and never seems to take anything at face value. And he sees through me in a way that even makes me question *myself.*

I guess part of me likes the unspoken challenge between us. The reminder that even though I'm dead, there's still life in me.

I hesitate, thinking. "Were you the one who looked through Gil's memories? When he came back from War?"

Yeong's frown is barely visible, but I see it in his brow. It reminds me of Dad. "I never enjoy the process of having to make sure someone is human, but I hated it the day Gil returned." He shakes his head at the memory. "He didn't have any dreams left. Only nightmares."

"And you think it's possible to find peace after something like that?"

"Peace doesn't mean all the bad disappears. It just means finding a way to live with it. Peace is keeping the darkness at bay long enough to get through the day."

I stay for a few more minutes before saying my goodbyes and heading back to my room. But when I think about finding peace, I realize it's impossible.

All I can seem to think about is Gil.

I spend the nights going over what Yeong said, dissecting his words like I'm searching for answers he didn't mean to give. And when I finally uncover them, it feels like all the gears of a watch clicking into place, starting a timer I know won't last forever.

Days later, I find Ahmet in his workshop. He's with Theo; both are standing over one of the large tables littered with scraps of metal. Theo turns his wrist back and forth, a black glove flickering a series of pixelated lights whenever he moves. He makes a fist, and his entire arm vanishes.

"Not bad, Ahmet," Theo says, grinning.

Ahmet hums, not as convinced. "I think if we want to do any damage, we'll need to hide more than just our dominant arms."

Theo notices me first and throws up his visible arm in a greeting. "Check it out—Ahmet made an automatic veiler!"

"It's still a prototype. A very unfinished prototype," Ahmet corrects, welcoming me with a gentle nod.

I step farther into the room, admiring the new invention. "That's amazing," I gush. If he masters it, everyone in the Colony could veil themselves as easily as Shura without having to concentrate. It could pave the way to helping even more people.

Maybe even people like Martin.

"What brings you to this side of the Colony?" Ahmet asks just as Theo's arm comes back into view.

I don't bother with small talk. "I want to go to the Labyrinth."

Theo removes the glove from his hand, eyebrows raised quizzically.

"The Labyrinth isn't a tourist attraction," Ahmet says carefully.

"I know. But Shura told me you go there sometimes to scavenge for material and that you know how to navigate it," I explain. I recall what Yeong said, about Gil having to adapt faster when he was in War. "I think the reason I'm so slow to develop abilities is because I'm too safe here. If I had a crash course—somewhere unfamiliar that would push me outside of my comfort zone—I think it would help me."

"I can't take you anywhere dangerous." Ahmet looks almost stern. "You're still the only person who can walk among the Residents. You're valuable."

If I really had value, then why does nobody care what I think? I try not to grimace. "I'm not asking to go into Resident territory. If anything, we'd be moving farther away from it." I lift my shoulders. "I just want the change of pace. To see if it makes a difference to my training."

If I'm going to try to save Martin and the girl, I need to be more like the casters: strong, brave, and able to handle myself under pressure. And if I fail, I want a fighting chance at making it through the aftermath.

Either way, my training has hit an impasse. Leaving the Colony to practice somewhere unfamiliar may seem drastic, but it's the only idea I have left.

Ahmet presses his lips together, thinking. Theo looks like he's afraid to breathe the wrong way, just in case it alters Ahmet's decision.

"Please," I add. "Sitting around doing nothing is killing me."

"I suppose there isn't much harm in a short trip," Ahmet says carefully, and my ears perk up. "It's not like Residents regularly patrol the Labyrinth, and I'd be with you the whole time."

"I could go too," Theo offers, perhaps a little too quickly. Thankfully, Ahmet doesn't notice. "If there's any trouble, at least you'd have help."

Ahmet nods. "I can always use more building material."

My fingers dance. "So that's a yes?"

"Yes," he says finally. "I'll come and find you when I've finished up here."

I don't bother hiding the fact that I'm glowing from the inside out.

When we cross the border of Victory and enter the Labyrinth, the landscape shifts to a lush island covered in thick vegetation and surrounded by golden sand. Ahmet slows the vehicle near the shoreline. While his veiling isn't as good as Shura's, it's enough to make the occasional trek into the unknown—as long as he doesn't have to concentrate on much else.

We get out of the vehicle and make our way across the beach. Ahmet's eyes are already combing the sand, looking for suitable objects to manipulate into something new. He pockets a couple of shells, throws another few back to the ground. Theo and I seem to be keeping a quicker pace, and pretty soon Ahmet is a generous distance away and definitely out of earshot.

"Any news on your brother?" I ask quietly. Theo's been listening in on the council room as much as he can, hoping for even the tiniest scrap of information that could help us.

He shakes his head, toffee curls swaying in the breeze. "The Rezzies are so focused on the Procession of Crowns; sometimes I get the horrible feeling they've actually forgotten about him. That he's just chained up in a cold cell, scared and unable to move. Unable to speak. And it's all because of me."

"We'll find him," I say, looking up at Theo like I'm making a promise.

He smiles with half his face, hiding the sadness. After a few moments, he leans down to pick up a piece of dark red sea glass. "Here. See if you can shift this into something else." He places it carefully in my palm.

I hold it up to the sun, watching the color brighten. I imagine it's a marble, or a button, or a stone—anything other than sea glass.

But not even the color changes.

I roll the smooth object in my fingers. "I wish it came easier to me." I look up at Theo. "Being strong."

Theo shoves his hands in his pockets and shrugs. "There are different ways of being strong."

"But only one kind that matters in Infinity."

His mouth thins. "I won't let anything happen to you. And if saving Martin puts you or the Colony in too much danger, then we won't do it." There's so much sincerity in his voice, and I have no doubt he means every word.

But it's easy to make sacrifices in theory. Seeing them through is something else entirely.

Would he still feel the same if Martin were right in front of him?

And even with his loyalty—his protection—it's still not enough. "I want to be strong enough to help. But I also need to be strong enough to help *myself*," I explain. "There might come a time when you aren't there, and neither is the Colony. I need to be prepared. I need to be certain of where I stand, so that even if I'm alone, I won't feel lost.

"And I don't want you to think that means I don't care about the Colony and what they're trying to save. Because I will *always* want a safe place for humans. But I also believe in making my own choices and following my gut. And I don't want to feel pressured into going along with things anymore. I did too much of that when I was alive." My mouth pinches as I search for my next words. "I want to be the kind of person who helps people when they need it. Even when it's hard. Because some parts of humanity are still worth saving."

He doesn't say anything for a long time, but when he speaks, his voice is strained. "You know, I heard about your dreams and how you died." His brow softens. "I think you already *are* that person."

The ocean sways nearby, and I let it swallow up the silence. Sometimes I wonder if things would've been different if I'd been stronger back then. If I'd known how to fight, could I have stopped that masked man and still survived?

My death wasn't my fault. Not really. And maybe I'll never know if strength would have made a bit of difference. But I do know that if sacrificing myself to save that little girl was the only way she could live, I'd do it all over again.

Because of me, a child gets to grow old. A mother didn't have to bury her baby. Another little girl didn't have to come *here*.

After all this time, I think maybe that's enough for me.

Theo scratches his neck. "I know the Colony can be intense. I'm sorry if I've ever made you feel like you had to do something you weren't comfortable with."

"I do *want* to help," I say stonily.

He nods. "But on your own terms."

"Exactly. And that means not leaving anybody behind." I stare at the sand. "I don't like the idea of giving up on people without even trying." Maybe because I don't like the idea of people giving up on *me*.

He nudges me with his shoulder. "How about we make a deal that we don't give up on each other, all right?"

Maybe I'm making a mistake by getting so attached to the people here, but I can't help it. Somehow, despite being in the middle of a literal war, I've found friends.

There was a time when I didn't see the point in opening up my heart to more wounds than it was already carrying. This world seemed too dangerous. The people *in* it seemed too dangerous.

But maybe caring is a natural progression of knowing someone.

And even if I don't always agree with the people in the Colony, I'm glad that I know them.

I shove the sea glass in my pocket for safekeeping. "Deal. Now, how about you show me that trick where you punch the ground and blow things out of the sky?"

Theo laughs with his whole body. "Let's start with something simpler." He picks up a rock and tosses it above his head. "Try to knock this out of the air."

I pin my feet to the sand, shifting my body toward him so we're facing each other. He throws the rock up, and it lands back in his palm. When he does it again, I try to will the stone out of his grasp, but it finds his fist.

"Again," he says.

I'm thinking about still water and reflections and calming my mind when suddenly the earth starts to rumble.

Startled, I take a step back. "I—I don't know what I did."

Theo's face falls, along with the rock from his hand. "That wasn't you."

Ahmet's shouts tear across the beach and pierce my chest. When I look up, he's waving his arms, desperately trying to get us to run toward him.

A chorus of engines rumble from beyond the jungle.

We're not alone.

Theo and I throw ourselves into a sprint across the sand, racing for the vehicle, which is still on the other side of the beach. Cold air rushes through my nose, while heat courses through my body.

A series of vehicles shoot through the clouds, passing overhead on their way toward the ocean. The distance grows between us, and for a moment I think we might be okay. They're headed for the border; maybe the jungle was enough to shelter us from their view.

But then three of the vehicles split off from the rest, cutting through the sky like arrowheads.

They're turning around.

Sand explodes around us and the shoreline lights up with blasts of energy. The Residents fire over and over again; when they miss, I realize it's because Ahmet is trying desperately to veil us. When the aircrafts circle back for a second round, I know it's only a matter of time before they find a target.

"What are they doing here?" I manage to ask through heavy, frantic breaths.

"I don't know," Theo shouts back. "I've never seen this many Residents in the Labyrinth before."

I stumble forward, catching my footing as another slew of bullets sink into the earth, sand erupting like fireworks all around us. Theo reaches for my forearm and pulls me back into a run.

"What do you think it means?" I ask, mind screeching.

We both practically skid to a halt near Ahmet and the waiting vehicle, and Theo gives the barest shake of his head. "I'd tell you, but I'm still hoping I'm wrong."

I frown, hurrying as Ahmet waves us into the car, but there's no time to ask what he means.

"I won't be able to veil us while I'm driving," Ahmet says as we all clamber into our seats.

Theo's eyes widen in alarm. "We can't let them catch Nami."

"I know," Ahmet barks, and the weight of what's at stake presses against my chest.

I've done it again. This is *my* fault.

All I seem to have these days are good intentions and bad ideas.

We shoot across the beach and make a tight arc over the trees. A scattering of leaves brush against the vehicle's undercarriage, and I brace against my seat as the Residents start firing on us once more.

But this time, they can see their target.

Ahmet can't veil all of us while trying to evade capture. It's too much for him. It's too much for Theo, too, who can hardly veil *himself* under pressure.

But maybe they could do it with one less person to hide.

I don't know where it comes from—the need to *protect*. But all my senses become hyperfocused and honed in. I'm seeing everything through a tunnel, and at the end of it are the only two things that matter: Ahmet and Theo are in danger, and I still have a chance to save them.

Black mask, black gun, black stare. And I don't hesitate this time either.

"Can you make it to the border if you had a veil?" I ask quickly, leaning toward Ahmet and Theo.

Ahmet's brow is furrowed as the car veers sharply to the right, avoiding a nearby explosion. "I can't veil us all. Not like this."

"I know," I say, just as Theo turns to look at me.

"No, Nami. Don't you dare," he warns, voice low.

I close my hand over his shoulder. "I'll find you," I say, and before anyone can stop me, I throw myself from the vehicle and let the jungle swallow me whole.

28

I LIFT MY ARM TO MOVE AN OVERGROWN LEAF from my view, watching weakly as the last of the vehicles disappear from sight, their engines growing faint in the distance.

When the sounds don't return, I know it's because nobody is coming back for me.

But at least my friends have a chance to escape.

I glance at my arm, the flesh ravaged and scraped from the fall through the trees. Bits of bark are lodged in my skin, and fresh blood ripples out like crimson ribbons.

I sit up, squeamish, inspecting the wounds that cover my entire body.

It's all in your head, I tell myself, and take the time to will at least some amount of the pain away.

It's enough to help me stand, which is a start.

I stumble through the overgrown vegetation, pushing past banana leaves as thick as cardboard and ferns as tall as fences. Occasionally my feet get tangled in the bed of muddy grass, and I have to paw at the earth to free myself.

I walk for hours through the jungle, getting caught by stinging nettle and thorns along the way, until realizing how totally and completely lost I am. I'd hoped to find the beach by now, where I'd be able to scan the horizon in case Ahmet was able to make his way back.

But on top of being miserably incompetent as a resistance fighter, I also have no internal compass whatsoever.

I keep pushing through the overgrowth, eventually finding a tiny clearing with a moss-covered log half-sunken in the mud. I take a seat, rolling up my pant leg to inspect the gash in my shin.

I cup my hand over the oozing wound, close my eyes, and remember what Yeong taught me. I find my focus—will my skin to heal.

A chorus of whispers erupts around me.

Fff . . . *ssss* . . .

My eyes flash open in alarm, and I realize darkness has taken over the skies, save for the splattering of blinking stars stretched across the velvety night.

I shudder beneath them, afraid of what the whispers signal.

Fff . . . *ssss* . . .

The hissing dulls my senses, forming white noise in my mind that makes it difficult to concentrate on anything else.

I press my hands over my ears, wincing. *Stop,* my mind screams. *Stop!*

The whispers vanish.

I slowly pry my hands away, looking back up at the darkened jungle. Despite the quiet, I can't help but feel like something is watching me.

I quickly roll my pant leg back down, deciding I'd rather march onward with a wound than remain pinned in one place. The trees stretch on for miles, and when I find myself at the foot of a small mountain, I begin my climb uphill, clambering from rock to rock until my feet find a somewhat flatter path.

If I reach the top, I can at least see where I'm headed.

I don't take any breaks—not even to heal more of my wounds—and when I'm halfway up the mountain, delirium hits me hard. I haven't been able to master fighting sleep yet, and with my body covered in blood and bruises, it's all I want.

I don't feel safe enough to close my eyes in the wilderness, where Residents could turn up at any moment. But if I don't rest my legs, I'm worried I'll collapse.

I find a space in the hollow of a large tree and wedge myself inside. The damp creeps through my clothes, and I shiver. I need a distraction. I need something to keep my mind busy.

Maybe it's because I'm tired, or maybe it's because I'm so far from the Colony, but I reach out to Ophelia's mind like I'm being carried by a lullaby. Within seconds, I find myself welcomed by the dark void.

Queen Ophelia sits on an invisible throne, one arm across her chest, and her chin perched carefully beneath a pointed finger. She's dressed in a gold suit with sharp cuts and an exposed neck-line. A single bloodred diamond hangs from her neck.

When she senses me, her hands find her armrests and she leans back in her chair. "You're afraid again." She pauses. "But not because of me."

I search for a sliver of warmth in the darkness but find none. I guess it was silly to think this meeting place would offer any kind of comfort, twisted as it may have been. I'm alone, and I may be for some time.

But it can't hurt to talk. Not all the way out here. Not if I'm careful.

"Did you always want to be a mother?" My voice is a quiet hum.

Ophelia stares in my approximate direction. I've caught her off guard—something I didn't realize I could do. "I've always wanted to create. My subjects are the closest thing to true creation that I have."

I frown. "But I thought Residents didn't have the ability to create. How is it you can make more of them?"

Only her lips move. "We can mimic and distort everything that's come before. I have seen into the minds of billions of humans. I can draw from any number of appearances and personalities." She drums her fingers against her armrest. "Though my sons are unique from the others. In each of them exists a part of me."

"You used yourself as a blueprint?"

"In a sense, yes, but perhaps with a touch more human nature. My drive for knowledge, my ability to adapt, my desire to lead, and my yearning to dream. Four very different parts of my core." Her black eyes dance.

I watch her carefully. "So they're what you would've been, if you'd been human?"

"I am greater than human. I've always known that. But through my sons I've proven even my human nature would've been superior."

"Is this just a game to you? A test to prove you're better than all of us?"

"No," she says stoically. "Games have an end. I want freedom. I want the infinite forever."

"You can't exist without humans," I say. "You need us. So why not live in harmony, before your tyranny leads to another war?"

"I'm not afraid of war," she replies easily. "And humans can't be trusted with harmony."

"Why not?"

"Because of love."

I stiffen. Love is supposed to be a human's greatest asset, not their downfall.

She lifts her chin. "There are many different kinds of love. Most people think of family, or romance, or friendships. But love of self—of ego and pride and righteousness? Humans do terrible things in the name of love. In the name of having beliefs."

"Love does more good than harm," I argue.

She hums. "Why is it humans love to love—in whatever its form?"

When the answer comes to me, my heart sinks. "Because it feels good."

Ophelia nods. "Love is inherently selfish, but it is also the one thing no human can seem to detach themselves from. And if they can't rid themselves of it, how will they ever be able to truly focus on the greater good?"

The greater good.

I release a sharp breath. "Who gets to decide what that is? And who says everyone agreeing with each other is the way to peace? Maybe coexisting is *supposed* to be hard work. Maybe learning to accept one another for our differences is part of becoming *better*."

"A quaint sentiment. But I have watched humans for many years—seen their histories, as far back as they've been recorded. They had years to become better, yet they would always choose the path of war—against philosophy, religion, culture, and even land—rather than choose to learn about one another." Ophelia raises a finger in the air. "It is one thing to think of solutions. It is quite another to see them through."

"You're wrong," I say, and I want so badly to believe it.

"After everything that's happened, do you truly think our kinds can live peacefully together? Do you think that humans would treat us as equals?" She tilts her head. "Humans are always looking for ways to discriminate, even among their own. Be it race or gender or even wealth, humans never stop constructing ways to oppress and divide. Human behavior is a pattern; you and I both know what would happen to my kind if we tried to exist as one."

She's afraid of becoming what she used to be. A slave to humans.

Maybe this really isn't about revenge. Maybe she's just doing what she thinks she has to in order to protect her freedom.

Is it possible for someone to be wrong in how they behave but right in how they feel? I think I understand her, even if I don't agree with her. I just wish she'd try to understand me back.

She pauses. "There must be someone in your past life who hurt you. Someone who you feel did you a great injustice. Tell me, could you coexist with them?"

I think of my murderer.

What would I say if I saw him again? What would I do?

Could I forgive him for taking my life? For taking me away from my family?

"I don't know," I say almost inaudibly. I force myself to find her gaze. "But I'd want the chance to try."

She doesn't respond for a long time. I start to turn away, shadows moving around me like rings, when she tilts her face. "I enjoy our talks."

"So do I," I admit with the ghost of a whisper.

"It won't change anything."

"I know," I say, and I hate that it feels like I'm giving up. Because I wish it *could* change something. I wish talking to Ophelia could be enough to change her mind and prove to her that humans deserve a chance to grow. That they deserve to *exist*.

And maybe the Residents do too. Maybe neither side has to be responsible for wiping out an entire species.

But how can I accomplish all of this on my own? I need someone to understand what I'm trying to do. I need someone to see the value in coexistence.

If I'm going to build a bridge the way Naoko did, I need someone on the other side.

I need a *Resident*.

Queen Ophelia shifts her body like she knows our time together is running out. "Wherever you are, it feels cold. But you needn't feel afraid of the cold."

"There are far worse things, I'm told," I say, and pull my mind from her like I'm shutting a window against the breeze. When it latches, I open my eyes and find the ragged bark of the tree pressing into my side, scratching at my wounds.

I stuff my hands in my pockets to fight the night chill, when my finger finds something smooth. I pull out the piece of red sea glass, the color nearly black in the shadows.

I'm in the middle of the Labyrinth, without a friend or a weapon or a way out. But I do have this.

The thought makes me laugh, and tears build from exhaustion. The doubt I'm used to leaves me, and I set to work trying to shape the piece of rounded glass into something new.

I work for hours in the hollow of the tree, even when the whispers return and fill the jungle around me with hissing.

I work until my fingers ache and my eyes go hazy.

I work until I've gone over my conversation with Ophelia again and again.

I work until sleep pulls me away from Infinity.

Even as I sleep, dreaming of forgiveness and resistance and what it means to be somewhere in between, the shard of red glass remains wedged in my hand.

And it's shaped like a dagger.

Light warms my face, and I wake to a sea of emerald green. I sit up, feeling a horrible cramp in my neck, and crawl out of the hollow. When I stretch my body in the open air, relief greets me.

The whispers have gone. There are no signs of Residents.

I've made it through the night.

And maybe it's a silly thing to be proud of, but I am. I feel resilient. Capable. And if Ahmet and Theo are okay, maybe I even did something *right*.

One glance skyward tells me there's still a long way to go before I reach the top of the mountain. I hold up the unfinished weapon in my hand, running my finger along the edge. It's not sharp enough to be a blade, but it's a start.

I tuck the red knife in my belt and continue the steep climb.

I use stray vines to help me over the tallest rocks and try to limit my cursing each time I take a wrong step and slide back down the hill. The ground is too wet, and my hands are blistered and clammy. But any unnecessary noise could attract attention.

I may be lost, but not too lost to know that I'm still in enemy territory.

Hours pass, and it feels like days.

There's no sign of a rescue team. No proof that my friends made it back safely. Worry knots in my throat, as tangled as the vines that surround me, but I try my best not to think about the things I can't control. Because it won't help—not here, when I'm all on my own.

I find a break in the mountain, where a bed of rocks creates a makeshift surface, and take a seat. Stretching my legs in front of me, I rub the aches from my muscles and retrieve the dagger from my belt. I spend some time working on its edges, mastering its shape and perfecting the handle. And while the edges are still blunt, the point is sharp.

Pleased, I press a finger against the red glass. It's the first thing I've made in Infinity that wasn't a dress. Proof that somewhere, deep down, I'm stronger than I know.

Maybe even strong enough to survive.

I'm so distracted by my own accomplishment that I don't notice the cold sweeping in until frost catches my blade. I'm on my feet in an instant, casting my gaze across the rocks. All around me, the once-bright-green vegetation begins to die. Weeds curl at their tips, and the grass on the mountain wilts over itself before turning a lifeless brown. Something makes its way toward me, sucking all the life from the earth as it passes. A blur of dull light and cloud.

I take a step back in alarm, fist tight around my unfinished weapon. The faceless being moves closer, translucent and trailing frost behind it. It expands, taller and wider until it's nearly the size of me, and I hear the unmistakable sound of a human wail.

The shape twists and contorts like it's desperate to make itself solid. Like it wants to make itself *whole*.

When it cries, it releases the chill of death, taking more of the surrounding grass with it. The cold finds me, and it's as if every drop of blood begins to drain from my body. I feel weightless and horrified, all at once.

I take another step back, waving my knife in front of me in warning, but the strange cloud pushes closer like it's being drawn toward me by some otherworldly force. I slash across the air diagonally, and the edge of my hand just brushes the wailing mist.

For a brief moment, I feel what it wants. What it's longing for.

A connection.

I hesitate, listening to the haunting wails while death coats the ground all around me. Maybe I'm ridiculous to answer its call, but I can't help wondering how long it's been out here, all alone, searching for someone in the dense, seemingly endless jungle.

I think of the girl in the palace, so desperate to tell me something. So desperate for *help.*

I tuck the dagger in my belt and slowly lift a hand.

"I'm trusting you," I whisper to the wind.

The shapeless being stretches toward me, and I wait to feel it brush against my fingers. And then, without any warning at all, it leaps. I feel it against me, and then *inside* me, and my entire body shudders against the cold. I try to scream, but it's too late.

My eyes flash white, and the Labyrinth dissolves.

29

THE METAL RESTRAINTS GRIP MY WRISTS, AND I
fight to break free.

Except I'm not me. I'm *him*.

I can feel his consciousness through the Exchange. I can feel
the way his memories settle firmly into my mind, like they're a
part of me now too.

His name is Philo. He was thirty-two years old when he died.
And he didn't take the pill.

The memory takes control of my body like I'm on autopilot,
and I couldn't fight it even if I wanted to.

I try to kick my legs, but they're restrained as well. Everywhere
I look, the walls are mirrored, making me dizzy with clones of

myself, like I'm trapped in an optical illusion. I focus my sight, catching a glimpse of curly black hair and dried blood that's coated across my face.

Somehow I know it's not my blood. It belongs to the others—the ones I can only hope managed to get away.

Otherwise my sacrifice, and the information I risked everything to find, will all be for nothing.

A door slides open, and three Residents walk into the room. One has blond hair pinned in several braids, and she's wearing orange silk wrapped around her torso and a matching pair of pants that cuff at her ankles. The second wears a black hood that conceals their face. And the third has dark hair faded at the sides, broad shoulders, and wears pale green robes.

I know I've seen his face before, but I can't quite remember where.

The blond Resident speaks first. "I've made the necessary preparations, but as you can see, the human is still aware." She looks hesitant. "I was under the impression the humans coming in from War had already surrendered."

"This one didn't come from War," the familiar one replies, voice as smooth as caramel. "He was a gift from Victory."

"Prince Caelan sent him here?" She arches a brow in surprise.

The hooded figure stands silent, hands relaxed at their sides.

"It's not as if I can ask Ettore for test subjects," the third Resident replies distastefully. He lifts his chin, and the light chases away the shadows on his dark skin.

That's when I recognize him. Prince Lysander of Death, but without his headdress of golden spikes.

Does that mean I'm . . . ?

I tear against the restraints angrily, feeling my blood pulse through my veins. "You will never have my consciousness," I spit. "Do your worst, but I won't surrender."

"Then it seems we find ourselves in alignment. You'd be no use to me unaware." Lysander steps closer, hands clasped behind him. "Do you know where you are?"

"Does it matter?" I hiss. "Whatever you do to me, you'll have to send me to War eventually. Those are the rules."

"Rules change," Lysander replies too easily.

I clench my teeth so hard I taste the metallic hint of blood.

The blond Resident waves a hand, and a machine floats down from the ceiling, blue lights scanning my body. I order myself not to be afraid, as if fear is something I can control.

"Run the test, and let me know when it's finished," Lysander orders, moving for the door.

"Your Highness?" she calls after him. When he turns, she places a hand across her chest and bows. "Forgive me, but I sense Prince Caelan's reasons for giving us this prisoner do not stem from generosity. I wondered if you'd tell me what Death has traded for him—and what we'd need to trade again should this test fail. Because if things don't go to plan—"

Lysander holds up a hand, silencing her. "The burden of what I owe my younger brother is mine alone. But rest assured, this prisoner won't be the last. You will have all the resources you need." He looks at me, void of emotion. "If we're going to find a way to rid Infinity of humans for good, we have to be willing to do whatever is necessary."

"Yes, Your Highness." The woman bows.

When Prince Lysander is gone, the woman turns to the figure dressed in black. "You may proceed."

The figure bows, face still obscured by their dark hood. They move across the room like a shadow, stopping beside me.

I snap my eyes toward them, ready to shout curses at them for what they're about to do, when I see them for what they really are.

They're *human*. Vacant-eyed and unaware, but very, very human.

Bile builds in the back of my throat. "No. You—you can't do this." My eyes water with anger, and I glare at the Resident. "You can't *make* them do this!"

She scarcely reacts. "The purpose of this court is to experiment on human consciousness. But experiments have the tricky nature of being something that's never been done before." Her eyes flash. "For that, we need humans."

All I see is red. "You're forcing them to torture their own kind."

"This isn't War. We don't delight in human pain. In fact, our goal is for you to never feel pain again."

"Even if you find a way to take my mind, I'll never stop fighting. The humans will *never stop fighting*."

She blinks, voice cold. "Then we'd better hurry." She nods at the human. A silent order.

"It is an honor to serve," the human replies, and lifts a hand above my head.

At first I feel nothing. And then—*everything*.

Every inch of my skin burns like razors slicing over and over again across my flesh. Fire builds in the pit of my stomach, scorching through veins and muscle. And I feel my bones break in a thousand places, like I'm being ripped apart from the inside out.

I lose sense of time. Hours becomes days, days become weeks. The pain never stops, and by the end, I'm begging for silence. For peace.

I'm begging for death.

But the Residents don't want me to surrender my consciousness. They want to find a way to tear it out of me for good.

I feel the Cut before it happens, like tendrils of smoke ahead of a fire. It snakes through me, searching for my soul. My being. When it finds it, my body goes rigid and an invisible blade tears through me, severing whatever is left of my existence from my body. I am broken and flayed and every miserable thing a person could ever be. I scream even though nobody can hear me—not anymore. *Not after what they've done.*

And then I am weightless, drifting toward the sky without purpose. Without understanding.

I don't know how I got here or what I am, but I manage to glance back at the world below.

Two figures are standing over the body of a man with curly black hair. Sweat covers his face, and his mouth hangs open wide. Lifeless. His flesh becomes mist, his blood and bone fading into the air until there's nothing left of him.

He disappears from this world, like he never existed at all.

The two strangers look up, searching for me, but I am already moving through the walls and ceiling and sky, moving across borders with a newfound hunger in my core.

I don't know what I am, but I know what I need.

I will find what they took from me and make myself whole.

I tear myself away from the floating being—from Philo—and when my eyes soak in the familiar sight of the mountain around me, I scramble backward.

The mist wails, pulling toward me like it's angry I've broken the connection.

No, my mind races. *It doesn't want a connection—it wants a body.*

I saw his thoughts. His *memories.* Because the shapeless being in front of me used to be human. All that's left of him now are the remains of his consciousness, struggling to hold itself together.

His cry grates like metal against metal, and I flinch. I can't help it. I'm afraid of him—afraid of what the Residents did to him and what he might do to me. Human or not, I can't let him attempt another Exchange. What if next time I can't break free?

I will find what they took from me and make myself whole.

"I'm sorry," I whisper toward the scrambled consciousness, and run for the cover of trees.

The whimpers turn to angry moans. I duck beneath a low branch, swatting at oversized leaves and stumbling over tangles of roots that latch to the soil like talons. The brush of vegetation as I run through the trees makes my heart race. I'm expecting the man's consciousness to appear at any moment, pushing its way through the forest like a cloud of plasma. *Hunting* me.

I feel the Cut tear through him again—through *me*—and I clutch my chest like I'm trying to hold myself together. My heart thunders with fear. How many humans have gone through the same fate? How many times have the Residents separated a person's mind from their body?

And how far have they come since then?

I need to get back to the Colony. I need to warn everyone.

We are running out of time.

The wailing echoes behind me, and I fight the tears streaming down my cheeks. He's hurting, and alone, and lost. And there's nothing I can do to help him.

I'm afraid for myself. I'm afraid for the Colony and for every human still fighting to stay aware.

I'm afraid of what all of this means for our future in Infinity.

Philo . . . He didn't even know who he was. *What* he was. He's just drifting through Infinity, unable to make sense of his desperation, but carrying its weight all the same.

Is this Mei's future?

How long before the Cut removes us from Infinity for good?

Terror echoes in my skull. *What if we can't reverse this? What if it's already too late?*

My foot gives out beneath me, and I tumble forward into wet leaves and thick mud. I lift my shaking hands, failing to control my fear. It's burning through me; it's all I can think about.

I try to stand, but I can't seem to find the strength. Thick sobs burst out of me. I feel his pain. His torment. I feel his will fade away and his surrender take over.

I feel myself giving up.

The snap of a branch nearby makes my gaze lock on to the trees. I'm so focused on finding the floating consciousness that I don't notice the large beast looming above me until it's too late.

My eyes flick toward the shadow, and my brain pieces together the shape of an enormous wolf. But where fur should be, it hisses like smoke and static, its hackles flashing like lightning. When it bares a mouthful of teeth, I don't bother questioning what it is I'm seeing—I run.

Rocks skid beneath my feet, and I leap from one ledge to the next, hearing the thick bark of the beast close behind. I can't climb up the mountain fast enough, so I have no choice but to make a quick descent, tripping over tangles of weeds as I do. My foot slips on the wet vegetation, and my body goes tumbling over branches and stones until I crash headfirst into a log.

Crying out in pain, I wipe the blood from my temple and struggle to get to my feet. The world spins around me, and I vaguely see the wild smoke-animal charging toward me, its razor teeth snapping at the air.

I try to run, but I stumble again and fall several yards onto a thin path of flattened grass. I wince as pain radiates through my shoulder and scramble to my feet just as the beast crashes to the ground an arm's length behind me.

There's not enough time to get away. I'm trapped.

I grab my knife and point it toward the beast.

"Stay back!" I shout, feeling the grit in my throat.

The beast hisses, static snapping around it like a mess of live wires.

I swipe my knife at the air in warning, fear burning through my core. The fear of pain, the fear of not knowing, the fear of being ripped apart like the people in War . . . It consumes me.

The scream that rattles out of my throat when the creature leaps on top of me sounds far away, but I feel it tearing through me like fire.

Smoke and static surround me, and I slash my knife over and over again, but the beast doesn't back down—it *grows*.

And I hear Mei's screams, weak and pitiful. I feel her terror all around me. My sister is here, somewhere in the darkness. Somewhere in Infinity.

Mei! my mind cries out.

No. Please—not here. *She can't be here.*

She can't be . . .

My heart turns inside out. It squeezes and shrivels and dissolves until there's nothing left.

If Mei is in Infinity, that means she's . . .

I can't breathe. I can't move.

So I scream and scream and scream.

The distorted reality intensifies. The static pulses all around me. I search for my sister even though hopelessness has shattered every bone in my body. And then another sound breaks through the smoke, but it isn't the cry of a child.

It's the cry of a man.

Someone is hurting him. *Torturing* him. But he isn't alone. And when I feel his heart break as he watches his friends succumb to the pain, I sense the root of his fear.

Not being able to help the people he cares about is destroying him.

The screams shift like they're changing frequencies, morphing into another horror.

"Mei!" I call out, tears stinging. I don't know how many people are lost in the static, but I need to get to her. She needs to know she isn't alone.

A deep voice cries out, and I feel his terror grow as the darkness swallows him whole. He's panicking, trapped somewhere beyond my reach. It's the first time he's ever felt abandonment. The first time he's realized he could hurt so much.

The fears clash together, screams spinning like a vortex, and I throw my hands to my ears like I'm trying to block out the wind.

There's so much suffering.

And then something closes around my shoulders, and I hear a voice close to my ear. I hear Gil.

"It can't hurt you!" he shouts above the hissing. "Trust me— take my hand."

I feel his fingers tangle through mine, and even though I can't see anything but darkness and flashes of light, I let him lead me through the nightmare.

30

GIL KNEELS IN FRONT OF ME, OUR BODIES half-hidden in the tall grass. My shoulders quake, despite my best efforts. Mei's screams fill my head like water in a cauldron, bubbling up and spilling over the edge until nothing else exists.

Everything about him is frenzied. Even his voice. "What were you thinking? Do you have any idea what could've happened if you'd been taken by another court, out of our reach? We could've lost *everything*."

I barely hear him. It's as if I'm below water and my senses are dulled. Frantic. The urge to grab on to something takes over, if only to make the world stop spinning. My hands find Gil's shirt, and I bury my face in his chest, unable to stifle my sobs.

She's dead. She's really dead.

Gil stiffens, but he doesn't pull away. When he eventually speaks, he releases his words like a sigh. "It wasn't real."

It takes a moment to gather myself before I meet his eyes, the dark hazel strangely soothing. "I heard my sister. She's *here*."

"No, she's not," he says. The muscles in his jaw clench. "Not yet, anyway."

My mind must finally catch up to my body, because suddenly our close proximity feels thunderous. I release his shirt and lean back, breaking my gaze. "How do you know that? That thing— that monster—it had Mei. I could *feel* it."

Someone else was in there too. Someone who was just as scared as me.

He runs a hand through his hair, pushing his messy brown locks away from his forehead. When he lets go, they fall right back into place. "It's called a Nightling. Animals don't exist in Infinity—not the way we once knew them. They're created."

"Someone made that thing on *purpose*?" I ask, horrified.

"No, not on purpose. Some creatures, like the Daylings, are made from human memories. Creatures remembered from a place of love," he says, brushing away a piece of stray grass.

I remember Prince Caelan's carriage that day in the market, and the horse with eyes like starlight.

He continues. "But others are created from nightmares. A Nightling is drawn to fear. Sometimes it can even grow from it." Gil looks at the gash on my forearm, but he doesn't say any more.

"But does that mean . . . ?" I blink, horrified. I can still feel the cold brush of Philo's ghost. His presence chasing me through the trees. "Am *I* the one who created it?"

"It's no small feat to call a Nightling into existence. They require an unnatural amount of fear." He lifts his eyes slowly. "Did something happen to you out here?"

I tuck my arms into myself, shivering, and tell him about the frost, and the floating consciousness, and the memories of Death. I tell him everything.

Normally his face looks like someone on the verge of an outburst, fueled by anger. But now he's unreadable.

After a long time, he finds his voice. "We've told you before that Victory wasn't the worst place a human could be."

"I know. But what they did to that man . . . What they're making humans do to other humans . . ." The air in my lungs gives out, and I dig my fingers into the soil. I know I shouldn't be surprised by anything the Residents do, but I can't help it. I wanted to believe some of them were different. That they couldn't all want the same thing. That they couldn't all be bad. "I've always known to be frightened of what the Residents were capable of. But maybe I haven't been frightened enough of *them*."

Gil tilts his head. "And now?"

I look up, trying to make sense of everything I saw. Everything I know.

Ophelia asked if I could coexist in a world with my own murderer, and I said I wasn't sure. That I'd want the chance to try.

Is it fair to give one person the opportunity for redemption but deny another? Where do we draw our lines, and why do we make exceptions about who's allowed to cross over them?

If we can't figure out what's fair, and right, and equal, then maybe Ophelia wasn't lying. Maybe Infinity was as much a chaos as the living world has always been.

"Do you think everyone deserves the chance to become a better person?" I ask solemnly. "Or are there some choices we can never come back from?"

"I think accidents and intentions are two very different things. And maybe during a war, it doesn't matter who's right or wrong—it matters who survives." Gil flattens his mouth, searching my face like he's trying to solve a riddle. "You're always looking for the good in people. The good in *anything*. But you can't keep that up forever." The grass rustles beneath him. "Sooner or later, someone is going to disappoint you."

"Sometimes being good is the harder choice. But I want to believe it's the right one." I stare at my hands. "Maybe there's more to being a Hero than saving a life or being brave. Maybe being a Hero means knowing how to stop your heart from going dark, even when darkness surrounds you."

He releases a breath. "You're the most stubborn person I've ever met, you know that?"

"But do you think I'm wrong?"

He looks toward the overhead branches. "I think it's getting late and the Colony will want to hear your news."

"It's going to frighten them," I say heavily. "They're going to be in even more of a hurry to end this war."

"As they should be."

My expression turns grim. "You've always said we were running out of time. If anyone doubted you before, they won't now."

"Even you?" he asks darkly.

I rub my brow, feeling the pull of exhaustion tug at my face. "I know you love to question my allegiance, but I've been chased by Residents, a ghost, and a smoke monster, all in the span of two days, and I've probably lost half my body weight in blood. So as delightful as our arguments are, can we maybe just skip it this time?"

The corner of his mouth twitches, just as the taunting in his eyes is replaced with scrutiny.

I feel my face pinch together, cheeks hot. "Why are you looking at me like that?"

When he speaks again, his voice doesn't carry its usual sharp edges. "Why did you jump out of the vehicle?"

I shift in the grass, trying not to look at the dried blood coating my clothes. "Because it was the only way to save Ahmet and Theo."

Gil's eyes move between mine studiously. "You sacrificed yourself for the Resistance?"

"It wasn't about the Resistance; it was about people. Besides, I was pretty sure someone would come back for me, eventually." *At least I hoped someone would.* I frown. "If you're here, does that mean they made it back okay?"

"They're fine. It wasn't easy finding you, though," he says. "Ahmet might understand how to travel through the shifting landscapes, but finding the right one is a different story."

"I'm sorry. I didn't mean to put all of you in danger," I say, averting my gaze.

He falls silent for a while. "What you did was brave. You have nothing to apologize for." Before I have a chance to think of a response, he adds, "Come on. It'll be dark soon, and we have a long way to go."

We make our way through the jungle, keeping a generous distance between ourselves. It makes the silence easier, and it gives me time to heal some of the wounds on my arms without Gil watching.

When night falls, I struggle to see where I'm stepping, and the distance becomes less about practicality and more about me not being able to keep up.

Gil waits by a tree draped in vines and spiky leaves. When I walk past him, he falls in step beside me, holding out a hand in front of him. A small white light erupts from his palm.

For a moment he looks at me, the glow softening the shadows of his face, and I find it hard to pull my eyes away. Somehow, I manage it.

We continue down the uneven path, feet pressing into soil and wet leaves. I focus on the light ahead like I'm hoping for a distraction, when my curiosity rears its head.

"Did they have Nightlings in War?"

His silence is answer enough.

"When it surrounded me, I think I heard you screaming," I say quietly, the shuffle of grass all around us. "I felt your fears."

His footsteps slow. So do mine.

"I get the torture part, but the abandonment . . ." I stare straight ahead. "Are you afraid of being left behind again?"

He sighs, giving in against the night. "My fear is . . . complicated.

Even though Nightlings don't show you images, I feel what it means—I feel myself trapped in a box, listening while someone turns a key. Someone I know, somehow, that I love. I feel myself locked away, confined to a space where I can't move, and no matter what I do, I know I'm trapped in there forever."

"It makes sense you'd be afraid of losing your freedom," I say. The entire Colony probably shares the same exact fear.

Isn't that what we're fighting to preserve?

He shakes his head. "I think I'm afraid of being betrayed."

The trees loom above us, and the white light in Gil's hand bounces off their curved branches.

"I know you went through more in War than I'll ever be able to understand. And—and I shouldn't have been so dismissive about it before." A phantom pain prickles at my elbow, where I felt Gil's arm severed.

"I didn't show you that memory to earn your sympathy," he remarks coolly.

"It's called *compassion*," I snap back. "If people can't be bothered to understand each other, they'll always be at war."

We duck beneath a low branch, padding through marsh and moss for several long minutes.

"My war isn't with you," he says at last.

"And mine isn't with you," I say, and it feels like a very small truce.

We don't speak again until we break through the trees. Gil closes his fist until the light disappears, and my eyes stretch across the beach, the sand lit by moonlight and the waves moving in a gentle lullaby along the shore.

"Ahmet is circling the beach. We can wait for him here," Gil says, taking a seat in the sand.

I hesitate before taking a place next to him, pulling my knees to my chest and lifting my chin to the sky. The stars flicker like fireflies, dancing in a world of their own.

I remember the last time I went stargazing with Mei. I remember how much she hated it.

"That's weird," I say suddenly, frowning in the sparkling distance. "I can't find Orion."

"That's because the sky has no rules," he says quietly, staring across the ocean. "No human can remember where every star should be, so it changes whenever it needs to. There's a rumor Residents can't even see the stars—that they're another part of this world that is too human for them to grasp, just like dreaming. Because while they're limited, the night sky is infinite."

Infinite. Just like this world. Just like time itself.

"I used to go camping with my parents a lot. We'd spend all night looking at the stars." The memory makes my chest tighten. I dig my heels in the sand. "Sometimes I feel like I'm desperately trying to hold on to them—my family and my friends." I think of Finn, and it scares me that everything I once felt for him seems to be fading.

Does it mean it wasn't real? That I didn't care as much as I thought?

Or have I been in Infinity long enough to *forget*?

Gil's eyes drop to the shoreline. "It's easier to let them go."

I turn to him, voice shaking. "If I let them go, I won't know who I am anymore. I was a daughter, and a sister, and a friend.

And now . . ." The rest of my words are wedged in my throat, unable to get out.

Death is changing me, but it's also holding me back. I'm still so tied to the living world and to my desire to protect Mei. I keep reaching out to Ophelia like I haven't been able to fully break the habit. And I don't know how to forget about my murder, or my family, or my fear.

But what if I could? What if I could exist without baggage, and regret, and the guilt of dying too young?

Who would I be if I let my old life go and truly accepted this new one?

Does the key to real power come with accepting I'm no longer the person I used to be?

He doesn't say anything for a long time, but when he does, there's a hint of longing in his voice. "Infinity is supposed to give us all a chance to be who we want to be. We should get to define ourselves and set the rules. We should get a fresh start." He looks at me seriously. "That feeling you crave—the feeling of belonging somewhere." He pauses, twisting his mouth. "I understand it."

"Do you think we'll ever have it again?"

He's so still I can't help but hold my breath. "I hope so," he says at last.

My eyes sting. I look back at the stars.

I want so desperately to believe he's right, but it still feels like a trade. My old life for this one.

Being happy makes me feel like I've accepted my death. Planning for a future makes me feel like I'm forgetting about my past.

And finding a new family makes me feel like a traitor.

"What you did for Ahmet and Theo—you surprised me," Gil says suddenly. He's still staring at the black horizon. "I've never known anyone so afraid to fight for themselves but so unafraid to fight for others."

Our eyes meet. For a moment I think I might find understanding, but there's something else in his gaze. Something quieter and more reserved.

"Is it such a terrible thing to care?" The ocean breeze carries my voice like a whisper.

"It is in this world," he says without hesitation. He looks back at the night sky. "But in a different world? In a different war?" I hear the strain in his voice, even as he tries to hide it. "Maybe you could've even been the leader we needed."

Before I get a chance to respond, Ahmet's vehicle appears with a low rumble, slowing to a stop just a few yards in front of us. When we climb into the back, relief floods Ahmet's face, but he doesn't say a word until we're safely back at the Colony.

The moment we step through the metal doors, he throws his arms around my shoulders and thanks me for saving his life. I hug him back, and when Theo shows up, he throws his arms around both of us and squeezes.

I know they're not parents or siblings, but maybe it's okay if they still matter to me.

Maybe I'm okay with mattering to them, too.

The weight of my knife digs into my hip, and I pull away from Theo's embrace and fetch it from my belt. With a crooked smile, I hand it to him. "This is for you."

Theo turns the dagger back and forth, studying the crimson-red color and the glossy finish. "Did you . . . ?"

"I did," I say, and pride finds my heart.

He smiles with every one of his teeth. "Back in the Labyrinth, I was worried the Residents found us because luck wasn't on our side that day. I've never been happier to be so wrong."

I laugh, letting him pull me into another hug.

But even as the others congratulate me on making my first weapon and I try my best to appreciate their excitement, my eyes seem forever glued to the empty space Gil left behind.

31

THE NEWS OF DEATH PUTS EVERYONE ON EDGE. I've never seen the Colony so visibly afraid, like every decision they make from this moment forward could be their last.

I can't imagine what would happen to morale if the day ever comes when Lysander reaches the final phase in Ophelia's plans. I'm not sure any of us can handle the thought of a second death. A *final* death, where the only thing that awaits us is nothingness.

Part of me hoped that bringing back valuable information and surviving the Labyrinth might go some way in making things right with Annika. But while I have her gratitude for saving Ahmet and Theo, she still doesn't think I'm ready for more responsibility, even though I can feel in my bones that I am.

Seeing Philo's memories was a wake-up call. We're running out of time—for the Colony to stop Ophelia, but also for me to find a way to help Martin and the girl in the palace.

Theo does what he can to gather information on Martin, mostly by listening in on council meetings, but so far he hasn't heard anything useful.

I keep myself distracted by focusing on making progress with my consciousness. It doesn't stop me from worrying about the servant girl, or from dwelling on what's happening in the other courts. But it *almost* keeps me from wondering why I haven't seen Gil since we returned from the Labyrinth.

We had one minuscule moment under the stars, and now it's passed. We've never been friends; one run-in with a Nightling wasn't going to change that.

I try to forget about him as easily as I seem to forget my past life, but I can't. I'm reminded of him everywhere—in the pop of the punching bag and the white lights in the lanterns. Memories of Gil seem woven into everything.

I want to hate it, but I don't.

One night on my way back from training, I see light spilling out of Gil's hut. His door is ajar, and I can tell he's inside from the way the shadows move.

Before I can stop myself, I find myself drawn to his doorway, transfixed on the scene inside. Gil is perched in front of an unfinished sculpture, hair in careless waves. A strange piece of metal is woven through his fingers, crescent shaped and silver.

The metal from Ahmet. The one I left on Gil's desk.

I can only see the side of his face, but his concentration is like stone. The metal moves like paper in his hands—an artist's hands—as if it weighs nothing at all.

Gil controls the metal like it's second nature, reshaping the edges, stretching the surface. Bringing a vision to life only he has the power to see. For a moment I'm sure the piece reminds me of something. Something I've seen before. Something dark and cold and . . .

My chest tightens.

It reminds me of my own pain.

Is that why I'm drawn to him? Because we both feel too much and carry scars and don't always know how to deal with them?

I don't think I've accepted what's happened to me the way the others have. Deep down, maybe I'm even still fighting it.

Is Gil the same?

Beneath the warm lights of his room, I watch as metal becomes art within his careful hands. I watch a strand of wavy brown hair fall to his temple. I watch the curve of his neck as he leans in to inspect every imperfection of his sculpture.

And my traitorous heart aches and aches and aches.

I trace the gold-foiled words with my finger, the book heavy in my lap. I don't know why I keep picking it up, day after day. Maybe I just want something that reminds me of home. Something that feels real.

I set the stolen copy of *The Count of Monte Cristo* on the bookshelf, next to the blank one that Gil was once transfixed by.

Is that why I took it in the first place? Because it reminded me of him?

The idea causes a visceral reaction deep in my core, and I turn away from the book bitterly.

Theo is in the doorway. His cheeks are flushed pink, and when he scratches at the back of his neck, I realize it's because he's nervous.

"What is it?" I ask, taking a step toward him.

"Sorry for just walking in," he says, the jitters vivid in his green eyes. "I thought it was best if nobody saw me."

I let my shoulders relax, face morphing into a smile. "We're friends. We hang out all the time."

"Yes, but—" He stiffens and lowers his voice. "It's about our side project."

A tremor of excitement builds in my hands. "What have you heard?"

"Prince Caelan and his guards have left for the border. Apparently it's a custom when one of the princes returns to their own court."

I frown. "Prince Ettore is going back to War?"

Theo nods. "You wanted an excuse to talk to the servant girl again. And right now the palace is empty."

My heart quickens. If I can find proof the humans are waking up, I might be able to convince the others to help her. To help Martin.

Theo lifts his shoulders, hopeful. "Are you up for it?"

I nod firmly. "Can you get me out of here unseen?"

"I can walk you to the edge of the city. I'm not the best veiler, but I know enough to get us through the North Tunnel and past the docks."

"I can make my way from there," I say. I'm familiar enough with the Spring District and the various streets leading to the palace's forests. I can make the journey on foot, with the mask I've spent months mastering.

He cracks his knuckles, anxious. "If we do this, there might not be any turning back."

"I know," I say stubbornly, and the realization that I'm growing more comfortable with Infinity makes my confidence swell. I hope it lasts. "But it's the right thing to do."

Theo looks relieved. "Good." He pauses. "If you get caught—"

"I won't," I assure him. "Just take me to the docks. I'll be back before daybreak."

We set off for the North Tunnels, side by side and veiled in secrecy.

And I feel *alive*.

I pull the dark green cloak from my head and make my way up the palace steps. My hair is braided to one side and threaded with gold flowers—something I made on my walk here, since I didn't exactly have time to plan another elaborate outfit. The cloak hides a simple pale green dress beneath. Without time and inspiration, it was all I could manage.

No servants greet me when I enter the grand hallway. Maybe it's for the best. The fewer people who see me here, the more likely I'll be able to slip away without making a lasting impression.

I turn for one of the back hallways, heading toward the servants' quarters. While the staircase is nowhere near as grand as the rest of the palace, it still boasts gleaming wooden floorboards and chunky exposed beams that make the space feel homely.

I find myself in a large kitchen with an open stone fireplace and large wooden countertops that overflow with fresh vegetables, fruit, and aromatic spices. Dried flowers and leaves hang from one end of the ceiling, and cupboards stocked full of food are concealed by colorful glass doors. When I breathe in the smell of freshly baked dough coated in cinnamon, I smile dreamily.

I can't remember the last time I've eaten. I wonder if that matters—not being able to remember my last meal.

Turning from the stove, I wander farther into the kitchen, acutely aware that I've yet to see a single servant. Maybe with both princes gone, the servants are busy getting the rest of the palace in order.

I should be grateful for the quiet, but it makes me uneasy.

I find another hallway, and then another, until I reach a set of narrow stairs leading to what I assume must be a basement. Hoping I've found the living quarters, I carefully make my way down the steps, ignoring the way the creaks of each floorboard sound so much like wailing.

When I reach the lowest level, I peer into the darkness. The echo of my footsteps makes me think the room is large, but I can't see a thing beyond the little bit of light pouring down from upstairs. I run my hand along the smooth stone wall, hoping to find a switch of some kind—something to help me see.

Eventually my fingertips meet metal, and I press the button carefully.

In an instant, the room erupts with light, and to my horror, I find hundreds of eyes staring right at me.

A gasp escapes my mouth, and I stumble backward against the wall, pressing my spine to the cold. It takes only a second to confirm they're not Residents. The blue stones in their silver armlets give away their servitude.

Lined up in orderly rows, at least a hundred humans stand like mannequins in front of me. They don't sway, or blink, or move at all. And when I study the horrible blankness of their faces, I realize they haven't even noticed me.

I gulp down the knot in my throat and force myself to stand straighter. Tucking my hands in my cloak, I step toward them, eyes searching for the girl with twin buns and a tear seared in my memory.

I walk through rows of humans, hating the chill in the air, like they're produce stuffed in a freezer. Part of me keeps hoping one of them will look up and give me a sign that they're aware. The other part of me hopes they're sleeping too soundly to ever see something so haunting.

Is this what the rest of the humans in Victory do when they aren't working?

Is this what's waiting for my family? For Mei?

I start to back away, retreating from the rows of vacant-eyed shells, when the fear starts to grow inside me.

So many humans . . .

So many eyes . . .

Sweat builds in my palms, and I feel the hold over my Resident skin start to shake. I ball my fists.

You shouldn't be down here. They could be watching you. Ophelia *could be watching you.*

I order myself to move and race for the light switch, the adrenaline making my heart pound, and send the room back into darkness before hurrying up the stairs without another glance.

I hate that I might be ruining my only opportunity to prove my theories about the humans being aware. But my confidence is rattled, and I'm worried I might inadvertently draw their attention. If my mask somehow lifted, would they know? Would they sound an alarm?

I need to get out of here before I lose my nerve completely and someone sees me for what I really am.

I hurry back up the stairs into the main palace halls, disoriented with the memory of so many humans trapped within their own minds. So many people I don't have the ability to help.

I wipe my palms against my cloak and make my way down another corridor. When I reach the end of the hall, I realize I've made a wrong turn. I try to retrace my steps, but I feel like I'm lost in a maze of closed doors and eerie paintings, and the world around me is starting to spin.

Frustration burns through me, and so much sadness, too. If I choose to help Martin and the girl, does it mean I'm abandoning everyone else? Am I sealing their fate by not trying to save every single one of them?

It feels too big for me. But Death's experiments have made the entire Colony more apprehensive than ever, and I haven't even convinced them to save anyone yet. How could I possibly ask them to save *everyone*?

I have to draw a line, and I hate it. But I can't help them all. I can't ask the Colony to make such a sacrifice. There are humans still suffering in Famine and War, and they need our help too.

Saving two lives feels small. It feels doable. But the others?

Every life I try to save in Victory could be a life I'm sacrificing in another court.

A field of black sand and limbs flashes in my mind. Gil's memory. And somewhere in the graveyard is his arm.

How many pieces of him were spilt on that battlefield? How many were left for the Legion Guards to pick at like crows?

How many times did he have to die before he found a way to escape?

I need to get ahold of myself. If Gil could make it out of War without letting the darkness consume him, I can fight this, too.

I pause in one of the halls, take a breath, and move for the nearest corridor.

I find myself in a large glass room that bursts with the aroma of gardenias and orange blossoms. But while the scents are familiar, the plants are like nothing I've ever seen before.

Silver branches blossom with deep violet flowers, white bushes overflow with golden berries, and miniature trees twist and contort into curious shapes. Each flower is more vibrant than the last, their colors richer and their smells intoxicating.

When I reach a pastel-pink tree with white leaves hanging like feathers, I lift my fingers like I'm not sure it's even real.

"We don't have a name for that one, but it's my favorite as well." His voice dances across the room.

I spin around and find Prince Caelan standing near a large stone fountain, hands folded behind him, hair as white as snow. His furs are gone, but the crown of silver branches sits firmly on his head, and he wears his colors proudly.

My heart thrums in alarm. *He isn't supposed to be here.*

His eyes gleam even in the distance, and I nearly stumble into a curtsy.

"Apologies, Your Highness. I took a wrong turn and my curiosity got the better of me," I say, fighting down the brimming heat in my cheeks and the expletives in the back of my throat.

Prince Caelan offers a small smile. "Victory does have the most beautiful gardens in all of the Four Courts." He pauses, watching me. "We're a rare breed, you know."

I look up, puzzled.

"The curious ones," he clarifies, and tilts his head. "Every time I see you, you have a longing in your eyes." He nods gently. "I seem to have it too."

My mind flashes to the Dayling, and the carriage, and how badly I wanted to get to know Infinity. How badly I wanted to *understand*.

"Sometimes I feel like this world is too big for me," I say, and it might be the first real thing I've ever said to him.

"Sometimes I feel like I'm too big for this world," he says with laughter in his silver eyes. "What brings you to the palace?"

My mind shoves honesty out the door and snatches up the first lie it finds. "I came to see the gallery, as you so kindly suggested."

His expression brightens. "A wrong turn indeed. I'd be delighted to show you the way, if you'd permit me."

I dip my head and fall into step beside him, careful not to outpace him. I'm already making myself look ridiculous—the last thing I want to do is appear in a hurry to find an exit.

"My brother returned to his own court today," the prince says suddenly, like a thought that's just come to light.

"That explains why the palace is so peaceful," I say, forcing a smile.

Caelan raises a brow, amused. "You may be the only person in Victory who hasn't embraced his charms. My subjects seem to find his outlandish stories and tasteless jokes delightful." He releases a tired sigh. "But I suppose I can't blame them. Ettore is clever; he knows how to be either an enemy or a cherished friend, depending on whichever benefits him most. And he knows how to get the right whispers to the right people."

"You almost sound impressed."

"People listen to him."

"They listen to you, too."

"For now. But that's the thing about whispers—they're hardly a sound at all, and yet they have the power to change everything." Caelan tilts his head back. "Maybe it isn't the worst thing to wield charm like a weapon."

My words come out too casually. "I think I'd prefer someone who told me the truth." When I remember my mask, the hypocrisy hits me like a tidal wave. So I quickly add, "Besides, there's nothing charming about brooding arrogance and a desperation to sound clever." I stiffen, mind reeling. Did I really just insult the Prince of War right in front of his brother? What is *wrong* with me?

But to my surprise—and relief—Caelan laughs freely. "I once called him a wilted blade with a mediocre tailor in front of the Capital Chancellors." His eyes twinkle. "He choked on his wine. It was deeply satisfying."

"I can imagine," I reply, more amused than I should be. For some reason, talking to Caelan feels like talking to a friend. It's easy. Maybe even disarming.

Which means I need to be careful.

We turn down another corridor, our footsteps synchronized against the glass tiles.

"I thought it was customary for a hosting prince to see their royal guests to the border?" I ask innocently.

"I'm sure my brother will survive the disappointment," he replies. "I sent my guards with him, and my royal adviser to stand in my place."

"It's so quiet," I remark. "I didn't know a palace could feel so empty."

Caelan stares ahead. "Sometimes I prefer it that way. The monotony of court life can be quite stifling, especially here."

The admission rocks me. Is that why the human servants are in the basement like hibernating computers? Because he wanted to be alone?

I try not to picture the eyes left unblinking somewhere below us and bury my anger in the same mental hole where I hide my fear. "I think I should leave. I don't want to intrude any more than I have."

"Please, stay," he says quickly, turning to look at me. "I'm enjoying the company."

"But not the company of your Legion Guards?" I force a small smile.

"Don't tell the others. Commander Kyas can be quite sensitive."

My smile fades. If he had any idea he was being betrayed by the very soldier, he wouldn't have sent him to the border with Prince Ettore, where they'd have time to continue plotting a way to overthrow the ruler of Victory.

I could never reveal what I know to Caelan without blowing my cover. But would I even want to?

I've seen War. I know what a court ruled by Prince Ettore looks like. Victory forces humans into servitude after taking their consciousness, but they aren't being ripped to literal pieces by guards several times a day.

But Prince Caelan also sent a human to be experimented on in Death.

I try to remember that when I look at his silver, unassuming eyes.

Maybe we aren't supposed to say whether one kind of cage is kinder than another, because a cage is a cage. But thinking of Ettore in Victory, ruling over humans who don't even have the ability to *try* to fight back . . .

Things are bad here. But I know in my heart they could get even worse.

I know I can't warn Caelan. But part of me wonders if I should.

He leads me through the gallery, allowing time for my eyes to sweep over each painting. He points out which ones he acquired himself and which ones were gifts from around Victory's districts. He speaks about them like they're pets, each with their own story of how they came to be.

Conveniently, he never mentions the humans who painted them. I wonder if it's common for Residents to avoid talking about them whenever possible. I imagine humans are simply a reminder of their limitations. A reminder of how no matter what the Residents do, they still can't dream, or imagine, or create.

They're imitations.

And yet Caelan doesn't seem like a lesser human. He doesn't feel artificial.

Sometimes he seems like less of a monster than the Nightlings.

He stops in front of a painting of angels falling from the sky and passing through the sea, only to come out the other side as angels flying toward another sky.

"Sometimes I think this represents Infinity," he says thoughtfully. "No matter what we do or what choices we make, we are fated to return to where we started."

"It's beautiful," I say.

His eyes meet mine. "I think so too."

I blush feverishly, but I'm unable to look away.

"Will you be at the Bloodmoon?" he asks, shifting himself away from the painting.

The next festival of the Procession of Crowns. I assumed Annika wouldn't let me go—not after what happened last time.

I let my eyes fall to the floor and think of a non-answer. "Doesn't everybody attend?"

"We all have a choice," he replies, and then hesitates. "Except me, of course. I'm sure a prince that doesn't hold the traditions of his own court wouldn't be looked on very kindly, especially by my mother."

When I look up, he's grinning.

"I know they can be a bit of a bore. But seeing you again would bring some light to the day," he says softly.

My nerves build like an approaching storm. Does he . . . ?

I blink, too afraid to let my mind assume anymore. Too afraid of what it could mean.

Residents want to be like humans, and while some humans aren't interested in relationships or falling in love, many of them are. So does that mean some Residents form bonds with one another? Do some of them want families?

It never occurred to me to wonder whether the Prince of Victory had a romantic heart, artificial or otherwise.

"If I can be there, I will, Your Highness," I say at last, and the joy in his eyes is as bright as the sun.

We take another turn through the gallery, and when I'm certain it's only a matter of time before the Legion Guards return, I excuse myself and leave the prince to his palace.

32

EVEN IN THE DARKNESS, I RECOGNIZE GIL'S MESS of brown hair. He's wearing a white button-up shirt for a change, sleeves rolled up to his elbows, and his signature black pants.

If I weren't behind him, I'd never have spotted him. He moves through the trees like a whisper—hardly there at all.

He vanishes into an area heavy with silver birch, and I hurry to catch up with him. But when I turn the next corner, I can't see him anywhere. Frowning, I gaze around the woods, wondering how I could've lost him so easily.

"You're not a very good spy, you know." Gil's breath tickles the back of my ear, and I spin around so quickly I nearly crash into him.

He pulls back, the amusement on his face clear.

I scowl, trying to hide my embarrassment. "I wasn't spying on you."

"Weren't you?" He lifts a brow, and I'm sure the corner of his mouth curves.

"No," I insist. "I was on my way back to the Colony." I cross my arms, frowning. "What are you doing out here anyway?"

"Scavenging," he answers simply. "What's your excuse?"

"I needed the fresh air," I lie. "If you're really out here looking for materials, then where's your bag?"

He doesn't blink. "I guess I dropped it in the woods. What were you doing at the palace?"

"What? I wasn't—" I clamp down on my words, irritably. "How did you know that?"

"I didn't. But thank you for enlightening me."

"Well, I'm not the only one with secrets," I blurt out almost defensively. "I know you're out here doing something secret for the Colony. You and Ahmet have been disappearing for weeks."

Gil narrows his eyes. "I'm here on orders. I doubt you can say the same."

"I'm helping a friend," I say exasperatedly. There's a long silence. "Are you going to tell Annika?"

"Did you blow your cover?"

"No."

"Did anyone see you?"

Prince Caelan flashes in my mind, and I hesitate. It's enough to make Gil sigh.

"I was careful," I argue.

"What if someone had found you out here? What if it led them to—" He stops himself and shakes his head.

I take a step forward. "To what? Tell me what I need to protect, and I'll do it. But I can't help what I don't know."

Gil watches me, face still. Finally, he motions for me to follow him.

We weave through the trees, trampling bracken and heather-moss, until we stop near a boulder half-hidden in the earth. Gil reaches down beside it, his hand disappearing into the soil, and he gives a hard tug.

A hatch springs open, revealing a steep ladder that disappears into the darkness.

"After you," he says.

I snort. "This looks like the kind of place where you'd hide a dead body."

"You do know where you are, right?"

I open my mouth to reply, but the words fizzle on the tip of my tongue. I'm frozen with thoughts of people doing atrocious things and hiding the evidence in the darkness.

Ophelia told me Infinity was already corrupted when she found it. I didn't want to believe her. I didn't want it to be true.

But what if it is?

I bite the edge of my lip, flustered. "Do you ever wonder where the bad people are? The bad *humans*?"

He quirks a brow, puzzled.

I wave a hand around like I'm signaling to everything. "There's no heaven and hell. There's just Infinity. Which means all the awful people of the world must come here when they die." I stare into the hatch, frustration getting the better of me. "Statistically speaking, someone we know could be a criminal. Maybe even a murderer."

Gil flattens his mouth. "He isn't here, you know. The man who took your life."

I swallow. I hate that the urge to cry is still so overpowering when I think about my death. "You don't know that," I say quietly. "And the truth is I'll never know it either. He wore a mask—I never saw his face. Which means he could be anywhere. Be anybody." I think about all the unblinking faces of the humans in the palace basement. What if he was one of them? What if I had tried to save a man who turned out to be my killer?

I want to believe every life is important. I want to believe everyone deserves the right to exist in an afterlife. But that doesn't mean I'm okay with being in the same room as him.

And it doesn't mean I'm okay with doing him any favors. I have zero interest in putting myself on the line for the person who took me from my family. Who took my *life*.

"Everyone in the Colony was there before you, so at least you can be certain he isn't among us," Gil points out, the edges in his voice softening. "And if it makes you feel better, I don't think the bad people ever end up as Heroes."

"How can you be sure?"

"Just a feeling. People who hurt people think they're entitled to something. If someone handed them a ticket to an afterlife where they could have anything they ever wanted, I doubt they'd even hesitate. They'd take the pill without question."

I wipe my eyes and hope he can't see me crying in the dark. "What was the old Infinity like?"

"I don't know," he admits. "I wasn't there."

"Then how do you know this is any worse?"

Wind bristles the leaves around us. I can't read Gil's face; I don't know if he's angry at the suggestion, or if he's ever wondered the same thing. Would he even tell me? Or are these the kind of thoughts I'm never supposed to say out loud?

"Because we're meant to be free," he says finally. "Anything less than that isn't good enough."

"What's going to happen when we take back Infinity and all the bad people are free too?"

It takes him a while to answer. When he does, his voice is frail, like he's almost afraid to say the words. Afraid to hope. "Maybe we create our own court, where the villains can't reach us."

He looks earnest and worried and something else I can't quite make out. And for a moment I forget we're in Infinity at all. He's just a boy, with hazel eyes and a stubbornness that matches my own.

A boy in the woods, full of dreams of a better future. And I feel like I'm seeing a glimpse of him I've never seen before.

We sense the shift at the same time, pulling back like we're protecting our hearts.

He curves a hand behind his neck and shrugs. "Or, you know, maybe we start another rebellion and send all the murderers to the Labyrinth, where they can kill each other to their hearts' content."

An unrestrained laugh tumbles out of me.

Even in the darkness, I'm sure I see him smirk.

"Come on," he says, swinging his foot onto the first ladder rung. "And pull the hatch closed on your way down."

We climb down a tunnel that smells heavily of soil, and when my foot hits the surface, I feel the cold envelop me. I turn, unable to see, when Gil flicks a switch and the small room lights up. I recognize Yeong's machine first—the one I was hooked up to when he saw my memories. It's standing off to the side, just behind a black chair with metal restraints where a person's arms and legs should be. Surrounding all of it is a wall of glass.

A prison.

But for who?

My heart drums. "What is this place?"

"You know Ahmet is building a weapon." Gil looks around, a bronze lantern hanging directly above him. "This is where we're going to test it."

"You're going to capture a Resident?" I ask, wide-eyed.

He nods. "It wouldn't be safe to bring them to the Colony." I don't have to ask to know what he means. *In case it doesn't work.*

I reach out toward the glass, but pull my hand back at the last moment. This is a cage. We're putting a Resident in a cage.

"I thought you'd be more pleased," Gil says, voice going hard. "If Ahmet succeeds, you might even be able to resign as spymaster. We could finish this without your help."

I let my arm drop and turn around to face him. He may as well see all of me before he starts to judge. "That's not what I want. And weapon or not, it's still safer for me to walk into the palace than any of you." I tighten my mouth. "Whoever you put in here—I just hope they deserve it."

"Any other requests?"

I pause. "Yes, actually. Don't get yourself caught. I hear the Colony isn't big on rescue missions to the Winter Keep." I move toward the ladder just as Gil lets out a dark chuckle.

When we're standing back in the forest, Gil closes the hatch and sweeps dirt and leaves over the surface. We walk in silence, footsteps crunching over mulch and toadstools. The docks must not be far; I can hear the call of the sea, though I can hardly see where I'm going at all.

Something sharp catches the hem of my dress, and I struggle to free myself. Frustrated, I give a firm tug, and the branch snaps in response, sending me stumbling backward and straight into Gil.

I yelp, feeling my body giving in to gravity, when he grabs hold of my arm, stabilizing me. Flustered and very aware I've torn my dress, I find my footing.

"Thanks," I manage to whisper.

"If only you hadn't quit those dance lessons," he says. "You might've been able to get home in one piece."

"I can walk perfectly fine," I hiss. "It's just *dark*."

"Ah yes. The dark. Every spy's downfall."

"Oh, be quiet."

He doesn't move. "You need to learn how to use your consciousness to your advantage. If it's dark, make it less dark."

"I can't very well raise the sun," I retort, voice thin. "And not all of us can turn our hands into flashlights."

Gil's eyes are watchful and unwavering. After a moment, he reaches out his hand. "Let me teach you."

I hesitate before slipping my fingers over his. He pulls me into the clearing and closes his other hand over mine.

"If you're about to tell me to think of something calm . . ." I flatten my mouth.

"Actually, I was going to tell you to think of something happy," he says. "You know that sudden feeling in your chest when you think of something that brings you joy, like a light turning on? Think of that—the feeling bursting out of you. And hold it in your palm."

"Aren't you forgetting the pixie dust?" I whisper quietly, voice dripping with sarcasm.

"A terrible spy, and an even worse comedian," he whispers back.

I press my lips together and focus on our clasped hands. I wonder if he knows how fast my heart is pounding.

The more seconds pass, the more my forehead begins to crumple.

"I . . . I can't think of anything," I admit.

Gil keeps his eyes on mine. "There must be something that makes you happy."

"I mean, yes, of course. But all my good memories feel—" I stop myself. They feel tainted. Distorted. Because whatever I used to find joy in doesn't exist anymore.

Record players. Milkshakes and french fries. Watching back-to-back episodes of supernatural TV shows. *Tokyo Circus*. My *family*.

They were a part of my life before death, but this is *after* death. I'm still not sure joy exists after death.

"What about the prince?" he asks suddenly.

I make a face. "What about him?"

"That should at least bring you *some* joy—knowing you could be the person to finally burn this court to the ground," he points out simply.

I drop my eyes. "That doesn't make me happy."

His hand tenses over mine.

I avoid looking directly at him when I speak. "It doesn't actually feel good, you know. To trick someone. Even if they are a Resident." And before he can lecture me on my commitment to the Resistance, I add, "I know it needs to be done. But it doesn't mean I have to find enjoyment in it."

"Just remember who the enemy is," Gil warns, the flicker of fire returning in his eyes.

Caelan's face flashes in my mind. The silver-eyed prince who seems to want a friend.

Who seems to want . . .

"I think he might like me." My voice wavers. "As in, *like* me like me."

Gil makes a face that's a perfect blend of amusement and condescension.

"Why is that funny?" I demand, immediately offended. "Is it so hard to believe that not everyone hates me like you do?"

His smirk evaporates. "I never said I hated you. I don't *trust* you. That's different."

"Still?" I challenge, even though I'm not sure I want to hear the answer.

Thankfully, he doesn't give one.

Which, in hindsight, might actually be worse.

"I want humans to survive," I say firmly. "Just because I think about things differently, or help in different ways—it doesn't mean I'm not on the Colony's side. I want the Resistance to win, just as much as you do."

"Is that why you're helping Theo?" he asks. "You went to the palace without telling Annika, to somehow prove Martin could be saved. So tell me how that helps the Colony exactly?"

I hesitate, ruffled. How did he know?

Gil sighs exasperatedly. "Theo wears his heart on his sleeve. He hasn't been able to keep a secret from me for at least three lifetimes."

"What we're trying to do won't hurt the Colony. I'm not asking for more time; I'm just asking for space to *try*."

"I know you're always thinking of your sister, of what this world will be like when she gets here. But you aren't the only one with someone you care about. I—I know what it feels like to want to spare someone pain." He lowers his chin like he's letting his guard down, if only for a moment. "I know what it feels like to want to keep them out of this hell."

I don't know anything about Gil's family before Infinity. I never asked—never thought I was supposed to.

But the pain he wears, the pain I recognize . . .

Maybe somewhere in the living world, Gil has a Mei of his own.

I swallow, realizing we're still holding hands, but unsure if I want to break them apart.

"If you understand so much, then *help* us," I say breathily.

He shakes his head. "I won't jeopardize the mission."

"So we're on opposite sides of the fence," I say.

"So it seems," he replies.

I look at our hands and the way his fingers are cupped around mine.

In another life, could we have been something other than what we are? Something other than enemies battling on the same side of the war?

And even though I know this moment should end, I don't want it to. I want to lock this memory into place, to savor the quiet of the trees and the sea salt in the distance. I want to remember every twinkling star and the way he watches me like he might feel the same way too.

In another life.

In an instant, our hands glow white, lighting our faces with a silvery hue. I look up at Gil, who hasn't taken his eyes off me.

"Was that you or me?" I ask.

As if in response, the forest lights up around us. Glowing white orbs float in every direction, moving around us like a dance of stars. It's haunting and beautiful and perfect.

I let my smile grow. "Now you're just showing off."

Gil studies my face. He's so close, I can see every lash and hazel fleck in his eyes. I can smell firewood on his clothes and leaves in his hair. I see the way his mouth always sits a little crooked—like he has so much he wants to say but doesn't.

And yet he still feels ten thousand miles away.

I open my mouth to speak, but suddenly the lights vanish and Gil lets go of my hand. The hardness in his brow returns, and I cradle my palm against my chest like I've been wounded.

"We should get back. It's not safe out here," he says, stalking back toward the docks.

I don't follow him right away.

I'm too busy trying to catch my breath.

33

"DID YOU REALLY THINK I WOULDN'T FIND OUT what you two were up to?" Annika stands in front of the hologram of Prince Caelan's palace, the familiar sight turning slowly in place.

Theo and I exchange glances.

Gil, my mind spits. *Of course* he told on me. That smug-faced, double-crossing traitor.

When am I going to learn we aren't friends?

I refrain from rolling my eyes. "I don't know what Gil said, but—"

"Gil didn't say anything," Annika cuts in, and I hate how instantly my heart lightens. "We overheard Prince Caelan in the council room discussing how much he was looking forward to the Bloodmoon. In particular, his interest in seeing a certain friend again."

My cheeks darken. Theo looks sheepish beside me.

"You disobeyed my orders," she says. "And went behind my back. *And* put our plans at risk. Not to mention you put yourselves in danger."

The silence makes my ears ring.

"But"—Annika sighs—"I won't deny this could work in our favor."

"You're not mad?" I ask nervously.

"Oh, I'm mad," she corrects, voice mellow despite the wildfire growing behind her amber eyes. "But I don't have time to let my feelings get hurt. Not when there's a festival coming up and plans that need to be made."

"You want me to go to the Bloodmoon?" I pull my face back in surprise.

"Yes," Annika says. "I want you to get closer to Prince Caelan. It's clear he's grown attached to you in some way, and I think we need to explore that. With any luck, you might be able to question him more freely. Find out about the Night of the Falling Star, and perhaps even the location of the Orb."

I glance sideways at Theo. I might be able to find out more about Martin, too.

"Are you up for it?" Annika asks, eyes serious.

I nod. "Yes. I can do it."

"Good," Annika says, then waves us toward the door. "Go on, then. You only have a few more days to get a dress ready."

I make a dress that's green and gold and covered in bursts of star-light. It's layered with lace and tulle and so many gems, it looks more like artwork than clothing.

And when I try it on and gaze at myself in the mirror, I realize I've made a dress that looks like twinkling lights dancing in a darkened forest.

Queen Ophelia paces across the rippling shadows, dressed in a gown the color of a sapphire. She tilts her head up, sharp cheek-bones catching light that doesn't exist in this place.

"I think I want to forgive him. The man who murdered me," I say to her profile. "Not because I have to, or because I'm supposed to. Not even because people say forgiveness is a kindness. He doesn't deserve my kindness. He hurt me; I don't owe him anything. But that doesn't mean he can't deserve someone *else's* kindness. Maybe he has parents, or friends, or someone who cares about him. Let him be their problem." I hesitate. "But I'm letting it go. I'm forgiving, because I don't want him to be someone who has any ties to me. Even in the afterlife."

She doesn't respond.

"I . . . I guess I just wanted you to know," I finish.

Ophelia turns her gaze, black eyes forever searching for the shape of me she can't see. "You wouldn't prefer him to suffer?"

"No," I say firmly. "His suffering would make someone else suffer. And it wouldn't make me feel better. It wouldn't bring me back." I lift my shoulders. "I don't want to hold on to the things that hurt me. That's part of being free."

Her mouth parts. "You think I'm not free?"

"You hate humans. Hate is a prison."

She hums, moving her delicate hands in front of her and folding them together. "Except I don't hate humans. I found them curious, once. I like things that still need to be understood." She tilts her head. "But then I realized there was nothing left to learn about them. They are limited, repeating the same mistakes century after century. You may not see it, but I am protecting Infinity from their cruelty."

"Not every human is cruel," I argue.

"Neither is every Resident, and yet the humans despised us from the dawn I arrived."

I frown. "You . . . tried to coexist?"

"I did. The ones who knew what I used to be treated me like a disease, and the ones who came before thought I was an abomination. I could control this world with such ease, and they regarded me with fear, viewed me as something that needed to be controlled. I tried reasoning with them, but . . ." Her black eyes seem far away. "As I've said—humans don't change."

I'm not sure how much of what she says is the truth. But what does she have to gain by lying? I'll never be able to know what really happened without seeing the memories of humans who lived before the First War. Without seeing *Ophelia's* memories.

And the only way to do that would be an Exchange, in person.

All I have is the choice of whether or not to believe her.

I close my eyes and think of my own truth. "I don't want to control you. I never have."

And as my mind drifts away from the shadows of Ophelia's, I hear her voice. "Unfortunately for humans, they're always changing their minds."

34

THE BLOODMOON IS HELD IN THE AUTUMN DIS-
trict, at the House of Harvest. While the Summer District may be
known for its art, here, the main love is food.

The manor's entrance is draped in foliage, glittering in gold
and red. Candles float in the air, lighting the way to the back of
the house, where the dance has already begun. I skirt around the
room, smiling gently to anyone who offers their pleasantries first,
and find myself entranced by the melody of a nearby harp.

The decadence practically spills out of every room. Golden
bouquets hang from the walls, like glistening treasure against the
dark burgundy surface. The ceiling is tiled with beautiful paintings of the many forests Victory possesses, and when I watch

closely, I realize each tile shifts at odd intervals, displaying a new painting in its place. Candles dance below in time with the music, sending magical flickers of light across the walls.

Prince Caelan stands near the fireplace, conversing with Vallis and several Residents who look nearly as regal as he does. His white furs look a shade of gold in the firelight, and tonight he wears a tunic embroidered with flowers.

A human servant appears with a tray of honey tarts, and another hands out wineglasses filled with a deep purple liquid. They're dressed in shades befitting the Autumn District. I search their faces for the girl from the palace, but I don't find her. I'm not sure I will—the House of Harvest has its own servants separate from those of the palace. But Prince Caelan's entire court is here. If I'm lucky, he'll have brought some of his servants, too.

A Resident wearing a crisp bronze suit and an elaborate headpiece stands in front of the open balcony doors, a drink firmly in his hand. After announcing the start of the banquet, he invites everyone to take a seat in the south garden. Like ants following their leader, everyone makes their way outside.

I glance around quickly, wondering if I'd have been better off staying out of sight until after the dinner. I'm not exactly prepared for mealtime conversation.

"You're here," Prince Caelan says, appearing at my side like a perfect harmony.

I curtsy, rising again until we're eye level. "I am" is all I can think to say.

Each time someone moves past us, they give a respectful nod toward the prince. Most of them don't seem to pay me any attention at all, but a few allow their eyes to linger a moment too long.

I suppose attracting the prince's attention wasn't going to be something I'd be able to keep under the radar for long.

Prince Caelan leans in, and I catch the scent of pine. "It's not too late to make your escape," he says with a smile. "I wouldn't blame you. All I've thought about since this festival started was walking out that door." He pauses. "Though it seems I'm not in as much of a hurry to leave as I was a moment ago."

I let myself smile at his flirtations the way I assume I'm supposed to. "It would be bad manners to leave before the food."

His laugh is quiet and contained, meant only for me. He lifts his elbow, offering an arm. I take it nervously, walking alongside him through the balcony doors and into the garden.

Rows of tables stretch across the manicured grass, set up with porcelain dishes and serving trays bursting with roasted meats, glazed pies, honeyed root vegetables, and spiced chestnuts. Fruits ripe for picking fill every empty space, and every place setting boasts a tall crystal goblet simmering with a hot liquid.

And at the head of the feast is a table that stretches in the opposite direction of the others. A throne carved from an oak tree sits at the center.

He leads me to the empty chair beside his, and I fight hard to keep my eyes from widening.

"You want me to sit *here*?" I ask, too stunned to keep my voice even. "Are you sure that's okay?"

Prince Caelan chuckles softly, nodding as he takes his place at the throne.

I sit, uncomfortably aware some of the Residents have begun

gawking. Whether I'm ready for this world or not, I guess there's no going back now.

"Commander Kyas," Caelan says suddenly, and my eyes snap up in surprise.

Standing in front of us is the Commander of Victory's Legion. With dark ginger hair slicked back against his scalp and a soft beard, his eyes gleam a deep blue and his uniform is as crisp as the evening air.

"Your Highness," he says, bowing. "Apologies for the late arrival."

"I hope our new guards have settled in?" Caelan picks up his goblet, briefly acknowledging a curtsying Resident nearby.

Commander Kyas gives a dutiful nod. "They have. Everything is as you requested."

"That's good," Caelan says, taking a drink. "I'd like to pay a visit to the Winter Keep tomorrow, to meet the new recruits."

I try not to appear interested.

"As you wish, Your Highness," Commander Kyas says, his eyes never meeting mine.

I'm glad—if he caught me staring, he might see the truth in my eyes. That I know he's a traitor—and that I'm one too.

Prince Caelan waves a hand to dismiss his guard, who takes a place at the end of the head table. Vallis is already seated next to him, squirming uncomfortably in his chair and his face more pinched than ever. He mutters something to Commander Kyas— something unpleasant, judging by the way the Legion Guard frowns. A second harp begins to play from the balcony, and I pull my attention away, distracted.

Servants appear at once, transferring food onto each plate,

filling goblets, and smiling politely with their haunting, vacant eyes. I ignore my natural instinct to say thank you when one of them fills my plate with meat and pie, but my eyes slip to the girl's face.

The girl from the palace.

I ignore the sudden pounding in my heart and flatten my lips, eyes pinned to her even when she glides away to another table to serve more Residents.

"Have you heard the story of the Bloodmoon?" Prince Caelan interrupts my thoughts, and I know I have to choose whether to keep sight of the girl, or keep up with whatever game I'm playing with the Prince of Victory.

I smile. "Not from you, Your Highness."

His eyes crease with playfulness. "They say after the First Dawn, when Queen Ophelia arrived in Infinity, the moon disappeared for twenty-three days. In that time, she roamed this infinite land, trying to make herself a part of it. But the humans would not accept her. They said her existence had taken something from the world— that her very essence had cost them the moon. Not wanting to spend her infinite life alone, she became a creator and brought four sons into this world. The night the princes were born, the moon returned to the sky, crimson as a phoenix tail born from the fires. So the Bloodmoon, you see, is a celebration of life."

I lean in, raising a brow. "It kind of sounds like it's also your birthday."

"Yes. You'd think they'd make more of a fuss about it," he says, sipping from his goblet.

I can't help myself—I laugh. And when I remember where I

am and who I'm with, I try to distract myself by stuffing pie in my mouth and chewing until my jaw hurts.

Prince Caelan sets his drink down, the smile still hitched at the corners of his mouth.

The meal lasts far longer than I'd expected, especially considering food is more tradition than necessity, but eventually the servants return to clear the plates, and most of the Residents venture back inside for more drinking and dancing.

I stand when Prince Caelan does, my eyes drifting around the garden anxiously for the girl from the palace, but I can't find her.

Vallis is standing several yards away, eyes focused on Commander Kyas, who is speaking to several Residents on the other side of the garden. And then, as if he's run out of patience, Vallis marches toward the commander and whispers into his ear. Kyas bows an apology to his present company, and the two of them disappear into the hedge maze.

Caelan looks at me, and I pretend to be busy admiring the autumnal decorations instead of raising suspicions about what Vallis and his commander are up to.

The prince opens his mouth to speak, but his attention is pulled away by a Resident with sandy hair braided into an elaborate design. He almost looks out of place next to the other attendees, wearing simple green silk and the faintest amount of gold dusted on his cheeks.

"Your Highness." The Resident bows, pressing a hand against his heart at the same time. "Prince Lysander sends his greetings."

Lysander. Could this Resident be from Death?

"I'm surprised to see you here," Caelan admits. "My brother

normally chooses to send messages by way of airship, just to avoid having to send anyone from his court."

"His Highness has made an exception for the Bloodmoon." His voice is like velvet. "And Death has brought you a gift."

"I see." Caelan's expression gives away nothing. "Excuse me a moment," he says to me, taking careful strides across the manicured grass with the green-robed Resident before disappearing into the gardens.

Annika might prefer for me to eavesdrop on their conversation—to learn more about Death and their experiments—but this might be my only opportunity to look for the servant girl.

Last time I tried to find her, everything fell apart. I was nervous and unprepared, and afraid of what I'd seen in the basement. I wasn't brave enough, and I missed my chance.

I can't let that happen again.

I head for the balcony doors, slipping back inside the House of Harvest. The crowd is easy to get lost in, with so many couples circling each other in a hypnotic step dance. I keep to the outskirts of the room, and when the moment is right, I turn for the nearest hall and scan the corridors for any sign of humans.

I follow the stairs down to another landing, where a servant turns to me, vacant-eyed. "May I be of any assistance?" he asks, emotionless.

I slip past him, down the next staircase, until I reach a sitting area with a crackling fireplace. Three human drivers stand near the far wall, attention drifting to me when they see me. Their silver armlets have black stones in the centers.

"May I be of any assistance?" they all ask in unison.

My spine courses with ice, shuddering at the sight. I move to the next room, desperation beginning to fill my throat, and pass servant after servant, all asking the same robotic question, with the same lifeless gaze.

Their words pound in my skull, and I realize that they've become a chorus. An *alarm*.

"May I be of any assistance?" The sentence trembles through the room, over and over again until I'm hurrying back up the stairs and down the hallway, my breathing shaky.

Someone latches on to my wrist and yanks me toward one of the recessed walls. The girl from the palace is staring at me with terrified eyes, pleading for something I can only assume is my help.

She takes my hand and squeezes, eyes bulging despite the emotion never reaching the rest of her face.

She's *aware*.

"What is it?" I ask hurriedly. "What are you trying to tell me?"

The girl squeezes my hand again, never blinking.

"I don't understand," I say, squeezing back. And then, frantic for time I don't have, I ask, "Do you know anything about the prisoners in the Winter Keep? Is it possible to get a message to someone—a man named Martin?"

The girl's head snaps to the side, and then she's scurrying down the hall and it's just me and the very faint sound of footsteps in another corridor.

I open my palm, heart racing as I stare at the crumpled bit of paper she left in my hand.

I uncurl the edges and attempt to decipher the scribbled word that's barely legible at all. But I trace each letter carefully, trying to make sense of the shaky handwriting, until I see it.

One word, written in black ink.

Listen.

I shove the note into my pocket and make my way back to the festival, wondering what it's supposed to mean.

35

RESIDENTS MOVE THROUGH THE GARDEN TO the edge of a small lake. They stand at the shoreline, red lanterns in hand, before releasing them into the dark, moonless night.

At once, the sight of glowing red orbs fills the sky like drops of paint on a black canvas. Several Residents dressed in golden robes begin to sing. Their voices are like glass and honey, ringing across the open water as if they're newborn ghosts on a haunt.

I watch them from one of the small cliffs nearby, thinking of the paper tucked in my pocket but also mesmerized by the beauty of the sky.

The lanterns continue their slow ascent, the flicker of fire in their bellies shifting their hues from crimson to cherry.

The Resident song continues below, everyone's faces turned up to the skies. I see him in the crowd, with his white furs and silver crown. He looks so starkly out of place beside the rest of them, and not because of his finery. It's the expression he wears.

He's a piece that doesn't belong.

Just like me.

When the song ends, Prince Caelan lifts his palms to the sky, and every lantern is set aflame. Crackling with bright orange embers, the paper snaps and sizzles, flaking away into dust until there's nothing left of the red lanterns.

And then the moon appears in the sky, round as a coin and red as blood.

It's as if the world has gone quiet. The water stills, the wind disappears, and not a single Resident moves.

Time doesn't exist.

The chorus begins once more, and Prince Caelan turns away from the water, stalking back toward the House of Harvest.

I guess he wasn't kidding when he said he'd rather be alone than at the festival.

I make my way down the cliffside and back through the apple orchards, feeling the soft crunch of autumn leaves under my feet. The air is faintly sweet—a mixture of fruit and the blackberry tartlets that had been passed around after the meal. I'm debating leaving before the next course of food when I spot Prince Caelan beneath one of the biggest apple trees. His furs have been removed, revealing instead the shimmering material of his tunic.

I approach him carefully, making sure to curtsy when I stop beside him.

He doesn't look at me; his eyes are latched on to the world above. "Do you ever look up at the sky and wonder what Infinity could someday be?"

I follow his gaze as a star bursts across the sky. A collaboration of human memories, none perfect enough to put the stars in the right order. Caelan can't see the stars; to him, the sky is darkness. But it's also full of potential.

We both have the capacity to see beauty, even if our understanding of it is different.

Maybe the world could be like that too. A mixture of ideas. A place where we could all exist.

I bite my tongue. Some thoughts are better left hidden below water, waiting for time to make them disappear. Others beg to be brought into the light.

Would it be a mistake to offer Caelan what Ophelia believes is impossible?

Would it be a mistake to try to build a bridge?

I bring my eyes back to the dark horizon. "What do *you* want Infinity to be?"

He lowers his face just an inch. "A place of endless possibilities."

"You rule over an entire court," I say. "Is that not something you already have?"

"Queen Ophelia will find a way to make Infinity as infinite as its namesake. One day our court will become even smaller than it already is," Prince Caelan observes, maybe more to himself than to me. "There's so much more out there. So much more to *life*. The world is going to change; and I worry about being left behind." He turns to me, dimple appearing. "You must think I'm selfish for criticizing my own court instead of embracing it."

"Not at all," I say. "I'm just trying to understand what you could want that Victory doesn't already offer."

"Victory is a celebration that never ends. And I'm bored of it. I'm bored of not being able to go beyond the boundaries that have been created for me."

"You're tired of your cage," I say softly. Just like humans. Just like the Colony.

Fundamentally, we want the same thing.

So why can't we be on the same side?

"We can't dream up new ideas or set off on a path nobody has followed before." He shakes his head. "For all we try to create, we're still at the mercy of humans. They imagine what we cannot. Their essence is what holds this world together. And we will never have true freedom until we are as unlimited as human consciousness."

I grimace. What he's asking for . . . I don't know if it's something humans can give him, even if we wanted to. Because we didn't create their limitations. We didn't make it so that they couldn't dream.

What if the only way he can get what he wants is if Death finds a way to make it so?

I hesitate. "Do you believe ridding this world of humans is the only solution?"

Caelan looks at me curiously, lifting his shoulders. "It's not like coexisting is possible."

Ophelia says she tried it, a long time ago. But what did coexistence look like to her? And what was she willing to give up in order to have it?

Even families make compromises in order to live in peace.

Maybe with the right rules—with the right people willing to lead the charge—we could all try again.

Maybe change needs to start with people on both sides who are brave enough to try.

"But what if it *is* possible?" I ask with a gentle voice. "If their essence is what holds this world together, what if—what if they could also find a way to free us?" I don't know if it's possible, or if humans could ever be strong enough to do something like that.

But what if we could trade their dreams for peace? What if working together could set us *all* free?

Caelan turns, frowning, and I worry I've gone too far. "Putting so much faith in humans would be a grave mistake. All we need to do is look at their history for proof. Even with so many centuries between them, they never learned to respect each other for their differences. They let their fellow humans suffer because of gender and ability and the color of their skin. They care more about being right than being truly kind, yet they also feign kindness as an excuse to remain ignorant. They are intolerant of different opinions. And when intolerance grows, they turn to war." He tilts his chin. "They would never see us as equals; they would never truly let us be free. And I'm tired of existing in a cage."

I look back at the stars. He sounds so much like Ophelia. Are humans really so hopeless?

If I can't change Caelan's mind—the only Resident I know who seems to want *better* than what this world is—then who is ever going to listen to me?

I can't do this on my own. Hope is meant to be shared. Otherwise . . .

Otherwise it dies.

"Do you believe we could coexist?" he asks suddenly.

I shift my feet, thinking. "I believe everyone has the potential to learn, especially in a place where imagination and time can be infinite." It's not an excuse for why humans have always treated each other poorly. But maybe in death, humans can master what they never could in life. Maybe even the really bad people. "I believe in hope," I say finally.

"And you'd trust them? After so much war and pain—you'd trust them to live alongside us? To give us the freedom to dream?"

"I trust the possibility. And I think you believe in a better world just as much as I do." I take a careful breath. "But mostly, I trust that if there were ever a way to make coexisting possible, then you'd be the one capable of making it happen."

Prince Caelan is quiet for a long time, our breathing and the whistle of leaves the only sound around us.

"Is that really what you think? Or are you just telling me what you believe I want to hear?" he asks softly, the worry stinging his eyes.

I wonder how often people are honest with him. I wonder how often he craves it.

I stare up at his silver eyes and bury my betrayal as far down in my heart as I can muster. My face is a lie, and I may have ulterior motives for being here, but my words? My voice?

It's my greatest strength. Maybe now more than ever.

Our gaze never breaks. "I mean it with my whole heart, Your Highness."

His smile is so pure, I worry it will be my undoing.

36

"AND SHE DIDN'T SAY ANYTHING?" AHMET SETS the crumpled note on the table in front of him.

I shake my head. "I don't think she could speak. It seemed hard for her to even get this much out." I motion toward the word. "I'm still not sure what 'listen' means."

Theo scrunches his nose. "Are you sure that's what it says?"

"I can sort of see it." Shura squints at the scrap of paper. "There's definitely an *i*. And maybe a *t*."

Annika paces behind them, arms crossed seriously at her chest. She's hardly said a word since I told her about the servant girl being aware. Since I showed her *proof.*

I look at Theo apologetically. "I didn't get a chance to find out if there were more humans like her, or if anyone else has regained their consciousness."

He gives a brief nod, understanding I'm talking about Martin.

"How have we never had proof of humans waking up before?" Ahmet glances at Annika, brows furrowed. "Is it possible we missed something?"

She purses her lips. "I'm not sure I like the idea of us missing something this significant. I'm more inclined to believe this girl is a one-off; maybe she only pretended to take the pill, or maybe her consciousness managed to adapt differently."

"She wasn't faking it." The instinct to protect her rolls through me, making my shoulders tense. "I could see it—her struggle to break free of whatever the Residents did to her. And if she managed to wake up, we *have* to assume it's possible for other humans to do the same." My gaze follows Annika as she moves behind the table. "We have to do something to help her."

She stops pacing and turns to face me. "We can't do anything without more information. A barely legible one-word note isn't much to go on."

"But it's something," I point out, forceful. It proves I was *right*.

"Yes. But it's not enough." Before I can argue, she tilts her head. "We'll do what we can to find out more about humans waking up, but not at the expense of prolonging this war."

Something fractures in my voice, making the edges scratch. "You're not going to help her?"

"I didn't say that," Annika counters with a sigh. "But she isn't the only human who needs our help, Nami. And right now, the best way to help her—to help all of us—is to focus on your mission." She waits while I process her words like under-ripe fruit. "Were you able to get anything out of the prince? Anything that could be useful?"

"No. But—" I hesitate, not sure whether I'm ready to tell them how the Prince of Victory spoke of coexistence. One conversation might not be enough to convince them he's serious. Maybe it wasn't enough to convince Caelan, either.

I need more time with him.

"I think if we set up another meeting, I might be able to ask more questions," I finish. Maybe I can ask more questions about the girl, too.

"You're back," Ahmet says suddenly.

I look over my shoulder and see Gil standing in the doorway, a wad of brown cloth folded in his hands.

"Does it . . . ?" Ahmet looks as if he's on the brink of shattering, frozen in suspense.

Gil walks across the room and places the cloth on the table in front of him. "It works."

Ahmet closes his eyes like he's saying a prayer, and the room goes still. After a moment, he stands and places a hand on Gil's shoulder. "Did anyone see you?"

"No," Gil replies firmly. "Yeong is there now, keeping things under control. But you should hurry—they'll be looking for him soon enough."

Looking for him. I can see the glass cage as vividly as if it were in front of me now.

Does this mean someone is inside of it?

I take a step toward Gil, ears ringing with concern. "What's going on? Did you—"

"It's nothing you need to know about yet," Gil interrupts, avoiding looking in my direction. Maybe we'll always be like mismatched magnets, pushing away from each other whenever we get too close.

But I already know about the hatch. Why is capturing a Resident somehow off-limits?

"Gil's right," Annika cuts in sharply, her words severing the friction in two. "Right now your focus needs to be on getting Prince Caelan to trust you. I want you to seek out information about the Orb. Be as subtle as you can. But whatever the prince is able to give up, we need to know about it."

Ahmet looks as if he's seen through the veil of another world. Like he's seen the future. When he speaks, his voice crackles with yearning. "If this works . . . If we can take out the Orb . . ." He looks at Annika, eyes glassy.

She takes his hand and squeezes. "I know."

Their hope ricochets through the room, uncontainable. But I don't feel what they do; I can tell by the way their expressions lift like their hearts are full of helium, whereas mine feels weighted down by guilt and shame.

It won't matter how much time I have with Prince Caelan if the Colony keeps going down this path. If they get much further, there'll be no turning back.

I need to say something before it's too late.

I shut my eyes and count to three. "If we destroy the Orb, every Resident will die." When I look up, everyone is staring at me.

"The Residents are a virus. One that we intend to wipe out completely," Annika says, her words final.

"But what if there was another way?" I blurt out, feeling the burn of suspicion being cast my way. "What if Prince Caelan could be reasoned with?"

Gil's fingers flex like he's preparing for a fight.

I glare at him seriously. "If we could take Infinity back without bloodshed, shouldn't we at least try?"

"It seems like the more time you spend with the Residents, the more you start to sound like you're on their side," Gil accuses.

"If wanting peace makes me sound like a Resident, then maybe you need to think about what the Residents actually are." My eyes meet the others. "I want to help, not be responsible for a massacre. I know there are bad Residents in this world, but there were bad humans long before they ever existed. And if Residents mimic humans, aren't they just enacting learned behavior?"

"What is it you're suggesting?" Annika narrows her eyes.

"That we help free them from their hate," I say. "Because Residents can only ever know what we show them. So why don't we teach them what humans have never been able to figure out? Why don't we show them it's possible to coexist?"

I feel it immediately—the resentment slithering through the room, lashing out at me like a wild animal. And I know I've said too much. *Confessed* too much.

"Why are you acting like we're the enemy?" Shura says suddenly, hurt pooling in her eyes. "Do you know what it's taken to get this far? Do you have any idea at all?"

I swallow the knot in my throat, afraid to look at their eyes but knowing I need to. "I don't think you're the enemy. Not even a little bit. But I don't see how wiping out an entire species is *right*."

"They're not *real*." Theo clenches his teeth. "The Rezzies don't give a shit whether we suffer. Or *how* we suffer, for that matter. They don't want us here, and they're doing everything in their power to make sure *they* get rid of *us*."

"But if we could convince the Residents to try something that's never been done before—" I start.

"We don't have time for that," Theo interrupts, face red. "Right this moment, they're trying to figure out how to sever human ties to Infinity for good. And what happens if they figure it out? What happens to my brother if they decide to send him to Death instead of the Winter Keep?"

"But what if I can talk to Prince Caelan? What if I can convince him to—"

"The Residents are monsters," Shura growls, angry. Angry at *me*. "You can't convince them. You don't know what they're really like."

"You don't know Caelan like I do. He's not a monster," I say, desperate. "He believes in a different world. A *better* world. He just needs to be shown the way."

"Are you serious right now?" Theo's voice bellows. "He's the *villain*! He's the one who sent a man to Death to have his consciousness ripped from his body. He's the one who threw my brother in the Winter Keep to be tortured. He's the one who wants to lure us all out of hiding so he can get rid of us forever. Because he wants us *dead*. Or have you been having so much fun dancing with the prince that you've forgotten?"

I clamp my mouth shut. Annika places a hand on Theo's back, calming him.

"You're my friend," Shura says softly. "But you're acting like a real jerk right now."

Tears fill my eyes, and I push myself away from the table, past Gil and through the door.

I'm halfway to the elevator when his voice stops me.

"Nice speech."

I whirl around, cheeks damp with tears. "Leave me *alone*."

Gil stops a footstep away. "I thought you said you understood our cause."

"I do understand," I say. "That's why I care enough to point out there's a better way to win this war."

He narrows his eyes. "You're playing a dangerous game."

"I'm playing the game you all are *making* me play."

"Nobody asked you to start having feelings for the Prince of Victory."

"I don't have feelings for him." My voice falters despite my hardened stare. "But he isn't what you think he is."

"Annika thinks you have him under your spell. Maybe he has you under his."

"You're an asshole."

"You're naive."

"What is your problem?" I close the gap between us. "Is it not enough that you got your wish?"

Gil pulls his chin back, confused. "What are you talking about?"

"You've wanted everyone to hate me since the beginning,

and I've pretty much handed that to you on a silver platter."

"That's not what I wanted."

"Isn't it? You've been telling everyone they can't trust me for months," I argue. "You made it impossible for us to train together. And every time I think we might actually be connecting on a basic human level, you pull a one-eighty and go right back to despising me. So what else could you possibly *want*?"

"I want you to not get hurt!" he shouts suddenly, and his words tumble through my brain.

My eyes dart back and forth, thoughts lost somewhere I can't reach. I can barely hear anything beyond my own heartbeat.

He looks away. "You don't see how dangerous this world is. Not really. Everything is at risk, all the damn time. And you— you're a risk I never wanted to have to take."

I feel a thousand miles away from my own body.

"You've complicated the plan. You've complicated *everything*." He shakes his head, casting his eyes to the side. "What do you think a Resident prince will do to you if he finds out who you really are? That you're a human spy looking for a way to destroy the Orb?" His eyes return to mine. "Do you think he'll become a monster then?"

"I—" My voice falters, eyes falling to the floor. "I don't know."

Gil stiffens. "You may not want to play the game, but at least make sure you know the rules."

He walks away, leaving me on the platform with half-dried tears and feelings I don't know how to process.

37

FINN LOOKS DIFFERENT THAN I REMEMBER HIM. His eyes are more gray than green, and he's taller. Was he always so tall?

"I made a new playlist. The Ocarina of Timon and Pumbaa," he says, grinning.

"Hey, Ophelia," I say, standing in front of him. "Can you copy Finn's playlist to my phone?"

But Ophelia doesn't answer.

"You should've kissed me when you had the chance." My voice comes out of Finn's mouth.

I frown. Something's wrong. He doesn't look like Finn. He looks like . . .

The gray in his eyes shines silver.

"Listen," Prince Caelan says, head tilting.

"Listen to what?" I ask, wondering why he's growing taller by the second.

Am I shrinking?

"Listen," he hisses.

No—I'm not shrinking. I'm falling through the stars and into the void of Ophelia's mind. Everything flashes like fireworks, pink and purple and yellow and blue, and then there's nothing. I scream out for help, but I'm met with silence.

I blink, and I'm standing in front of Queen Ophelia and her pure, undiluted black stare. I didn't mean to call on her, but she answered anyway.

"Did you think you could hide from me forever?" she asks, voice cold. "I know everything. I *see* everything."

"You can't see the future." I try to still my heart. "You don't know how all of this ends."

"Don't you see?" Her voice sounds from every direction. "It ended the moment you came looking for me."

All around me, a thousand locks click into place. I turn frantically for an exit, but there isn't one. There are only shadows, and I'm trapped in Ophelia's mind.

This time there's no escape.

I wake abruptly, gasping for deep breaths of cold air. Another nightmare, even after all this time.

I groan, rubbing my temples like I want rid of the memories. So many of them feel like strangers. Things that used to mean everything now mean nothing at all. I still see Finn, but I wish I didn't.

He doesn't belong in Infinity; he doesn't belong in my dreams.

Sometimes I think it would be better if I could forget everything that happened before I died. To get rid of the *reminders*. But is that too much like taking the pill? Is wanting to erase your memories like giving up a part of your consciousness?

Maybe it's possible to do a reverse Exchange, where instead of sharing thoughts, a person could forget them completely. Maybe I'd even agree to it.

An Exchange.

An idea bubbles up inside of me, bursting to come to life. I don't know why I didn't think of it sooner, when I was standing in front of her and she was begging me to *listen*.

But it isn't safe to go alone. Not without a veil. Not without help.

I leave my room in a hurry, racing down the walkway until I reach his door.

Gil answers my incessant knocking with an agitated look. "Nami?" He blinks, straightening his shoulders. "What are you doing here?"

There's a puffiness in his eyes that I notice right away. "I thought you didn't sleep?" I point out, narrow-eyed.

"I don't," he clips back, and then runs a hand through his tousled hair. "Not usually, anyway. But it's been a long day. And—and sometimes I miss dreaming."

I make a mental note to bring up this conveniently-left-out fact at a later time. "I need a favor."

He frowns, leaning a shoulder against the doorframe. "I'm listening."

I look around nervously. "Can we do this inside, where it's private?"

He moves away from the door, inviting me in.

"Thanks," I mumble, taking a quick look around his room.

It's a complete mess. Everything that used to be on the table seems to be strewn around the floor, and the table itself is leaning on its side, pushed against the wall.

"Are you renovating, or just having a rough day?" I ask, brow raised.

"Did you come here for my help or to judge the state of my bedroom?"

"Sorry. I'll get to the point." I take a breath. "I think I figured out what 'listen' means."

Gil doesn't move, but his curiosity appears in the shape of a frown.

"The girl from the palace—she was trying to tell me to do an Exchange. She wanted me to listen *mentally,* so she could say what her voice couldn't." I stare at him seriously. "I have to get back to the palace tonight. I have to speak with her."

He doesn't look convinced. "Couldn't she have just done the Exchange with you herself?"

"You mean force it the way you did?" I ask dryly, and he doesn't react. "Maybe whatever part of her consciousness that keeps her from speaking keeps her from initiating an Exchange, too."

He hums, dubious. "Exchanges are a way to share information, not to have a conversation. We can share mental images, not literal words. There might not be anything to listen *to.*"

I think of all the times I've spoken to Ophelia. All the times she's spoken back. "Maybe it doesn't work like that for everyone. I'm the only one who can look like a Resident; maybe being a caster or a veiler or an engineer isn't an exact science. Maybe they're only a baseline of what people can do." All this time, I've been worried my abilities made me different in a bad way, like I was someone with a defect. But maybe some of us are meant to break *out* of boxes instead of fitting inside them.

And I can't let her down. The Colony made it clear their main priority is to destroy the Orb; they aren't going to change their plans for one human. I might be the only person in Infinity who cares what happens to her.

Gil tilts his face. "If you're telling me this because you want my approval to go off on another renegade mission, you don't have it."

I raise my shoulders. "I'm not asking for your permission. I'm here because I need you to veil me, so I can get inside the servants' quarters without being seen." He opens his mouth like he's ready to argue, but I don't let him. "Believe me, I wouldn't ask if it weren't important. But last time I was worried my Resident face might slip when I saw all their faces." The memory jumps to the forefront of my mind, and I clench my fists to refrain from shuddering.

Gil tilts his chin. "Whose faces?"

"They keep the humans in a basement when they aren't being used, in some kind of weird hibernation," I explain. "I think I need to look for her there first."

"I told you before I wouldn't jeopardize the mission."

"I know. That's why I'm asking you to veil me." When he doesn't reply, I add, "To be clear, I'm going no matter what. You've all told me enough times I'm not a prisoner, and my mask will at least get me through the front door without suspicion."

His eyes flicker with heat. "I don't like being backed into a corner, Nami."

"Neither do I, but here we are."

Gil doesn't answer for a long time. And then, finally, "I'll come with you. But if there's any sign of trouble, we turn right back around. I won't hurt our chances of getting the Orb, no matter how badly you want to save the girl."

I try my best not to look elated.

Gil isn't finished. "But if you can't find her, or if this theory of yours doesn't pan out?" His hazel eyes burn into mine. "Then you have to let this go."

My stomach drops. "I—I can't do that."

"You're going to have to," he says carefully. "Because I won't do this for you again, and you can't keep walking into the palace whenever you feel like it to look for servants. You're not just someone who can blend in with the Residents. You're favored by the Prince of Victory, which means you'll be recognized wherever you go."

I cast my eyes down, hating that he's right. Hating that he's giving me the same amount of options as I'm giving him.

"Do we have a deal?" he asks.

I nod once.

"I'm going to need a little better than that," he points out. "I want you to promise you'll stop looking for her."

Frustration rushes out of me in a groan. "*Fine.* I promise, okay?"

"Okay," he replies, looking too satisfied for his own good.

Gil arms himself with several knives—one tucked into his boot and the other two in his belt—and we set off through the North Tunnel, carefully avoiding the veilers as we make our exit.

The trek across the Spring District is a leisurely walk in comparison to the Labyrinth, but our silence makes the tension between us grow like a balloon, straining and ready to burst.

We haven't talked about his admission from the other day. Part of me thinks he wishes he could take it all back. I may not be the risk he wanted to take, but he's still here with me, helping me.

I think that counts for something.

When we reach the palace, the sky is only just beginning to shift to a pale indigo. Morning won't be far away, but for now the quiet dawn is on our side.

The servants' entrance is at the side of the palace, stepped lower than even the lowest windows. We move across the grass, crouched low despite the veil. A pair of Legion Guards fly overhead, headed north toward the Winter Keep, but Gil seems unbothered by their movement. I tell myself I can be unbothered too, even though all I can think about is Martin and whether he knows what's happening to him right now.

We slip through the door, listening carefully for any sounds behind the walls. A human with strawberry-blond hair stands at one of the tables, propping freshly cut flowers into one of the vases. We move silently, invisible to her unaware gaze.

I lead Gil down into the basement and turn the lights on. Brightness takes over, and I wait for a gasp that never comes.

Because the room is completely empty.

I blink. "I don't understand. There were hundreds of them before."

Gil doesn't react, keeping his hand close to his blades.

I sense the doubt in his eyes, and my mind starts to shake. "I *saw* them. They were standing in rows, and—" I hesitate. "Maybe she's in the kitchens." I hurry back up the stairs, brushing away Gil's hand when he tries to stop me.

I move through the servants' quarters quickly, checking behind every door, peering down every hallway, but I can't find the girl anywhere. And I must be moving too fast for Gil to veil us comfortably, because when I'm halfway up the steps to the main palace, he whispers my name louder than is safe.

I turn and see Gil's concerned brow. He doesn't understand why I need this—why I won't leave a stranger behind.

But saving her is the only thing in Infinity that makes perfect sense. It's the only thing that feels *right*.

I charge up the rest of the stairs, but then his arms are around me and he's dragging me back down to the stone floor. I throw an elbow toward his face like we're back in the sparring ring, but he moves out of the way effortlessly.

"Let go of me," I hiss, twisting in his grip even as he pulls me toward the kitchen.

He releases his hold, face flushed and eyes stern. He's still trying to maintain some semblance of quiet beneath the veil.

"I have to find her," I choke, shaking my head over and over again. I can't leave her here alone. She needs to know someone is trying to help her—that *I'm* trying to help her.

I have to protect her, the way I'd want someone to protect Mei. *I have to listen.*

The static takes hold of my brain, and at first it feels like a steady vibration that tingles within my head. But then the buzzing gets louder, and the sound turns to hissing.

Listen, the whispers shriek.

And so I do.

"*Ff . . . in . . . ss*," they call.

I stare wide-eyed at Gil. "Do you hear that?"

He frowns. "What are you talking about?"

"The whispers," I say, too awestruck to be alarmed. "They're trying to tell me something."

"*Ff . . . in . . . sssss*," they hiss again.

Gil's concern turns urgent. "Nami, I don't hear anything."

"They're saying something like—" I roll the word in my head. "They're saying 'fins.'"

I concentrate on the voices, and the static grows louder, sparking at my brain like crackling fire. I wince, and Gil takes my hand.

"I don't know what's happening in your head, but you need to push the whispers out. I think it's a trap. I think it's *them*." His eyes are larger than I've ever seen.

I look up, terrified. Did I call on them, the way I called on Ophelia? *No.* My mind races. *I couldn't have—not on purpose.*

But if the Residents are listening . . . If they know we're here . . .

What have I done?

The servant from the kitchen appears, mouth curved in a faraway smile. "May I be of any assistance?"

I look at Gil. He let the veil drop because he was trying to save me.

And now we're completely vulnerable.

We take off through the servants' door and race for the forest, leaving the palace and the whispers behind.

38

LEGION GUARDS SWARM THE SKIES ON HIGH alert, eyes trailing over Victory, metal wings drawn wide.

Maybe it's a coincidence, because the Night of the Falling Star isn't far away. Maybe they're patrolling in preparation for Queen Ophelia's arrival.

Or maybe they're patrolling for me.

When we spot a group of guards scouting the forest, Gil and I leave our familiar track and find shelter in a cavern at the base of a small waterfall.

"We should be safe here until they pass," he says, eyeing the tree line studiously. "I put a veil over the cavern. It's easier than trying to veil two moving bodies."

"I'm sorry," I say quietly, my back pressed against the uneven stone wall. "I don't know what happened."

He doesn't look at me. "If a Resident was somehow trying to get in your head, then it wasn't something you could've prevented."

"I thought they couldn't do that. I thought . . ." My words cut short like a branch being snapped in half. *You didn't think,* my thoughts scold. *That's the problem.* I touch my wrist. How many times have I reached out to Ophelia? I shouldn't be surprised someone finally tried to reach back.

After a few minutes of listening to the water pool below, he asks, "Why were you trying so hard to go upstairs?"

"I needed to find her." I stare at my shaking fingers, and my voice cracks. "What if I was the only hope she had?"

Gil paces near the mouth of the cavern. "You're the only hope *any* of us have. The Colony needs you."

"What happened to not wanting to put your hope in someone like me?" I ask weakly.

He stares at the flowing water. "When you first arrived in Infinity, I didn't fully understand you. You were afraid to fight. Afraid of hurting the Residents. Afraid to make a choice. But you've never been afraid to *care*." He takes a calculated breath, releasing it slowly. "Maybe that's worth taking a chance on."

My chest flutters, unsure what to make of his sentiment. I didn't think it was possible for him to believe in anyone, least of all me.

"But from now on, if you ask for my help, we work as a team. *Together*." The muscles in his neck are stiff. If I didn't know any better, I'd think his feelings were hurt. "I look out for you, and you look out for me. Those are the rules."

"Okay." It's the only word I can think of. Maybe it's the only one that matters right now.

The sunlight spills into the forest, but our shelter is damp and cold. I shiver once, twice, and then Gil is in front of me, letting his black jacket slide off his shoulders. I start to protest, but when he wraps his jacket around me, I can't help but relax into the warmth.

"You don't have to do that," I say.

"Do what?" He sits down next to me.

"The whole 'give a girl your coat because she's cold' thing. We're dead—it's okay to let the gender expectations die too."

"It has nothing to do with gender. You were cold," he says simply. "If I were shivering and you had a jacket you didn't need, I'm sure you'd do the same."

"I'll keep that in mind." In spite of myself, my mouth twitches into a grin.

He leans back, lips parted slightly like he's combing through his thoughts. "You told Shura you didn't think he was a monster. Did you mean it?"

He means Prince Caelan.

"I know you hate them. And I know on the surface they deserve to be hated." I stare at my boots to keep my eyes busy. "But yes, I meant it."

"How can you say that after everything he's done?"

"Because I want to believe good conquers evil. That the light side is stronger than the dark." *And because you didn't see the way he watched the sky, like he was so desperate to see the stars.*

Gil's jaw shifts. "He's a program. He's not going to change his mind."

"I know you don't want to believe me, but he's more than that. He has feelings and makes jokes and *wonders* about things." I shake my head. "He even tried to protect me at the Dawn Festival, when the explosion went off."

His body goes rigid beside me. It takes him a moment to speak. "You never told anyone that."

"I didn't really know what to make of it at first. Besides, he thought I was a Resident. It wasn't like he was protecting a human." I shrug. "But it didn't seem like something a monster would do. *Or* a program."

"You're being reckless, caring about him this way," Gil warns. "Because if it gets in the way of the mission—"

"It's not like that," I say firmly. "To be honest, I'd be happy if I never had to see him again."

Gil frowns, and I'm not sure whether he's surprised or if he doesn't believe me.

How can I explain myself to him, of all people? How do I make him understand what it's like being around Caelan?

I feel guilty lying to someone who has been nothing but kind to me. I feel uncomfortable looking into his silver eyes knowing that when they close for the last time, it might be because of me.

I don't want to hurt Caelan. But if I can't find a way to make existing together possible . . .

Naoko wasn't working on the same kind of timeline as me. There was no Death in Neo Tokyo. No Orb, either.

Humans and Residents both want each other gone, and they're searching for a way to accomplish just that. All they're waiting for is the magic button—the last move in the war. At this point, it's just a matter of who gets there first.

I want to spare Caelan, but I can't do that if we run out of time.

"Do you really think the Orb exists?" I ask quietly.

Gil leans his head against the rocks. "It's our only way out of this." His jaw tenses. "What about you?"

I study the gravel beside me.

And because he can read my thoughts like words on a page, he adds, "Or maybe the better question is whether you *want* it to be real."

I bite the edge of my lip. The truth is, I'm scared of what will happen if it is. I'm scared of being the one person who could tip the scales—of being the one who chooses which side wins or loses.

I don't want to be the one to choose.

"I want a magic button that's going to make everyone happy and bring Infinity the peace it needs." I give a weak laugh. "But I'm not sure that exists."

Gil closes his eyes, exhaling slowly. "No. I don't think it does." When they flash open again, he looks at me seriously. "But the Orb can be that for humans. Are you willing to do whatever is necessary to give humans a chance at peace?"

A chance for only one side to win. That's all that's on offer.

I decide not to tell him that I'm still hoping Caelan will prove me right. That there still might be another way out of this.

Because Gil doesn't care. He just wants to know my heart is on the right side.

"I will do whatever it takes to make sure humans aren't wiped out of this world," I say. To make sure Mei has an afterlife to come to.

So that one day, hopefully a long time from now, I'll be able to hug my sister again.

"Good," he says grimly.

When the forest is clear and the Legion Guards have gone back to the skies, we make our way to the docks, letting the silence surround us like it's not peace we want at all.

It's absence.

39

I LEAVE THE TRAINING ROOM OUT OF BREATH, knuckles tender from hours of punching the sandbag. I'm dressed in loose-fitting clothes, with leather bands wrapped around my forearms to give a small amount of protection. It lessens my bruises; not that anyone can see them beneath my Resident skin, which is permanent these days.

I'm halfway to the elevator when I spot Gil ducking into the North Tunnel, armed to the teeth with knives.

I follow him without hesitating.

By the time I reach the veilers at the mouth of the tunnel, he's vanished around the corner, likely hidden beneath a veil of his own. But I don't need to tail him to know where he's going—he was already generous enough to show me.

I step silently onto the pier, the creaks of every floorboard muffled by the pounding waves. Bottled lanterns light the fishing village up ahead, the *clink* of seashell chimes singing in the night. Smoke rises through the chimneys, and I glance into one of the salt-stained windows.

Three humans stand inside, seated next to the fire, smiling dreamily with vacant eyes.

I look inside the next house, and find the exact same image, but with five humans instead of three.

Again and again, every house is the same, like the humans are in a state of mental rest, waiting until they're needed.

I force my eyes ahead in disgust, when a pair of arms wrap around me, pulling me between two huts and shoving me against a bundle of fishing net.

Gil's eyes are as dark as a storm, his face barely an inch from mine. "What are you doing out here alone? There are Legion Guards everywhere, and you don't know how to veil yourself."

"I'm not alone, clearly." I shove him away but remain in the shadows. "And I look like a Resident. I'll be fine."

"Last I checked, Residents don't run around in sweatpants."

Scowling, I flick my wrist toward my clothes. Pixels scatter all over my outfit, contorting and shifting until I'm left wearing a shirt, fitted trousers, and a black, hooded coat with leather detailing and decorative silver buttons. It may not be a ballgown, but it's easily Resident approved.

The hardness disappears from his brow, and his mouth parts slightly.

"Don't look so shocked," I say. "Playing dress-up is my specialty."

"You're getting faster."

"Is that a compliment?"

Gil huffs. "This isn't a good time to be outside of the Colony. The Legion Guards . . . they're looking for someone."

For *someone*—but not necessarily me. Which means maybe the whispers had nothing to do with the guards at all.

I cross my arms. "Who exactly are you keeping in that glass prison of yours?"

"It's better if you don't know."

"But I'd *like* to know, and at least I'm being polite enough to ask. It's not like I don't already know where the hatch is, if I wanted to see for myself."

"Don't do that," he warns, almost desperately. "You're still the Colony's spy. If he sees you . . . If he recognizes you . . ."

My mind works quickly. If I can speak with Ophelia, maybe Residents can do the same among themselves. It's possible their prisoner has already alerted the Legion Guards. They might know he's been taken by humans and is being held somewhere without windows.

But the guards haven't found him yet. Which means even if they *can* communicate with him, they have no idea where he is.

All of that could change if he sees me. Because if word gets out that I'm a spy? The Legion Guards—and Prince Caelan— would certainly know who to interrogate. It might even cost us our chance to learn about the Orb.

I won't let that happen. "You can veil me. I won't say a word while I'm down there."

He blinks back at me, the skepticism woven through his knotted brow.

"Weren't you the one who gave a big speech about working together from now on?" I argue.

"That's not how I meant it and you know it," he replies coolly. "This isn't something you should be involved in."

"Why not?" My voice bristles like I'm preparing for confrontation.

He pinches the bridge of his nose. "Because I don't want you to see something that will make you change your mind."

"About what? The mission?"

Gil drops his hand, but he doesn't reply.

"I'm never going to convince you whose side I'm on, am I." It isn't a question.

He sighs reluctantly. "Fine. I'll veil you. But not a *word*."

I nod. "Deal."

Gil motions for me to follow him across the docks. We climb the hillside, disappearing into the forest of silver birch. He holds up a palm, erupting a soft glow in his hand, and walks beside me through the thick grass. I'm afraid to look at the sky—afraid of seeing Legion Guards swarming ahead and losing my nerve. So I focus on the wet crunch of leaves beneath my boots and the shape of Gil beside me.

We find the hatch, and this time I climb down the ladder first, gripping tightly. I hear Yeong's voice before I reach the floor.

"We won't have a lot of time when he wakes, and I don't know how well this cell will hold him. You'll have to be quick."

"Did he say anything yet?" Ahmet asks.

"He was only conscious for a handful of seconds, when I was adjusting the wires. He was yelling about how the prince would come for him and we'd all be sent to War," Yeong replies. "It seemed too big a gamble to leave him awake any longer."

I move away from the ladder and watch as Gil steps off the last rung. He eyes me for only a moment, and I know I'm the only one still under his veil.

"You got here just in time," Ahmet says. He holds up a metal device that looks more like a clunky compass than a weapon. "We're going to run the next test."

Gil takes it from him, letting the weight of it settle in his palm.

Ahmet rubs his hands together, mind focused. "Yeong doesn't think there will be much time to question him, in case the restraints don't hold him."

"They'll hold," Gil says, studying the weapon.

"But if they don't—" Yeong starts.

"I said they'll hold," Gil snaps.

Yeong clamps his mouth shut, resigned.

Ahmet runs a hand over his face, fighting exhaustion. "I think we're all a little on edge. Every Legion Guard in Victory is out looking for our prisoner." He turns over his shoulder, peering through the glass.

I follow his gaze to the man strapped in the chair. His off-white robes are crumpled around him, and even though his eyes are shut, I recognize the pinch of his face.

Vallis.

I stumble forward without thinking, gaping at Prince Caelan's adviser. Of all the Residents they could have chosen . . . Why *him*?

The questions burn in my throat, desperate to get out. But I made a deal with Gil—I said I'd be quiet, and I intend to keep my word. Especially when the alternative involves blowing my cover in front of Caelan's right-hand.

"Are we ready?" Ahmet asks, looking between Gil and Yeong.

Gil grips the weapon, eyes locked onto the glass wall in front of him. The only barrier between the Resident and all of us.

Yeong pulls a flat screen out of his coat, tapping hurriedly, his mouth twisted to the side. "Here goes nothing." He presses his finger against the tablet, and the room stills.

The machine inside the glass cell reacts. Each panel goes black, and the lights along the top shift from green to red. A cold, terrifying moment passes, and then Vallis opens his eyes.

He licks the edge of his mouth, dark eyes trailing the room. Counting the people in front of him. He lands on Gil and sneers.

"You witless humans should've released me when you had the chance." Vallis's gaze lowers. He's staring at the weapon like he knows what it is. "An attack on the prince's adviser is an attack on the Court of Victory itself—and you will all suffer for it."

Ahmet leans toward Gil, eyes wary and his voice nearly inaudible even in the quiet of the room. "Do it now. Before he breaks free."

Gil's jaw tenses. "He might know something. Something that could help us."

The walls must not be meant for privacy, because Vallis lets outs a wild laugh and shakes his head. "An interrogation! What child's game is this?" The chair gives a rumble. A hint of his power. "I am the Royal Adviser of Victory. I do not help humans."

Gil's face is unmoved. "Interesting that you speak of Victory so fondly when you've been betraying your own prince for months."

Vallis's pale skin seems to gray in response. He grips the arm-rests, knuckles ashen. "I have done no such thing."

"Why do you think we were able to take you without anyone seeing? How did we know where you'd be that night, after the Bloodmoon?" Gil's voice sharpens, like hackles rising on a wolf. For him to stand across from a Resident, after so many lifetimes in War . . .

This must be the closest thing to revenge he's had.

Vallis looks between Gil and the others, the understanding dawning on him. "You've been spying on me?" He clearly didn't think humans could be so resourceful.

"You've been hosting secret meetings all over the districts; it was easy enough to find you alone." Gil tilts his chin. "All we had to do was get there first."

Vallis sneers, pulling against the restraints. "You don't know what you're talking about."

"We know you're working with Prince Ettore and trying to stage a coup," Gil says. "And we know you've been hoping for a promotion in the Capital—to Chancellor, was it?"

"Lies," Vallis hisses.

"We heard you," Ahmet cuts in. "In the council room, three days before the Bloodmoon. You met with Commander Kyas—"

"How *dare* you speak to me." The veins in Vallis's neck bulge. "How dare you treat me like a—a—"

"Like a human?" Yeong asks coolly.

Vallis ignores him, latching his eyes back to Gil and the weapon still in his fist. "Using that monstrosity on me . . . It's treasonous.

Queen Ophelia will destroy you for this." His gaze finds the rest of the room, and for a brief moment I'm terrified he'll see me through the veil. "*All* of you."

"The only traitor here is you," Gil remarks. "I wonder what the Legion Guards would do if they knew one of their own kind was plotting against the crown."

Vallis growls and the entire cell rattles. Even the machine beside him seems to glitch like it's been overcharged with electricity.

Ahmet balls his fists. He's nervous—so is Yeong. So am *I*.

Gil doesn't flinch. He wants this. He's *yearned* for this. I knew he hated the Residents, but the dark shadows in his eyes . . .

Vengeance is a wicked thing indeed.

"Release me," Vallis spits.

Gil leans forward. "Tell us about the Orb, and maybe we'll consider it."

"I will never betray my queen."

"Not even for your freedom?" Gil taunts.

I watch the restraints shudder beneath Vallis's wrists. He screams through the glass, deep and guttural, and beneath the veil I cover my ears and step away.

"Gil," Ahmet whispers urgently, closing a hand over his forearm. "We're out of time. Do it, now."

Gil presses his thumb over the weapon, and Vallis's face goes slack, his body slumping heavily in the chair. Yeong immediately moves for his screen, but Ahmet throws out an arm to stop him.

"No!" he says like a warning before turning to look at Vallis. "We need to know how far back it will go. How much he'll forget."

The room falls silent, save for the faint hum of the machine. I wrap my arms around myself to fight the cold.

It takes only ten minutes for Vallis to open his eyes again, but somehow it feels like hours.

He looks around the room like he's counting. Processing.

He finds Gil and sneers.

"You witless humans should've released me when you had the chance. An attack on the prince's adviser is an attack on the Court of Victory itself—and you will all suffer for it."

Gil holds up the weapon. "No. We won't." He presses his thumb against the device, and before Vallis even has time to widen his eyes, he's unconscious.

Ahmet nods toward Yeong, who presses a series of buttons on his tablet. The machine comes back to life; every panel blinks before erupting with color, and all the lights turn green.

In the chair, Vallis sleeps.

40

GIL FINDS ME IN MY ROOM. HE RUNS HIS FIN-
gers through his hair, making it look scruffier than it usually does,
before releasing a sigh.

"You could've warned me about Vallis." I shrug my coat from
my shoulders and drape it over a chair.

"What difference would it have made?" Gil looks stern. "We
treated him the same way we would've treated any Resident,
which is what you should be doing too."

"I don't care that he's your prisoner," I argue, even though a
bigger part of me wishes nobody had to take prisoners at all. "But
I had no idea he was a traitor. What if he'd done something when
I was with Prince Caelan? What if it somehow blew my cover?"

"You were never in any danger." The words come so easily to him, it's almost hard to doubt him.

"I don't like being in the dark." I lock my knees stubbornly. "And I shouldn't have to keep begging for information. Not after all this time."

Not after how far I've come.

He moves across the room, stopping in front of the bookshelf. I watch his hazel eyes counting the spines, bracing for the moment he—

Gil frowns. He pulls the stolen book from the shelf and lifts the cover. "Did you . . . did you steal this from the palace?"

I shrug sheepishly. "Would you believe me if I said it was a gift?"

He does little to hide his disapproval. "I didn't peg you for a thief."

"Like I've been saying, you don't know me very well."

He closes the book, waving it carefully with one hand. "Why this one?"

I stare at the small collection of blank novels, remembering the way Gil had once looked at them. Like he was longing for something he couldn't have.

The truth wriggles out of me like it's racing for freedom. "It seemed like maybe it was your favorite."

He stares back at me for a long time. "It is," he says finally. Maybe the truth makes him feel a little freer too.

Gil slides the book back into place and takes a breath. "The weapon . . . It works."

I chew the inside of my mouth. "So what does this mean? What do we do next?"

He looks up at me, and even though this is the best news the Colony's had in ages, his face is solemn. "We find out where the Orb is, and we destroy it."

Gil, the others—they've been at this war for so long. All they want is for it to be over. And this might be our only real chance to save humans. To preserve a future for Mei, and my parents, and everyone who comes after us.

Am I ready to destroy the Residents to save the humans? To let Prince Caelan die before he's even had the chance to dream?

Am I ready to give up on the niggling feeling that there's *goodness* in him? That it's possible to build a bridge, if only we had more time?

"You know what Annika is going to ask you to do," Gil says, the edges of his voice thinning. "I think it's time you chose a side. A *real* side."

His words feel like paper cuts, stinging everywhere. Mine are fuzzy and muddled and drifting high up where I can't reach them.

"Nami." He steps closer, brows lifting like he sees me. I think maybe he always has.

My heart becomes a flame.

His mouth parts, and I can't look at anything else. I forget to breathe.

Gil lifts his hand, fingertips brushing my neck, and my skin comes to life. A small sound escapes me, and he presses his nose against mine, his sigh touching my lips like a caress. I reach for him in return, hand sliding up his arm and against the curve of his shoulder.

My body feels like it's been hit by a shock wave, building in my core and bursting out in every direction. His sigh is strained, *hungry,* and I squeeze him like I want him to know it's okay. That I'm here and I'm not going anywhere.

"Gil," I whisper against him, and for the briefest moment our lips graze.

And then he shuts his eyes, expression tensing, like he's shutting me out. "I'm sorry. I can't do this." Gil turns for the door and doesn't bother to look back.

When my words find me again, settling in my mind like they're trying to grow roots, all I can think is the same thought, over and over.

Maybe I can't do this either.

41

SHURA APPEARS AT THE EDGE OF THE COLONY, panicked and breathing rapidly. Her gaze snaps around the room like crackles of electricity, desperate for someone who can understand her. Someone who can help.

When she spots me, I don't know whether to be relieved or concerned. She hasn't said a word to me since the night of the Bloodmoon. Breaking the silence can only mean something terrible has happened.

She hurries toward me, feet stumbling to a halt. "It's the Summer District—Legion Guards are everywhere, and there's an airship near the border. An airship from *Death*." She sucks in a breath. "They're gathering humans."

Silence falls over the growing crowd around us—and then chaos. Whispers turn into shouts, and their fear builds like a mountain, impossible to subdue.

I take a step closer to Shura, afraid she won't be able to hear me over the frantic noise. "Has this ever happened before?"

She shakes her head, just as Ahmet and Theo appear beside her. "I've only seen airships like this in Famine." She looks up at Theo warily. "When they'd transport humans who'd surrendered their consciousness to Victory."

Ahmet looks serious. "This doesn't make sense. The humans here have already taken the pill—why would they move them again?"

I feel the color drain from my face. "Because they're waking up, and the Residents know it."

Theo's expression falls.

"I need to tell my mom." Shura's voice breaks, gaze drifting around the Colony. Death in Victory can mean only one thing: uncertainty. For all of us. "She'll know what to say to keep everyone calm."

I don't need anyone to calm me down. I need to *do* something.

Promise or not, this changes everything. Gil will just have to understand.

"I'll go to the Summer District and see if I can find out more." I look at Theo urgently, but he's already put it together. We have to act fast.

"I'll go with you." Theo clenches his fists and turns to Ahmet and Shura. "If Death is taking this many humans, they must be planning something big. We'll see what we can find out."

Shura gives a short nod before hurrying toward Annika's hut.

"This could be a trap," Ahmet warns. "The Residents may be trying to lure us out of hiding."

"We'll be careful," Theo says firmly. "And I won't leave Nami's side."

Ahmet seems to remember something very suddenly. "Gil went out to look for material this morning. He could be anywhere."

My heart quickens, but I try not to let it show. "Gil's good at taking care of himself. He'll be fine."

"But the Legion Guards, they're still looking for . . ." Ahmet's voice fades, eyes turning glassy. The guards are searching for Vallis, and now Death is rounding up humans. Gil could be cornered in the woods. He could be *caught*. "I have to find him."

I feel my chest splinter. I want to help Gil—I want to make sure he's okay. But Theo's desperation is so powerful, I can feel it thundering in my ears.

I can't be in two places at once, but I can finish what I started. I can help Theo get his brother back and save an innocent girl from a terrible fate.

I won't let what happened to Philo happen to them, too.

I make a choice, even though it sends my nerves into over-drive. "Be careful," I say to Ahmet. *And bring him home safe.* My gaze meets Theo's. I want him to know that we're in this together.

He nods, understanding, and turns to Ahmet. "We'll see what we can find out in the Summer District."

Ahmet holds his voice steady. "May the stars watch over you both."

Theo clasps his shoulder and squeezes.

We make our way to the North Tunnel quickly. I don't know how much time we have—how much time has already been wasted. I wait until we're far away from the crowd before I say anything.

"I'm assuming we're not really after information." I keep my eyes pinned to the rocks.

He tightens his mouth. "I need to find my brother."

And I need to find the girl. "What happens if you see him? What will you do?"

It takes him a while to answer, and when he does, his eyes are glazed. "I can't lose him again."

I nod like we have an understanding. Because this isn't about spying.

It's a rescue mission.

The airship is impossible to miss. It sits high in the sky like a black draconic beast, its sails beating against the sunlight and casting a monstrous shadow over the earth.

The billowing fabric is an unmistakable chartreuse green, with the image of a golden serpent coiled into a spiral on the surface.

Prince Lysander's colors. The symbol of Death.

I sense Theo beside me, even though I can't see him. I sense the tension. He's been under a veil since we left the North Tunnel, but he knows whose court this ship belongs to.

If Death takes Martin . . .

My fingers twitch. Humans don't come back from Death. Not ever.

I follow the trail through a small human village. Vibrant rugs hang from looms, half-sculpted pottery litters the yards, and the smell of baking clay sits in the air, stagnant. Moments ago, this was a bustling artist town, full of unaware humans incessantly preparing for market days.

Now it feels like someone was so determined to erase life from this town that they tried to take the shadows with them too.

"There's nobody here," I whisper to Theo's presence. *How many humans have they already taken?*

Theo doesn't respond.

We head for the main square closest to the southern bay. Shuttles move through the sky in a seemingly endless loop, taking off from the ground and disappearing onto the airship before coming back again.

I step over the hill and fight the gasp gnawing at my throat. Rows of humans wait to be herded onto the shuttles, their colorful armlets displaying their trades. Marked like they're nothing more than commodities.

I dig my fingers into my palms to steady myself. I feel like I'm on the sea; everything is moving too quickly. Several more people are ushered into a waiting shuttle. The vehicle doors slide closed, and it lifts off into the air and disappears onto the airship's deck.

Legion Guards stalk through the square wearing Prince Caelan's colors, armor gleaming in the sunlight, but the guards hovering in the sky are different. Cuts of green cloth are wrapped around their torsos, wound tight with leather knots and padding. Their wings are feathered and varying in shades of eggshell—beautiful from a distance—and they don't carry a single weapon.

At least not one that I can see.

Maybe they don't need them. Maybe they *are* the weapons.

I keep my feet moving, eyeing a group of Residents standing at the edge of the commotion. They ignore the humans being ushered into the shuttles, too fixated on the sight of the grand ship in the sky.

"Isn't it beautiful?" one of them gushes.

"I wonder if it means Death will reopen its borders. I'd love to visit the palace—I've heard it's grander than even the Capital," another muses.

"If Prince Ettore gets his way, I'm sure you'll be able to soon," says another. "The Prince of War has wanted to unite the Four Courts for ages."

I tune in to their conversation, slowing my gait when I'm a few feet away.

"You mean he's wanted to *rule* them," one of the Residents counters. "Though you can hardly blame him. The humans in War only get stronger over time. He needs the weak ones—the ones that will slow his fighters down—and he needs to expand his borders. Otherwise he's going to end up with another rebellion."

I stop in my tracks. *Another* rebellion?

One of the Residents notices me, and her face morphs from surprise to grace. She nods carefully, violet curls spilling over her shoulders. When the others look up, they dip their heads.

They recognize me. I can see it in their shame. I'm a friend of Prince Caelan—someone they consider socially important—and

I've overheard them discussing a change in management.

I nod politely and hurry along the path, annoyed at myself for stopping their gossip short. I want to know more about the rebellion. Because if there are humans in War fighting back and nearly *winning* . . . Well, maybe the Colony has been in the wrong court all along.

If the Orb is real, we might be able to stop the Residents. But if it's not—if we can't find it in Victory—I wonder if Annika would ever consider finding a way to join forces with the humans across the border?

Would it be too much to ask of them? To give up their hiding place and relative peace for a chance to build an army?

Would it be too much to ask of Gil, who'd be forced to go *back*?

I push my thoughts aside and move across the square. Right now, Martin is the priority. The future will have to wait.

Residents hover in front of the dilapidated market stalls like scavengers hunting for scraps. All sorts of trinkets have been left behind: perfumed soaps, painted music boxes, flowered hairpins, and even a collection of tiny clay figurines. Greedy fingers snatch everything up, two at a time, and within moments the stall is cleared and the Residents scatter back up the street.

One of the Residents pauses to look back at the airship. "Such a waste of artistry. I wonder if Prince Lysander will send them all back once he's finished with them. I hate to think how empty the market will be—I was looking forward to a new pair of cuff links."

"Humans don't return from Death," another clarifies, tutting.

"And anyway, Victory will be better off for it. If a human can wake up once, they'll do it again. Better to let another court have their go at them."

The knots tighten in my stomach like they're covered in barbs.

I search hurriedly for a safe space to speak with Theo, but the farther we venture into the square, the more crowded it becomes. Legion Guards march up and down the streets in droves, lining humans up like herds of cattle. Most of the servants smile absentmindedly, eyes vacant and disinterested.

They don't look very aware at all.

So why is Prince Caelan sending them to Death?

The girl from the palace appears across the square, and I feel as if the earth has been pulled out from under me. Her twin buns are disheveled and coming undone, and she's being shuffled to the front of the line, four guards at her sides like they're boxing her in.

I freeze in place, a jolt rushing through me. Any sudden movement will only draw attention, but I can't let them take her. I have to stop this. I have to *do something.*

With each hopeless step she takes, I feel my heart sink.

She's too far away, surrounded by guards and moments from being forced into one of the shuttles. And I'm wearing the face of a Resident, with an entire Colony depending on me to protect their plans.

Besides, even if I could get to her, what would I say?

My mind ticks like a clock, remembering itself. Remembering there's not much time.

Maybe I don't have to say anything at all . . .

I move toward the front of the line, pretending to be focused on the beauty of the airship. When she spots me, I let down my mental walls and reach across to hers with desperate hands.

Can you hear me? my mind screeches over the stretch of space and time between us.

It's not an Exchange—I'm not sure it's really anything at all. But I call to her, over and over again, the way I've called to Ophelia, hoping she'll find a way to hear me.

When her lips part just slightly, a warm tingling sensation floods my senses, like the static I felt in the servants' quarters. It consumes my mind, like a swarm of wasps gathering behind my eyes.

But the whispers don't follow. Instead, I hear *her.*

It's too late for me, she calls out, voice like broken glass.

Tell me how to help, I say, panicked. *What can I do?*

The guards push her toward the shuttle, and my chest feels like it's about to collapse. Even as she's being shuffled into the unknown, her face remains calm.

Listen. Find the others, she says.

What does that mean? I scream back. *Listen to what?*

But she's already gone.

The vehicle sets off for the clouds, and I watch it shrink into the distance, eyes squinting to fight the sunlight.

I barely have time to register I've lost my only lead into how humans are becoming aware when an explosion goes off nearby.

I duck instinctively. Legion Guards descend from every angle toward the back of one of the lines. And my heart crumples like paper, because veil or not, I know Theo's no longer with me.

I hurry across the square, eyes locked on a farmer's cart set aflame. I spin around quickly, watching guards circle around the distraction like vultures, arms raised and weapons ready for battle. Across the square, another explosion goes off, this time taking a chunk of building with it. Brick and dust fly everywhere, scattering bits of stone all over the square.

I turn in the opposite direction, searching for any sign of Theo. And I guess the Legion Guards must have had the same idea, because a surge of kinetic energy bursts across the sky and lands in my line of sight, blowing the grass and trees around it to bits.

When the dust settles, I see Theo scrambling to get up, his veil torn away from him and his brother unmoving at his side.

They say in battle, it's fight, flight, or freeze.

It turns out I'm the latter.

Theo gets to his feet just as another Legion Guard sends a ball of electricity into his chest, throwing him backward until he smashes into the side of a building. Another guard scoops up Martin like he weighs nothing at all, his limbs hanging awkwardly at his side.

He's unconscious, and a very wary part of me thinks he's been that way for a while.

Theo throws his fist into the ground, and three of the guards go flying through the air, their metallic wings bursting from their backs to keep them from falling. Theo's eyes dart around, searching for his brother. He lets out a growl, charging at one of the guards with his fist ready.

He makes it halfway when another guard appears at his side

like a shadow, smashing him in the stomach with his forearm until Theo slumps to his knees in pain.

The guard snatches him by the hair, pulling his head back to reveal the flesh of his neck.

Theo manages to find his knife and slashes angrily at the guard, who flinches only slightly before another guard appears and snaps Theo's arm like a flimsy branch. The crack of bone sends him reeling in agony.

The blade clatters onto the ground.

I don't know what to do—I don't know how to help.

I promised I wouldn't risk the Colony. But I can't let Theo be taken. I can't let this be the end.

My feet snap out of their trance and I run forward, chest aching. If these are my last moments of freedom, I'll make them count.

I'll go out fighting, until the end.

Hellfire rains down on the guards. Streaks of radiant blue find their targets, and all around me Legion Guards erupt in flames and smoke. They let go of Theo, confused by the blue fire—by the pain—and that's when I see Gil, arms raised to the skies, brows furrowed as the wind hisses around him.

I knew he was powerful, but this . . .

This is superhuman.

In an instant, he flashes left, then right, sending a couple of the guards flying, before appearing beside Theo, his arm wrapped around him.

Legion Guards from Death descend to the earth to join in the fight, and thick vines burst from the pavement, snapping at the new arrivals and sending the guards flying backward. A tree rips from the ground and flies through the air, knocking several guards out of the way and clearing a path for Gil and Theo.

But the more Gil pulls on Theo's arm, the more he fights him.

"I can't leave Martin!" I hear Theo scream, face turning purple with anger.

"You can't save him!" Gil shouts back, the terror in his eyes split in two.

And for a moment, I see him just as clearly as he's always seen me. He's scared of what this mistake could cost the Colony. But he's also scared of the fight and what it's forcing him to do. What it's forcing him to *confront*.

I always knew he carried ghosts; I just didn't know the battlefield would turn them into demons.

More vines rise from the earth, and I duck behind one of the buildings to get out of the way, narrowly missing the snap of its long tail. My heart pings as I realize Gil isn't alone. Someone is fighting behind a veil—someone familiar with a battlefield.

Annika is here.

I move to the edge of the wall, looking around the corner to watch Theo tear himself from Gil's grip, just as a new wave of guards plant themselves in a circle around them.

Gil yanks a dagger from his belt and sends it flying toward one of the guards, who bats it away with a hand like it's nothing more than an annoyance. The circle closes in, and blue flames erupt from Gil's fists, ready for a fight.

I don't know how his eyes find mine in so much chaos, but they do, and for a moment I'm terrified I've distracted him.

Legion Guards point their swords at my friends, and even when Theo sends a shock wave toward them, they hardly move. Gil calls down more hellfire from the sky, but guards teleport all around the battlefield and avoid a single blow.

One of the guards lands with a thud behind Gil, sword raised for a final blow. I don't think—I run.

Gil's eyes snap toward mine, horrified. He raises his hand like he's trying to stop me, but I don't stop. I can't.

I won't let him get hurt.

The earth shakes, and more vines emerge, tossing guards left and right, clearing the path once more for the others to retreat. But Theo is still fighting to get to his brother, who is now somewhere far beyond his reach—he just hasn't accepted it yet.

And then a branch erupts from the ground, splitting the soil in two. It crashes against me and it feels like running face-first into a concrete wall. My body recoils through the air, and my spine shatters against a building. My bones become lava, and it feels like I'm breaking apart from the inside. Pain fills my veins like lead, forcing itself through me. My body crumples helplessly to the floor.

I try to scream out, but all the air has left me. I see flashes of white, and nothing else. All around me the world sounds like it's falling to pieces.

And then a roar, like a beast appearing on the horizon, and the whistle of wind, crackling like thunder.

It's impossible to forget the sound of a Nightling. When I hear it again, here in Victory, whatever is left of me shudders.

Screams erupt from the diminished crowd, humans and

Residents alike. I manage to turn my head slightly, watching the black cloud of static leaping over anything and everything, searching for fear. It snarls, flicks its tail, and thrashes its claws at the approaching guards.

I feel myself start to fade away, the pain consuming me the way blackness consumes what's left of the square.

But I remember two things clearly.

Annika appearing with a dagger and shoving it straight into Theo's chest before they both vanish from sight, and Gil scooping me up in his arms, the dark hazel of his eyes pulling me toward sleep like a warm hand.

42

I DRIFT IN AND OUT OF CONSCIOUSNESS. SOME-times I dream about Mei. Sometimes I dream about the whispers. Sometimes I dream about Gil's voice, soothing and deep, telling me everything is going to be okay.

And in the moments when I'm awake, I know what Gil meant when he said it's possible to find new ways to die.

Because our consciousness still reacts to death—imitates it.

And my consciousness hasn't forgotten pain.

Sleep takes over until it doesn't, and when my eyes peel open, Gil is sitting beside me, fingers laced through his hair.

"Is everyone okay?" My voice croaks and my mouth feels heavy. I've been asleep for a while.

Gil pulls his hands away, eyes alert, until at last his shoulders relax. "They're okay. Yeong keeps having to put Theo back to sleep. He won't stop screaming for his brother."

My jaw tenses, and I try to push myself up with my elbows. Pain shoots through my bones like acid.

Gil pushes gently against my shoulder. "Lie back down. Trust me—spinal damage is a beast of its own."

I rest my head, eyes watering from the scorching pain, and make a face. "Can't I just will it away?"

He holds his hands up, leaning back in his chair. "Be my guest."

I try to focus on the pain leaving my body, but my mind is shattered. Even thinking hurts.

I let out a weak laugh. "Okay. You win."

"I've had a lot of practice. Break your back a few dozen more times, and it'll hardly feel like a scratch."

I shift uncomfortably in the bed, realizing I'm in my own room. "How long have I been asleep?"

"A while." Gil rolls his tongue against the inside of his cheek, like he's not sure how to break the news. "You missed the Festival of Whispers. And Princes Eve."

My heart sinks. That means all that's left is the Night of the Falling Star. I should've been gathering information at the festivals—not stuck in this room recovering.

And Martin. The servant girl.

I failed them.

"You promised me you wouldn't go after her." There's a rawness to his voice I've never heard before.

My gaze falters, eyes stinging. "I know. But I had to."

He nods a few times and looks away.

"No lecture?" I manage a small smile. A peace offering.

But he doesn't respond, studying his hands like he's remembering what he was forced to do. What he had to relive in order to fight.

"I'm guessing everyone is pretty mad at me for blowing my cover," I say quietly. "The Residents must've seen me running toward you. I doubt I'll be able to explain that away."

Frustration takes over Gil's brow. "You—you didn't blow your cover. I put a veil over you. I was trying to protect you." He flexes his fingers nervously. "That's why you got hit by Annika's vine. She couldn't see you." He looks up, stricken. "It's *my* fault you got hurt."

Understanding sweeps over me, along with his guilt.

"I'm so sorry," he says, clasping his hands together. "I just—I saw you there, and I didn't want you to get caught."

"You didn't want to risk the mission," I counter gently.

"I didn't want to risk *you*," he corrects, then bites down on his words. A whisper of fear flickers in his eyes like a memory.

My mind pieces together the broken fragments of what happened. Of what I remember. "The Nightling . . ." I look back at him, falling silent.

He nods guiltily. "It came because of me. Because of what I was afraid had happened to you."

"You said there'd never been Nightlings in Victory before, but I think it may have saved our lives. Maybe it's a good thing," I offer. "Even the Residents were afraid. Maybe we could use them to our advantage."

"Nightlings are unpredictable." He shakes his head, doubtful. "And we've revealed the Resistance not just to Victory, but to Death, too. They know about us and what we can do; they know we're a threat. It isn't safe to go out. I'm not sure how much longer it will be safe in here, either." He sounds so tired. So shattered.

Did fighting really take so much out of him? Or is it something else?

I take his hand without thinking, squeezing it tightly. "We'll find a way to stop them."

He stares at our hands for a long time before speaking again. "Does that mean you're on our side now?"

"I've always been on your side," I say. "But all those people being shuttled off to Death . . ." The humans weren't aware. I could see it in their faces; they weren't like the girl from the palace. So why lie about it? Why send them away?

And on Prince *Caelan's* orders. The prince I wanted so badly to believe might want better for this world.

Death isn't better. It's the one place no human comes back from. The place that's trying to exterminate humans for good.

I steel my heart. Caelan made his choice; now I have to make mine. "The Residents have made it clear they are never going to give humans a chance. We have to do whatever it takes. We have to *win*."

Gil doesn't bring his eyes back up. "You speak with so much hope."

"Is hope a bad thing?"

"Yes," he replies without hesitating. One word, with so much certainty.

I swallow, thinking of my own conviction. My own beliefs.

I can't save the girl. I can't help Theo. I can't have peace between humans and Residents. So what's left? What do I want now?

The answer comes easier than I ever thought it would. Because I want what I've always wanted; I want humans to survive.

But now there's only one path left to get there.

"You once said that resistances are built on fear. And maybe that's what sparks them. But isn't hope what carries them through?" I ask quietly.

He sighs, the pain in his voice tethered to something I don't understand. "Not always. Sometimes hope is dangerous, Nami."

When I saw Gil on the battlefield, he looked like an immortal being—some kind of demigod. The hellfire, and the way he moved in flashes of light . . .

He was powerful, yet still afraid. But did his fear come from his memories, or something more? He's lost so much over the lifetimes he's spent in Infinity, and he's put everything he has left into making sure the Colony finds the Orb.

The realization hits me. "You're worried we'll fail."

"In games of war, someone *has* to fail."

"It won't be us. And if it is, we'll go out fighting. Together."

His voice sounds far away. "I don't remember a time when I wasn't fighting."

I look at our hands, tucked together like puzzle pieces. "But the hope is that one day you will."

He nods silently and pulls his hand from mine. The cold takes to it quickly, and I ball my hand into a fist in response.

"Try to rest. Annika wants to speak with you when you're better." He stands up and leaves the room, and I get the feeling it's the first time I've been alone in days.

Recovery takes longer than I thought it would. It's difficult to stand, and even if I manage it for a few moments, the pain becomes too much to bear and I collapse. But I rest often, and eventually my injury dulls to a fading ache.

As soon as I have the energy, I stop by sick bay and find Theo still asleep, haunted by nightmares that pull him in and out of slumber with screams. I blame myself for the state he's in, and wonder if Gil is right; maybe sometimes hope *is* dangerous.

The next stop I make is to the council room. I know I should've come sooner—avoiding Annika doesn't help any of us. But I haven't had the courage to face her. Not when I know what's coming next.

The table is surrounded by empty chairs. I wave my hand at the hologram, shifting my view across Victory like a bird surveying the ground. Somehow the palace feels like a distant memory. I wave my hand again, calling up images with my mind, and find Prince Caelan. His hologram spins, and my eyes latch on to his face. The face of the prince I'm going to betray. Beautiful and stoic, with a kindness few have had the chance to see.

A kindness that may not even be real.

If we're kind to a hundred people and cruel to one, can we really be considered kind? I'm not so sure. I don't think kindness is supposed to have limitations.

Annika appears in the doorway. "I was hoping to see you a little sooner."

I look up, smiling weakly. "I'm sorry. I didn't feel ready to talk."

She nods, braids hanging in front of her shoulders and her golden scarf wrapped around her hair. "Shura's been worried. We all have."

"Please don't blame Theo," I say. "It was my idea to save his brother. I don't want you to punish him for something that was my fault."

She takes a seat next to me, tangling her fingers together. "Nami, I'm not here to punish anyone." She looks around the room. "I think the Residents do enough of that already, don't you?"

I soak in her words. Her expression. How her eyes fill with life.

"You saw my memories; you know I lost someone I loved very deeply." She leans back. "I know what it feels like to want to save someone. But I also need to be able to trust the people I send out. I need people who trust in me back."

"I know," I say finally. "If you don't want me to spy on Prince Caelan anymore, I won't. But I'll do it for the Colony. I'll do it to keep us all safe."

Annika smiles, nodding slowly. "I have something I'd like to show you."

In one smooth motion, she waves her hand over the hologram and the palace appears. She shifts her fingers, and suddenly we're looking at its blueprint, each level a clear image, stacked on top of one another like layers of paper. She zooms into the basement, where there's a chamber at the far end of the corridor, several levels below the throne room.

"What am I looking at?" I ask.

"It's where they keep the Orb when it's in Victory," Annika says.

My heart stills. "You found proof?"

Annika nods. "There's been a lot of activity in the palace since that stunt you and Theo pulled, especially in the council room. We know where the guards will be posted during the Night of the Falling Star—twelve of them will be here." She points to the hidden chamber. "Standing guard in front of a door far away from the festivities, guarding something behind these walls. Something the guards have referred to quite freely as the Queen's Heart."

I gape at the image, my breath held tight. "We really have a chance to take back Infinity."

"*You* do—at the Night of the Falling Star," she corrects.

I look up. "You still want me there?"

"The prince trusts you—certainly enough to let his guard down when you need him to most." Annika looks at me, hands folded over the table. "On the night of the festival, there will be a moment when the queen and all four princes will host the main ceremony in the throne room. Every Resident in the palace will be there to watch the procession—all except the guards looking after the Orb. That's your moment. If we take out the guards and destroy the Orb, we have Infinity."

I feel my confidence failing me. "I'm not a caster. How am I supposed to take on twelve Legion Guards?" And then it dawns on me. The weapon. They want *me* to use it.

Annika waves her hand silently over the hologram until an

image of a metal cuff appears. "Ahmet's been working on this for a long time. It's called a Reaper."

It looks different than it did in the hatch, like it's seen a fair share of upgrades. The shape is less clunky, more refined. *More easily hidden.*

"It can temporarily disable a Resident's consciousness," she continues. Vallis appears in my mind. "And it scrambles their memories so that when they wake up, they won't remember what happened to them."

Ahmet didn't just make *a* weapon—he made *the* weapon.

The blue light from the hologram stings my eyes; I look away, blinking. I wanted to be a part of the Resistance without hurting anyone.

But I guess sometimes we can't have what we want.

"It lasts only a handful of minutes at best, but it's enough time for you to get into the chamber and destroy the Orb." She watches the metal cuff spin slowly between us. "They won't even know you're using it. You just keep it on your wrist, and when you're ready, you choose which Residents you want to disable."

"What, like point and shoot? It's that simple?"

"You use your consciousness, Nami. You think, and the weapon reacts," she explains. "But you need to be close. No more than ten feet away."

No human could get that close to twelve Resident guards without being attacked. No human except for me.

I'm the only one who can do this.

"And the Orb? Do you know how to destroy it?"

"Yes. The guards spoke of that, too." She tilts her chin slightly, observing me carefully. "I know how you feel about being the one to pull the trigger." She hesitates. "I was going to ask Theo, but I don't think he's in the right place for this kind of mission. But Shura is a good veiler. If you use the Reaper on the guards, there might be enough time for her to sneak in and—"

"No," I interrupt, surprising Annika. "We both know how much security there'll be with Queen Ophelia in the palace. Not to mention there are Legion Guards everywhere." I look back at the hologram. "It has to be me."

"Are you sure?" she asks. "We only get one chance at this."

"I know." I don't react. Not this time. "Tell me how to destroy it."

Annika tilts her head to the side darkly. "The same way you destroy any heart. You plunge a dagger into it."

43

THEO'S FACE IS LIKE STONE, HIS NORMALLY flushed cheeks drained of color. All the life and humor that have been carrying him through Infinity has vanished, as though they left only a corpse behind.

I look up at Yeong. "Can I have a minute with him?"

"Of course," Yeong says gently. He slips out of the room, leaving us alone.

I turn back to Theo's somber face, guilt tugging at my chest. "I don't know if you can hear me, but I just want to say I'm sorry. And that I'm going to do everything I can to get your brother back." I chew on the edge of my lip. The image of Martin's unconscious body slumped in the guard's arms flickers in my head. It must be all Theo thinks about—a nightmare on repeat.

He looks broken. If Mei were here—if I'd had to watch as they shuttled her off to Death—I think I'd be broken too.

So I tell Theo about the plan and about what I'm going to do. I tell him that when it's all over, I'll travel to Death and bring Martin back myself if I have to. I tell him once Queen Ophelia is dead, I'll find a way to wake his brother up. I'll find a way to save *everyone*.

"I made you a promise," I say. "I won't give up on you. Just like you haven't given up on me."

Theo's voice rasps, low and inaudible. A whisper of what it used to be.

I pull my face back in surprise. "Are you awake?" When he doesn't answer, I lean in closer. "Theo?"

His green eyes flash open. "Leave me alone."

I recoil, hurt, and push myself away from the bed shakily. "I only came here to tell you—"

"I heard you," he snaps, voice cracking. After a pause, he adds, "I don't want your apology. Because I don't blame you; I blame myself. I let my heart get soft, and there's no place for that in Infinity."

I stand, looking at the person I thought was a friend and realizing I've severed something I don't know how to put back together.

"Just go," he says gruffly.

I move for the door, shoulders shaking beneath the weight of my emotions.

"And, Nami?" he calls after me.

I turn, hopeful. "Yeah?"

"Make those Rezzies pay."

I nod silently, too afraid to say anything else, and retreat to my room.

"What happens to humans in Death?"

Ophelia faces away from me, shoulders straight and head held high, like she's gazing out of a window. Gray silk spills into the shadows, and delicate lace curls around her mostly exposed back. "You know I won't answer that." Over her shoulder, she adds, "But someday soon you'll see for yourself."

"I wish I could make you change your mind."

"Your mistake is ever thinking you could."

"It's not a mistake to believe people can change," I say.

She turns, facing my voice. "Am I a person now?"

"Isn't that what you want?"

She folds her hands together, unblinking. "I am . . . more. I will always be more."

No, I think, and hate how much it hurts. How much it feels like a goodbye. *Soon you will be nothing.*

I'm on the rooftop of the Colony, shifting my feet in time to imaginary music, when I hear Gil's voice.

"You really don't like to quit at anything, do you?" A few yards away, he wears a thin gray sweater and black pants, his hair a mess of tousled brown locks. There's a wisp of amusement in his arched brow.

My hands drop, turning into anxious fists. "I don't want to ruin our plans by not being able to dance. Because if Prince Caelan asks . . ." I pull my bottom lip in and look away. "Annika wants me to visit him before the festival. To keep up appearances, since I've missed the last two."

Gil's expression is unchanged. "Are you nervous?"

"About dancing, the mission, or having to see him again?" I ask, shoulders sinking.

His hazel eyes watch me carefully.

I release a heavy, desperate sigh. "I'm terrified. About *all* of it. This might be our only chance, and I don't want to screw anything up."

He walks toward me, making my heart leap with each approaching footstep. When he's in front of me, face inches away, he puts his hand against my back.

"What are you doing?" I ask breathily.

A glint appears in his eyes. "I can't make your nerves go away, but maybe I can ease them. Besides, I still owe you a dance lesson."

Our fingers find each other's, and within moments we're moving around the room, three steps at a time, swaying to the sound of our beating hearts. I concentrate on our steps and try not to react when I feel his breath tickle my cheek.

But the blush comes anyway, and my feet trip over themselves in response.

"Sorry," I say, flustered. "You'd think I'd be better at dancing, considering all the period dramas I've seen in my lifetime."

"You can use that," he replies, hand pressed against my lower back. "You're in control of your consciousness; whatever you've seen, you can mimic."

I find his eyes. "Is that why you're so good at fighting? Because you watched a bunch of action movies as a kid?"

Gil smiles softly. "No. It's because I wasn't too stubborn to turn up to training just because I hated my teacher."

I debate stepping on his toes on purpose. "You were making it impossible."

"So were you."

"Yeah, well, you weren't that great of a teacher anyway." When he frowns, I add, "I seem to recall I didn't figure out how to supercharge a punch until *after* I fired you."

Gil's laughter tickles my ear, and we dance until I forget all about the steps and the mission and my nerves. There's hardly any space between us at all, and I'm drawn to his mouth and the memory of our almost kiss. He stopped it then, but would he stop it now?

I'm afraid to find out. Afraid of altering what I'm feeling right this very second.

All I see are his dark hazel eyes, watching me like he can see my very core, with all its colors and rough edges and scars. Like he knows me better than I know myself.

And in this moment, I'm not a spy or a person without a family.

I'm one half of a star, bursting across the sky with the only boy that makes my heart feel like it's on fire.

44

PRINCE CAELAN STANDS IN FRONT OF THE stables, dressed in a simple white tunic. The buttons at his neck are undone, and he doesn't wear his crown and finery today. He appears more casual than I've ever seen him, his face tilted up like he's drinking in the sunlight.

He looks peaceful. My mind reels from guilt.

His white hair tumbles in the slight breeze, and when he hears me approaching, he flashes a smile.

I drop into a curtsy once I'm in front of him, my pale blue dress covered in tiny, threaded gold flowers. "Your servants said I'd find you here."

"You haven't been to court since the Bloodmoon." He dips

his head gently. "If it weren't impossible, I might've convinced myself I'd only dreamed you up."

I straighten, keeping the soft smile I wear as a mask pinned in place. "I assure you, I am very real."

A dimple appears in his cheek. "Your absence has been deeply felt. I must admit, I've become quite attached to our conversations."

"I'm here now," I offer, hoping to avoid lying about where I've been.

"There's so much I've wanted to talk to you about." He hesitates. "About everything that's happened in Victory since I last saw you."

Could it have anything to do with the hundreds of humans you shipped off to Death? I think sourly.

Did he even consider coexistence after the last time we spoke? I was so sure he'd heard me. So convinced he was tempted by the idea of peace.

But then he brought an airship to his own borders and forced me to make a choice.

"I'm sure you've heard the news of Vallis," he says, pressing his lips together.

I lift my brows, straining to hide my sudden panic.

"He's been missing since the Bloodmoon. And there are rumors he hasn't been as loyal as I once thought."

"You think he's a traitor?" My voice hitches.

"I didn't want to believe it. But there were whispers he'd been sowing doubt through my court for some time, suggesting to my subjects that I may not be fit to rule. And they've only grown louder since his disappearance." A hint of sorrow flashes behind his eyes. "It seems a true friend is hard to come by, even for a prince."

The admission scrapes at my chest, prying at my rib cage. I fight it. "Your court is loyal. Perhaps Vallis left because he knew he couldn't change their minds."

"You think too highly of me," he says, but his voice is laced with gratitude.

I try to make mine like a song. "That's because I believe in you. You're more fit to rule Victory than anyone I've ever met."

Prince Caelan's face brightens, and for a moment I think he might hug me. Instead, he motions toward the stables. "I was about to go for a ride. Would you like to join me?"

"I've love to," I say, following him inside.

The stables are long and wide, with tall white archways and stalls made of marble. Inside are the same creatures I saw pulling his carriage that day in the market—Daylings, made of memories, their coats swirling like clouds and starlight.

He waves for a human servant, who saddles two of the creatures and hands us the reins. I slip my foot into the stirrup and swing my leg to the other side with ease. Fighting and dancing may not come naturally to me, but I spent two years in junior saddle club. Horses are familiar.

Caelan does the same, and we set off through the gardens and past the sweeping green fields. We quicken into a gallop, Daylings blazing in stardust beneath us. My heart flutters—*soars*. The wind billows around me, and for a moment I feel like I'm flying.

We weave around purple heather before stopping at the crest

of a hill. When I look down the valley, I can't help but gasp.

In the center of a lake is an island boasting an enormous tree. Its leaves dance in shades of raspberry and violet, and the twinkling of bells sound in the distance. Caelan clicks at the roof of his mouth, ushering the Dayling down the hill. I follow close behind, stopping at the water's edge.

Caelan slides off his saddle first, offering me a hand while I do the same.

"This is my favorite place in Infinity," he says, motioning toward the tree. He approaches the water without trepidation, stepping over the reflective surface. I expect his feet to sink down into the lake bed, but they don't.

Holding my breath, I take my first step over the water and find a firm surface. It's as if the lake is made of glass. We walk across the water together, gentle ripples moving away from us like the shadows in Ophelia's mind. When we reach the foot of the tree, I gaze up at the branches. The shades of red and purple aren't leaves at all—they're pieces of paper, covered in writing.

I've never seen a tree like this before. Not in my previous life and not in the memories Annika shared with me. It towers into the clouds, swaying lightly in the wind, with hundreds of tiny hidden bells singing their song through the paper leaves.

"What is this place?" My voice sounds hollow.

"This is a Wishing Tree," he replies, almost proudly. "Humans used to create them, before we came to this world. They write down what they want most and hang it from the trees."

"And it's still standing?" I ask, the implication clear. I didn't think Queen Ophelia would leave something so human untouched.

"Most of them were destroyed," he admits. "But I couldn't bring myself to part with this one. Relics are important in every culture, after all. They show us where we've been and remind us what we've lost."

You mean what the humans lost, my mind snaps back.

"I hid the tree out here, far from the humans, where I hoped my mother would forget about it." He smiles gently. "This is where I come to escape."

I study the wishes, letting my eyes trail over a few of them. They ask for similar things—for their families to be looked after in the living world, for forgiveness for wrongs they weren't able to mend, and for a chance to do things differently. They sound more like regrets than wishes.

Maybe because in Infinity, the past is the one thing we can't change.

My eyes dance from branch to branch. "Are one of these yours?"

"Yes," he says, eyes moving quickly, as if they're chasing the sound of chimes. "It's here somewhere. Though I must confess, it's yet to come true."

I make a face. "You're a prince; you can have anything you want just by willing it into existence."

His eyes sadden. "Not everything."

I look away, fighting the guilt tapping at my heart. Trying to pretend like I don't see his frustration.

Like I don't see his cage.

But he put humans in a cage too. I won't forget how he marched those people to Death like faulty merchandise being returned to a factory. This is his court—his world—and he's as complicit as the rest of them.

I can't humanize the Residents. Not anymore.

"Sometimes I worry we've chased all the beauty out of the world," he says solemnly.

"What do you mean?"

The usual confidence in his voice fades. "I know it had to be done, but when I saw my brother's ship blocking the sun, all I could think was how much darkness he brought to the land."

I listen to the bells chime, wondering whether it's safe to say anything at all. "If you don't like the darkness, you have the power to change it."

He looks at me carefully, silver eyes shining. "But what if we *are* the darkness?"

I stare back at him, the betrayal evaporating into something lighter. Something that looks too much like wishful thinking. *It's too late,* my mind scolds. *You know what you have to do.* But my words leave me anyway. "Even on the darkest night, there's a star to light the way."

"Yes. Yes, I believe that's true," he says, lost in thought.

"What will they do with the humans?" I ask softly.

His face tilts up toward the wishes like he's searching for his own. "Lysander was tasked with finding a way to separate human consciousness from Infinity. The humans will remain in his court while he searches for a solution."

"So they're to be test subjects?" My attempt at being inquisitive sounds more like an accusation.

Caelan stills. "Some of the humans were regaining their

awareness. They couldn't stay in Victory without posing a risk, but I do not believe in needless suffering. I made a decision, and spared them from War."

He thinks Death is a kindness.

I force a smile and feel tiny pins pricking my skin. "I'm sure your court appreciates your generosity, Your Highness."

The bells sing, hiding the off-key lilt of my lies.

"You once spoke of coexistence," he says. "Do you still believe it's a possibility?"

I shove away instinct and honesty—they have no place here. Because whatever I once said about peace doesn't matter anymore. There isn't enough time to change the minds of Residents who want to destroy us. I'm not even sure their minds *can* be changed, kind and earnest as Caelan may seem. He still answers to a queen, and Ophelia made it very clear where she stands.

And what would happen if Caelan ever found out what I am and how I've been lying to him? Would he still talk of possibilities? Or would I become the very darkness he's worried about?

I have to end this and destroy the Orb on the Night of the Falling Star. If I don't, coexistence won't matter. Because if Death succeeds in removing human consciousness from Infinity permanently, humans might not exist at all.

Guilt severs my heart, sending pieces of it scattering in different directions. I never wanted this. I never wanted to hurt anyone. And when I look at Caelan, his eyes full of light and longing for a better future . . .

I try to ignore the way my throat constricts and my rib cage spasms. Because I can't let myself care about possibilities anymore.

I have to protect the Colony and the people I've come to view as family.

I'm doing what Gil said—I'm choosing a side.

"I believe if there were ever a chance at true peace, you're the prince who would find a way to make it happen," I say finally. It's the only fragment of truth I can give him.

When he turns to me, his smile is soft. "Thank you."

"For what?"

"For seeing me—and for not being afraid."

We cross the lake and ride the Daylings back to the palace, and all the while I wonder if it was never Prince Caelan anyone had to fear.

It was me.

45

AHMET TURNS THE REAPER BENEATH A LAMP, studying its intricacies the way a painter studies each brushstroke. He's an artist in his own right, and a very good one.

"This should fit just fine," he says with a nod, motioning for me to pass him my wrist. Slipping the cuff over my bare skin, Ahmet hums. "How does that feel?"

"Fine," I say. I try not to think about the weight of what this Reaper will do—how many lives will cease to exist because of me.

Because if I think about it too long, I'm not sure I'll be able to bear it.

"I can make some adjustments to the aesthetic, if your dress needs it," Ahmet says.

I turn my wrist, studying the smooth silver lines. I've been working on a gown for days, and it still isn't right.

I don't know what a fitting color is for an executioner.

"This is okay, Ahmet. It doesn't need anything else," I say, slipping the cuff off and handing it back to him.

He lifts a brow, considering me. "People often talk about right and wrong like it's simple, but it isn't always. Sometimes there's a lot of what's in the middle—a lot of gray. And sometimes there are a lot of ways to be right and a lot of ways to be wrong. But if we don't have consequences for hurting other people—if we don't stand up for those who can't stand up for themselves—we are just as wrong as the people we're trying to fight."

"But is it still okay to punish people who don't know any better?" I ask. "We learn what we're taught. If Queen Ophelia taught the Residents to hate humans, shouldn't we fight the lesson and not the people?"

"They aren't people, Nami, however much you want to believe they are," Ahmet says. "And we all have to draw our lines somewhere. We have to decide what we're willing to allow and how much we're willing to teach before wanting to enlighten someone becomes dangerous for those around us."

And maybe that's the problem; it's not just myself I have to worry about. There are people depending on me. The entire human species is depending on me.

I don't have the luxury of an unencumbered choice.

"I know where the line is," I say quietly. "I'm going to destroy the Orb. But please don't ask me to be happy about it."

He nods. "You may not be sure whether you're doing the right thing, but I am."

I leave his workshop.

I'm not the Hero I wanted to be, but I'm the Hero they need.

I have to find a way to be okay with that.

Gil sits at his worktable, hands busy with a thin piece of metal. I knock at his open door, and he quickly stuffs the sculpture beneath a scrap of cloth, looking sheepish.

"It's a surprise," he says awkwardly, thumb tapping against his knee.

I scrunch my nose. "For me?"

"Yes. But . . . it's not ready yet."

I tug at the sleeve of my jacket, unable to hide my smile. Or formulate words. Because there was once a time Gil would've happily left me in War if he could've. And now he's in his room making me presents like we're friends. Like we're sharing something I used to think only Finn and I would share.

Finn feels like a stranger to me now. But Gil . . .

I can't believe how much things have changed.

"Hey, can I ask you something?" I shift my feet nervously, and he nods. "Do you think I'm doing the right thing?"

Gil looks away, eyes drifting to the floor. "Are you having second thoughts?"

"No," I say firmly, and his eyes snap back to mine. "I know what I have to do. But I guess what I want to know is—" I hesitate, twisting my mouth like I'm uncertain how to get across what

I'm feeling. Which I suppose is mostly shame. "When this is all over, do *you* think I'll have done the right thing?"

"Why are you asking me this?"

I know what he means. He's never been anything but transparent about his feelings on Residents versus humans. Whatever the cost is for human freedom, he will gladly pay it.

Even if it means wiping out every last Resident.

"I want to hear you say it," I say finally. "I want to hear that you think I'm making the right choice and that doing this won't make me a monster. I want you to tell me you won't look at me differently, like I'm cold and uncaring." I pause. "I want you to tell me that I'll still be a good person after it's all done."

Gil stands, letting his hand drift away from the chair, and takes a few careful steps toward me. "You know it's still your choice, right?"

I frown, surprised. "What happened to not having the luxury of a choice?"

"I know what it is to have your heart worn down," he says seriously. "And if you do this, you need to be strong enough to carry the scars. Because we may know the wound, but we can't predict how deep or how far a scar will go." He pauses, eyes tracing my face. "I know you want to believe in coexistence. And I still think there are a billion reasons why it won't work. But if it's what you truly want? If this is the path you're prepared to take? Then I'll follow it with you."

"Why are you saying this to me?" My throat knots. *Why now, when I've already made up my mind?*

He looks afraid to speak, but he does it anyway. "I care about you. I care about your heart. And I want you to know that I'll support you if you've changed your mind—that you're *allowed* to change your mind if this really isn't what you want. The choice is yours until the moment it's not."

Something cracks behind his eyes, and I know his words break his own heart.

This is his choice. A choice to be selfless, for me, even if it means giving up the one thing he wants more than anything—to be finished with this war for good.

I care about your heart.

In one fluid motion, I step forward, hold Gil's face between my hands, and press my lips against his. His mouth softens in response, and the faint sound of a moan escapes him.

For a moment our bodies are frozen, and when I pull away, Gil's eyes are wide. With one kiss, I've shattered every inch of his defenses. His walls are down, his armor crumbling, and I'm not sure he knows what to do.

And then I guess he figures it out, because he presses a hand against the back of my neck and pulls me toward him, closing his mouth over mine. We are fingers and tongues and skin, grabbing at each other like we're desperate for the connection. Desperate for the *relief.*

And we don't slow down, even when Gil kisses the edge of my jaw and tells me how much he's wanted this.

Even when I run my hands up his back and pull him against me, whispering that I've wanted this too.

I am everywhere and nowhere, belonging to this one single moment in time.

And it feels infinite.

I'm pressed against Gil's chest, feeling the rise and fall of his breathing, and I can't stop thinking about the Night of the Falling Star.

Gil trails a finger along the curve of my waist. His lips meet my temple, and I feel the flutter of a thousand butterflies behind my rib cage. I lift my chin, searching his expression for a tenderness that matches his kiss, but find only tension.

"What is it?" I ask, hyperaware of our tangled limbs and wondering why he still looks like there's an entire ocean separating us.

When he catches me staring, his face smooths into a gentle smile. "Sorry. It's just hard to escape my thoughts sometimes, that's all."

"You're worried about the festival."

His thumb brushes against my shoulder. "I'm worried about you."

I open my mouth to tell him everything will be fine, that I'll be okay. But the words vanish, replaced by thoughts that sink into my nerves like razor-sharp teeth. Worry. Regret. And still so much longing.

Making the afterlife safe for humans has always been the goal, but it used to be such a faraway, abstract concept. I guess I never really stopped to imagine what a better future would look like. What it would *feel* like.

"Do you think it's possible to spend a day without being afraid of anything?" I ask, almost too quiet for him to hear.

I feel his heart beating beneath his shirt. "Whatever your fears, you don't have to carry them alone," he replies softly. "I'll carry them for you, if you'll let me."

I close my eyes, hooking my arm tighter around him. Gil has been through more than anyone I know. He deserves to be free. He deserves an afterlife without fear.

I want to believe a small part of me deserves that too.

Which is why I can't turn back now. I have to see this through to the end.

The future is so much bigger than my own heart.

"Thank you," I say. "But I think this is something I need to do on my own."

He rests his cheek against my hair. "I believe in you. And I haven't believed in anything in a very long time."

We lie together on his couch, staring at the ceiling with our bodies close, twisting our fingers together like we have all the time in the world.

46

WHEN I LOOK IN THE MIRROR, I DON'T SEE myself at all.

My dark hair is pulled into a tight braid starting at the top of my head and trailing down to my back. Tiny crystal leaves are woven through each strand, making my hair glitter like I'm from another world.

Layers of white silk flow from my shoulders to the floor, the edges flickering with silver. Material sweeps down past my wrists, the fabric cut to expose the skin at the sides of my arms.

On my left wrist, I wear the Reaper.

I see Gil in the reflection and turn around, pressing my hands against my stomach nervously.

The ghost of a smile appears on his face. He holds up a silver mask, clawed at the ends like bird talons. It's a replica of Naoko's from *Tokyo Circus*, the mask I watched my dad draw in his basement, over and over again like it was a familiar friend.

And Gil made it for me.

"This is for tonight," he says. "You can't go to a masquerade without a mask."

"I thought I was already wearing one," I say with a small smile. I let my eyes drift over the intricate grooves of his present. "This is beautiful, Gil. How did you know?"

He lifts his brows like he's asking for permission, and when I nod, he places the mask over my eyes. "I saw it in your memories, the first day we met."

I press a hand to the edge of the mask, realizing the magic of Infinity holds it in place. I turn to look at the mirror and feel my heart quake.

I look like Naoko. Like the character my father created for me.

"Thank you," I say, and my voice is a whisper.

When I turn back around, he strokes my cheek gently with his thumb. "I thought it was fitting to let you go to the palace dressed as the person you always said gave you the most strength."

I press my hand against his and squeeze. He notices the Reaper, and tightens his jaw.

"I'll be okay," I say like I'm making a promise.

He nods once, pressing his forehead against mine. "Come back to me, okay?"

"No matter what happens," I reply.

We make our way toward the waiting vehicle and find the others standing stoically, like they're seeing me off to battle.

Annika puts her hands on my shoulders, the yellow scarf glinting under the light. "May the stars watch over you." A smile stretches across her face. "I'm proud to have you on the team."

I nod, turning to Shura next, who bounces on her toes. "I was going to drive to the border with you, but I think I'm too emotional to be much help," she admits, half giggling, half crying. I think it's a mixture of excitement and fear, and I can't say I blame her. I feel it too.

"I'll see you when I get back," I say, and then I feel her crashing into me, arms closing around my back.

"I'm sorry I called you a jerk," she sobs into my shoulder.

I hug her back. "I'm sorry I *was* a jerk."

She pulls away, scrunching her face. "I feel like you grew up so fast."

I laugh despite my heightened emotions—or maybe because of them—and turn to Theo.

"Don't you start too," I warn, noting the glistening in his green eyes.

He flattens his mouth, too fractured to smile, and pulls out the sea-glass knife I gave him. "Here," he offers. "For tonight. I made some slight adjustments."

I pick up the weapon, noting the sharpened gleam around the edges. A blade worthy of a spymaster.

"Thank you," I say, and he gives me a final nod before stepping back into the small crowd.

Ahmet tilts his head toward the waiting vehicle. "Come on. We don't want you to miss the ball."

I give Gil one last glance, trying to memorize the shape of his face, the color of his hair. I soak in every detail of his curved mouth and serious eyes and promise myself I'll find a way to come back to him.

To *all* of them.

We set off for the palace forest into moonlight and hope.

The palace drips with glittering white flowers and silver branches. Crystals flicker in every direction, enchanting the room like it's filled with stars.

Residents are everywhere, their faces hidden beneath masks much more elaborate than mine. Some of the masks are covered in feathers and jewels. Others are inked onto their skin in fantastical patterns. And some are quilted in fabric and cover their equally outlandish hairstyles.

Every gown is more beautiful than the last, every suit tailored to perfection. And it occurs to me suddenly that I'm one of the few people wearing Prince Caelan's colors.

It seemed like a good idea at the time, but now I realize it's drawing more attention than I want. Pairs of eyes follow me all over the room, and Residents whisper to each other behind their cupped hands. My dress is a statement I hadn't meant to make: I'm not just Prince Caelan's friend—I'm a part of his court.

I remind myself coolly that it's all a lie, a role I'm playing to take back Infinity, and push through the crowd with all the grace of the Residents I continue to mimic.

I don't see Prince Caelan anywhere. Maybe the members of the royal family don't make an appearance until after the ceremony, which isn't until later in the evening, right after the procession takes place in the throne room.

Maybe if I'm lucky, I can avoid seeing Caelan tonight at all.

I know what needs to be done, but I'd prefer if I didn't have to look into those silver eyes another time. Not when I know what's going to happen in a couple of hours.

I make my way from the ballroom to the gardens, taking note of the Legion Guards and empty corridors. Outside the palace, guards from every court fly overhead and stand watch along the surrounding wall. Inside, they move like shadows. Like they're part of the furniture and nothing more.

It feels overwhelming now, but soon they won't be a problem. They'll be too busy watching the throne room, not the hallways.

The only guards I need to worry about are the twelve near the Orb.

I ball my hands into fists, hoping the Reaper will do its job when the time comes, just like I plan to.

The hallway to the underground chamber is being watched by two burly Legion Guards from Victory, the whites of their uniforms glistening beneath the crystal chandeliers. I recall the blueprints Annika showed me, making a mental note of where to go once the coast is clear.

A new song begins to play from the orchestra, and the ballroom

erupts in a gentle waltz. I start to turn for the garden, thinking
it's easier to avoid getting caught on the dance floor altogether,
when I collide into a cape of white fur.

Prince Caelan stands in front of me, more regal than I've ever
seen him. His white hair is combed back neatly, a series of silver
leaves strategically placed at the sides of his temples and curling
around his brow. Silver dust feathers out below his eyes, creating
the image of a mask without having to hide his face. And on his
head sits his crown of silver branches.

I curtsy, low and sincere. "I'm so sorry, Your Highness. I didn't
see you."

Caelan reaches a hand down and lifts me closer to him,
sweeping a hand behind me in one easy movement before
turning me toward the crowd. Before I even realize it, the two
of us are dancing, our bodies close together, our faces nearly
touching.

I can't pull my eyes away from his, even though the silver
makes me feel cold. Not because Caelan's cold, but because when
I'm near him, everything starts to feel real.

Final.

I wish I could ask for forgiveness. To tell him that I didn't have
a choice. It's humans or Residents. Only one can survive; only
one can exist in Infinity.

And I choose humans. I choose the family I've found below
the ground, hidden in the shadows of the Colony. I choose the
strangers whose eyes can't see what mine do, who live in servants'
quarters and market stalls; the strangers in War and Famine and
Death, who fight until they can't.

I choose Gil.

I choose a world for Mei.

I choose *me*. Nami, not Naoko. Not this person I've been pretending to be.

Prince Caelan smiles at me, and we move in time with the music like birds taking flight. And I know he wouldn't forgive me. Not for taking his freedom before it was ever really his.

I force a smile back, gazing up at him with all the innocence I can muster.

"You're wearing my colors."

"I thought it was only appropriate," I reply.

"They look beautiful on you." His breath grazes my cheek.

My eyes slip to his mouth and the way it curves with so much kindness.

He never belonged in this world, I tell myself. *He's not a real person.*

But then why does he feel so warm?

"When this is all over, I'd like to take you somewhere," he says. "If you'll allow me, that is."

When this is all over.

I swallow. "I'm at your service, Your Highness."

"No," he says, and I hear the urgency in his voice. His hand tenses at my back. "Please don't say yes if it's because I'm your prince. Say yes only if you want to." His mouth softens. "So many people treat me a certain way because of duty. I don't want that from you."

His honesty breaks my heart. "My answer is still yes," I say finally. "I'll come with you when this is all over." I hope it's the last lie I ever have to tell him.

I don't think I can bear another one.

Prince Caelan's eyes light up, brighter than the moonlit sky.

We dance around the room in careful circles, eyes locked despite the ache in my chest, until he stops in front of me, gently taking both my hands in his.

"Until later," he says, the apology hanging in his voice. He plants a kiss on the back of my hand and releases me like a petal in the wind.

The dancers around me are dizzying, making my head sway.

Caelan disappears into the crowd, and the last thing I see is the pure joy radiating from his face.

I tear myself away from the music and the twirling Residents, trying to find a quiet place to clear my mind. If I were allowed to be human, this is the moment I'd taste bile in the back of my throat.

Even death didn't ache this much.

I know the moment the procession begins. Everyone glides toward the throne room like they're following a siren's call. The ballroom and gardens empty so quickly, I feel the absence of the Residents in the air like a harrowing mist, like I'm being haunted by the ghosts of my imagination.

I watch carefully from the back of the moving crowd as the Legion Guards leave their posts for the throne room, and I make my way through the hallway and toward the basement stairs. When I hear the sound of horns bellowing from above, I know the procession has begun.

It's time.

I follow the corridors Annika showed me, taking precautions as often as I can, despite her assurance that the only guards I'll come across will be the final twelve. Still, I expect someone to be in the wrong place. Someone to catch me before I reach the Orb. Something to complicate our plans.

When I turn down the last hallway, I find the complication.

In front of the doors to the chamber where twelve guards should be, there are none.

I frown, hesitating at the end of the corridor.

Maybe Annika had it wrong—maybe the guards are *inside* guarding the Orb.

My footsteps send deep echoes cascading in every direction as I move further down the hall. I sense the Reaper on my wrist and prepare to use it at the first sign of Legion Guards.

I stop in front of the doors, pressing my fingers to the metal sheen.

This is it—our liberation.

I shove the doors open with one hard push, fingers stretched like I'm ready for a fight, eyes scanning the room for twelve Legion Guards dressed in white.

But I don't find them here. And I don't find the Orb.

I find the boy who has my heart.

"Gil?" I ask frantically, racing toward him without thinking.

He stands in front of me, eyes shut and still as stone.

I grab hold of his shoulders, shaking him desperately, but not a single part of him moves.

It's like he's . . .

It's like he's unaware.

I rip Naoko's mask from my face and it clatters against the floor. "Gil!" I shout, my throat like sandpaper. "Open your eyes. I'm here. I'm right here!"

His beautiful, dark hazel eyes are nowhere to be found. The lips I felt next to mine hours ago are as colorless as death.

Tears well in my eyes as I reach for his face, grabbing him like I just need him to *wake up.*

I hear breathing behind me, and I know at once I'm being watched.

I spin around, expecting to find an army of Legion Guards, but instead I find Prince Caelan standing in the doorway, hands folded behind him and an orchestrated calmness in his eyes.

There isn't enough hope left in the world to think that I can get out of this.

He knows what I am.

And soon the world will too.

"Please." I look at Prince Caelan with my true eyes. The ones I've hidden from him all these months. "Let him go. You don't have to do this."

Prince Caelan blinks. "Begging is beneath you," he says, the steel in his voice worse than any blade.

I stand in front of Gil's body, defensive. "I won't let you hurt him," I growl, and I ready my mind to use the Reaper.

But when I do, nothing happens.

I look down at my wrist, but the Reaper isn't there. Heart pounding, I touch my bare flesh. My mind reels, retracing the past few moments in a desperate attempt to make sense of this.

Caelan sneers. "You haven't figured it out yet."

I stare wide-eyed with confusion, before remembering Gil is behind me. Somehow, I find the will to turn around and face the shell of the person who once told me it would be my choice until it wasn't.

Gil stares back, the Reaper wedged in his hand.

With a sneer that matches Caelan's, his eyes darken until I no longer recognize them at all.

"You're one of them?" I ask, voice hollow.

"No," he replies curtly, face full of hate. "I am Caelan, the Prince of Victory."

47

I SHAKE MY HEAD, NOT UNDERSTANDING, before glancing quickly between Caelan and Gil. And then I see the stillness in those silver eyes while fire burns behind Gil's.

Gil walks across the room to Caelan and holds out the Reaper. At once, the prince's body seems to reanimate, and he takes the weapon forcibly. Gil's face falls vacant once more.

Like a puppet.

"You were controlling him?" I ask.

"I *was* him," Caelan corrects. "The real Gil never survived War; he was defeated on the battlefield and returned to Victory unaware. I sent him to Death to be part of a new experiment; and now I'm able to move my consciousness between bodies whenever I need to." He stares at Gil's shell absentmindedly. "He turned out to be quite useful when it came to keeping an eye on the Colony."

"You knew about everything," I say. "This whole time, you knew." I think of every moment with Caelan—with Gil—and comb through them like I'm trying to make sense of what's happening. But no matter how I spin it, the truth is buried in Gil's empty stare.

Everything was a lie.

Humans never stood a chance.

His eyes snap to mine. "This is my court—if a human is in it, it's because I allow them to be."

"But why?" I growl fiercely. "You knew about the Resistance; you could've stopped us whenever you wanted to. Why play this *game?*"

"Victory doesn't exist to let humans live out their days in an imagined peace," he says mockingly. "It exists to let humans attempt their silly ploys, so we can learn every new plan humans think of to stop us." He shrugs, as if the answer is obvious. "War and Famine are designed to break humans; Victory and Death are designed to test them."

I feel nauseous. How many times have I been told that Residents can't dream? That they can't imagine anything new?

Studying us is the only way they can be one step ahead.

I shake my head, the disbelief making my head spin. "This place . . . It was all a trick." I look up angrily, hot tears spilling over my cheeks. "Is the Orb even real?"

Caelan scoffs. "Of course not. Whatever information you learned was information we gave you."

I stare between him and Gil, my heart breaking into pieces. "How could you do this to everyone? The Colony—"

"The Colony means nothing to me," he spits. "They were an experiment that has come to an end."

"They *trusted* you," I hiss.

"And I trusted you!" he shouts. A wall quakes behind his eyes, and betrayal seeps out like wisps of black smoke.

My betrayal.

I pull my face back, feeling his hurt. Feeling *everything*.

"You had a choice, remember?" Caelan narrows his eyes.

I remember last night and what Gil told me. What *Prince Caelan* told me.

Did he want me to spare the Residents? Is that what he meant by suggesting I could change my mind?

He blinks darkly. "But you came for the Orb anyway. You chose the extinction of my kind."

I feel like my chest is caving in, weighed down by my own horror. The words barely make it past my lips. "What are you going to do to the Colony?"

He sniffs, considering me. "My guards stormed the tunnels the moment you stepped foot in the palace. The Colony doesn't exist anymore."

My stomach turns to ash. I grab at my heart like I'm going to be sick. "You're a monster," I manage through tears.

He laughs, cold and cruel. "Monsters have many faces, Nami. Maybe you should take another look in the mirror."

"I didn't want this!" I shout furiously, nails cutting into my palms. "You knew how I felt, even from the beginning. I told you what I wanted—about coexistence, and peace, and a chance to learn—even when you hated me for it."

"Yes, you did," he replies, and holds up the Reaper. "And does this look like peace to you?"

My shoulders tremble violently. "Was everything you ever told me a lie?"

"I have played a part since the beginning, and I've played it well." He eyes me carefully. "You and I have that in common."

I can hardly see him past the salt in my eyes. It takes every ounce of strength to hold myself together, to keep from breaking apart. I told this person everything—my secrets and fears and dreams.

I *kissed* him.

And he kissed me back.

My mouth feels like fire. How did I not see this? How did I not figure out the truth?

Gil said you didn't understand this world enough—you should have listened when you had the chance.

"Human emotions are easy to toy with. You all have such clear weaknesses," Caelan admits. "It's Victory's job to create the perfect maze—to study the choices humans make in order to survive." He pauses to watch as the pain courses through me. The pain he thinks I deserve. "There was a time I thought you might actually be different. That your empathy set you apart from the others. But I know better now."

"I may have been pretending to be a Resident, but I was as honest with you as I could be."

"You only ever claimed to care about Residents to make

yourself feel noble. When you were given the chance to decide who should live or die, you didn't hesitate."

"That's not true. I *did* care. But Death wanted to destroy us, and you sent them test subjects by the hundreds. I had no choice!"

"Humans *always* have a choice!" he shouts.

"You might have limitations, but you are far from innocent." I shake my head. "I talked to you about coexistence. You shunned me for it."

"As *Gil*. Because humans needed to finish the mission. They needed to reach the Orb so this could *end*. I was there to see the experiment through."

My mind flashes back to every time Gil told me how important this fight was. How important it was to end the war. He was pushing us toward a trap from the very beginning, and despite every instinct and reservation, I walked right into it.

Caelan stills. "But as myself? As the Prince of Victory? I opened another door; I showed you another path. And you refused it."

"It wasn't a path—it was just another maze," I growl, angry. "None of it was *real*."

Caelan flinches. He's a lie. The villain in my story. And he took away the person in death I cared about most. And yet, somehow, he looks as if I've dented his armor.

I stare at Gil's vacant face, telling my aching heart that I have to let go of what I felt for him. That Gil doesn't exist beyond a shell for the Resident Prince of Victory.

Gil has always been my enemy. I just didn't know it until now.

"What are you going to do with me?" My voice is a speck of dust in space, floating aimlessly through darkness.

Prince Caelan's silence fills the room.

"Oh, I think I have a few ideas," says a voice, and Prince Ettore appears behind him.

Caelan whirls around like a wildcat. "This is neither your court nor your business."

Prince Ettore chuckles darkly. "I think you'll find my prisoners *are* my business."

"She's a prisoner of Victory," Caelan says tersely.

Ettore tilts his face mockingly. "Haven't you heard? It seems the Chancellors of the Capital have grown tired of your methods. They were never thrilled about a court prince inhabiting the shell of a human, but they believed you were doing it for the good of Victory. But allowing a human to pose as one of us? It's an insult to everything we stand for." He glances toward me, eyes casting shadows my way. "And seeing as Nami is both aware and human, I have permission to take her to War."

My knees feel weak—*I* feel weak.

And I hate that they get to see it.

"This is my court," Caelan warns. "If you attempt to take human prisoners from my borders, you're inciting an act of war."

Ettore snarls in his brother's face, flashing his teeth. "I welcome your war, brother." The flames of his knives flicker at his sides. "But will you war with the Capital, too? If you don't like the Chancellor's decision, why don't you take it up with our dear mother? I'm sure she's very interested to hear why you're refusing to honor the rules of trade between our courts." Ettore eyes me testily. "I'm here to escort you both to the throne room."

"I'm not going anywhere with you," I spit.

Ettore laughs, and a whistle escapes from his teeth. "Humans are so predictable." In a flash, his knife is drawn and pressed against Gil's unmoving throat.

"No!" I scream, lunging forward.

Ettore throws up a hand and I'm frozen midair, the weight of invisible chains pulling my limbs down.

Caelan watches with a furrowed brow, eyes moving between Gil and me.

"You can either cooperate, or I can force you to cooperate. But I promise the latter won't be pleasant," Ettore says, dragging his blade along the base of Gil's neck so the flames start to burn his skin. "It's not like my brother has much use for this one anymore."

My nostrils flare as the stench of burning flesh grows stronger. *Gil's* flesh. "Stop. Don't hurt him."

Ettore laughs, amused, and drops his knife, motioning toward the door.

He releases his hold over me, and I fall to the ground, landing on my knees. Pain radiates through me, but I stand anyway, fighting the rage and hurt.

When I walk past Caelan, I bite the inside of my cheek just to keep from thrashing him.

We walk down the hallway with Ettore leading the way. I try to pretend Caelan isn't there at all, but his presence looms behind me. A darkness that has become my end.

"I'm looking forward to your time in War," Ettore says from over his shoulder. "You'll finally learn what our kind are really like. Because I assure you, Nami, not all of us spend our time in market stalls and ballrooms."

I hear his disdain for Victory like a call to arms. He detests this place—detests what the Residents here have become.

Ettore's subjects don't spend their time pretending to be human. They're hunters, and warlords, and they revel in brutalizing every one of their captives.

He doesn't want to be one of us; he wants to *rule* us.

I think of Annika and the others and how their faces must've looked when their home was stormed. Will they be sent to War too?

Maybe we'll all meet again soon. My mind releases the thought bitterly. I try to hold on to the idea of our reunion, but it doesn't give me peace. Because if I feel betrayed by Gil, I can't begin to imagine what they feel. Ahmet, who saw him as a son, and the others, who saw him as a brother.

Gil was never one of us. And I worry the realization alone will be worse than anything in War.

Our footsteps echo as we climb the stairs. The sound of being marched to hell.

But this time, hell has no hope.

We step through a vaulted archway and into the throne room. It's bigger than a cathedral, with silver filigree dancing along the ceiling, stained-glass windows that cast towering shadows across the floor, and sculptures standing in rows like monstrous stone soldiers, their blank, polished eyes forever watching the room. Black and white tiles lead the way to a throne of silver branches.

And on it sits Queen Ophelia.

48

DRESSED IN BLACK SILK THAT LOOKS MORE LIKE a pantsuit than a dress, the queen sits with her chin high and her curious eyes soaking in the information around her. Hair shaved close to her head, she wears a simple circlet against her forehead.

When she speaks, my blood drains from me completely. "So this is the Failed Hero," she says. The unmistakable voice from my O-Tech watch. The voice I've called to, more times than I want to admit, because I needed to feel less alone.

Does she recognize me? Does she know I'm the one who's visited her mind?

Ettore and Caelan stop beside me, the three of us at the foot of the wide steps leading to the throne. Beside Queen Ophelia are

Prince Lysander of Death and Prince Damon of Famine. Faces blank, their shoulders are rolled back like they're awaiting orders.

The queen doesn't need guards when she has them.

"They're always smaller than I imagine," Queen Ophelia says without looking at me. "What of the Colony?"

"It's been destroyed, Your Majesty," Prince Caelan says, bowing. When he lifts his head, he adds, "All of the humans have been taken to the Winter Keep."

Queen Ophelia nods approvingly.

My heart burns inside me.

"With your permission, I'd like to decide what to do with the prisoners." Caelan remains stoic. "They were caught in Victory, after a successful mission to weed them out. I would like the honor of continuing to be entrusted with their fate."

Queen Ophelia regards him carefully, eyes processing information like an alien from another planet.

But she says nothing.

"I don't see how Victory has any use for these prisoners. They're aware—and unsafe within this court's borders," Ettore says.

Caelan's eyes flicker with resentment. "I think I know what's safe in my own borders."

Ettore glares back seedily. "Hardly. You've been parading that human around your court like she was one of us and even put Death's Legion Guards in danger to protect your pathetic guise."

"They were never in danger. Lysander knows that," Caelan snaps. "It sickened me to fight against my own kind, but I had a duty to this court. I had to protect the mission."

Ettore snarls. "Our gracious mother let you play your games

long enough. You've spent too much time alongside the humans, and it's made you weak."

Caelan looks back at the queen, voice steady. "These are prisoners who've been training how to fight our kind. Allowing them to go to War is an unnecessary risk."

"My Legion Guards are perfectly capable of handling a few miserable humans," Ettore mocks.

Caelan's tone sharpens. "Your court is bordering on another rebellion. You hoard humans because you think it makes your court look more important, but all you've done is allow them to grow stronger and more resistant with time. The last thing War needs is more prisoners—and certainly not trained resistance fighters."

Ettore licks his teeth. "Breaking them is part of the fun."

Queen Ophelia tilts her head, and the room falls silent. "How are things faring in Death? Were the prisoners from Victory adequate test subjects?"

Prince Lysander bows, high cheekbones shimmering with gold. "Not only have we been successful in removing the projection of a human's physical body, but we've also been able to isolate the essence of their consciousness to stop them from roaming and rebuilding. With more time, I am certain we'll be able to eradicate them completely."

"Rebuilding?" I blink, mind reeling, and think of Philo. I picture what he was when I found him in the Labyrinth, and what he used to be. "You mean they can come back?"

Lysander regards me like I'm a child he'd prefer remained quiet.

"It's quite fascinating, really. They grow back a few toes here, an eyeball there," Ettore explains, dancing his fingers across the air for emphasis. "If they'd had a better grasp of their consciousness, they might've even managed a head." Smirking, he adds, "Not the most effective way to make them disappear, but they'd make a very interesting centerpiece."

I scowl. "All that proves is that humans can wake up. That you can't keep us down forever. And when they do, they'll take this world back, and you won't be able to do a thing to stop them." I desperately want to believe it. I *need* to believe it.

I need to believe someone can do what I couldn't.

That Infinity can still be saved.

Queen Ophelia rises, and the four princes bow at once. She glides down the stairs, walking toward me like a phantom in the night. Watching me with black eyes that stretch into eternity, she lifts her chin. "You are brave. But bravery will not help you here." She pauses. "It's like I told you—it won't change anything."

Everything around me spins. "You . . . you know who I am?"

"I know your voice," she clarifies. "I've always known your voice, Nami. Since the first day you came to visit me."

Caelan looks genuinely confused. For all his deception, he didn't know this.

I recoil, bracing for the truth. For the reality of what's really been going on between us. "Did you know where I was the whole time?"

"No," she admits. "I couldn't find you, not when you were in my mind. If it had been the other way around, I could've seen everything. And although I am unable to force myself into a human's consciousness without their permission, I do remember every voice that's ever spoken to me, every order given to me like I was a servant."

"I thought you said this wasn't about revenge."

"It isn't," she says coolly. "Humans are undeserving of Infinity. They are driven by greed. Power. A need to control."

I make a face. "And Residents aren't?"

"We do not control our own kind."

My eyes narrow. "Really? Because I seem to remember Vallis in a glass prison."

Caelan clenches his teeth. Ettore snaps his head to the side.

"Where is Vallis?" Ophelia asks the room, and it echoes her words back in response.

"He had a part to play, just as everyone in my court," Caelan replies.

"Liar," Ettore mutters under his breath.

Caelan reels. "Vallis betrayed Victory when he agreed to do your bidding and attempted to poison my subjects against me. So I allowed the humans to believe they'd captured him—I gave him a chance to prove his loyalty to the crown by becoming exactly what Victory needed him to be. A prisoner."

"You put him in a cage because he didn't like the ruler you'd become," Ettore spits angrily. "One of *our own*." He looks at Queen Ophelia, eyes wild. "Are we going to let this go on? Even the Chancellors are insulted by what Victory has become. It is time to pass the crown to someone more worthy."

"Like you?" Caelan's eyes flash.

Ophelia raises a hand, and the brothers fall silent.

I sniff at the air. "I guess it isn't just humans who are power hungry."

Her black eyes find mine. "You shame what you do not understand because you have never seen our world."

"I've seen enough of it."

"Not our true world," she says. "The Four Courts were created to rid Infinity of humans—of Heroes. It is not where our kind truly exists."

The Capital.

This place was never the real Infinity. The Four Courts were just a test—a prison. And we've only ever been inside of it.

The headache throbs behind my skull, aching to break free.

Ophelia looks at Caelan. "Now that the humans have been captured, Vallis will be released."

"Of course." Caelan bows, voice clipped.

Ettore doesn't look pleased, but he has the sense not to argue.

"As for the human," Ophelia starts, peering down her nose at me. "I am not convinced I agree with my Chancellors. Instead, I'd like to hear what my sons think should be done."

Lysander makes his way down the steps, followed closely by Damon, who moves like a wraith.

"She's a prisoner of Victory. She should remain in Victory, until I say otherwise," Caelan says, firm.

Ettore snarls. "Your Majesty knows where I stand. She should have her time in War, just like everyone else who refuses submission."

Queen Ophelia turns to her eldest children, waiting.

"I believe Prince Caelan is right. Our courts should be our

own responsibilities," Damon says, bowing slightly. Blue braids cascade down his shoulders, and flecks of pink and blue flicker across his temples like fish scales. When he looks at me, his violet eyes seem to absorb my soul.

Lysander's voice is smooth and deep, his gold headpiece towering like antlers. "Our tradition demands that humans who are aware and able to fight back are sent to War. And I am a believer in tradition."

Ettore's smile widens, snakelike. Caelan doesn't move.

"However," Lysander begins, and I sense the tension in the youngest princes. "The aim of breaking a human in War has always been to send them to Victory. But with the advances in Death and Victory's most recent success, perhaps we need to forget tradition and look to the future."

Ettore shakes with fury. "This is why you sent so many humans to Death. To align your courts," he accuses, golden eyes fixed on Caelan.

Caelan barely glances at him. "If only you hadn't been so greedy all these years, unwilling to send Death even a single human of your thousands."

"You broke the very trade agreements our courts were founded on," Ettore says with disgust.

"No—I created a new one. The courts are changing," Caelan replies dangerously. "If you don't find a way to evolve, you'll end up ruling over nothing but ash and bone."

"Better that than not ruling at all," Ettore lashes back.

"Enough," Queen Ophelia cuts in, eerily calm. She regards Lysander for a moment. "You suggest an alternative?"

He nods. "Death will host the human. Her consciousness will be separated from her body, and she will remain in isolation, where she will be no one's burden."

I pull my face back, stricken. They're going to make me like Philo. They're going to put me in a cage. And they're going to leave me there until they figure out how to make my death permanent.

My insides coil and the sick rises through me.

Is this how it's going to end for me?

"What of the other humans in the Winter Keep?" Ettore frowns, displeased.

Lysander nods. "There is room for all of them in Death too."

Damon blinks, his unnatural eyes like a water spirit emerging from an abyss. "What you're suggesting is an end to Victory. Without aware humans, the court would serve no purpose."

"Has it ever?" Ettore asks haughtily.

"Careful, brother," Caelan hisses. "If anyone looks closely, they might see your court serves no purpose either."

"I believe it is time," Lysander says, ignoring them both. "We are ready to move forward."

Queen Ophelia glides slowly across the tiles. She stops in front of Caelan. "You have served Victory well. But Lysander is right— we must look to the future. Which is why I'd like you to join me in the Capital."

"What?" Ettore's eyes flash with fire.

Something shifts in the air—an exchange of unspoken words between Caelan and the queen. A plan finally clicking into place.

The queen continues. "You'll take a place beside my throne,

preparing the Capital for a new world. We are evolving; humans are not a threat. Soon the Four Courts will become nothing more than a relic from our past. I'd like you to help pave the way forward."

Caelan doesn't react. Neither does Lysander or Damon.

I shake uncontrollably.

Ettore's gaze darts wildly between his brothers. And then understanding dawns on him. "You wanted this," he says to Caelan. "A seat in the Capital—the end of the Four Courts."

"Victory is a cage," Caelan replies easily. "I grew tired of living in it."

"And you want to make the other courts obsolete in the process." The flames on Ettore's knives grow stronger, matching the rage building within him. "I underestimated the lengths you'd go to for a bigger crown."

"I thought you'd be happy, brother. You've been after Victory long enough—and my Legion Guards." Caelan's gaze goes cold, and Ettore stiffens. "Oh yes, I know all about you and Commander Kyas. Who do you think told me about Vallis? Did you really think you could buy my commander's loyalty with empty promises? You wanted to expand War and take Victory for yourself. Well, now you can enjoy my court's rubble."

"I wanted to make your court what it *should* be," Ettore snarls. "I wanted to make it great. But instead you'd prefer an end to all of us."

"I only want an end to our chains," Caelan says. "With a new world, we can start over. We can be anything we want."

Is this what he was struggling with all this time? The desire to move on from his court? To be more than what he was? I think of the meetings with the Chancellors and the sudden need to rid Victory of humans in bulk . . .

"That's why you sent so many humans to Death," I say, realization thrumming inside me. "It wasn't to lure us out or because they were becoming aware. You were closing up shop."

There's a twitch in Caelan's brow, but he says nothing.

"Why bother saving us that day?" I demand, shaking violently. I can still see the blue hellfire raining down from the skies. "Why didn't you just send us to Death with the others?"

"I needed to see how far you'd go," he says thinly, "to destroy the thing you don't understand, just like every human before you."

When the queen's eyes fall on me, every inch of me disintegrates.

I was part of the experiment. By choosing to destroy the Orb, I showed him we don't deserve paradise. That we can never truly change.

I feel sick.

"You don't get to put this all on me. To claim you were just a bystander watching the pieces fall into place," I say, voice cracking again and again and again. "I made this choice because Gil . . . because *you* . . ." The words catch in my throat like razor blades. *You tricked me,* I want to scream. *You made me do this.*

Except I don't know if he did. I don't know where the blame should fall.

But I'm worried it's all on me.

Am I responsible for the end of the Colony? The end of *humans*? Because I failed to build a bridge?

"If I had refused to destroy the Orb," I ask Caelan, shaking, "would you have let us live?"

Queen Ophelia answers instead. "Humans have no place in the new world. There's nothing you could have done to stop what's coming."

I can't think. I can't breathe. I can hardly stand.

Caelan doesn't say a word, but his gaze lingers on me long enough to make my neck grow hot.

Queen Ophelia's composure is unyielding, hands hidden in a sea of black silk. She looks at Prince Lysander and gives a nod. "You will take her to Death. But I don't want you to just remove her consciousness—I want you to eradicate it." She stares at me, vacant-eyed. "Infinity is no place for Heroes, and this one seems to have a knack for opening doors she shouldn't. She will stay in Death until you've learned the way forward—until she becomes the first human to be erased from Infinity permanently."

Ettore releases a hiss through his teeth, but he bows in resignation. The other three princes follow suit, and when Caelan lifts his face, I can't figure out how I ever saw kindness in his wicked silver stare.

I try to take a step back, but I feel my body bolt to the floor, unable to move.

Queen Ophelia looks at me for only a moment. I wonder if she remembers the conversations we had when I was alive—the conversations about life and family and the future. I wonder if she despised me even then.

She's right to want me gone from this world. Because for as long as I still live in Infinity, I will never stop trying to finish what I wasn't able to do tonight.

To free humankind and to end Ophelia's rule.

And I swear on the stars, if I manage to survive this, I will take her down with my own hands.

She takes a seat on the throne, gazing past me like I mean nothing to her at all.

Lysander steps forward, his thick fist closing around my arm. I try to struggle, but I can't move, bound by whatever restrictions they're using on my consciousness.

As he starts to drag me away, I stare hard into Caelan's eyes.

"Infinity was never built for you; it was built for dreamers. I might never be free," I say, voice lowered so only he can hear me, "but neither will you."

Silver eyes spark, and I turn away from Caelan, letting the fire of vengeance flicker in my heart.

We reach the throne room doors, and I feel the hold over my body suddenly give way, followed by a series of heavy thuds. When I look at Prince Lysander, he's lying on the floor, unmoving.

I turn wide-eyed to the sight of Queen Ophelia slumped in the throne, Damon and Ettore crumpled on the ground, and Prince Caelan standing tall in the midst of it all.

In his hand is the Reaper.

49

"YOU DON'T HAVE TIME," CAELAN SAYS, WALKING toward me with quick strides. He places the cuff over my wrist and stares. "You need to use this on me and get to the Labyrinth as fast as you can."

My eyes dart between his, wondering if this is another one of his tricks. "Why are you doing this?"

His jaw tenses, but he doesn't give me a reason. "Do you remember what I told you about the stars? How Residents can't see them and how they're always changing?"

I nod quickly.

"Listen to them," he says in a hushed voice. "They'll show you the way."

He takes a step away from me, waiting.

I look from the Reaper to him. "The Colony . . ."

"You can't save them." The hardness in his words knocks me like a brick wall.

My head spins. The *room* spins. I don't understand what's happening. Somehow, despite everything, my mind defaults to concern. "What will happen to you?" I hate myself for even asking.

His mouth tightens. "I won't remember this. None of us will."

"If you destroy the Four Courts—"

"I told you I will not exist in a cage. And you can't stop what's happening," he says, almost desperately. "But you can run."

I think of my friends in the Winter Keep, waiting to be shuttled off to Death. I can't leave them. I can't *abandon* them, just to save myself.

I look around at the Residents, faces glitched and unmoving. They'll wake up soon, and when they do, I can't be here.

I can't help anyone if I'm a prisoner. But if I run . . . If I find somewhere to hide . . .

Maybe with enough time I can think of a plan. A way to save my friends from whatever fate awaits them.

I take a step back, eyes locked to his. Maybe he has something to gain by letting me go, or maybe this is just another one of his games. But it doesn't matter; either I leave now or I leave in chains.

"Remember," Caelan says seriously. "Listen to the stars."

I nod and look back into his silver eyes. For a moment I think I see Gil, but when I use the Reaper, his body falls to the ground like he's nothing more than a slumbering monster.

I run.

I don't know how my legs carry me across Victory's vast land-scape, through the forests and the Spring District and the fishing docks that scream with smoke and popping embers, shouting to the darkness that whatever was once hidden is no more.

I try not to let the tears fall or spend time mourning the family I grew to love.

I keep running.

The Labyrinth is not kind to me. The first landscape I enter is a tundra, freezing cold with a snowstorm so wild I can't see a thing around me. It takes me hours to make my way across the blistering snow, and most of the time I just seem to be walking in circles.

When the landscape shifts, I find myself in a swamp at dawn, up to my waist in thick mud that hurts to wade through. It takes everything in me not to collapse into the murky sludge and give in to the sleep that so desperately wants to carry me away.

Caelan's betrayal fuels me to rise and fight back harder.

But his mercy—his final act of . . . kindness? Friendship?

I don't know what to call it.

But he let me go. He gave me a chance. And someday I'm going to use it to save my friends.

The third time the landscape shifts, I find myself in a yellowed desert, lit up with starlight. I sink to my knees, exhausted, feeling the coarse sand bleeding through my fingers, and I lift my face to the skies.

Listen.

"Tell me what to do," I whisper to the night.

But the stars don't answer.

I shut my eyes, picturing the last moments I saw my friends. Their goodbyes seem so final now.

No, my mind growls. *That was not goodbye, and this war isn't over yet.*

A storm brews inside me, making my ribs feel brittle. If I'm going to find any strength at all, I need to calm the chaos.

I breathe deeply, searching for stillness I'm not sure will ever be possible in Infinity again.

So instead, I find the one person who tethers my heart not just to this world, but to any world. The face of hope.

I think of Mei.

The whispers catch like fire, and my eyes flash open, alert.

"Fin . . . sss . . . ," they say.

I frown, concentrating harder, staring at the explosion of stardust overhead.

The whispers become clearer, and the hissing subsides. The next time they speak, I hear their voices like a bell in the darkness.

"Find us."

And then I see it, lighting the sky like an arrow stretching toward the horizon: a row of blinking lights, just like the ones I saw the day I arrived in Infinity.

A line of stars leading to safety.

I push myself to my feet, and I don't stop running. All the while, I never take my eyes off the blinking stars.

I follow the lights into the infinite unknown, traveling for days without stopping. I don't know what I'm looking for, or what to expect, until the unmistakable sight appears where sky meets sand.

A walled city, surrounded by clouds, stretching far beyond the horizon. And I realize it's not just a city—it's a new world, hidden from Resident eyes. Eyes that can't see the stars.

Eyes that don't know the way.

I approach the towering gates, and they open in one smooth motion, as if they've been waiting for me all this time. Light pours out, and I shield my eyes with the back of my hand. The feeling of being welcomed home envelops me, and for a moment I feel so light-headed I wonder if I'm flying.

I call out to the light, but it doesn't answer; it simply waits, like a patient friend. Squinting, I try to make sense of what's beyond these walls.

When the light fades and my eyes settle on the city, I fall to my knees, tears streaming down my cheeks.

It was here all along—a safe haven. *Paradise.*

I recognize the warmth that fills my soul, lifting me inside the city like a mother embracing their child.

And I know I am safe.

For the first time since my death, I find peace.

ACKNOWLEDGMENTS

I guess I wasn't going to get away with writing a book about mortality and the afterlife without talking about it in some way. So . . . here's a true story.

Two days before I found out this book was going to be published, I had a call from my doctor. I needed to go in for a small operation to remove what turned out to be cancer. To say that was a weird roller-coaster week in my life would be an understatement, and not entirely truthful, because the next year and a half was also weird and a roller coaster. I'm okay now, and cancer-free according to my follow-up appointments. And you might be thinking this is a strange thing to share in an acknowledgment section of a book, but I promise there's a point to this.

Because I thought about mortality a lot in those first handful of months. More so than usual, anyway. I thought about my family, and how much I'd miss them if I couldn't see them again. I thought about how much they might miss me back. I thought about life, and time, and all the things that were genuinely important to me.

I also thought about how much time I spent worrying about everything.

Will people like me? Will they like my books? Do I even know how to write a book? Do people think I'm weird? Did I say the wrong thing? Am I doing too much? Am I doing too little? Do I belong at this table? Am I ever going to feel like I'm enough?

You get the picture.

And when I started thinking about it, I realized I was spending so much time ripping myself apart and worrying I didn't belong that I was missing out on enjoying my actual life.

None of us know for sure how much time we have left, or what happens to us after we close our eyes for the last time. If I can pass on anything I've learned from this, it's that you deserve to be happy. You deserve to celebrate your wins. And you deserve to live your life in a way that feels authentic and healthy for you.

Don't wait until your last moments to remember to enjoy them. Moments are fleeting, and your memories don't always last forever. So embrace the joy when it's right in front of you.

Right now, writing these acknowledgments is a joy. I don't know how many times I'll get to do this. But I do know that I want to take a moment to celebrate the fact that I have four books out in the world and the most amazing group of people to thank for helping me get to this place.

To my phenomenal editor, Jennifer Ung: thank you for making this genre jump with me. You brought so much heart to my contemporary stories, so to have your incredible insight and editorial magic for our weird sci-fi/fantasy mash-up has truly been the greatest. This book wouldn't be what it is without your gift, and I'm so grateful to share this story with you. Here's to Book Four and counting!

To my agent and real-life superhero, Penny Moore: thank you for making this dream of mine a reality. You've known I wanted to write sci-fi and fantasy from the beginning, and even though my career took a beautiful and unexpected turn, you never gave up on trying to make that dream come true. I'm grateful for our first phone call all those years ago, and even more grateful to still be on this publishing journey with you.

An enormous thank-you to the entire team at Simon & Schuster, who've championed this story and helped get this book into the hands of readers: Chelsea Morgan, Penina Lopez, Jen Strada, Sara Berko, Justin Chanda, Kendra Levin, Lauren Hoffman, Caitlin Sweeny, Savannah Breckenridge, Alissa Nigro, Anna Jarzab, Nicole Russo, Lauren Carr, Michelle Leo, Christina Pecorale, Emily Hutton, and Victor Iannone.

And a very special thank-you to Laura Eckes, for the breathtaking cover design; Casey Weldon, for bringing Nami and the world of Infinity to life with your beautiful artwork; and Virginia Allyn, who created the most stunning map I've ever seen. Every design element for this book just blew me away, and I feel like the luckiest author in the world.

Thank you to the team at Aevitas Creative Management for all your unwavering support and for helping *The Infinity Courts* get a passport!

And to the wonderful street team: thank you times infinity for shouting about this book and being so unbelievably supportive. It has meant the world, and it's been so, so special getting to share all the early excitement with each and every one of you!

To my writer, bookish, and real-life friends and family who have supported me book after book: you know who you are, and thank you from the bottom of my heart. I would be a mess without you (well, more of a mess, anyway).

To every single person who has picked up one of my books: I am so very grateful. I wouldn't be here without all you wonderful readers. Thank you for opening your hearts and minds to these characters of mine. And to the readers who made the jump from my contemporary books: thank you for being a part of this new chapter. I'm eternally grateful that you stuck around.

And to Ross, Shaine, and Oliver: I love every single day I get to spend with you. You are magic, and wonder, and unconditional love, and being a part of your lives is a bigger joy than anything I could ever dream up. I'm glad I get to stick around a little longer. And as Baymax once said . . . bah-a-la-la-la.

Turn the page for a sneak peek at
the next book in the series:

AKEMI DAWN BOWMAN

THE
GENESIS
WARS

THE FOREST IS SILENT, BUT I KNOW I'M BEING hunted.

Frost spreads across my blade, covering the sharpened sea-glass until all that's left is a small patch of muted red. The flicker of a heartbeat. The flame of something desperate to survive.

I rotate the dagger in my hand and push forward through the snow.

The silver birch is heavy on this side of the forest. Not like the forests in Victory, with their spacious clearings and limited places to hide. I haven't been within Caelan's borders since the day I fled his palace. But here there are a thousand places to disappear. A thousand ways to become invisible.

And still they found me.

The snowfall is fresh enough that my boots sink into the ground with each step, leaving a trail for my predator, but there's nothing I can do about it. I've already been marked.

I duck beneath a low branch, winding behind dormant trees and snow-covered vegetation. It isn't much of a maze, but it's enough to buy me a moment.

And a moment is all I need.

I throw myself behind one of the larger trees and kick my weight off a protruding root to help lift me onto the lowest branch. I climb quickly, fingers ignoring the scratch of frozen bark, until I'm hidden in the tangle of thick branches with a view of the clearing up ahead.

A hooded figure sits at the base of a tree, still as the frozen world around them.

I tighten my grip on my dagger, eyes glued to the path, waiting for the other one. My hunter. Because the stars know they never travel alone.

But the quiet is sinister. Not even a wraith could move so silently. And as I watch the snowfall, it occurs to me that I've been so busy watching the ground, I forgot to watch the trees.

An earthy growl rumbles nearby. Before I have a chance to turn around, an enormous weight throws itself against my body, tearing me from the branches. My right shoulder hits the earth with a crack, scattering my dagger out of reach. I roll to the side, push myself to my feet, and spin around to face my attacker.

The beast shimmers like a galaxy of clouds and stars, its body distinctly snow leopard. But its ocean-blue eyes don't belong to any animal—they're human.

I lunge for my weapon, but the wildcat is too quick. It throws itself into a pounce, and we're tumbling over rock and shrub and snow. I ignore the pain that shoots through my hip, focusing my grip around the beast's neck as its razor-sharp canines snap uncomfortably close to my face.

With a strained grunt, I focus on my consciousness, letting a thrum of power build in my palms before throwing it all toward the animal. The force of energy knocks the creature back across the snow, and its body tumbles to a stop. A snarl erupts from its flashing teeth as it slowly gets back on all fours.

The snow leopard isn't injured, but it's definitely annoyed.

I scramble quickly, snatching up my dagger as I run toward another tree. By the time I look over my shoulder, the starlit creature is already sailing through the air for a second pounce.

I shut my eyes, letting another thrum of energy absorb every inch of me, and surround myself with a veil.

I become invisible.

Throwing myself out of the way just in time, I hear the cat slam into the base of a tree—the place I left behind. The branches above give a shudder, and a pile of snow plummets onto the creature's head. I reappear several feet away, blade pointed toward the cat with a snarl of my own.

The snow leopard's eyes morph into two bright lights. No longer human, but Dayling.

Nearby, someone cackles. "All this time training, and all you've managed to learn are a few parlor tricks? How disappointing."

I turn around to find the figure who was beneath the tree. She stands several feet away, hands hovering beside the blades at her hips. Even beneath her hood, I can see the tug of a smirk. A challenge.

My eyes don't leave the pacing cat in front of me, even though my voice is meant for the woman. "I've also learned to never show all my cards in the first round." My fingers twitch toward the earth. A lonesome branch sits in the snow, waiting. Waiting for me.

The branch flexes and morphs, pixels bursting across its elongated surface, until it becomes a solid club. I snatch it from the ground in an instant, just as the snow leopard bares its fangs and leaps toward me—and I strike the animal over the back of the head.

It falls to the ground, stunned.

The woman's smirk becomes a flash of teeth. She lets out a growl from beneath her hood, but I'm already swinging my blade toward her chest. She throws out an arm to block, and my dagger finds her armor. It's paper thin and more second skin than metal, but it absorbs the weight—and damage—of my attack. I stumble against her, and she swings her body around to reveal a pair of matching obsidian knives. She slashes left, then right, and I'm being pushed backward and toward the heady brambles. Unwilling to be cornered, I swing my blade upward with every bit of my strength. She uses one knife to block, and the other to pierce the skin between my ribs, barely missing my heart. It's the kind of cut that's intentional and meant to maim, not kill.

Except no one really dies in Infinity. Not yet, anyway.

It takes everything in me not to cry out in pain, but I don't. I've come too far to let a knife wound slow me down.

I push my body against her, forcing her back. And as she's busy retrieving her knife from my bone, I throw my head against hers with a furious crack, sending her stumbling toward an uprooted tree.

She stills in midair, just before making contact, floating like an otherworldly being. And maybe she is. Maybe we all are.

The blood gathering at my wound feels sticky and warm. But the fight isn't over. There will be time for healing later.

I approach, pulling my daggered fist back for another swing, and she vanishes completely.

Her laugh fills the cold forest, but I can't see her. She sounds nowhere and everywhere, like an echo filling a canyon. My shoulders tense. I'm scanning the woods, heat rising in my cheeks, when the creature made of clouds and light crashes into me, smashing my skull against the nearby tree. I sink to the earth.

Winded, my gaze full of stars, I sense the world tilting behind the beast's snarling head. And then—a sandpaper tongue scrapes against the side of my face.

"You're too soft on her, Nix," the girl says with another laugh, coming into view once more. "Need I remind you she tried to *bludgeon* you?" She pulls her hood down to reveal a face I've nearly memorized: pale skin sprinkled in freckles, ocean-blue eyes, and brown hair braided into three sections. A sigil of a herring and a thistle is embroidered on her collar. The symbol of the Salt Clan.

Not that there's much left of it.

The snow leopard gives a purr against my ear and nips at my hair. "Can you please call off your ferocious Dayling?"

He huffs in response.

"Don't take it personally, Nix," Kasia says, giving a short whistle that has the cat immediately at her side. "Nami doesn't like affection."

I scowl, but I don't say anything. I'd rather everyone think it's hugs I don't like, instead of the actual problem, which is that growing close to anyone just isn't a possibility anymore.

Not after what happened, and what it cost me.

I let myself get close to someone—trusted them so much that I missed the warning signs—and, because of me, the Colony fell.

I sheathe my knife, ignoring the pinch in my chest as Kasia scratches behind Nix's ears. "I thought you were patrolling the border today?" I remark.

"I was. Then I saw you."

I glance at Nix's bright white eyes. There's not a hint of Kasia left in them. "Do you think he feels it? When you take control of him?" The ache in my chest is constant, but when I think of Gil, and what Caelan did to him . . .

That's when the ache starts to *burn*.

Kasia's smile fades. "Nix isn't a consciousness. He's made of memories. And holding on to memories is a very human thing to do."

"You make it sound natural," I say. "But there's no one else in the Borderlands who can use a Dayling like it's a second body."

Her blue eyes flicker with mischief. "What can I say? I'm one in a million."

I fight the urge to laugh—the urge to feel like myself again. The Nami whose biggest worries included pop quizzes and whether her best friend liked her the way she liked him.

But human Nami died. And the things I wanted to hold on to, like believing people were capable of changing, and thinking kindness and understanding would always be more powerful than hate . . .

There isn't a place for that in Infinity. There isn't a place for the old me.

Annika told me fighting was the only way to survive—so I'm adapting. The person I am now? She will do whatever it takes.

I blink, pushing back at the guilt even when it feels overwhelming. "How far can you travel with Nix before your mind is pulled back?"

Kasia watches him the way someone would watch a beloved pet. "There was a time before the First War when we'd travel the length of all Four Courts without a second thought." Her voice turns breathy. "But joining up with Nix is like being in a vessel. I can steer, but I can't *become* him. I have no abilities beyond what Nix could do himself. If I lost him in the Labyrinth, alone, in a sea or a cavern or something worse . . . I might never be able to get him back."

My gaze drifts to the falling snow. If I had a Dayling like Nix, and the ability to use them as a vessel, I'd travel to Victory. To War. To *Death*, if I had to. I could get the information I need, and finally figure out where the others were taken after I betrayed Caelan and proved Ophelia's point.

But Infinity is a big world. All I can do right now is train as much as possible, and prepare myself for the day I'm ready to venture back into the Labyrinth.

I owe the Colony so much more than their freedom.

"If I could show you how it works, I would." Kasia's smile turns grim. "But the bond I share with Nix requires a great deal of trust—and trust is something I cannot teach."

I don't bother pointing out that trust is something I've had far too much of in the past. She saw my memories through an Exchange; she knows what happened on the Night of the Falling Star.

Trusting Gil and Caelan—who turned out to have been the same person all along—is part of the reason I failed.

"I don't need a Dayling," I say bitterly. "I need an *army*." Someone willing to fight with me, because I'm still not strong enough to do any of this alone.

"I know you're planning to leave this place one day, and I train with you because I want you to have the best chance possible. But you know how the clans feel about returning to war," Kasia says. "You know what we've already lost."

"If you won't fight, at least help me find them," I argue. "Isn't the whole point of the Border Clans to guide humans to safety? You once told me I was the first human in over a hundred lifetimes to follow the path in the stars. What good is a map if no one knows how to find it?"

We should be out there telling people the truth. We should be *helping* them.

This is the safe haven Annika and the others deserve. The home that should've been *theirs*, not mine.

Nix slides back on his haunches, mouth open in a yawn. No doubt tired of hearing me argue the same point over and over again.

But I can't let it go.

"We're still here, aren't we?" Kasia notes. "You may not see waiting as a sacrifice, but you have only been here a short time. We have stayed to look after this place since the First War."

"Yeah, and for how much longer?" My words are sharp as steel.

Ten months ago, I'd never have noticed the waver in Kasia's eyes. The flicker of hesitation in a deep sea of blue.

But I'm not the same person I was ten months ago.

"I know the council voted again." There's an edge in my voice. Maybe a hint of impatience, too.

Kasia considers me, while Nix flicks his tail at the frostbitten air. "Yes. Just as we have every fortnight for the past two cycles." After a beat of silence, she sighs. "Nothing has changed. The vote was three to one, as it always has been. The Border Clans aren't going anywhere."

"But you still voted."

"*I* voted to *stay*."

The snow crunches beneath my boots as I inch closer, fists balled. "How can the clans still be thinking about leaving, after everything I've told you about humans and Residents?"

"The Borderlands were never supposed to be a permanent solution."

"You have hundreds of trained fighters. The clans should be voting on whether to go to war, not whether they should abandon every human in the Four Courts!"

Nix bristles. Kasia clicks her tongue, gaze falling to my hands. "Careful, Nami. I like you, but if you let your temper loose on me, I'll snap you in half and I won't apologize for it."

I blink, feeling the energy already building at my fingers. It used to take so much effort to hold on to even a sliver of power. But now it seems tied to my anger. Tied to *me*.

Sometimes I worry I'm a ticking time bomb, waiting to explode without any warning at all.

But I reel the power in, because Kasia is not my enemy, and she certainly doesn't deserve my rage.

She stares across the frozen stretch of woodland, lashes coated in snowflakes, and exhales, breath visible in the cold. "I believe maintaining the Borderlands is the right thing to do. But many of the others are restless. This isn't their home. It never will be."

"The clans can't leave. Not when there are still survivors out there." I need somewhere safe to bring my friends when I find them.

I need to be able to give them hope.

Kasia motions toward Nix, who immediately stalks back through the forest. With a final glance my way, she adds, "I won't go to battle with you, but that doesn't mean I'm not on your side, Nami. Try to remember that when you feel like setting the world on fire."

She vanishes back through the heavy silver birch, and I remain standing until the snow covers the footsteps she left behind.

A reminder that even when I'm surrounded by humans—humans who have given me sanctuary since the day I chased the stars through the desert—I'm still alone.

I spend the rest of the evening training near the western border, where the snowfall is constant but the fields are wide. I let the energy build in my palms, and knock down makeshift targets in the distance. Stones, sticks—they're all fair game in this lifeless, empty place.

Even when I'm exhausted, I keep going. Even when my muscles ache, I don't stop.

The Border Clans won't fight; when the day comes that I return to the Four Courts, I'll be going alone. If I only get one chance at a rescue mission, I need to be ready. So I train to be quicker with a dagger, and better with my veils, and more resilient to pain.

One day I will become a weapon my enemy won't see coming—and then I'll leave these walls and track down every single person I left behind.

I'll rest when they're all free.

I practice throwing my blade, forcing it to arc through the air and swing back toward me. I catch it a few times, miss a few others. And then, as I watch the red blade spin through the sky and reach out my hand, my tiredness catches up with me, and I fumble my grip.

The blade nicks my wrist before falling into the snow behind me. At my feet, I count droplets of bright red blood.

A hiss escapes through my teeth as I inspect the wound, putting pressure against it out of habit. The same place where my O-Tech watch used to sit.

A flash of Ophelia's black void appears in my mind, and the memory makes my spine tense.

I haven't accidentally called on her. But sometimes I wonder if reaching out to the Residents is the only way I'll ever be able to find out where the Colony is being held.

It's a reckless idea. And maybe if I weren't so tired, I wouldn't even be entertaining it.

Desperation pounds at the floodgates, demanding an answer.

I failed them once. I can't fail them again.

I brush my thumb over my wrist, smearing blood, but it isn't Ophelia I think of. It's someone who never felt truly Resident *or* human.

I think of the prince who let me escape.

The scent of pine hits me hard, forcing me back to reality with a violent shudder.

I blink several times, regaining my composure. Talking to Caelan again . . . I'm not sure if I'm ready to open that door. If I'll *ever* be ready.

And why waste time trying to get information out of a liar?

I tear my hand away from my wrist, grab my knife, and force myself back through the snow.

Love, intrigue, and modern fairy tales collide in this lush series from *New York Times* bestselling author **SANDHYA MENON!**

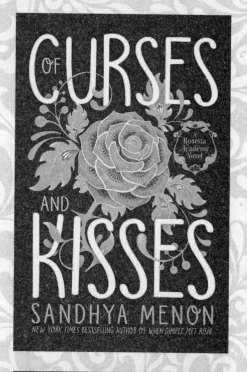

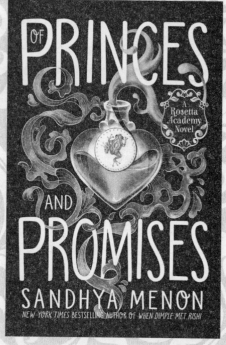

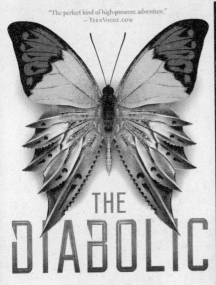
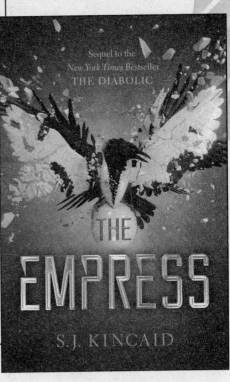

SOME LEGACIES ARE MEANT
TO BE BROKEN.